Pompeii Man

Other books by Paul Ruffin:

Lighting the Furnace Pilot (Poetry)
Our Women (Poetry)
The Storm Cellar (Poetry)
The Man Who Would Be God (Stories)
That's What I Like (About the South) (Co-edited with George Garrett)
After The Grapes of Wrath: *Essays on John Steinbeck* (Co-edited with Donald Coers and Robert DeMott)
A Goyen Companion: Appreciations of a Writer's Writer (Co-edited with Brooke Horvath and Irving Malin)
Circling (Poetry)
So There You Are: The Selected Prose of Glenn Brown (Edited work)
Islands, Women, and God (Stories)

Pompeii Man

Paul Ruffin

Louisiana Literature Press
Southeastern Louisiana University
Hammond, LA

Printed in the United States of America

FIRST EDITION, 2002

Cover design by Kellye Sanford
Cover Photograph © Bert Sirkin

Author's note: The circumstances and characters of this book are purely fictitious. Any resemblance to people living or dead or to any actual circumstances resembling those in this narration are coincidental.

Selections from John Crowe Ransom printed with permission from *Selected Poems of John Crowe Ransom*, New York: Ecco Press, 1978.

Library of Congress Cataloging-in-Publication Data

Ruffin, Paul
Pompeii / Paul Ruffin.-- 1st ed.
p. cm.
ISBN 0-945083-03-3 (alk. paper) -- ISBN 0-945083-04-1 (alk. paper)
1. Gulf Coast (Miss.)--Fiction. 2. New Orleans (La.)--Fiction. I. Title.

PS3568.U362 P66 2002
813'.54--dc21

2002038756

For Sharon

The images of the invaded mind
Being as monsters in the dreams
Of your most brief enchanted headful,
Suppose a miracle of confusion:
That dreamed and undreamt become each other
And mix the night and day . . . .

—from John Crowe Ransom

Pompeii Man

POMPEII MAN

I

New Orleans is a city of magic old and new, a dreamland where to the casual eye it would seem that people come only to play. But people play and people prey, and this is ancient law, stretching far beyond written memory, no less real for steel and concrete and glass, the shadows of slanted wings rippling across buildings, exotic fragrances that ribbon the streets, the noise of commerce, and brilliant colors that light the night. Here fantasy and reality blend and twist together in a great swirl until one is inextricable from the other, a vortex that will pull the unwary toward its tightening center and down to black.

In the dead of summer on a cloudless day New Orleans is only in weather like any other large city of the Deep South along the Gulf: as the cooler mists of morning burn away and the night breezes die, the sun climbs steady, reaching its zenith and leaning out the shadows of buildings, then starts its slow slide toward the western horizon, and the heat builds and intensifies, creating a vast shimmer of streets and sidewalks, along which people move slowly, if at all, on their many missions. The day is merely to be endured as a mild sentence of the gods, for in this city one escapes the issues of the outer world, finds himself lost in its charm, its panorama of smells and sights, wearing away the sun as he must, waiting for the night to come.

Heads almost touching, hands linked beneath the table, a

couple sat quietly in a hotel bar sipping icy drinks cold enough to burn going down. Their voices were low, inaudible to the bartender, whose dark eyes flicked across their faces from time to time, reversed in the mirror through which he saw them. The woman, with light blond hair, was strikingly dressed in black, her skin so white against the sleek fabric that the bartender thought it could almost hurt the eyes. Her face was lovely in proportion and color and texture, her eyes large and expressive, and from what he could recall of her as the couple came in, her body was wonderfully sculpted, with a dancer's legs and small but perfectly shaped breasts, whose nipples declared to anyone who might notice that she was wearing no bra beneath the dress. *Angelic* was the word that came to his mind as he rinsed and dried glasses for the evening crowd. *Divine.*

In time the couple finished their drinks and rose, and the man leaned and kissed the woman lightly on the lips. As they left the bar, he winked at the bartender, whose eyes swept over the woman. The man smiled and nodded good-bye and conducted his companion through the lobby and out into the noonday heat, the light so surprisingly bright that at first he could see the buildings only through a tight squint. The woman removed her sunshades from her purse and put them on. He wished that he had his. A palpable heat rose from the sidewalks and streets and made them wave and ripple so that distant traffic and buildings danced like apparitions, surrealistic, distorted, shapes blending, and when someone crossed a street a few blocks away, he appeared to be wading in a thin transparent sea.

Because it was a weekday, Jack Stafford supposed, and only early afternoon, there was little traffic along the narrow streets as they made their circuitous way to the Quarter. He had chosen a back way that took them even beyond North Rampart, which marked the northernmost boundary of the French Quarter, because he wanted to see if a particular curio shop was still there, one he remembered from years ago, with huge brass telescopes and models of the solar system, one in particular that stuck in his mind: a burnished brass sun the size of a softball around which the planets spun on steel rings. The owner of the store had positioned it in the center of the shop window, suspended the model in a large three-sided box lined with black cloth, and directed a spotlight beam on the highly polished ball of brass so that it reflected a brazen ray directly on the little green, blue, and brown earth and the yellow moon behind it, lighting one side, leaving the other in shadow. It was almost exactly like one Stafford had seen one time at a university science exhibit his father had taken him to. He recalled wondering how, with all that spinning and rotating, the center could hold and the bright planets keep from being flung off into space.

On his way back from the Quarter late one night, walking along with a girlfriend, both of them quite drunk, they had passed the shop and he spotted from across the street the fiery ball in the darkened window. Mesmerized, he weaved over and stood with his face pressed to the glass. Against its black enclosure the solar system looked so very real to him, the sun and planets and moon perfectly balanced in the middle of the bleakness of space. When he returned to the girl, who had waited across the street, he told her he wanted to check on the price of the model the next day.

But swept up in the passions of youth and still foggy about the night before, he spent the next morning in bed with the girl, forgot about the little solar system, and left New Orleans that afternoon. The memory of that night, of the arrogant flaring brass sun in its black prison bouncing a ray of light off the earth and moon, came back to him time after time over the years. In the few brief trips he had made to the city since, usually with limited funds, he had never taken the time to check on the model. The scale was, of course, way off, but he didn't mind that—he had always wanted that toy, and now, far beyond his impoverished student days, he could probably afford it. After all these years it was doubtless long gone, but he wanted to see. Perhaps the proprietor had kept it in his window as an enticement and never intended to sell it at all, or maybe he knew who had it now. If it was still there or could be found, he would make an offer. He could fancy it on the table by their front window, which looked out on the Gulf.

He found the building easily enough, but the street had run down dreadfully and the shop was no longer there. In its place was a small, dimly-lit antique store through whose front window he could see furniture and little else. He tried the door, but it was locked. "Why would they be closed in the middle of the afternoon?" he asked his reflection in the glass.

"I think you have to ring the bell," the woman with him said. "The sign says so." He could see her lovely face immediately behind his.

He pressed the pearl-colored button and waited. Whoever had painted the facade last, in a somber, shadowy green, dolloping it on in coarse strokes the way someone would paint a barn, had painted right up onto the brass rim that housed the button. It was a wonder that it still rang—and perhaps it didn't. But Stafford could see motion from deep in the store and eventually a woman with heavy legs shuffled to the front and squinted through at him, nodded, and opened the door.

"Help you?" she asked. The wide, sallow face was pleasant, but her eyes made a quick and penetrating assessment of this man who had interrupted whatever it was she had been doing. In one hand she held a slender book of some sort, but she had it turned so that the title wasn't visible. She stepped back.

"My wife and I here—well, I'm not sure." Stafford leaned inside the doorway and looked around. Nothing but heavy, dark furniture and dim lamps. The place smelled like ancient furniture and dust and old people. His companion stood close behind him.

"There used to be a curio shop here," he told the woman. "Had telescopes and stuff. Lots of brass. There was a display." He motioned. "A solar system display, right here in the window."

She swiped at a desk with her dust rag. "Well, I been here eight years, so it must of been a while back it was here. I don't know nothing about a place around here that sells things like that. I just got regular antiques, furniture and glassware and such, lots of old stuff but nothing curious." She laughed. "Unless you count me."

"Yes'm." He nodded to her. "I guess things have changed since I was down here. Thanks. A good day to you." He stepped back into the glare of the sun.

"Things have changed a lot," she said, closing the door behind her. Stafford could hear the deadbolt slam to.

They started walking again. "That's a shame," he said. "It was a wonderful shop. I think you'd have liked it."

"We should have gone on in." She squeezed his hand. "She did have some glassware I'd like to have looked at. Mother's got me hooked on glassware."

"You don't talk much about it. I mean, I know she has a lot of it and sells it in her shop, but you haven't talked about it often, and we don't have much at the house."

She smiled. "Well, I have several pieces scattered around, more than you've probably noticed, but you don't care much for it, so I don't talk about it. It hardly compares with all your shelves of artifacts from Europe and Asia. And we don't antique much, now, do we? How many times have we been in an antique shop together?"

He shrugged. "Well maybe we should start doing it more often. And it's not that I don't care for the glassware—I just don't *know* anything about it. Books I know about, but I didn't see any old books in there. I'd like to know what she was reading."

"She was reading *The Old Man and the Sea*. I saw the spine. And you know all about *everything*, Jack Stafford. And what you don't know about glassware I'll be happy to teach you, if you really want to know. How to tell the age and patterns and all. What it costs, how to know when you're getting a bargain."

"There's a lot we don't know about each other." He pulled her close to him.

"Right," she said, "like I didn't know you were interested in model solar systems and such. You've never mentioned that."

"Like I say, there's a lot we don't know about each other, but we'll learn." He stopped and kissed her hard and held her to him. Then they walked on again.

They passed almost no one on the sidewalk, and the occasional balconies were vacant, though here and there he saw a pale geranium blooming or the brighter bougainvillea, and a few ferns drooped in the hot, dead air. Even the proverbial winos, who usually stumbled along clutching their paper bags of Ripple or Thunderbird or Boone's Farm or sat dozing in doorways, seemed to have retreated from the heat.

Or from something else, Stafford thought. He was suddenly a little uneasy about being off the beaten path. Streets that a few years ago would have been as safe as his own back yard were now part of the jungle. But that was after dark, not in broad daylight, and surely not just a few blocks from the center of the bustling Quarter. He could see quite a lot of cross traffic at a distance, in the general direction of Jackson Square, so with a slight urgency he nudged his wife toward the cars and people.

"I wish I had put up more of an argument about this black dress." She wiped perspiration from her cheeks with the back of her hand. "The white one would have been a lot cooler."

"If you just knew how enticing you look in that thing. I'm already turned on again. If you'd left your panties off, you'd be more comfortable." They were on the shady side of the street, but the heat was merciless, with not so much as a trace of a breeze.

"God, all you think about is me without underwear." She was smiling. "It's enough that I'm not wearing a bra. Look—" She thrust her chest out.

"I *love* the way your nipples stick out. Maybe we can find a dark alley . . . ."

"Not in this heat," she said. "Besides, you've already had some, you maniac. Wait till tonight. Can we slow down just a little? These shoes are not very comfortable." She stopped and opened her purse and took out a tissue, dabbed her cheeks and forehead. "You know, we could have waited till October." She snapped open her compact and looked at her face.

"Your face is fine," Stafford said. He leaned and kissed her on the cheek. "You look just fine. By October we'd be an old married couple and the honeymoon would be over and all we'd be doing would be talking. Things are still fresh. We're still in love."

She smiled at him. "Do I need more lipstick?"

"No. You look great."

She was a truly beautiful woman, as blond as sea oats, thin but well-proportioned, her legs marvelously formed, a bit muscular like a dancer's, her waist not much thicker than Stafford's thigh. Even with little wisps of perspiration across her upper lip and under her eyes, her face was a delight for him. And her *body*. He found himself glancing from time to time at her, loving every motion she made, every gesture. Perhaps it was New Orleans, being away in a strange town with her, or maybe he was recapturing the initial thrill he felt when he first saw her. Perhaps it was both. They should have made a trip like this sooner, just for the two of them, spontaneous and a bit juvenile in a way, but exactly the way a trip to New Orleans ought to be for young lovers, with no obligations to anyone and no one back home even knowing where they were.

When she closed her purse, he took it from her. "Better let me carry this. It's safer." Often enough he had heard stories about how a thug could snatch a purse from a woman, break the strap, and be gone in a flash. He trapped it with his right forearm, like a football, so that anyone making a lunge for it would have one hell of a time taking it. His other arm was hooked through his wife's.

He pointed. "It's not far now. That traffic's near the Quarter." He urged her forward.

They had just crossed over a street and begun a new block, not a particularly attractive one, with old faded buildings towering over them—some with traces of paint from decades ago, others of bare brick, some recently blasted for repainting—and beneath their feet skewed and cracked slabs of concrete-patched stone, littered with cigarette butts and beer caps and tabs and stains of tobacco spittle and God only knew what else. They were in shade now, where at least it was cooler. He steered her around a vile-looking smear just as a flock of pigeons blustered from an alcove. Winged shadows circled briefly on the street, then blended into the shade of buildings.

He hurried her along. "Jesus. Scared the shit out of me."

"It was just pigeons."

"It sounded like a herd of buffalo," Stafford said.

Even here, on this back street, conducting his new wife through an area where he felt vaguely alien and alone, the edge of the known world within his view but distorted by afternoon heat and moving so slowly toward them, he felt a strange exhilaration, the way he felt at times standing on the edge of the beach in front of his house facing the night Gulf, beneath whose water creatures of another dimension moved. Soon, he knew, the mysterious sounds and scents of the Quarter would engulf them, the smells of fruit and coffee and incense, the jangling of horses' harness and bells, the clopping of their hooves, and the twitter of happy people, arousing in him memories of parties and girls and women, drunken nights on the levee, a drowned but persistent past that would resurrect itself like something rising bright and winged from the sea.

"God, I love this town," he said.

They were only a few feet down the next block, a similar stretch of shadowy, vacant-eyed buildings with an occasional gay curtain or a plant perched on a wrought-iron shelf, when three kids turned the corner toward them, one a bit older than the other two but none looking over high school age. Black kids, skinny, with their hair cut close on the sides and back but left full on the top, like stick men you might draw in school, and wearing jeans and white basketball shoes and jerseys with team logos. They were moving along in a rhythmic slouch as if walking to music, chattering, intent on their conversation, when they saw the couple. Then they stopped, looked at each other, and spread out shoulder to shoulder to form a phalanx across the narrow walk, the tallest one half a step ahead in the middle, spearheading.

Stafford glanced at the boys, then to the other side of the street.

At a time like this, with such a threat bearing down on him, real or merely perceived, a man alone with his woman and with no weapon at hand envisions nothing but escape, an outlet. This he does not formulate as thought, only as an image, instinctive and spontaneous, like a pre-language savage bolting from some creature with unsheathed claws and bared fangs, his mind intent not on confrontation and combat but on deliverance from the threat: some tree to climb or stream to plunge into, where he knows the animal following him cannot or will not go.

Any notion Stafford might have had of screwing up his courage and continuing his pace directly toward the boys or moving to the edge of the street trying to sideslip them, all the while conducting his wife with whatever dignity he could—such ideas, squelched even before they became thought, were overwhelmed by the urgency to be gone, to wish the scene away, to turn and leave the three in the shadows of the stark-faced buildings and flee to the sunlit side of the street, where there was an iron gate opening into some sort of garden, and above the gate a sign, for a restaurant or a bar.

And the second thing that comes to a man in such perilous circumstances, this more clearly and more persistent finally than the visceral urgency to escape, if only because it comes as thought and not as impulse, is the rational assessment of his situation: a man alone with his wife in a strange town facing three street toughs who, for all he knows, carry with them guns or knives and who might be high on drugs.

Stafford was larger than the boys and in reasonably good shape, but this was their territory, and they were younger and more agile, probably well accustomed to violence. He had no time to try to read their eyes, to determine their design, if indeed they had any, and he knew further that eye contact might provoke action when none had been intended. It was the right and proper thing to do, he reasoned, to follow his initial impulse and swing his wife out of their path and across the street while there was still time, with a good quarter block of sidewalk between them and the boys.

But a man knows further that yielding to such an impulse will leave him beaten just as surely as he might be in a confrontation with the threat, and beaten more completely, more permanently, than he would be by fists and feet, knives and clubs. In short, he knows even before he takes one step out of harm's way that to run from such danger is to prove himself not a man at all, but a simple coward, who in future years will return to the scene time after time, with shame and with disgrace. And the woman he had thought to defend by steering her out of this perilous path would recall him merely weak and feeble to attend, noble in cause but withered in the bright light of circumstance. These things a man knows innately, in the blood, at the stem of the brain, far below the surface prattle of the conscious mind, for he is the male, the stronger of the two, and it is fundamental law that he must stand between his mate and the threat. Besides, these were little street punks who would either back down at the least sign of resistance or pursue across the street if they wanted trouble. It would happen or it wouldn't. Either way, foolish or not, he could not run.

So Stafford pushed his wife to the inside of the walk and behind him, linked a hand in hers, shifted the purse to his left arm, still cradling it like a football, and squared his shoulders and stared straight ahead past the three oncoming boys to the sunlit opening that marked the next intersection, beyond which he could see cars and people moving. The woman, saying nothing, walked as close to the buildings as she could and as she walked she brushed against the bricks. When he turned to look at her he saw terror on her face and streaks of brick-colored powder on the black dress. She moved closer to him as they approached the youths and Stafford could hear her breathing fast and shallow.

The boys came on, silent and slow, each with a cocky grin, eyes fixed on the blond woman. Walking at the same deliberate pace, Stafford looked from one face to the other, then back to the intersection ahead. With each step his wife's shoes scuffed his heels. Here, pinned against the dusty brick wall but still moving, he felt a burning begin deep in his throat and lungs, pronounced by the banging of his heart, which in its terrible urgency seemed to pump more blood than its valves and veins could handle and was strangling on its own precious fluid. Focused on the street corner ahead, he struggled to keep his balance as he placed one foot straight ahead of the other, flattening against the building, allowing the boys all the room they needed to claim the walk.

It seemed interminable to him, this closing of ranks, as if the scene were cast in slow motion, the three thugs still shoulder to shoulder before them and Stafford squeezed as close to the building as he could walk, tugging his wife along like a child.

Then the one on the inside stepped in front of the other two and swept his body down into a bow, allowing the man and woman to pass.

"Thanks," Stafford mumbled. He moved to the middle of the walk and pulled his wife up alongside him.

"Yo," a voice came from behind. "Nice purse." Stafford did not turn, did not break stride.

"Hey, muthafucka," the voice yelled.

Oh shit, Stafford thought. *Keep it cool, man, just keep on walking*. His heart was racing.

"Yo, muthafucka! Nice *pussy* too."

Stafford stopped at that and spun and glared at the boys, one of whom was standing looking at the couple. It was the one who had bowed and let them pass. The other two still shambled along, nearly halfway down the block. Somehow they didn't seem like such a threat any more, with the intersection only a few feet away and the boys at a distance.

His wife was tugging at him. "Jack, Jack. Come on. Let's get out of here."

"What the hell did you say?" he shouted to the boy, who was standing there with a toothy grin, his eyes all over the woman.

"*Jack!*"

The boy yelled back, "What'd *you* say?"

"I said, what exactly did you say to me?"

"You said somethin' to me firs', when I passed you. What'd *you* say?"

Stafford stared at him. "I said *thanks*. That's all." He could feel his wife pulling at him.

They stood glaring at each other while the other two boys retraced their steps to stand shoulder to shoulder with the one who'd been talking. "What the hell goin' on here?" one of the others asked.

"He say I said somethin' to him. He said somethin' to me firs'. Didn't sound like *thanks* to me."

"I *heard* what you said," Stafford snapped.

"Then what the hell you axin' me what I said for?" The boy had his chin thrust out, his teeth bared, as if he were growling. He pushed the sleeves up on his jersey to reveal a thin wrapping of muscles about the bones, overlaid with ropey veins. His fists were balled tight. Even at that distance Stafford could see the slick surface of scars on one forearm, and a jagged ridge of lighter tissue that crossed his right cheek. The boy held his pose but did not move.

"I want you to apologize to the lady." He could feel his wife tugging hard at his hand. "And to *me*."

"Come on, Jack," she urged. "Let it go. We've got to get out of here."

"He ain't *got* to 'pologize," one of the others said. "You say somethin' to him firs', he can say anything he want to to you."

The one who had spoken first took a step toward the couple.

"Whon't you take yo' woman and get on out of here before we make you wish you had? We'll take the purse *and* the pussy away from you." One of the other boys, younger, was looking up and down the street.

"You Goddamned little punk. All I said was thanks."

"Sound like *fuck you, nigger* to me," the first one said.

"Jack, come on. *Please.*" She was pulling him hard toward the street corner.

In his concentrated fury, eyes locked on the boy, short and lean and angular, with a wispy juvenile mustache across his lip, Stafford did not even see where the car came from, it was on them so quickly. One of the blacks shouted *oh shit oh shit* and there was a squealing of tires at the corner they had just passed and a light-colored blur from behind the boys, a huge grill shot up beside him, then screeching as the car slid to a stop, doors exploding open, and someone knocked him against the building. He still had the purse clutched under his forearm as he slid down the wall and forward onto the walk. A black man—he had seen part of a face emerge from the back seat just before a dark fist, glittering with rings, caught him in the temple—straddled him and hammered him on the side of the face as he tugged at the purse with the other hand. Stafford's head flashed with the blows. He twisted his body over onto the purse and tried to turn his head toward the muffled screams of his wife. A punch to his left side rolled him up in a tight ball.

A voice came from somewhere: "You little sonsabitches better get on outta here!" Then, "Leave the muthafuckin' purse, man, leave the purse." He felt the weight of the man lift from his body.

"Susie!" Stafford tried to straighten up, to raise his head, to see something, anything, but before he could focus, a foot caught him behind his right ear and he saw lightning and he went down again.

"You just stay down, muthafucka, keep your eyes closed." The man's mouth was right at his ear. "And give me that *purse.*" He tried again to wrestle it away, but Stafford kept his body across it.

A voice boomed out again, "Leave the purse. Get in the car. We got her. Get in the Goddamned car!" There was a final scuffling of feet, a door slamming, and the car squalled off down the street.

Stafford lay in silence awhile, uncertain whether to move or not. He still hugged the purse to his chest. There was little feeling in his face—the left side had been slammed against the walk by the fist that pummeled the right. The sharp pain in his ribs told him that he probably had something cracked or broken, at least badly bruised, but he had not moved enough from his fetal position to assess the damage. He turned his face in both directions but saw no one, not his wife, not the boys, not the car, no one.

Finally he managed to uncoil on the sidewalk and sit up. There was no one nearby, though way down the street he could see a couple of workmen carrying a piece of plywood or sheetrock, something large and rectangular. Then they disappeared and he saw only the distant traffic of cross-streets.

"Susie . . . Susie," he managed and slumped onto the walk again, where he lay curled up in pain, his head throbbing, eyes clenched. When he looked down the street again, he saw two people turning the corner. They stopped when they saw him, disappeared briefly, then came back around the corner with a policeman.

The sleek white car with flashy grill eased along side streets, the driver intent on his route and all traffic signs and lights and careful to keep his speed right at the limit. Two men in the backseat kept the woman pinned to the floorboard with their feet. They had spread a blanket across her. Gliding finally out of the Quarter, deeper and deeper into the dark heart of New Orleans, the car began to pick up speed, zipping easily now past the rows of look-alike houses, small, with chain-link fencing around their yards, then clusters of tenement buildings alike in color and design, everything shimmering in afternoon heat.

"Keep it down," the driver told them once in reaction to something the two men were saying. His eyes were cold in the mirror. "Don't want no shit now. We got her and we got away. Don't want no shit coming down on us. Keep her face on that floor and keep her covered up, but don't smother her."

"Wish we'd got that purse," one said from the back seat.

"Forget about the purse," the driver said. "You'd tore his arm off before he turned aloose of that purse."

"You reckon them little turds know who we are?" the man directly behind the driver asked. He kept the blanket pressed down on the woman's head.

The driver glanced through the mirror at him again. "Them boys?"

"Yeah."

"I don't care whether they know or not. If they do, they sure as hell know better than to say anything. If they don't, they got to have a pretty good idea, enough of one to know to keep they mouf shut."

"I hope you right," the other man said. He had lifted the woman's dress and run his hand between her legs. She was making a sound.

"Be still, bitch. I ain't hurtin' you."

"Benny, keep yo' hands off of her. Leave her alone." The driver had turned and was glaring over the tops of his sunglasses.

"Ain't tetched nothin' yet. Bitch got her legs clamped like a Goddamn oyster." He brought a foot down hard on the girl's calves. On the other side his companion had one foot on her neck and one in the middle of her back. She cried out.

"Shut up, bitch. You gon' moan later." He looked at the other man. "Can't you turn her over and pull that blanket back so I can look at her?"

"She alright," the other one said. "You can look at'r later. There'll be plenty of time to look. We gotta keep her down like this and that blanket on'r so she don't draw no attention."

"Then keep it over her head. I don't care about her head. She ain't gon' scream nohow. She scream and I'll kick the hell out of her. You hear me, bitch? Just turn her over."

"Let her *alone*," the driver said. "And don't smother her with that blanket. Y'all kill her and the Man—y'all just let her alone."

The one named Benny said, "This the bes' lookin' woman I seen in a long time. Turn her over, Roy Gene. You can keep the blanket over—"

The driver glared at him. "Shut yo' fuckin' mouf, nigger! Ain't gon' be no mo' talkin'. The mo' she hear, the mo' she gon' remember. Now shut the fuck up! And leave her alone."

"You done called me Benny in front of her. And quit callin' me a nigger, nigger."

The driver's eyes flashed in the mirror. "Then quit acting like one. And I don't give a shit if they get *you*, nigger. *Or* Roy Gene, now that you've introduced him. I just don't want them to get *me*. Now shut the fuck up. You say another word and I'll stop this car and shoot *both* your dumb asses and run by the zoo to pick me up some help. Coupla fuckin' gorillas or baboons or something. Anything be better'n y'all." He held up a black pistol and waved it. "You don't believe I'll shoot y'all's asses, you keep on."

He drove in silence then, weaving through narrow streets scattered with dilapidated apartments and houses and great gaps where uncut lots lay festering with mounds of refuse and abandoned cars, until he was on a street dotted with buildings under construction. In a short while he pulled up before a tall hurricane fence, beyond which there was a massive brick structure with high windows. A thin margin of knee-high grass grew around the perimeter of the fence and clumps sprang out of the lot between slabs of concrete. He stopped before a locked gate.

"Somebody gon' have to mow this place one of these days."

"Shut up, Benny, and unlock the gate," the driver said, handing back a key. "Be yo' ass quick about it or I'll make *you* get out here with a mower."

"Yas-suh!" The black grinned and saluted. "You de boss." He sprang out and unlocked a padlock and swung the gate wide, watched while the car came through, then closed the gate and relocked it and got back in and handed the driver the key. "Nex' thang you know I be pickin' cotton for you."

"You don't shut yo' mouf you gon' be *pushin' up* cotton somewheres over in the Delta," the driver said. "Shoot yo' black ass and plant it in a cotton patch somewhere where they won't never find you. Be cotton roots wrapped around yo' ribs and runnin' thoo yo' eye sockets. Be the best crop they ever had, feedin' off such a big pile of shit. Be better'n a whole ton of cowshit." He eased the car up to the front of the building and stopped before a set of large double wooden doors. "Open up, Benny." He was grinning when he handed back the key.

After the doors were swung wide, the driver pulled inside the great dim garage area and killed the engine and got out. He took the key from the one he called Benny, who had closed the doors behind them, and handed a pillowcase to the other man, still sitting with his feet on the woman's neck and back.

"Put it over her head before you let her off the floor," he directed. "Pull her arms behind her and put these straps on'r." He handed him two long nylon ties used to secure electrical cables. The man pulled the blanket back and slipped the pillow case over the woman's head, then forced her arms as close together as he could behind her back and put one strap around at the elbows, cinching it tight. He put another strap around her wrists. She winced and groaned but said nothing. Satisfied, he dragged her out of the car and yanked her to her feet.

"You want me to gag her?" he asked.

"What the fuck for?" the driver asked. "She inside now. Can't nobody hear her." He reached and placed a hand around the woman's throat. "You better not scream, though," he said to the pillowcase. "You wouldn't want to unnerve me."

The one named Benny backed the woman against the side of the car. "Lordy, look at the way her titties stick out with her arms pulled back like that. And look at them legs. Swan meat, man." He reached and tweaked her nipples, grinned, and kissed the pillowcase below the outline of her nose.

"Ain't *yo'* swan," the driver said. "Leave her the hell alone and bring her on. And bring that damn shoe."

"Please," she said, her voice muffled through the pillowcase, "please loosen the upper strap. It's hurting my back and arms."

The man who had strapped her nudged her along behind the other two toward an old freight elevator. "You better shut up. Shoulda gagged her. Shit, she whinin' already and ain't even *started* to hurt. We ain't loosenin' nothing till we get you upstairs. Then we gon' loosen you up alright—"

The one who had driven turned around and studied the woman. "Roy Gene, shut yo' *mouf.* You talk too Goddamned much." He pulled out his knife. "Man, you can't pull nobody's elbows together behind they back like that. People won't bend that much. You gon' break her in half, fool, like my momma break a chicken up, gon' break her shoulders." He cut the upper band and the woman's arms relaxed.

"Thanks," she said.

"Don't thank me, bitch." He pushed her before him. "I'd do the same for a dog."

They led her onto a freight elevator and the door closed.

II

She was simply too beautiful, too graceful, for words, like something not really meant to be bound to this earth, a fact that Jack Stafford acknowledged to himself the first time he ever saw her, stepping delicately across a rain puddle in front of the Fine Arts Building, her umbrella out to counterbalance the fistful of pencils and brushes she held in the opposite hand. She landed lightly on the ball of her left foot, which shot out from under her, sending the leg high and her already wind-billowed dress above her waist, leaving her legs completely uncovered for anyone passing by to see, one thrown out in a perfect kick, the other neatly dropping a foot into position, so that when the pale-green gauzy dress descended and the leg had recovered from its startling thrust, she walked on as if nothing had happened. She should have taken a bow. She had not seen him, or at least had not looked his way, so he merely kept to his coffee and watched her go on across the street and get into her car, his mind still trying to focus on the splendid legs and the black, lacy French-cut panties that would not go away.

"I'll tell you, Em, she was—she *is* something." He was still pointing to the spot where he had seen the girl.

In the Commons, at a table facing Fine Arts, Stafford quietly blew across his coffee cup while Emily Miller cradled her chin in her hands and smiled her special, knowing smile, which was not really a smile at all, but something a mother might use to mildly chastise a wayward boy. One of Stafford's steady lovers, Emily was married to a homosexual history professor named Howard who taught at a small private college in Mobile. It was not unlike her to drive over and drop in at the Commons during his coffee break every week or so—she cared little who saw them together, and neither did he. They enjoyed their talks.

Emily was a tall brunette, mid-forties, thin and attractive and as free a spirit as Stafford had ever seen in a married woman. Her hair, close-cropped and swept back, gave her face an almost heron-like quality, and her quick eyes darted as if searching for a flash of silver just beneath the surface. Stafford never felt entirely at ease with Emily, whether wrapped up in bed with her or sitting at the Commons having coffee. Her life with Howard had not been a pleasant one since her discovery a few years into their marriage, her second, that he had a male lover. She had returned unexpectedly from a trip to New Orleans and found the two of them showering together. Rather than at nearly forty seeking another mate or managing alone, she had decided to settle for whatever security he could give her, but she declared that she owed him no allegiance whatsoever and sought her comfort wherever she could find it.

Stafford had met her at a faculty reception for a visiting writer at the little community college where he worked as a librarian, and before the evening was out her husband had left for New Orleans with some chap, cheerily announcing to her that he would not be back until the next day. Later that evening Emily ended up at Stafford's house, where after they had finished off a fifth of bourbon on the beach across the street he found himself sprawled out in the sand kissing her as she lay atop him. He led her back to the house and upstairs, where they undressed and he discovered that her body was still in its prime. They showered to wash off the sand, and he took her to bed. Since that night they had been together frequently, at least five or six times a month, and neither of them particularly cared whether Howard knew about it or not. They were fairly certain, in fact, that he didn't care at all.

"You're just helping Howard out, keeping our marriage together," she once told Stafford while she was dressing to leave. "You're doing what he can't bring himself to do."

They had sex when they wanted it, and it was comfortable, without commitment. She always came over to his place for a toss, and often they had coffee in the Commons, chatting like the old friends they had come to be.

Emily sipped her coffee and looked over the edge of the cup at Stafford. "It's finally happening to you, isn't it, Jack?"

"What?" His eyes were on the double doors of the Fine Arts

Building across the street. "What's finally happening to me, Emily?"

"The skirts. I wondered how long it'd take for the skirts to get to you. Had to happen sooner or later. So many of them around, twitching their little butts." Her voice was hoarser than usual. She was now nursing a cigarette, carefully cupping it in her hand and bringing it to her lips, then easing it under the table again, letting the smoke drift out of her mouth and nose. Twice before she'd been asked by management to put her cigarette out and not to smoke in the Commons again. But she smoked when she wanted to.

Stafford sipped, exhaled, and glanced once again at the building across the street. "Maybe so, Em. She's something. Just like she'd rehearsed it. Up goes the leg, almost as high as her head—hell, higher than her head—like a ballerina, down comes the other foot. Or more like a goddess descending onto a stage somewhere, gently dropped by wires, that's how smooth it was, how effortless, only she did it without wires. Whew. Grace, pure grace."

"Maybe she did rehearse it, Jack."

"Hmmm?"

"Maybe she knew you'd be sitting here and decided she'd stage a little drama just for you, a ballet called *Identify the Panties*."

"Em, you're getting tacky."

"Well, at least it's a *girl*," she said. "If I have to find something positive in it."

He smiled.

"You *boyzzzzzz*." She rolled her eyes. "I do like the panties part, though. How your eyes latched onto them."

"Come on, Em."

"How could you tell they were lacy or French-cut or anything, as fast as it had to happen? Nobody's that quick, Jack."

"Quick enough, my dear. The legs and panties—all of it's locked in here." He tapped his temple. "You know, like when you glance at the sun and close your eyes and the image stays, the bright spot stays?"

"Bullshit," she said. "You'd better stick with what you know is real, my boy. Open your eyes and you'll find that the bright spot is gone. And remember, too, that looking at the sun will blind you." She eased her coffee cup under the table and extinguished the cigarette. It went out with a quick hiss. "Goddamned things are so bitter." She wiped the tip of her tongue on a napkin. "I don't know why I bother with them."

"Why *do* you?" Stafford asked.

"You find your pleasure where you can, Jack. Age just drives you to pursue things you might not have a few years before—and pursue them harder. The disgusting comes with the sweet." She pushed her chair back and rose. "Usually."

"You're a bit cynical this morning, more than I've seen you in a while. What's the problem? Howard acting up?"

She shook her head and looked out across campus. "Howard rarely *acts*," she said.

"Methinks Emily's jealous," he said, reaching and grabbing her arm and pulling her back into her seat.

"Oooooh, Jack, I like it when you're rough."

"You're not in that big a damned rush, Emily. Talk to me. I need somebody to talk to. Help me get a focus on this thing."

"Oh, you're focused enough, Jack. When you can determine that a girl's panties are French-cut with lace in a tenth of a second, you're genuinely focused."

"Emily."

"No, I'm not exactly jealous," she said softly, maternally. She appeared tired, looked her age. Her skin, sallow in the glare from the window, seemed to hang looser than it did only a week ago. "I'd have to be a fool not to know that this would happen. Sooner or later. But you're acting just like a high school boy, Jack—you've gone stratospheric over a little girl that you know nothing about and might never touch. You are PW'd, pure and simple. And she's probably dumb as a duck."

"PW'd? What does—"

"Jesus, Jack, you're a librarian and you've certainly read enough trashy novels. I ought not have to explain the alphabet to you. *PW*'d. *Pussy whipped*. You've never heard the term?"

"Yeah, I've heard the term. I thought it meant *uxorious*."

"Whatever the hell that means. You Goddamned librarians."

"Henpecked, then. I thought it meant henpecked."

"It does mean what it has always meant—I was just adding a little dimension to it. She's got you whipped and whining like a puppy and you haven't even seen her up close or touched her or talked to her, unless you're lying. You're like a damned dog that's got a whiff of a bitch in heat."

Stafford nodded and smiled, though he was not amused. "I'm not lying. I've seen her once. And I think you're making a hell of a lot more of this than what I intended. I just saw this gorgeous girl—*woman*—do something cute. That's all."

"Howard's *DW'd*. Get that one?"

"You're getting mean, Emily."

"No, I'm getting ready to *go*, Jack. I have someplace to be—an appointment."

"A guy?" he asked.

"A guy."

"Now, do you see *me* getting jealous? Who is he?"

"A damned dentist, if you have to know. And not all that attractive. Balding and hairy chested with gold chains and just brimming with goofy talk—reminds me of a used-car salesman. He's got a dozen trains of thought running at the same time, and they're running in all directions on no particular schedule. All he'll be sticking in my mouth will be his gloved fingers and his little metal tools—always a real turn-on. Sort of like having a Pap smear. You boys just don't know the thrill of those cold instruments slicked with K-Y rammed up in you. All *you* ever get is a single finger, if I've heard right, and that just long enough to see whether your itty bitty walnut has gone nasty and sprouted into a tree. Does that finger ever turn you on, Jack?"

"Emily . . ."

"Howard doubtless gets a kick out of it. He'd probably get eight or ten examinations a year if the insurance company would pay for them, only he prefers something larger than a finger."

"Em, you're getting loud."

She glanced around the room and blew into her palm, then rubbed her teeth with a napkin. "You got any breath mints?"

"No," Stafford said.

"Never mind. I'll just run by a drugstore and buy some mouthwash. Forgot to floss too, damn it. And hear this, Jack Stafford—I am not, by God, jealous of any little dew-drop cunt with lacy French panties."

"If it's not jealousy I'm hearing, what *would* you call it, Emily? Exactly what do you call it when an older woman talks like a sailor and makes remarks like that about a younger woman when the man the older woman's involved with is attracted to the younger one? And what makes you think that because I saw someone I find exciting I plan to do anything about it or that she'd pay any attention if I tried?"

"You'll try because you *can*, Jack. That's the bottom line. You are single and young and intelligent and good-looking and you have wonderful social skills, so you probably *can* do something about it. Guys like you are rare enough in an area where most men work at the shipyard and look like it. You'll get in her pants if you try hard enough. Work out your own ballet. It'll take a little time, but you can have her, if you want her bad enough." She twisted her face into a grin that wasn't a grin. "I probably know you better than you know yourself. Want me to coach you through it?"

"What I hear is jealousy, Em."

"Not jealousy, Jack. Not exactly." She stood again and gripped the chairback until her knuckles whitened. "By the way, you and I were never what I would call *involved*—Honey, we just *screwed*." With a toss of her head and a little wave she breezed out.

"Bye, Em." Stafford stared at the doorway she had gone through. "Jesus," he whispered, "that really got to her." He shook his head. "Very, very jealous, I'd say."

He could not rid his mind of the girl for the rest of the day. He returned to the library after his coffee at the Commons and spent the afternoon engaged in menial cataloging, leaving his office only twice, once for water and once for a bathroom stop. But no matter how diligently he attempted to concentrate on his work, he kept seeing the flash of her alabaster legs as she performed that unexpected flourish before him, landing as lightly as a ballerina who had practiced the routine all her life, not even breaking stride. Her face was a bit nebulous yet—he had only glanced at her before her foot slipped—but she was one gorgeous girl, or woman, whatever the hell she was. That much he knew. Her image was fixed in his mind like the flash of some exotic bird, the rush of bright wings against a wall of jungle green, or a darting, dazzling fish in blue water. On impulse he took a longer route to his car after work, passing slowly by the Fine Arts Building, but the car he had seen her get into was gone.

When he saw her the next day approaching the same building, he surmised that she must be new on campus, since, it being his custom to walk across to the Commons for coffee and a light reading break that same time every afternoon, following the same route, he would certainly have noticed her, as any man in his right mind would. The fall semester had just begun—fierce summer still clung stubbornly to the Coast—so she was probably a new student, maybe just out of high school. He hurried across the street and walked toward her, studying her face as he approached and passed her, averting his eyes when she looked his way.

Jesus, he thought, as he drank his coffee, the paperback still unopened on the table—her hair, the eyes, the nose and cheeks and chin, everything was so perfectly in proportion. She was thin, with wonderfully developed calves, and astonishingly blond, but not the too-fair, freckled blond of the farm girls he'd seen, whose hair was really more red than blond and whose skin without makeup looked anemic and sickly. Her hair was a bright straw color with no hint of darker roots, with matching eyebrows, her skin without blemish, cheeks slightly rouged, but he was not certain that the blush was not natural. Scandinavian ancestry, Swedish probably, but *angelic* was the word that came to mind as he sat there sipping his coffee. It was almost more than he could do to resist watching for her the rest of the afternoon, then following her to her car and introducing himself. God, he wanted to hear her speak, wanted to see her face and legs up close, wanted to ask her out, wanted . . . .

Maybe he'd been too long without a woman he could call his own. Maybe he needed a wife, someone young like the blond girl, someone innocent and pliable whom he could add dimension to and teach life's many mysteries. Sometimes the older women he slept with, as intrigued as he was with them, vaguely intimidated him, as if they knew more than he did. There was very little softness to them, and when he tried to say something clever or deeply philosophical, or recited lines of poetry that meant so very much to him, he often got the feeling that they merely tolerated him, the way one does a preacher or teacher, whose message, indisputably true and delivered with intoxicating passion, has very little relevance in the real world and makes a mark no more lasting than a stone flung into the night sea.

And then there was the stark loneliness he had come to feel those times when after a tryst with Emily, still wearing her smell, he lay alone in his bed and imagined what it would be like to have a wife again, to wake up day after day beside a woman with whom he shared more than an occasional romp. Someone to add color and sound and warmth to the rooms. Many a morning he had lain staring up at the ceiling, noting how dreadfully silent and cold a house was without a woman. Nothing was the way a house was supposed to be, with the delicious smell of her things in the bathroom, panties on the shower rod drying, a bra dangled over a chair, her clothes hanging in the closet, and a kitchen fragrant and warm. The bright trill of her laughter. Maybe he was just feeling his age, but Jack Stafford needed a wife, not just a lover. He shook his head and downed the rest of his coffee, picked up his paperback, and went to the library to finish out the day.

He did not see her at the customary time and place the next afternoon, though her car was parked in the same row of vehicles as before, so he stationed himself at a handy table with his coffee and book and watched. After reading along a few lines, he would glance up at the steady trickle of students moving across campus, then return to his reading. There were lots of other girls to entertain his eyes, all dressed in their light summer dresses or skirts or tight shorts. God, how he loved to watch them, their bare legs and arms, their hair gleaming in the sun, their lovely faces. There was simply no place on earth like a college campus to witness perfect beauty, especially in the summer.

She came out several minutes after he had taken a chair and assumed his vigil. Accompanied by a male companion—a student, Stafford judged by his age and general demeanor and the armload of books that he carried—she stepped lightly through the door of the Fine Arts Building and walked on ahead down the steps and to the curb and never looked at the boy. Whatever he was saying to her seemed to be of little interest—she said nothing back that Stafford could see. Hesitating at the curb only long enough to avoid a passing maintenance truck, she crossed to the car and unlocked it, allowing him to shift the armload of books and swing the door open for her. Then she took her books and got in, at that point turning and waving lightly. The boy returned the wave and stood watching her back out and drive off. He had been carrying her books for her like a high school kid.

"I know how you gotta feel, little hard-leg," Stafford said quietly, picking up his book to leave. "You'd trade your pickup for a night alone with her, wouldn't you? Your pickup, a six-pack of beer, a can of Skoal, and your first paycheck from the shipyard."

Over the next week he made it a point to look for her around the Fine Arts Building every day, on two occasions spotting her, each time briefly as she walked to her car. Both times she was alone. He chose not to walk near her, for fear that seeing him too often might frighten her into thinking that he was stalking. That is, *if* she saw him, there being no indication that she saw anyone at all.

She looked at the concrete before her or straight ahead, as he supposed any beautiful woman must do. All it took to prompt a male into action was eye contact, especially with someone of her exquisite beauty. It was really unfair, these girls parading their assets as if they were on some sort of auction block, then acting insulted when some fellow ventured a bid. Of course, this girl, whoever the hell she was, could wear anything of any size and shape and still be enticing. All someone that lovely had to do was *appear*, and every male in the vicinity would lift his nose to the wind.

What they didn't realize, or refused to acknowledge, was that at work here were dynamics dating from way before any big-brained upright ape thought about cotton dresses and tight shorts and college campuses. A man had to treat one of his own most fundamental biological urges like a pet wolf, feeding and soothing it, hoping to subjugate it to the useful and the good, praying that it would not snap its chain in some heated frenzy and go for the kill. Sitting quietly in his office, his feet kicked up on the desk and the back of his head resting against his interlaced fingers, Stafford suddenly felt strange and a little embarrassed, silly and juvenile, almost as if he had been pursuing her like an animal. Hell, he was above that. He wasn't that desperate. Besides, she had to be nearly twenty years his junior.

So he simply decided to forget about her and change his route and schedule, facing away from the windows of the Commons when he went for coffee. He was too old to let a young thing like that get into his head. She probably *was* dumb as a duck and, because of her incredible beauty, conceited. There were plenty of other girls and women to concentrate on.

Stafford did not look like a librarian, as Emily had pointed out a few times, was in fact over six feet tall and rather well-built, handsome enough, with a full head of short brown hair and a neat mustache, and he wore glasses only for reading. His clothing was always fashionable and fit him well, and weightlifting and long runs on the beach across the highway from his house kept him lean and in good shape. Several weekends a year he fished in the surf out at the barrier islands with a friend, and he spent a great deal of time on the beach across the street from his house, so he maintained a tan all year, in the summer darkening to an almost Amerind shade.

The convertible Mustang he drove, though far from new, was nonetheless fast and sleek and he had never known a woman to complain about it. A Renaissance man, he had bought the car and restored it himself in a little garage behind the house—rebuilt the engine, repainted the car, even reworked the upholstery, all by himself. There was little he couldn't do when he set his mind to it. Jack Stafford, Greco-Roman in mind and body, a marvelous balance of intellect and muscle, was proud of himself. He had a right to be.

He worked a normal weekday shift at the library, from eight until five, and as he could afford it took long vacations off in Europe or Australia or wherever. He admitted no allegiance to anyone or anything. Since his divorce had involved no children and was a neat severing of ties and equal splitting of property, he had no financial obligations other than rent and household expenses.

His qualifications were such that he might well have taken a job at any number of libraries, but he loved the Mississippi Coast—not yet spoiled by the kind of strident commercialism of the East Coast beaches but developed enough that a man might have any kind of night life he preferred, from fantastic food to gambling, now that floating casinos dotted the beaches of Biloxi. Mobile lay just to the east, a thirty-minute drive away, and New Orleans was less than two hours off, so he had the charm of Old South cities close by and the comfortable down-home atmosphere of Biloxi, where he lived.

The Mississippi Coast had become a Gold Coast, where a man of moderate means and an education and good looks might live any sort of life he wished with any kind of woman he wanted. The beaches were pleasant most of the year, the restaurants plentiful and improving in service and range of offerings, and the whole stretch of waterfront from Biloxi to Gulfport was now throbbing. Old beach-front homes with columns and verandas, their lawns shaded by huge liveoaks whose moss-draped limbs defied nature and grew straight out from their trunks, were part of his daily vista as he drove the coast road to and from the college.

And the campus itself was thronged with lovely girls and women, scantily dressed most seasons, usually in only shorts and thin pullover shirts, through which their typically braless breasts presented themselves, little nipples straining like late spring buds. Their legs white-scissored along the walks and across the grass, as inviolate in form as anything an artist's eye might fashion. And their faces were studies in human perfection, noses and eyes and hair, skin without blemish. He sat as often as he could simply watching them, as one might study birds, not intending to capture or harm, merely to admire. And as he watched, the lines of a poem would sometimes come back to him:

> Tie the white fillets about your hair
> And think no more of what will come to pass
> Than bluebirds that go walking on the grass
> And chattering on the air.

Stafford's life was one of essential leisure, and he loved his bachelorhood, except for those long silences in the house, the hours and hours of solitude when he found himself sometimes wishing that he had his wife back, someone to break the silence. The only thing that truly took great chunks of his spare time, that filled in his hours of silence, was his reading, to which he was addicted. When he traveled, his books went with him; when he was home his books were there by his bedside, in the bathroom, on his kitchen table, on the coffee table. Even his car seats were littered with them, front and back. He read incessantly, starting a new book the minute he finished the last.

From his early high school days he had been a devotee of the sciences, and but for a couple of dismal mathematics professors at Mississippi State would have pursued, no doubt to a successful end, a degree in engineering. A keen rationality his finest virtue, he analyzed what he saw, and what he analyzed, he eventually understood. He subscribed to *Discover* and *Omni* and *Popular Science* and read everything he could on the universe or seas or paleontological issues, venturing occasionally into histories and biographies and books on psychology. The world's great mysteries were for him simple phenomena that, if he did not presently understand them, in time he would. This included people.

His most profound weakness, if it could be judged a weakness, was for novels—mysteries and thrillers, especially the lurid paperbacks that the library displayed in the main browsing area, arranged in black wire racks that turned on a shaft, books that two decades earlier no librarian would have allowed near their sacred ground. He did not understand his appetite for them, nor did he try to—they were something he enjoyed, an escape, and that was enough. Once a week he deliberately spun through them, looking for something new, his eyes taking in titles and cover designs, and he cared little whether what caught his attention was the sort of thing the English professors might approve of.

In fact, he often sought out the ones that he knew had no literary merit, preferring the simple plots and stock characters that slipped so easily through his eyes and mind. Whatever the conflict they were involved in, every fifty pages or so some man and woman were undressing each other and making love, and he was there with them, watching, taking in every undone button and open fly, every flung undergarment, and he writhed with them until the woman yelled, "Oh God, yes, oh God," and the man shuddered and moaned. He was, admittedly, something of a voyeur, poking his head—by invitation, of course—into these bedrooms and executive suites and cabins of ships, and he relished the incredibly alive, exotic worlds that the men and women made their unencumbered love in, these powerful, lusty men and beautiful, mysterious women. And the most delightful thing was that the women, almost always profoundly complex, seemed to understand the world of sex better than the men did. They were delectably appealing creatures, these female spies and oil barons' wives and duchesses, the young and not so very young, and sex was safe and easy, perhaps arrived at only after long and convoluted scheming by one or both, but it came naturally at last, the two falling into each other's arms, naked and throbbing, wherever it might happen.

Above all else Stafford loved deep, enigmatic women whose lives had followed a tortuous trail—battered women, bitter women, wronged women whose beautiful surface was underlain with plumbless waters of stark despair and confusion and anger, women who, even when they gave themselves to a man, held something back, the dark core private and unassailable. Women with a deep hurt, like those he read about in his books, or like Emily Miller, loved deeper, at an almost animal level. Women had deeper currents than men anyway—this he believed—and they were more acutely attuned to the world they moved through. A man might be trapped all his life far from the primal forces that determined the directions and intensities of animal life, but not women. When he thought of women, he thought of cheetahs and leopards, lions and tigers, creatures of surface beauty whose claws, though sheathed, were ready to arch to the surface and rend any flesh that came near them, and whose passive eyes belied the smouldering passions of the heart. Women were moved by the moon and by the seasons, their bodies following deeper urgencies than men could ever know. When the woman he was with failed to offer the depth and dimension he needed, he simply transformed her through his white-hot fancy into one who did.

Now fixed in his head was a real woman, one of the most incredibly beautiful women he had ever seen—a girl really, couldn't be more than twenty—and uncertain whether he should avoid or pursue her, he decided finally to do neither and go about his business as any decent man should. As much as he wanted to make contact with her, as much as he lay awake nights and mornings daydreaming of that woman sharing his house, he would not rush into anything. He came to work and did his job, went for coffee under the old regimen, and in the Commons chose a table facing the windows as before, where he could watch the girls go by. If he saw her, fine; if not, fine. For days he did not, and he did not care.

III

The officer on the passenger's side turned and studied Stafford in the back seat. He had a wide, avuncular face. "You sure you're OK? It's not too late for us to run you by the hospital to get you checked out. Might have a concussion or something. Broke ribs maybe. This ain't nothing to mess with." He turned back to study the people on the sidewalk.

Stafford, hunched over, favoring his left side, winced. "I'm not sure of *anything*, except that my head and side hurt like hell, but I suspect the worst I've got is bruises. It's not me I'm worried about. I want to know what has happened to Susie—to my wife."

He touched the knot on his right temple, moved his fingers to the lump behind the ear, then dropped his hand to his side, lightly wrapped with a compression bandage they had put on him at the precinct station. It hurt to breathe, so he took shallow little breaths like a puppy. The purse and Susie's sunshades and one of her shoes lay beside him on the seat.

"Why don't we just run you by for a check-out?" the cop driving asked. "Won't take but a few minutes. There's nothing you can do about your wife right now. No need to try to be a damned hero. It's in our hands. We'll find her."

"You don't know what she looks like." Stafford swept his eyes up and down the streets and walks as they drove slowly along. Now the quaint little shop fronts and balconies swirled with ornamental iron seemed sinister and the faces of the people who slid past the car blank and passionless.

"We've got a pretty good description," the other policeman

said. "Too bad you don't have a picture on you."

"You've got the one on her driver's license."

"You said her hair's a lot longer now," the driver answered. "Besides, them pictures never look much like the person. Usually several years old, hair's different. You know."

"Her hair's longer, but—"

"If I had a wife that good-looking, I'd sure have pictures, *lots* of'm." The shotgun-seat policeman was holding Susie's driver's license.

Stafford nodded. "I'll have some made."

"What about it? You gon' let us run you by the hospital?" the driver asked.

"No. I'd like to ride around with you a little longer. I just want to keep looking, you know?"

"Yeah, we know how you feel," the other cop said, "You feel like you're responsible for what happened, but you're not. It wasn't your fault. This kind of shit just happens. It's not your fault."

"Yeah, I know that," Stafford said, "but . . ."

"Look," the driver interrupted, "we got lotsa people working on it. Half the uniforms from the Eighth are looking for your wife, looking for the guys, for the car, for the boys. They made copies of this license picture and blew it up, and every uniform out on the street has got one or will get one soon. We're *looking* for her. But since nobody seen anything—and you didn't see much yourself—we ain't got a whole lot to go on. If you're not going to let us take you to the hospital, it's best for you to go back to the hotel and wait until we got something to report. You can bet she's not on the street now. No sense in wasting time riding around, and no sense in you hanging around down at the station feeling the way you gotta feel." He was a large man too, paternal looking, his eyes kind and empathetic in the mirror. Stafford could imagine that he probably had a nice wife back home, and kids.

The other officer turned around again. "For all we know, your wife got away from those bastards and took off around the corner or across the street, probably scared to death. Our guys may find her in a cafe or bar or hiding behind a dumpster or a damned potted plant in somebody's garden. Could be sitting having a Hurricane at Pat O'Brien's, wondering where the hell you got off to. Looking like she does, they'd let her in with one shoe—or with *no* shoes—and *give* her a damn Hurricane. They'd figger she'd be good for business." He belched and winced. "You can bet she ain't out on the street walking around. You might get back to the hotel and she'll be there."

"Or there'll be a message from her waiting for you," the driver added. "This kind of shit happens sometimes down here. It's a big city with lots of strange people. They probably let her go when that guy couldn't get the purse from you."

"Look," Stafford protested, "I heard them say that they *had* her. 'We *got* her' is what one of them said. They dragged her into that car and took off. I told y'all that. They wanted *her*."

"So she may have got away from'm, man." The driver was looking at him through the mirror. "Or, hell, they may have let her out a few blocks down the street, once they figured she didn't have any money or valuable jewelry on her. If all she had was a couple of rings and a watch, like you said, and them not really expensive, what the hell would they keep her for?"

They had driven slowly in an expanding circle until they were about eight blocks away from the scene of the abduction, then begun tightening the circle, moving back toward the center. As he talked, Stafford flashed his eyes up and down the sidewalks running parallel and perpendicular to the street they were on.

"She's a beautiful woman," he said, picking up the purse and clutching it to his right side. "They might do anything—"

"Sure she is," the other cop said, holding up the driver's license. "But this town is *full* of pretty women. Nobody's gon' snatch up a woman just because she's beautiful. Risk a kidnapping charge for snatching up a woman like that and doing whatever with her. These guys might get a little crazy going after drugs or money to *get* drugs, but not over a little poon—"

"Larry!" the driver said.

"I'm sorry, man. Didn't mean anything by that. It's just—"

Stafford nodded. "It's all right. I know what you're saying."

They drove on in silence. The patrol car slowly weaved through narrow streets until Stafford saw the hotel sign ahead.

The driver eased up to the curb out front. "You want us to go in with you, just in case there's a message or something?"

Stafford stepped out. "No. Y'all just sit here for a minute, if you don't mind. I'll go in and see if there's a message and let you know. I'm pretty embarrassed over all this anyway, and it might prove embarrassing to the hotel. I'll see."

The driver leaned out his window. "The hell with the hotel. Call the room again, see'f she's there, and if she don't answer the phone, you might go on up and check out the room. She might be too scared to answer. May be hunkered down waiting for you."

Stafford picked up Susie's things and nodded and went in. As he passed through the glass door, he could see a reflection of the police car and the two officers, their heads leaned toward each other, talking.

There was no message at the desk and no answer when he phoned their number, and when he went upstairs and swung open the door to the room it was exactly as they had left it. He laid the purse and sunshades and shoe on the dresser and went back down and out to the patrol car and told the officers. They nodded.

The driver smiled thinly at Stafford. "Well, don't give up. It's too early to worry about it much yet. This kinda thing usually comes right in a few hours. It just usually does." He held out Susie's driver's license. "You might as well go ahead and take this."

"OK, thanks." Stafford shook hands with the driver. "I sure hope you're right. I'll sit tight until I hear from you."

"That's best," the policeman said, putting the car in gear. "Somebody from the Eighth will call to let you know if anything happens. But don't count on them calling until tomorrow unless something does break." He had an ingratiating smile. "Normally nobody panics until the missing person has been gone for twenty-four hours. After that things tend to get serious."

"She is not just *missing*, damn it. I told you, she was *taken*. I was there. They took her right off the street. A hell of a lot could happen in twenty-four hours." He glanced uneasily up and down the street.

The other policeman leaned over. "Look, man, I don't mean to get nasty about this, but for all we know you and your lady got in a fight and she took off—"

"That is absolute *bullshit*!" Stafford slammed the roof of the car with his open hand.

"Quit beatin' on the car," the driver said. "The Department ain't got the money to fix it." He reached out and laid a hand on Stafford's arm. "I know you're upset and all, man, but just calm down and think about our position in this. You wouldn't believe the shit that goes on down here. Look, nobody seen her snatched. We got just your word for it, and frankly, so much goofy stuff happens down here that we can't hit the panic button everytime a couple—everytime something happens between a couple, you know. They're havin' trouble at home and they come down here to get over it, but you don't leave shit like that back home—it comes with you, just like you packed it with your clothes. They bring the trouble with them, and then they get to drinkin' and the next thing you know—well, sometimes it starts up again, even on the street."

Stafford pointed to his face. "What about *this* then? Doesn't this prove anything?"

"Sure it does," the driver said, "it proves somebody knocked you down or you fell down on your own. We don't know where the bruises and scrapes come from. It don't prove that a black guy in a big car did it."

"This is *bullshit*. You aren't taking this seriously."

"Oh, hell yes we are. We always do. But we don't call out the Marines and Air Force the minute something like this happens. Look, man, usually the missing person shows up. That's the way it almost always happens. If we went into all-out-battle mode every time somebody thought we should, the Quarter would look like a war zone with tanks and machine guns. We just can't get worked up until we know for sure that something really bad has happened. We drove around looking all over for your wife, and people are *still* looking for her. But we're not going to go ape shit just yet." He took his hand away. "And neither should you. Give things a little time to come right again."

Stafford shook his head and backed away from the car.

"Now, if your head gets to hurting you too bad, or your side," the other policeman said, "you call us and we'll run you over to the hospital. It could be you got broke ribs. We'd feel better if you'd go on over there now, but I guess we understand that you need to be here."

"Yeah. I'll be all right. I need to be here, in case she calls."

The driver nodded and rolled up his window and they drove off.

Stafford went up to the room, pulled the curtains to, and sat down by the window, careful not to put too much stress on his injured side. The sheets were still pulled back, the pillow on Susie's side bore the imprint of her head. After what he had just been through there was something terribly comforting about seeing the bed where they had made love only a few hours earlier.

Jesus, what would we ever do without beds? For sleeping or making love or convalescing in—soft and silent and sweet-smelling beds, with their sheets and blankets and pillows. Beds are female, they are women, they are where we go when we have to rest or rejuvenate or heal. We slide into them and snuggle and lose ourselves to dream or to love or to toss in the wild delirium of fever. And from them we rise renewed, ready to start over. Beds are sanity. We are born in them and we die in them. They are the final reality.

He took Susie's license from his shirt pocket and laid it on the dresser beside the purse and sunshades and shoe and opened the closet and looked at the white dress hanging there. He knew how it would feel if he touched it to his bruised face, knew how it would smell, but he was afraid of soiling it so he closed the door and walked to the window, where the cracked curtains admitted a slender beam of light.

He retreated a step and looked at himself in the mirror. His short-sleeved shirt, ripped at the collar, had two buttons missing at the chest, and both his shirt and pants looked like something he had sneaked from a dumpster. What a sight he must have been at the hotel desk.

"Jesus Christ," he said aloud. "What kind of Goddamned mess have we gotten into?" Stafford pulled his clothes off and shoved them into a paper laundry bag he took from a shelf from the closet, leaving on his jockey shorts. He went back to the window and flung the curtains open.

"*We*, white boy? *You*, you damned fool. You're the one who brought her to New Orleans." His voice echoed about the room.

Traffic was beginning to pick up, and there were more people on the sidewalks. Far off a siren wailed. He reached to close the curtains and almost doubled over with pain when he stretched out his arm. Favoring his side, he grimaced as he turned away from the window and, deliberately avoiding the mirror, sat down on the edge of the bed. His eyes came to rest again on Susie's things on the dresser, all that he had left of the woman who had walked out into that brilliant sunlight with him.

He eased off the bed and knelt before the dresser, taking the shoe and holding it to his face. *Why don't their shoes smell?* He knew that if he slipped his shoes off, they would smell like regular feet, the way tired feet were supposed to smell, like perspiration, fetid and sour, offensive. But Susie's shoes didn't smell like that, even though she might walk through the same heat the same distance as he. Her shoes would smell of leather, of dye, of powder, of *her*, but not of the odors you associate with feet. *Why don't their feet smell?* Susie could work in the yard all day and come in and kick her sneakers off, and Stafford would have been willing to stick her toes in his mouth. *Jesus, I'd put* any *part of her in my mouth.*

When he put the shoe back on the dresser and relaxed, hunched over, the pain was unbearable and his breaths came in shallow gasps. He crumpled to the floor and lay there a few minutes trying to make some sense of what had happened. The three boys, the car, some big black bastard pummeling him, the fleeting glimpse of Susie disappearing into the back seat—it was all a mad jumble.

Gotta have a drink. Gotta have a drink.

He dragged himself up off the floor and dressed in some shorts and a shirt and sneakers. Left arm pulled tight to his ribs, he took the elevator to the lobby, slipping as inconspicuously as he could to the car, where he removed his bottle of Seagrams from the trunk and returned to the room.

In the bathroom, he tore the paper sleeve from one of the glasses and poured a good three fingers of whiskey. There was no ice, and he didn't feel like going and getting any. Ice was for leisurely drinkers, not people who needed quick oblivion. He didn't even want to dilute it with water. He wanted it to burn going down, to sear his throat and stomach, to strike straight and deep like a little nugget of fire, then break up and spread its heat through every capillary, settling finally in his brain.

He held the glass of whiskey in front of him and watched his hand slowly raise it to his mouth. God, what a mess he was, with a bruise beginning to triangulate at the corner of his right eye, his jaw red and lumpy, and a discernible knot on his temple and behind the ear an even bigger lump that he could feel but could not see. There was no way of knowing how many times he'd been hit, but he figured around half a dozen solid blows and two or three that glanced off. The side of his face that had been against the sidewalk was scratched and abraded as if someone had worked him over with coarse sandpaper. He wished that somehow he had managed to get a lick in, a kick or punch, something to let his attacker know, as *he* well knew, that he had been in a fight.

Even while the first gulp was burning its way down he realized that as much as he needed to lose himself in the bottle, he needed even more to keep a straight head. He might get a call from her or from the hospital or police, or . . . hell, whatever, he needed to slow down, so he walked over to the window and cracked the curtains and set the glass of whiskey on the ledge.

From there the city looked so peaceful, so quaint, with its

grand mix of architecture, rooftops and facades, its smells and sounds, all the people from everywhere on earth. What an incredibly beautiful city it had been to him in years past, but now a pall had settled over it, black and suffocating. How much love he had made in this city, and how much love he had planned to make this day and the day following. As he gnashed down another deep shot of the whiskey, tears welled up into his eyes. He pulled the curtains wide and looked out across the rooftops to the river. A barge drifted down, held on course by a small tug. The river swung in a wide bend, but the water was turbulent, even without traffic on it, as if it ran over something jagged just below the surface.

An airliner, underside blazing with late sun, banked in its approach pattern and silently made its descent, almost hovering, until it fell out of sight behind a row of buildings. He wondered if Susie had seen it too, had watched it settle like the sun itself, almost imperceptibly, until it disappeared beyond the horizon.

Evening was coming on fast. What in daylight might be a reasonably safe city—at least here, close to the Quarter—at night would slide into the shade of the jungle. If they didn't find her now, while the sun still hung out there in the corner of the sky . . . . But he couldn't think of that. They *had* to find her. What were policemen for?

His head still throbbed. The lumps seemed larger, but he supposed it was simply that they were getting more and more sensitive—it would take more than two swigs of whiskey to change that. He went to the bathroom and washed his face and ran a wet hand over his hair. He thought about showering, but he was afraid the phone would ring.

"Why in God's name did this happen?" he asked the face in the mirror. "What kind of sorry mess is this?"

His ribs hurt. Maybe he should have gone on to the hospital as the foot patrolman suggested when he panted up with the couple who had spotted Stafford on the pavement. He offered to call an ambulance or have a patrol car take him, but Stafford had stubbornly refused, insisting that he was all right, that the man had hit him with nothing harder than his fist, that he'd been hit as hard before. "I'd rather start looking for my wife," he told the patrolman.

The officer had radioed for a patrol car, which arrived promptly, and they drove around the block twice, moved out in concentric circles until they had covered most of the area around the Quarter, then reversed direction and spiraled back to the spot of the assault.

They saw nothing—there was no sign of the three young blacks—and the foot patrolman reported that he had found no witnesses to the attack, though he discovered in the gutter an ivory-colored lady's shoe and on the sidewalk a pair of sunshades, which Stafford identified as his wife's. As they drove him to the Eighth Precinct station to file a report, he sat quietly in the back seat with her purse in one hand, her shoe and sunshades in the other.

Still dazed, he had filed his report. A uniformed officer directed him, but there was not much to say in it except that some black man had knocked him to the sidewalk and beaten him while someone else, presumably black, pulled his wife into the back of a car that he had seen so little of that he could not identify the make or, worse yet, even the color. It was long and had a prominent chromed grill and was a light color, white or silver or gray.

When pressed, he had to admit that he had not seen her pulled into the car, but one of them yelled out that they had her, and her shoe and sunshades were right there where the car had been, and she was nowhere to be found in the area, all of which was proof enough to him that his wife had been abducted. He gave as good a description as he could of the boys, regretting that he had not taken more note of what they looked like and what they were wearing.

When he had finished with the report, he asked if there were a private room where he could wait for word of Susie. Or perhaps someone could take him back on the street to look for her. The assisting officer nodded sympathetically and told him that it would be best for him to go to the hospital and then back to the hotel to wait for developments.

Stafford declined to go to the hospital, but he allowed another officer, one with some sort of medical training, to look him over. All were pleasant, polite, and very professional, and every one he talked to said that he probably had nothing to worry about, that such things happened, seldom with a tragic outcome, that his wife would probably be at the hotel by the time he got there. The whole thing had taken less than half an hour.

As the face in the mirror stared back at him, he hurt more and more, head and side, as if now, in the calm aftermath of such violence he had time to allow his body to feel fully what had been done to it. A passive man, he had been beaten up only one other time in his adult life, one night in Munich when he was really just a kid, right out of high school, overseas with friends for a lark before beginning college. Roaring drunk from an afternoon in one of the beer halls, he had lain back on the hood of some German's MG, to which the owner took great offense when he showed up. He yanked Stafford off the hood like a rag doll and punched and kicked him until finally his friends managed to pull him away and into their VW van. It was the next day before feeling returned—as it had now, after just over an hour—and he really hurt when he sat up in his sleeping bag in an abandoned barn where they had camped for a couple of days. He had given thanks for the anesthetic qualities of that German beer.

Now he had known the deep, raw, metallic taste of a sober beating, his head jumbled with stars and streaks of light and not enough liquor in his system to dampen the blows. He couldn't recall pain when the black man's fist struck him, just a dull concussive force like thunder and flashes of lightning in his skull, then another and another, and his head slamming against the sidewalk, again with no pain. Even the punch to the ribs, though it blew his breath away, came without real feeling, just a sudden force, like wind or water, almost as if there were no substance to what struck him, only the impact itself. But now there was pain, more intense with each passing minute, throbbing, shattering pain, which he knew only the whiskey would take care of until he found Susie again—and sleep, if he could get there, the wonderful forgetfulness of sleep.

Gradually the whiskey began to settle on him like a warm blanket and the pain subsided. He filled the glass half full again and moved to the window ledge, where he sat and watched the street, now alive with more people, fancying that he might at any minute see Susie turn a corner and cross the street to the hotel.

After a while, his body was quite numb. He staggered to the dresser and stared at the shoe and purse and picked the shoe up and smelled it again, breathing deep the leathery fragrance of its interior, then opened the purse, whose mixture of odors—makeup and leather and peppermints, the myriad smells of a woman's intimate holdings, the trappings of her home away from home—forced tears into his eyes.

Oh God, oh God.

He stepped to the closet and opened it and thrust his face into the folds of the white dress, drinking in the smell of the beautiful woman who had worn it earlier. He little cared now that he might soil it—he'd buy her another one. He'd buy her all the dresses in the world, anything she wanted.

"Oh, dear God, Susie, where are you? Where *are* you?"

He dragged out her travel bag and slumped to the floor and unzipped it and carefully laid her panties and bras and blouses and other soft things in a circle about him. He smiled as he held up the tee-shirt that she loved sleeping in, with SQUEEZE ME in large red letters across the chest, recalling how her nipples pushed out the U and M. "UM spells *ummmm*," he told her once when she wore it to bed. He repacked the bag, folding everything and placing it exactly as he had that morning.

After another glass of whiskey his side no longer hurt, and he had little feeling left in his face. "It's *me* that hurts now, not my body," he muttered and settled back onto the bed. He kept seeing images of Susie, all the vignettes that cluttered his mind. What a beautiful woman, so soft and so—so perfect. So pure, so innocent. And now where was she? What dark and sinister men had her? And for what purpose? It was as if she had been swallowed by some great sea.

Why won't the Goddamned phone ring? *Why won't somebody,* anybody, *call*?

He rolled off the bed and stumbled into the bathroom, this time tilting the bottle back and slugging it. It scarcely burned, not even to the point of watering his eyes. He did it again and again, until, steadying himself on the sink, he could barely focus on the face in the mirror.

"This is the face of *experience*, Emily, you bitch," he hissed, seeing the face of his former lover weaving in and out of his. "I wonder how *your* Goddamned feet smell?" He slammed his open hand against the mirror. "I don't want the dark side! I don't want anything under the cream. I want the cream, the *cream*. I want my wife. I want the cream back!"

Then Jack Stafford, alone in his hotel room, was sobbing like a baby, so totally out of control that he forgot for a moment where he was, the face of Susie looming before him, white as a lily and joyous with youth and innocence. He lunged for the face, reeled back, glanced off the door of the bathroom, and plunged headlong onto the bed, where he curled into a fetal ball and fixed his eyes on the strange ceiling and lost himself in her memory.

IV

It was early one Thursday while serving a boring turn at the reference desk, as everyone but the director had to do, that Stafford looked up from a torrid paperback right into her sky-blue eyes. She was holding out to him a piece of paper upon which were written some numbers and the name of a book, *Pompeii: Its Life and Art*, a title he immediately recognized as a book he had at home, Mediterranean history being one of his early passions. She said nothing.

Taking care to keep the cover hidden, he laid his book aside and reached for the note. His breath was caught deep in his chest.

"Can you help me find this?" she asked as he held the piece of paper.

"Could I—" he began. He noticed that his hand was trembling. "Uh, you need this book?"

She lowered her eyes to the paper and nodded. "Yessir, I do. Can you tell me where to find it?"

"Yes." Stafford said, looking vaguely at her, as if to look directly at her would blind him.

She smiled. "I found the call numbers, but I'm new on campus and I don't know where to find the book."

"No problem." He attempted to return the smile, "I'll be happy to do it for you. Things are slow here in the mornings."

He came out from behind his desk and walked to the table lined with monitors and keyboards, hit a few strokes and brought up the menu, punched a few more buttons, and the book title appeared. He jotted the number down and compared it with what she had written.

"There you go. You have the numbers right." He pointed to the number he had written down and nodded toward the stairs. "All you have to do now is go up into the stacks and track it down according to the letter-and-number system . . . ."

She shook her lovely head. "This is my first time in here. I'm just not sure I know how to do that. Can you direct me?"

"Well, all you have to do is . . . ." He looked about the first floor and saw little traffic, so he took the piece of paper and told her to wait while he went upstairs and found the book for her. He motioned to one of the chairs at a terminal. "If you'd like to take a seat, I'll go get the book for you. It'll take just a couple of minutes."

She thanked him and sat down and he went up the stairs toward the main stacks, pausing once he was out of her vision. He leaned back and looked at her. She was wearing a blue denim skirt and red blouse, across which her blond hair lay as she sat looking about the lower floor. She had crossed her legs so that he could see a marvelous expanse of thigh where the skirt was split up the side.

God-damn. Even at this distance he could appreciate the incredible architecture of her face, everything in perfect proportion, the delectable paleness of her skin. From here he could study her, something he would never have the courage to do up close, where she might take note. He watched her as long as he dared, then bounded up into the stacks.

He was halfway down the aisle the book should be on when he stopped and glanced at the piece of paper again. Turning it over and over in his hand, he leaned against a bank of shelves and stared down the corridor of books through a window that looked out onto the tops of brilliant green pines that studded the campus.

"Thank you, Jesus," he said quietly to himself. A soft white cloud blew in from the Gulf and passed across the blue upper half of the rectangle. He turned around, walked slowly through the stacks, and descended the stairs.

When he approached, she lifted her face to him.

He shook his head. "I'm sorry. It's not there. Somebody must have it checked out." He handed the piece of paper to her.

"Oh, dear."

"Do you need it right away?"

"Yes. I need it today. I have a report due on it Monday. Can you check to see when it might be back in?"

"Sure," Stafford said, "but there's no way we could get it back in here for you today. If we were lucky, maybe tomorrow." He laughed. "We can't just send the police out to pick it up, you know."

She shrugged. "I'll go and ask my instructor whether I can use another book, or maybe I can get an extension or something." She stood and slipped the piece of paper into a notebook.

"Have you got a second?" No one was waiting at the reference desk, only two people were at main circulation, so he motioned her to have a seat and sat down in the chair beside her.

"I'm Jack Stafford." He held his hand out to her and she hesitantly took it. Her hand was cool, creamy soft. "I'm on staff here in the library, and, believe it or not, I have that very book at home."

She smiled at him. "You've got this book on Pompeii?"

"Yes. I've traveled in the Mediterranean. Been to Pompeii. I have lots of books about Italy and Greece. Art, history, architecture, you name it."

"I'm impressed." She shook her marvelous head and smiled. Her teeth were very, very white and even. Stafford knew perfection when he saw it, and this was perfection.

"If you'll write down your name and phone number, I'll run in at lunch—I live over in Biloxi, just off the beach—and bring it back with me and give you a call. You can pick it up this afternoon."

"Well, sure, that'll be fine. If it's no trouble." Obviously relieved, she pulled out a sheet of paper, doubled it, and wrote her name and phone number across the top.

Now, damn it, he had to decide. Did he dare say, "Of course, you can have lunch with me and we'll drive over and get the book"? Or let it go at that and hope there could be some follow-up after she got the book or when she brought it back?

It was the sort of thing that required more thought, so he said, "No trouble at all. I'll give you a call this afternoon."

When she was gone he looked at the name: Susie Clayburn. "Well, well," he said softly, putting the piece of paper into his shirt pocket, "Susie Clayburn, I am going to spend some time with you. May take a little work, but I am going to date you. Bet your sweet little ass."

He called her mid-afternoon. She picked the book up late, just as he was getting ready to leave for home, and he walked her to her car, pretending, as he had to, not to know which was hers. She was friendly enough, so when he opened the door for her, he asked her whether she had any plans for dinner. For an answer she slid in and closed the door and rolled down the window.

"Mr. Stafford, you're the—you're about the tenth person

who's asked me out in the short time I've been here. Students mostly, but a couple of profs too. A girl gets tired of the propositions. If your book is simply a ticket to take me out to dinner, you can just have it back and I'll wait for the other one."

He stood there looking down at his feet. Above his head a mounting breeze was tossing the pines.

After long silence she sighed and dropped her forehead onto the steering wheel. "I have no plans for dinner, no, so what did you have in mind?"

"Well," he said softly, recomposing himself, "how many of those other guys have actually been to Pompeii, have pictures and slides of the place, have artifacts and ashes and pieces of stone from the streets and houses?" Smiling his warmest smile, he continued, "I'm sorry if I appeared to come on too quickly for you. I am a gentleman and scholar first, a lecher second, so why don't you go ahead and take the book with you and bring it back when you're through. I'm sorry I offended you. Keep it a week if you need to."

That was good. Really good. He couldn't have rehearsed it to greater perfection. Pleased with himself, he turned to go.

"Wait," she called out. "Wait, Mr. Stafford. Come back."

He took another step and stopped, pivoting slowly to face her. "You sure? I might put a little pressure on you."

"Yes. Come on and let's talk about it. I've been rude." She asked him to get into the car, and he went around and slid into the seat beside her.

"I'm the one who's sorry," she said when he had closed the door. "It's just that ever since I got on this campus it seems I have been hit on by every guy who walks past me. I am so up-tight that I don't date anybody. I just thought you were coming on too. I'm really sorry." Her small gold earrings caught the late sun and sprinkled it around the car.

"No, no, it's all right. I can see how you might perceive it." He was looking out through the pines toward the Gulf sky, where small clouds scudded along. "I hadn't intended to use the book as a—well, as you put it, as a ticket to get to go out with you. You just seemed very interested in Pompeii, and since . . . ."

She had turned in the seat and pivoted her knees toward him, her right one almost touching his leg. "And you've been there, and you've got artifacts and pictures, and I ought to be grateful to be able to visit with someone so up on Pompeii, right?"

"Hey, you're the one saying it, not me. But if you're interested in the place, I do have all kinds of small stuff that I picked up, some I bought. I was over there when I was just out of high school, before they had scoured the place and packaged everything and hauled it out to display it around the world. Before the place got vulgar. I've got some good pictures and slides, if they'd help you with your report—you know, if you need them."

"Well, whatever your intentions are, any report in art is better if you have pictures and artifacts." She was definitely softening.

"OK, then," Stafford said, playing it cool, "they're yours to use, if you'd like. I can bring them in tomorrow, if that won't be too late, or you can follow me over to the house and pick them up. While we're driving over there you can decide whether I'm safe to have dinner with or not. I mean, I *am* a librarian."

They did have dinner together, a modest chef salad that he prepared from what he had on hand—he generally kept such makings—and dark German beer served in frozen mugs, consumed on the second-floor screened porch just off his bedroom. Stafford's house was an older one, dating to near the turn of the century, nestled back among great oaks and within easy sight of one of the best stretches of beach west of Gulf Shores. The mantle of white sand ran perhaps five miles from the imposing Beau Rivage on the east to a large marina and a big three-masted casino on the west, broken only by a couple of public piers.

The porch was a perfect place for such a meal—quiet and romantic. The wind had fallen now to a steady landward drift, the night was soft and gentle, ready-made for such an occasion as this, the temperature a bit high but the humidity just right, and no mosquitoes or gnats had managed to get near the table.

As they ferried their trays of salad up to the porch, he noticed that she studied the bedroom very carefully when they passed through, and her eyes lingered on the bed. This girl, young or not, was no fool, and he knew that any chance of getting her into that bed lay well in the future. It would be one evening of good behavior for Jack Stafford if he hoped ever to add her to his list. OK: he could play the game. He could script it, and he could play it out.

As they sat and ate, she was slow to open up to him, as he expected, and he certainly did not intend to dominate the conversation, so their exchange was slight and patchy, she filling him in a little on her background as an art student and her childhood in

North Mississippi, he describing how he had happened on the house after moving to the Coast.

"I can't believe how little you're paying in rent." She swept her eyes across the lawn. "I mean, they could get—"

"Well, the couple who own it are quite old and living in Mobile near the wife's family. My father knows the guy, and I really just keep the place up for them. Yeah, they could get two or three times what I'm paying them." He smiled. "Besides, they like me. The lady is a former librarian."

"You're not married or anything, are you?" she asked suddenly, interrupting his description of the place when he'd moved in. "I mean, if . . ."

"No, no, *was*. Not now. I've been divorced for five years."

"Sorry. I felt that I had to ask. I didn't see any signs of a woman in your house. I've had married men hit on me before . . ."

"It's OK. I understand. I don't blame you."

"Kids?"

"No, thank God." He shrugged. "I mean, kids would really have complicated things. As it was, we just—it was an easy break."

"It just didn't work out?"

"That's the best way to describe it." Stafford reached for another beer and held one out to her, but she shook her head. He loved the way she used her napkin after every bite, delicately dabbing the corners of her mouth. "Mutual incompatibility, let's call it." There was no way to tell her how dull his first wife had been, how excruciatingly dull, in bed and out.

They ate on in silence for awhile.

"I've never met anyone who actually went to Pompeii before," she said after agreeing to a second beer. "You must have had an interesting life."

"Well, I've traveled quite a lot. My parents sent me to Europe for a high school graduation gift, and I got pretty much hooked on the place. I try to get back over there at least every couple of years. I've been to seventeen, eighteen foreign countries altogether."

"Is it expensive?" She was toying with a fired-clay spoon holder that he had watched a potter on Rhodes make. So strange that a man with such enormous hands, heavily veined and calloused to a dark yellow, could create delicate work like that, coaxing out the lip of the piece to almost razor thinness, then running his broad thumb across the edge and curling it lightly under and smoothing it with his saliva-wet fingers to the slickness of glass. Stafford had stood that day with sweat creeping into the corner of his eyes, his nostrils confused by the pleasant aroma of food from within the man's small house and the smell of feces ribboning the air from somewhere along the road beside it, wondering how a man with hands like those would love a woman, how gently his fingers might follow her delicate contours. The potter brushed the piece with something he dipped from a dark jar and added the holder to a rack of others in a brick kiln. Stafford picked it up the next day.

"It's—no, no," he said, "I gave maybe a dollar for it."

"I don't mean this," she said, putting the spoon holder back on the table. "I mean going overseas."

"Oh, well, yes, expensive. The air fare is, *always* is. And hotels and trains, everything is going out of sight. But there are ways to get along once you're over there. I've hitchhiked all over Europe, ridden trains, rented VW vans with friends. You can eat for almost nothing, if you don't mind a lot of bread and cheese and cheap wine, with a little stolen fruit from time to time. In Italy one summer I *lived* off peaches and cherries and a few loaves of bread. Cheapest trip ever. But I did get hungry a couple of times. I even tried to catch a sheep to roast, but the little bugger kept one bound ahead of me."

She laughed at that and after awhile poured up the last of her beer, which he noticed was loosening her tongue if not her morals. "You traveled alone over there?"

He handed her another beer, which she readily took. "Sometimes I did, especially when I was hitchhiking. Hitched all over Yugoslavia one summer. Back before all hell broke loose in the country. Generally I had a couple of people with me. It's a lot cheaper to rent a car that way."

"Girls?" she asked.

"Girls?"

"Did girls go with you?"

"Oh, yes, occasionally. One went over with me three times, another once. I ran into a few over there who traveled with me. You know, splitting expenses."

"Is that *all* you shared?"

Stafford looked at her.

"Were you lovers?"

Stafford pretended to be embarrassed, but he liked the direction this conversation was going. If she could talk freely so soon about lovers, maybe he was farther ahead in the game than he had thought.

"Yes, two or three were. Four maybe. I guess you could call them lovers. We, uh, we had sex, if that's what you mean."

"God, what that must be like, to be way off over there away from all the people who control your life, making love to someone." Her eyes were shining.

He smiled and took a deep swallow of beer. "Yes, it *is* something, something special, something delicious and exotic, like the first time you make love." That might not have been a wise thing to say, since she might *never* have made love. *Dear God, what girl over sixteen hasn't these days?* On the other hand, if she *was* a virgin this kind of talk could encourage her to loosen up, and if she wasn't, what the hell could it hurt? Besides, *she* brought the girls up.

"Just like making love for the first time," he reiterated, directing his eyes out toward the beach, which, scattered with people heading home for the day, was subsiding into the shadows of evening. "There you are thousands of miles from home, both of you, no boyfriends or girlfriends or parents to worry about, just the two of you rolled up in a sleeping bag, naked, or on a soiled mattress in some ratty hostel . . ."

"Well," she interrupted, "I've never been out of the States, except for one little dip into Mexico at El Paso. We drove down for an afternoon of shopping and came back with a bunch of straw hats and a leather purse and two big bottles of vanilla extract. And I was with my *parents*." She laughed. "There's real romance for you."

She had turned the conversation around neatly enough. He liked the direction things had been going in, but he knew better than to try to get back on that trail. What he really wanted to do was fling the table aside and sweep her into the bedroom, leaving pieces of her clothing dangling from bedposts and chairbacks, and make love to her until the sun broke through his window next morning.

"Would you like another beer," he asked. The meal was finished and they had sat in the quiet of the summer night for long minutes, she with her head thrown back looking at the gingerbread fretwork that decorated the eaves of the porch, he discreetly staring at the creamy curve of her breasts where they rose out of the low-cut red blouse.

"No. No thanks," she said. "I have a paper to do tonight, you remember. At least I've got to get started on it. Got to go."

"Well," Stafford said, rising, "it's been a great evening, and I hate to see you leave, but I understand such things."

She rose from the table and steadied herself against one of the porch supports. "Mercy, I believe that I had one beer too many."

He reached for her arm, which she willingly gave, and led her through the bedroom door toward the stairway, for one awkward instant almost spinning her around and kissing her square on the lips. Thinking better of it, he escorted her down to the study, where they gathered the bag of slides and artifacts, and out to her car.

"I enjoyed having you over, Susie," he said as he opened the car door for her. "I hope that we can see each other again sometime. At least when you bring my things back."

Over the Gulf the moon was out now, and the vast shimmering expanse of water was alive with light and motion. Far off on the horizon he could see two shrimpers trawling, their little lights dancing. What a shame not to take her down to the beach, to walk and talk, wade in the gentle surf, perhaps . . . .

"Mr. Stafford." She had started the car, then turned the ignition off. She was leaning her head out the window.

"Jack, please, just call me Jack." He was leaning over her, his hands on the roof of the car.

"OK, Jack. You're not at all what I expected." Her arms, pale and lovely in the glow from his porchlight, lay easily across the sill. "I kept expecting you to make a move or something. You know, girls just expect—"

"You sound disappointed."

She smiled. "No, no, not disappointed. Relieved. Happy, I guess. I've always heard that older men were different."

He lowered his face and looked at her. "Just how much older do you think I am?"

"You're old enough to be a gentleman. That's what matters."

He sensed that she was teasing him into pushing things a step farther. The moon was vying with the porch bulb to light her face, and Stafford, struck again by her almost divine beauty, determined that, wise or not, he was going to take that next step.

"Suppose we forget about the somewhat synthetic gentleman who's been restraining himself all night and unleash the real Jack Stafford, who would like nothing better than to suggest that you put off your paper another couple of days—I'll write a note to your prof explaining that the book was out—and take you down to the beach. That moonlight on the water's much too wonderful to waste. I promise you that I will not make any move, as you put it, that you don't want me to make."

"I suppose," she said, sighing, "that to refuse Gentleman Jack would be un-Southern of me." She reached over and patted the Pompeii book lying on the passenger's seat. "Pompeii can wait, then, but I would like that note, if you don't mind, just in case."

She got out of the car and hooked her arm in his and allowed him to lead her across the lawn to the highway, where they dashed over to the white-sand beach, made whiter by the intensely bright moon bearing down. Without talking, he guided her toward the darker end of the stretch of sand, away from the light-strung sweep that led to the marina and boat slips. Far down the beach to the east he could see the lighthouse that stood on the median beween lanes of the beach road and beyond it lights of the Beau Rivage.

Stafford stopped walking and turned back to face the house, where his little upstairs porchlights burned like beacons. Jesus, the number of times he had stood in that same spot with a woman beside him looking over at those lights, knowing that in a little while he would be using them as homing points to guide him back to his wide bed, where they would have their pleasure.

"You're not talking," she said finally.

"Oh, I'm sorry. I was just looking at the house," he replied.

"It's a beautiful place," she said.

They turned then and approached the gently swishing surf and removed their shoes, as if they had done it together a thousand times before, he rolling his pants cuffs up to just below his knees, she pulling her skirt up and holding it mid-thigh. In the light of the moon and glow of distant streetlamps he saw her legs up close for the first time, confirming what he already knew from the flashing instant when she had slipped in the puddle—that they were divinely shaped.

"You're looking at my legs."

"Even a gentleman is human." He laughed and reached out to take her hand. "Come on, let's walk out in the water a little. It's shallow. If you feel anything, it'll just be minnows nibbling at your toes or fiddlers scooting across them. If something big comes along, I'll rescue you."

They waded in the surf, hand in hand, just a couple like hundreds of others he had seen in the years he had been watching. The soft night swallowed them as they moved away from the lights on the beach road. He pointed out to her the lighthouse that stood in the median, then the one that stood just south of the Beau Rivage. The lights of shrimpers eased along far off the beach, trawling.

"They look so lovely and so peaceful out there." Her voice was dreamy.

"Yes, but they are working even as we watch, engaged in the urgency of making a living. Wearisome work. I spent a summer in high school helping on a shrimpboat. Dragging up those heavy nets with all kinds of sea-life, shrimp and fish and stingrays, everything you can imagine, mud lumps, beer cans . . ."

"I thought they just brought in shrimp." She was holding his hand tightly as they watched the boats work their way parallel with the beach.

"Oh no. They—from time to time they drag up huge dead fish that commercial fishermen have jettisoned, enormous manta rays, sharks with fins missing, mutilated porpoises, even *people*, dead bodies. It's happened. You never drag up just what you want."

She studied him.

"You know, life's just sort of like dragging a net. With the good things that come up in it, you've got a whole lot of the mediocre or bad, stuff you'd rather not have to fool with. But it's life and you have to go on dragging through the murk, hoping to keep catching enough of the good to make it worth doing."

"My, but you are the philosopher," she said.

"Well, it's kinda like dreaming, isn't it?"

She had turned to face him, her mouth just inches from his.

He continued, "You go to sleep and throw out your net and bring in whatever is down there. Sometimes it's what you want, sometimes it's not. You know? Do you know what I mean?"

Now he studied *her* moonlit face.

She smiled and said quietly, "Yes. Exactly like dreaming. You bring up the dark things along with the light—the ugly, poisonous, hideous creatures along with the things you're fishing for."

"Right, like at Pompeii, when they were digging through that ash. Some of the things they found must have set their hearts fluttering—jewelry and pottery, coins, statues, treasures of all sorts—and some of it must have been horrifying to them, the remains of men and women and children, twisted in their final agony. But most of it worthless ash, tons and tons of ash for every pound of anything worth keeping."

"But they kept at it," she said, "they kept going."

Then he simply kissed her, reached out and hooked his arm around her waist and pulled her to him, kissing her deep and long until she pushed him away with her free hand, gasping.

"I'm sorry." She leaned her forehead into his chest. "I'm so sorry. I had to get a breath. I—I just wasn't expecting it."

"I'm the one who's sorry," he said. "I got carried away. I know you've probably heard this a thousand times, but you are so beautiful . . ."

"It's all right, really. I just wasn't expecting it." She tilted her face up and placed her hands around his neck, letting her skirt drop to the water, pulling his mouth down to hers. The kiss was long, and deep.

"I was ready that time," she said when they drew apart. She turned toward the Gulf. "What are those lights farther out?" She pointed to an array of lights barely visible over the horizon.

"Probably a freighter, headed over to Standard Oil at Pascagoula, or maybe even a Navy ship coming back from sea trials. It's big, whatever it is." His breath was coming in shallow little gasps. Jesus, hadn't the kiss meant anything?

"That's too common. Why not a cruise ship loaded with lovers off to the Caribbean?" She laughed and leaned against him.

He kissed her again, and this time he pulled her so tight to him that they almost lost their balance and tilted into the surf. Afraid that she might feel his erection, something he wasn't ready to risk yet, he held her parted legs against the outside of his right thigh, noting that she bore her full weight down on him as he pressed his lips against hers.

She withdrew after a short while and said softly, "I believe we'd better go back. Things are moving awfully fast here."

He pointed to her skirt trailing in the water. "You're wet."

She gave him a quick look, then smiled. "I'll dry," she said as they waded out onto the sand.

They put their shoes on and walked up the beach to a spot across from his house, where the porchlights burned like points of flame. She raced him across the highway to her car and slipped in behind the wheel before he could reach her. He kissed her goodnight through the window, a quick, formal kiss, though he would have preferred to rip the door off its hinges and sweep her up and out and carry her to his bedroom, where in a few hours the sun would find them naked and wasted on his sheets.

She started the engine, then stopped it. "Sorry to mess the mood up with practicalities, Jack, but would you mind awfully writing that note to my instructor?"

He laughed and went into the house and returned in a couple of minutes with a piece of paper, which he handed to her. "Ms. Cooper, right? Matilda?"

"Yes," she said.

"OK. This'll get you off the hook a day or two. I know her."

"Thanks, Jack," she said and drove off into the night.

The easy and simple life turned completely around for Jack Stafford, who found himself profoundly infatuated by the incredible Susie Clayburn: Susie of the radiant blond hair and angelic face, whose every part was as perfect as a sculptor's hands might make it, whose long white legs stuck in his mind like the wings of a rising swan.

The following Friday, she returned his book and slides and artifacts, as she had promised, dropping them off at the circulation desk with a note thanking him for his kindness. Her car was parked along the same curb in front of the Fine Arts Building, but she had obviously changed her routine: when he went for his afternoon coffee the car would be there, when he left for home it would be gone.

Stafford was sensible enough to know that whether she had changed her pattern because of him or for another reason, the surest way to screw things up was to force the issue, so he neither called nor made an effort to see her. He had put his best foot forward and behaved himself with admirable restraint that night, yet he left no doubt that he was interested. That was the way it was done in his book. It was the most ancient dance of all and he had choreographed it well, the same old cat-and-mouse game that men and woman always played: silly and adolescent and frustrating, but part of the order of things. Insect or bird or beast, it was all courting and conquest, from both sexes: the male pursuing, flashing his brilliant colors, puffing and raging and bellowing, the female coyly keeping one step ahead but never out of sight for long, zig-zagging across his path, brushing past him, then leaping ahead again, knowing that the time would come when she would allow him to catch her and she would open up to him, present herself, and the time was *hers* to choose. *For this is the most fundamental law of nature, this is the order of things.*

Jack Stafford, who so well understood these truths, knew that lying back and waiting might not be the prescribed tactic of the male, and it might not work, but neither would a frontal assault, especially since he had no idea how strong her feelings were for him, though from the way she returned his kiss on the beach he was convinced that she felt at least *something*. If he had to make an error in tactics, it would be on the passive end of the scale. This was conquest Jack Stafford style.

For over two weeks he waited for something to break. He went on with his routine, having Emily over on the weekends. This time, though, when he made love to her it was not to some paper-back character with tumbling black tresses haunting his head but Susie Clayburn. He closed his eyes as he clung to his willing partner and returned to that night on the beach, kissing Susie more and more passionately, finally leading her across the highway and into his house, upstairs to the bedroom, then undressing her and laying her gently across his bed and making long and delicious love to her.

"Whew," Emily said, rolling free of him, "I must have been something really special today."

It was a Sunday afternoon and they had just finished making love. He went and got into the shower. Emily followed him into the bathroom.

"I was the new girl, wasn't I, Jack?" she asked the curtain, behind which Stafford directed the water full on his face.

He did not answer.

"It's OK, Jack. I'm glad that I was good. It's good to be young again."

He heard her at the lavatory, then the door closed. When he returned to the bedroom she was gone.

The point was, of course, Stafford admitted to himself one morning as he shaved to go to work, he was falling in love, resolutely in love, a fact that he had fought off as long as he could. It began the instant he saw the flash of her legs and panties that day, like a spark around gasoline or gunpowder, and now it had exploded and he was consumed. The danger had always been there for him—he was around so many beautiful women and girls—but he never believed that it would actually happen. He was too logical about such things, and it felt very, very strange to have to admit it to his face in the mirror, this face with the knowing eyes behind which steadily roared a furnace of a brain: he was in love.

However enslaved he was by romances and mysteries, however vigorous his imagination, deep-down he was a man of the sciences: archaeology, paleontology, psychology, astronomy.

Looking out across campus each day, if he allowed himself he could imagine what it had been like 200 million years before, under water and seething with primitive life forms, or just as easily project in the other direction and envision a desolate charred crust devoid of life, the lovely young things swishing before his eyes long since evaporated into nothing. The line from some long-forgotten poem came back to him: *We are all skeletons waiting for time to say "I told you so."*

In this great universe, where human beings were insignificant bits of matter brought to life through incredible moments of happenstance on a tiny planet in a small solar system in a medium-sized galaxy in what might be only an obscure corner of what scientists currently believed to be the whole universe, love was a riot of biology and chemistry that kept things going, there being no more mystery and dimension in human love than in the fiery, instinctive coupling of beasts, except for what men dreamed into it. And what they built on this planet—their war machines, their monuments, their empires—they built for women. They dreamed and fought their wars and built their civilizations to impress women, like some endless strutting parade of puffed breasts and fanned tail feathers, from the dawn to the doom of time, no matter how many thousands of souls might perish from their folly—dreamed and built on this silly little planet great cities and bridges and highways and rockets to reach the stars. All ultimately for women, maybe for *one* woman, for some astonishingly absurd notion that we like to call *love*. This Jack Stafford knew.

And when he thought this way, lines from Ransom's poem came back:

> Practice your beauty, blue girls, before it fail;
> And I will cry with my loud lips and publish
> Beauty which all our power shall never establish,
> It is so frail.

He hadn't been in love with his wife, who came out of nowhere at a time when he needed a woman to live with. She was warm and beautiful and the marriage worked out for a while, finally subsiding into a palpable tedium that neither of them could tolerate for long, so they divorced. No love there, no love lost. It was that simple.

He could recall brief infatuations with girls all his life, from the time a neighbor girl pulled the crotch of her panties aside to show him how he and she were different, but one girl led quickly to another on into junior high and high school and he never really felt that he was in love with any of them. He never wrote silly poems nor spent endless hours on the phone blissfully listening to some girl giggle and breathe. And when the time came, he had sex with his first girl, a delightful experience, but he felt nothing more than physical pleasure in it, a hot flurry in the back seat of his father's car one sticky May night on a rutted road by a cotton patch just beyond the night glow of the little Alabama town they were living in. It was as quick and to the point as the mating of farm animals, and he was almost embarrassed as he zipped up and crawled back into the front seat, leaving her still huddled in the backseat bewildered and tearful, then wove along the little country road and screeched out onto the highway toward town, still marveling that such a highly touted thing as sex could be done so soon.

Then came a steady flow of college girls, fifteen, twenty, thirty—he'd lost count—each coupling just a mechanical act not vastly different from performing other biological functions like eating and urinating, only with more passion, until the act was finished. In the aftermath he had no more feeling for the girl than he would have had for someone he had just shared a candy bar with.

Later came the more mature women, who wanted the passion, life having already burned them badly enough that they understood that the frivolous words of youth, the words of marital vows, were as brittle as their dreams. And with them came his rich and deepest fantasies, which they understood and, he was sure, practiced themselves. For these women he felt respect, and passion in its season, and nothing more. They wanted nothing more.

Now Jack Stafford, the best he could determine, was in love.

V

How long he lay there in the silent room, he had no idea, but when the knock at the door came, the building across the street was superimposed against a scarlet sky streaked with high clouds. He wasn't sure how many times whoever it was had knocked.

"Coming," he croaked.

His head swam as he sat up and slid off the bed and righted himself. He made his way to the door and opened it.

He had expected to see uniforms again but found instead two men dressed in sports shirts and ties and polyester pants, like used-car salesmen. They stood to either side of the door when he opened it, as if they routinely left the middle open for a charge of buckshot or whatever might come flying out at them. They had badges attached to their belts.

Stafford managed, "Do you have any word of my wife?"

"No, we don't," the short one said. "Not yet." He was a thin man, very fair of skin, his red hair sparse, face and arms pale and freckled. His eyes were quick to assess Stafford and move past him into the room. "We're detectives. Name's Oswalt." He did not offer his hand. "This here's Merchant." He motioned with his thumb. "I'm just guessing, but I figger you're Mr. Stafford."

The taller man, an African-American, was much heavier. He smiled and extended his hand. Stafford shook it, then offered his hand to the other man, who allowed his limp fingers to fall into Stafford's hand and jerked them back.

"Mind if we come in?" Oswalt asked. "We need to ask you some questions about your wife's disappearance."

"No, of course not." Stafford stepped back and motioned them into his room. "Have you heard *anything*?" They walked past him, the little one leading the way.

"No, not yet," Merchant said.

"Like I told you." Oswalt stood by the bed studying the room.

"You from the Eighth?" Stafford asked.

"Downtown," Oswalt said over his shoulder.

"Thank God you're here. I was afraid they wouldn't try to do anything tonight. You'll have to excuse the place. It's the way we left it. I just figured you wouldn't want me messing with anything until you had had a look at it."

"Considerate of you." Oswalt sniffed. "Trying to drown it, I see." He nodded toward the bottle on the bathroom counter.

"Yeah," Stafford grunted. "I had a few." He squinted at his watch and noticed that he still had on his wrinkled shorts. "It helps."

The two detectives walked slowly about the room, each sweeping his eyes around as if he intended to buy the place. Merchant leaned into the bathroom.

"Naw, this don't help." He hefted the Seagram's bottle and swirled it around. There was little liquor left in it. "Just makes things foggier is all."

"Look like anybody's touched anything since y'all left it?" Oswalt asked. "The clothes or bags or anything?

"No, not that I can tell." Stafford had backed to the end of the bed to give them room to look around.

"All your wife's stuff's here?"

"I think so."

"Anything been messed with in the bathroom or the closet?"

"No. No sir. Not that I can tell. I poured a drink—well, some *drinks*—in the bathroom and lay down for awhile, but that's it. Dozed off a few minutes."

Oswalt was studying the bed. "Was this made up when y'all got here?" He reached and patted it.

"Yes," Stafford said.

"It's not now."

"Well—"

"Y'all musta took a nap, huh, or did you pull the covers back when you took yours?"

"I lay down on the bed a few minutes after your guys brought me back here." Stafford looked at his watch again. "Well, for almost an hour."

"After you had a few drinks?" Merchant asked.

"Yes."

"You pull the covers back for that nap?" Oswalt asked.

"No."

"Then when did the covers get pulled back?"

Stafford swallowed. "Earlier. Earlier this afternoon. What has this got to do with anything?"

"Maybe nothing, maybe everything. When were they pulled back? You and the little lady in question take a nap?" Oswalt was now rubbing his hand slowly down the length of the bed, beneath the covers and above.

"Yes. We lay down a little while after the trip. Before we went out. Look here, I don't see what you're getting at." Jesus, his head was swimming, and the deep pain in his ribs had returned. "And what the hell are you *looking* for?"

Oswalt sniffed. "You done a lot of napping today, Mr. Stafford. You ought to be pretty well rested."

"What are you—"

Merchant pulled his head out of the closet. "Aw, relax, man. We just asking the kinds of questions that we got to ask to get something going, to get a direction, a slant on things. It's just the way we work. Routine, man. You know. We don't get the full picture, we got no place to *start*."

"That's all right. I know." Stafford nodded toward the bed. "We just lay down awhile before we went out. We were tired."

"And you drove from where?" Oswalt scribbled something in a little notebook from his jacket pocket and put it back.

"From Biloxi."

"All the way from Biloxi, huh? Yep, that'd wear you out for sure. What, hour and a half? Two? I 'spect most people would have to break that into two days. Maybe find a motel in Slidell or something. Yessir. A hell of a long trip."

"Just what are you guys after here?" Stafford asked.

"Calm down." Merchant held up his hands like someone asking for time-out.

"How can I calm down when this guy keeps on with his sarcasm?"

"Main thing is," Oswalt continued, turning away from the bed, "we want you to tell us what you know. Sorry about the sarcasm, as you put it. You wouldn't believe the kind of people we have to put up with. Why don't we set down and talk over what *we* know and you help us fill in the gaps. That all right?"

"Sure." Stafford motioned for them to take a chair. He sat back on the bed.

Oswalt's eyes were fixed on him. Intent. Penetrating. "Did that woman come down here with you, or did you pick her up down here somewhere?"

"My God, this is ridiculous. She's my wife! My *wife* came down here with me. Her clothes are in that closet. What in God's name are you guys trying to do here?"

"Calm down, Mr. Stafford," Merchant said. "Just calm down and answer our questions."

Oswalt pulled out his notebook again. "All right," he said, "here's all we got to go on." He carefully summarized for Stafford all they knew—precious little, he admitted—about the disappearance of his wife. No one on or along the street had seen anything, the three black boys were nowhere to be found, and but for the shoe and sunshades that the foot patrolman had discovered and the purse that Stafford had, there was no evidence at all that his wife had been with him, though, he said with assurance, there was no doubt in their minds that the wife had been along and that something had happened to her. If there had been anyone else on the street near there, they had simply vanished.

"You can see," he said in closing, "that we don't really have much to go on. Just a little ol' picture of your wife on her driver's license, which we've made copies of and distributed all over the Western World, and your account of her disappearance."

"Which is why we are here," Merchant added. "It's just that we need to try to fill in some holes in this thing, try to get a more complete picture. People don't just get snatched off the street for no reason."

"And you don't figure there's any connection between the three black boys and what happened to her?" Stafford asked. He glanced uneasily at Merchant.

"Maybe, maybe not," Oswalt answered. "Do you?"

"I don't know. You're the professionals here."

Oswalt said, "You didn't see them signal anybody, did you?"

"No, but . . . ." His head was pounding so bad he clamped his hands to his temples.

"Looks like you need some coffee, man," Merchant said. "Want me to call some up?"

"No." Stafford removed his hands.

"Some aspirin?" Merchant persisted.

"No."

"I wouldn't figure that the boys had anything to do with it," Oswalt continued. "They were there, just passing through, bopping along, and you made eye contact with them and said something to'm—"

"I said *thank you* to them."

"Which sounds a hell of a lot like *fuck you* unless you say it loud. Point is, you made eye contact and said something, which any damned fool—pardon me talking straight to you—any damned fool ought to know not to do, especially when he's alone on the street with them, and even more especially when he's carrying a purse and has a pretty woman on his arm. You may *use* these streets, and we may claim that we own them and control them, but the streets belong to people like them. That's the way they got it figured. You make eye contact with them, and then you go and *say* something to'm, which any mouth-breather shuffling along picking up cans knows better than to do. As far's I'm concerned, you are one lucky sonofabitch. It's a wonder they didn't jump you before the guys in the car came along. You know, they *could* have cut your nuts off and sliced you into strips of bacon. My man, you are *profoundly* lacking in street sense." He took a deep breath. "See, times have changed. Now what you don't know can get your ass *killed*."

Stafford shot him a look. "I don't have to be reminded of how big a fool I was. And I appreciate very much your reminding me how lucky I am. I sure as hell don't *feel* lucky." He sniffed and rubbed his nose. "I don't remember seeing anywhere in all those damned brochures you distribute at the travel agencies anything about not making eye contact with people on the street or not saying anything to'm. You don't show pictures of those little thugs or the ones cruising around in cars looking for good-looking white women, and you don't say anything about how *they* own the streets."

"They ain't what you come here to see, Stafford," Oswalt said, "and they ain't what you want to hear about. If the Chamber of Commerces in our cities put out brochures that told the whole truth, tourism would be dead. You figger Miami tells the truth or Washington or, hell, Phoenix or Seattle or anyplace else? Mobile? Biloxi? But anybody reading and watching the news knows what the truth is. The truth is"—he reached and laid a hand on Stafford's arm—"the truth is that this country's in deep shit and don't know how to get out."

"You're still the exception," Merchant interrupted. "Stay on the main streets in the right sections of town in the daylight and behind whatever walls you got at night and you are not likely to get hurt, not here, not Detroit, not anywhere. You just got crossed with the wrong people at the wrong time. It sometimes happens."

"I think that it would be good if y'all could find those boys," Stafford said. "They might not have had anything to do with it or know who took her, but they damned sure got a good look at the car and probably at the guys."

"Hey, man," Oswalt said, flipping through his notebook, "We'd *love* to talk to them. But you described them as young black guys with funny haircuts and wearing fucking—mind if I talk straight to you?—wearing fucking basketball jerseys and blue jeans and white basketball shoes. That ain't what I'd call narrowing down the field a whole lot. We could find about ten or fifteen thousand just like that in a couple of hours." He glanced at Merchant, who nodded. "Line'm up for you to look at and pick out your three. *That* I'd like to see."

"And even if you did miraculously pick them out," Merchant joined in, "I'll bet you a dollar to a doughnut that they didn't see a damned *thing*. Nothing. That car could have run right between them and flattened the one in the middle and the other two would tell you right out that they never saw *nothing*. With the one in the middle flattened like a Goddamned frog on the interstate, they'd tell you that they ain't seen *nothing*. And when you asked them just how the hell their friend got that way, mashed flat as a used rubber, with tire tracks right up his backbone, they'd just shake their heads and tell you that when they turned around to see what the noise was, what the car was doing that come right between them, that's the way they *found* him. They ain't telling you nothing about the *brothers* that did this or the car they were driving. And I can't say I blame them. It'd be suicide. Look, Stafford, you're getting a good dose of reality here, and you're not comfortable with it, you're confused, and you'll probably be more confused before it's over."

"Coulda been," Oswalt said, softening his voice, "assuming the woman with you *was* your wife, of course—"

"She was my wife. *Is* my wife. Why can't you get that fixed in your head?"

Oswalt continued: "Coulda been y'all would have made your trip down here, had a great time, and went back home thinking on all of this as one hell of a good vacation, something to look forward to next year. Just champagne and good food and roses and love-making with your lady, a *honeymoon.*" He nodded toward the bed.

"I mean, down here that's the way it usually turns out, which is why people keep coming back. That's why the two of *you* came. We got a reputation for a fun city. The Big Easy, remember? People have fun here. They come here to forget about how dull their lives are back home. And as cities go, ours is a fairly safe one. I mean, yeah, we got people killing each other, but that's mostly after dark and in sections of town you wouldn't be in anyway. Slicing each other up, shooting each other. They gon' do that. But we keep enough uniforms on the streets in the Quarter that if you got in trouble, all you'd have to do is yell out and one of them would be there. They're like the cavalry on the frontier. They gon' be there if you get in trouble. We gotta protect the tourists, no matter what. You took a back street, Stafford, way the hell off the beaten track. *Mistake.* And you just got crossed up with the wrong people. It happens. In Chicago or Houston or New York or any damned where. Every place has its dark side, man." The little detective spread his arms wide.

He continued: "You could thrash around in one of our bayous out there in the Atchafalaya Basin for twenty years without anything happening to you, and then one day a alligator snatches your ass under and tries to drown you and eat you for supper. Then you gon' go back home with half a leg and a bad disposition and tell folks what a horrible place the Atchafalaya is? You don't think about them nineteen years and ten months of swimming around and enjoying the water in the bayou, which, by the way, the alligators got figured out that *they* own—all you can think about is the feel of them big teeth on your leg and that dirty water closing over your face. It just *happens,* Stafford. The law of probability says that it can happen and it *will.* This time it looks like it happened to *you.* Add stupidity to a bad draw of the cards. That's the long and short of it. Which is not to say that your wife is not this very minute on her way back to the hotel, limping along with just one shoe and her hair all messed up, cussing you for bringing her down here."

"It almost always works out OK," Merchant said.

Oswalt started again: "You look out at that swamp while you're driving over it on the interstate, or by it, and you think, 'God-*damn*, what a pretty swamp.' But there's a law out there and everything in the swamp operates by it. That's how it works. There are things meant to kill and things to *be* killed. That's the law, that's nature balancing things out. No good and bad, just *nature*. You go out in that swamp and, likely as not, you gon' end up playing by the rules of the swamp. Now, we got laws here, but obeying them is left largely up to the individual and they're hard as hell to enforce. These sonsabitches out here in the swamp that we got to keep order in operate according to no law at all, which is why they're a lot worse than alligators. Or wolves or bears or wild Indians or whatever.

"The Indians that used to ride down off the high plains on moonlit nights in Texas murdering and raping and plundering at least operated out of a set of cultural laws that allowed that kind of behavior. And they looked on them white people as intruders, somebody screwing up their hunting grounds, killing their women and children. There *ain't* any predictable laws in our swamp, Stafford, except for the ones that protect the animals we got to deal with. They ought to declare open season on'm the way the country did on the Indians and let us take out every Goddamned drug dealer and murderer and rapist and child molester that we know are guilty of horrible crimes but can't prove it. Let us play by the jungle rules that they live by, which is none at all. We'd clean the streets up in a month and make it so safe that a woman wearing a see-through dress with a hem up to the crack of her ass and waving a stack of hundred-dollar bills could walk clear from here to the river and not have to worry about anything worse than sweatin' any hour of the day."

Stafford sat in silence as the little detective got louder.

"I'll guaran-Goddamn-tee you that we can solve the crime problem on our streets a lot quicker than Congress or the state legislatures can. They don't have the foggiest notion how to go about it. Don't even *understand* the problem, much less how to solve it. We could clean the streets up in a week in this country if they'd let us, but it ain't gon' happen. They're afraid they might violate the rights of a bunch of animals who have forfeited *their* rights by violating the rights of everybody else. Might socially *stimatize*'m. Hell, I think they ought to let the British send expeditionary forces into our inner cities, which are worse than any third-world country you can name, and colonize them, impose British law and manners and education, and then in a few decades, after they were civilized, we could accept them back into the Union. The British know how to do that. And they'd figure out how to make a profit while they were at it."

"You gotta forgive him, Mr. Stafford," Merchant said, "he gets worked up like this sometimes."

The little detective stood up and pointed out the window. "Let me tell you something, my man: I'd rather deal with alligators any day than the kind of animals we got out there. These sonsabitches kill not because they got to, not because Nature tells them to, not because you are invading their territory, and not because there's cultural allowances for it, but because you look at'm, say something to'm, get in their way, or you got something they want. Hell, they do it for every reason under the sun. There was this escaped convict, a burglar or some such, got hauled in one time for killing a family off in the country somewhere trying to get out of the state, shot the man and his woman and two children and ate right there at their Goddamn table and drank a six-pack of the guy's beer before he stole their car and left, and when they caught him and was questioning him, asking why the hell he would do such a thing, the first thing he said was, 'Because they was *home*.' You know, if they hadn't of been there, they wouldn't have been there for him to kill. It was their fault for being *home*. Said all he wanted was something to eat and a car. They got in his way, so he killed them."

Oswalt took Susie's license from the dresser and studied it.

"You two must have been there at the wrong time is all," Merchant said.

Stafford stood and looked out the window. "I just don't understand why they would bother *us*. And why didn't they just let her go when I wouldn't turn loose of the purse?"

"Well, you're right. Why indeed?" Oswalt was scratching his shoulder blade and sweeping his eyes around the room. "Maybe because you *didn't* let it go." He laid Susie's driver's license down, then picked it up again.

"Or maybe they wasn't after the purse," Merchant said. "There's something behind it, for damned sure." He leaned and looked onto the street below. "Things like this don't just *happen*. If an alligator comes up out of the water and takes your leg off, you can say that shit happens. Had to, sooner or later. You troll a purse down those streets out there long enough, one of them two-legged alligators is gon' grab it. But an abduction off the street, broad daylight, with the woman's man along. Naw. Something's wrong."

Oswalt held the license out to the light from the window and scrutinized it at different angles. "She's pretty, that's for sure, but folks don't just steal pretty women in this country. Maybe Tobruk or somewhere. Cairo. Istanbul. But not in New Orleans. There's too many of'm. Ain't nobody out there except crazies—and they operate alone—is going to yank a pretty woman off the street just to keep for a while and screw or screw once and throw back out on the street."

"Gary—" Merchant raised his hand.

"I'm sorry, but it just don't happen. One maybe, but not a carload. And *he* probably wouldn't do it with you along, even at night. Too chickenshit for that. The risk is too great for that. They might take big risks for drugs or money, but not for a piece—"

Merchant cleared his throat and shifted in his chair. He did not look at Oswalt.

"I get your point," Stafford said.

"Sorry, but I asked you if you minded me talking straight with you. You ever been in trouble with anybody, especially anybody in the mob? You got a *dark* side? Anybody in your *family* ever had trouble with them? What about the woman? *She* got a dark side?" He held the license out toward Stafford and tapped the picture with his finger.

"Jesus, no," Stafford said. "I am a librarian. A *librarian*, for God's sake. My wife's an art student. I don't know anybody in the *mob*. Neither does anybody in my family. We're peaceful people, and Susie gets along with everybody. I don't have an enemy in the world that I know of, unless it's a couple of pissed off students now and then that I've had to crawl for stealing magazines or books out of the library. Besides, I've already told you that it was a carload of blacks that took her, and that's not mob, is it? Are there blacks in the mob?" He looked at Merchant, then back to Oswalt.

"You never know. Depends on what mob you're talking about, I guess. Hey, Merch, any of your people in the mob?"

Merchant laughed. "Probably," he said. "If there's money in it. The mob's blind when it comes to color, except for one—green."

Oswalt started up again: "Blacks in a big light-colored car with a flashy grill. Man, that's pretty damned specific all right. Sometimes I wonder what kind of testimony we'd get from a streetful of Americans if a great big ol' spaceship plopped right down in the middle of one of our cities and snatched up a couple of people. 'Well,' they'd say, 'it'uz a average size saucer, kinda off-white, nothin' special about it, flashin' lights around the edge, some shiny windows, roared a lot, set down right there across from the Ace Hardware on Bell Avenue, and two or three—maybe a dozen or so, who the hell can count?—little farts, avocado shade, average-height, jumped out and take'n them two women right from in front of our very eyes. I wuzn't watchin' real close, you know, 'cause this kinda shit is always happenin'.'"

"Look, Goddamn it, I've lost a wife and I've tried to tell you everything you want to know." He sat down on the bed. "I don't know who took her or why or what they've done with her. All I know is I have lost one damned fine woman to a bunch of street thugs and you guys are all I've got to help me find her."

"Naw," Oswalt said, sweeping the room again with his eyes, "we're not *helping* you do nothing. *You* lost her, but *we'll* find her, whoever and wherever the hell she is, and it looks like we're going to have to do it without much help from you."

"What do you mean, *whoever she is*? Can't you get it in your head that we're talking about my wife? That's her purse and her shoe." Stafford pointed to the dresser. "Her bag's in the closet."

"All we know right now is that you were with some woman," Merchant said.

Stafford lay back and draped an arm over his eyes. "Look, guys, I've told you everything I know. I was getting the shit beat out of me while they were taking her, my *wife*. That big bl—that big sonofabitch had my face to the sidewalk slamming me silly."

"Let me ask you something else, Stafford," Oswalt said. "Assuming this was your wife, you two have any kind of fight earlier?"

"What do you mean?"

"You know, did y'all have a domestic dispute or something, anything that might have pissed her off enough to slap the shit out of you a few times and hit the road?"

"Jesus Christ! I told you what happened. If she had just taken off, I would have gone after her. I sure wouldn't involve you guys."

"Well, maybe you got scared. Big city, good-looking woman. Maybe you got to thinking about what could happen to her."

"We did not have a fight or argument or anything. It happened just the way I told you. The boys, the guys in the car, all of it exactly as I told you."

Oswalt, still standing at the window, studied the rumpled bed awhile. He sucked his teeth, moved to the headboard, switched the light on, then stooped until his face was just over the left pillow. Very carefully he reached and rubbed his hand across the pillow the way someone would sooth a child. He lifted something and held it above him and stretched it in the light. He turned and looked down at Stafford.

"Your wife's a blond, right?"

"Yes."

"And you're, what, brown?"

"Brunette, I'd say," Merchant cut in.

"Brown, brunette, whatever." Stafford sat up. "But not blond. Why?"

Oswalt stretched a hair between his hands. "Pretty long for you, ain't it?"

"So?"

"So, who the hell else has been wallering on this bed today? You got short brown hair and your wife's got long blond hair, and what I've got here is a strand of reddish-brown hair, roan or what-the-hell-ever, over a Goddamned foot long. So whose hair *is* it? It ain't the maid's—she ain't been in here. Besides, we've already talked to her, and her hair is black and it damned sure ain't long and straight."

Merchant took the hair from Oswalt and moved to the window, where the late-afternoon light reflected off the clouds spilled in. "Browner'n hell. And long."

"Shiiiit." Oswalt had swung his face back down toward the pillow. "There's more than one hair here. More like a Goddamned *tuft*." He plucked another strand from the bed, then another.

"Was this bed messed up like this when y'all got here?" Oswalt asked.

"No, I told you that *we* messed it up." Stafford was up and pacing now.

"Then y'all must have had one rough nap. Now, tell us what the hell you did up here and why and who else was in on it. Did y'all have a threesome, or what? A Meringue Detroit?"

Merchant cackled, then looked at Stafford and lowered his head.

"All right, whose *is* this?" Oswalt stretched the hair out. "Did the little lady come up here and catch you screwing another woman, then take off? Or was your wife even down here? This is gettin' weirder by the minute."

Stafford dropped his head and sat back down. "Hers. The hair's hers."

"Your wife's?"

"Yes, my wife's."

Oswalt snorted. "You said she's blond. Have you already forgot what color her hair is? The woman in that license photo is *blond*."

"Look, nobody else was in on it. It was just a private little game, a joke. She put on a wig, that's all. A wig. Just harmless stuff that men and women do together. Husbands and wives. It was just a game. Don't you guys ever—"

Merchant reached and laid a hand on Stafford's shoulder. "Now what's going on here, man? You stop the crap right now and tell us what this is all about. You're wasting our time and yours, and we ain't getting no closer to finding your wife. What gives?"

"I told you, she wore a wig," Stafford said quietly.

"*What* wig?" Oswalt leaned toward him. "Where's it at?"

"When we . . . when we made love this afternoon she wore a wig. I don't know where it is. She put it somewhere."

Oswalt exchanged a look with Merchant. "Now our nap has warmed up a little. They were tired from that long trip, so they—"

"What we did on that bed is our business, none of yours."

"And the wig bit?" Oswalt pushed.

"It's something personal, something we *do*. It's got nothing to do with her being grabbed."

Oswalt sat down on the bed across from Stafford. "Well, ol' son, I guess *we'll* be the judge of that. Now, where's the wig at?"

Merchant sat down beside Oswalt. "This ain't no game now, Stafford. Like Gary said, we want to know what went on here and who was in on it. Forget the private stuff and all that. Ain't nothing private now. It's all gon' come out. So why don't you go ahead and level with us?"

He spoke softly, like an old friend, like a grandfather, but Stafford felt like a man caught in some terrible sin. He didn't see how it was any of their business what he did in the privacy of his hotel room with his own wife. They were so damned pushy, like they had a right to know about the wig and the game, like they could spy on him and his wife. There was no doubt that they were enjoying what was shaping up. He twisted in his chair.

"Look, man," Oswalt said, "you might as well go ahead and tell us what happened here. We have to *know*. Otherwise we can't piece things together. Things won't fall into place. Was anybody else here?"

"It's the last time I'm telling you—it was just the two of us, me and my wife, and what we were doing was husband and wife stuff—private, you know, things people do in their own rooms."

Oswalt slammed his fist down on the bed. "And it's the last Goddamn time I am *asking you*, where's the wig *at*?"

Stafford shrugged. "I don't know. I guess she put it in one of our bags. What do you need the wig for?"

Merchant pointed to the closet. "The bags in there?"

"Yes. Yes, they are in there. Do you seriously want me to try to find the damned wig?"

Oswalt nodded, rising from the bed and crossing to the closet. "It's not like we're asking you to do the impossible. Do you want to find it, or do you want *me* to look?"

Stafford got to his feet. "Jesus Christ, I feel like I'm being spied on here, like I'm some kind of criminal myself." He took a step, doubled over with pain, then lurched to the closet. "You are not going to go through our bags."

"You need a doctor?" Merchant asked. "Man, you hurtin'."

"No shit," Stafford hissed. He opened the door and dragged out the two leather-trimmed green canvas bags.

"*Are* you?" Oswalt asked. He stood over Stafford, his eyes still busy with the room.

"Am I *what*?" He unzipped the first bag, his, and flipped the folded things out.

"Are you a *criminal*? Is it *you* we ought to be focusing on?"

"What the hell do you think? Do I look like a criminal?"

"You're sure *acting* like you got something to hide," Oswalt said. "What you got in them bags that you don't want us to see?"

"Nothing," Stafford shot back. "I just don't want you handling our things, Goddamn it. This is private. You'll have to excuse me, but I'm pretty touchy right now."

"Got a gun or something? Maybe they toked a little too, Merch. You got dope in there, Stafford?"

Stafford ignored the detective. "It ought to be in one of these. It's—it's not in here." He wadded the clothes into the bag and zipped it up.

"Do you mind if *I* look?" Oswalt reached for the second bag.

Stafford pushed his arm away. "I damned sure do mind. These are our bags, and what's in them is none of your business. And, no, I don't have a gun or drugs or anything else that's against the law. The wig must be in the other one."

Merchant got off the bed and walked to the window. "You may not be guilty of anything, Stafford, but you sure making it hard for us to believe it. Why don't you lighten up and let us do our job. We are not the enemy. Let him look."

"Not necessary." Stafford yanked the wig out of Susie's bag.

She had wedged it down into a corner. "Here's the frigging wig."

"That what you call it, a *frigging* wig? That's nice." Oswalt took it and held it like a dead animal in his palm. "Hell, Dave, look at this thing. Where'd you get it, Wal-Mart? I can't believe a woman that looks as classy as your wife would be caught even in the bedroom, alone with her husband, with this thing on."

"It wasn't a fashion show." Stafford snatched the wig away from the detective and flung it back into the bag and zipped it. "It's none of your business where we got it. Now, why don't you quit treating me like a street pervert and help me find my wife? You ought to be out looking for her instead of bruising me up." He thrust his face out at him. "I've *had* my lumps today, damn you!"

For the first time he saw real anger in the little detective, who had his head deep in the closet. He pulled his head back and grabbed Stafford by his shirt and shoved him against the wall. He lifted him onto his tiptoes. Stafford's side flared with pain.

"Man, you better get right with us. We don't even know that you *had* a wife here with you, much less that somebody stole her off the street. All we got is a wild-ass story about some niggers hopping out of a big light-colored car on a busy New Orleans street and snatching some beautiful blond away from her husband, if he *was* her husband, and the only one we know that saw it—and he damned sure didn't see it *well—was* the presumed husband, who don't seem to be able to explain about a wig that he didn't even remember to tell us about until we made him. I get a picture of a guy carrying a purse and a God-damned woman's shoe on the street, with a woman's clothes and wig in his room and no record what-so-damned ever of a wife being with him except for that bag of clothes and a shoe and a purse, which might not even be his wife's, with a driver's license photograph in it. And it's an Alabama license, not Mississippi, and the name on the license don't end in Stafford, and the address on it is Mobile, not Biloxi. You notice all of that? Maybe we ought to try to call your home number and see if the little lady ain't still *in* Mississippi or Alabama or wherever the fuck you're from and don't even know where you are or who you been with. If you are just messing around with us and wasting our time, for whatever reason, I'll shove a book up your librarian ass!"

Merchant tapped the little detective on the shoulder. "Gary, let'm down."

He couldn't believe that such a small man could be so strong. The detective shook Stafford as if he weighed nothing. He looked for help from Merchant, and the big detective grabbed Oswalt by both arms and held him.

"Would *you* believe you if you was us?" Merchant asked. Oswalt let him slide down the wall until his feet were flat on the floor.

"I don't know. Maybe not." He slid down to the floor, his back to the wall. Oswalt shook loose from Merchant and leaned over Stafford. "But let me ask you guys one thing." He glared up at Oswalt. "If I'm making this shit up, how the hell do you think this happened to me?" He pointed to his face, then to his side.

"Man," Oswalt said, "we ain't doubting for a minute that you got your ass beat up on the street. It's the woman we're not certain about." He was crouched before Stafford, rocking on his heels. "You got to tell us everything you know. Who *was* she? Lotsa guys walk these streets with good-looking women that ain't their wives."

"All right, all right. I'll tell you what went on here. Not that it makes any difference in what's happened, but if it'll make you get on out of here and look for my wife, I'll do it." He pulled himself up defiantly. "And she was—*is*—my wife."

"How come it's an Alabama license, the name on it ain't Stafford, and her address is different from yours?" Oswalt was in his face.

"Because we haven't been married long. Her maiden name is still on it. And she's been in Mississippi only a few months. She hasn't had a chance to get everything changed yet."

Merchant returned to the bed. "Come on, Gary." He patted the mattress. "Come on and set down and let's let the man talk."

With the two detectives sitting quietly on the bed, both busy with their notebooks and pencils, Stafford tried to piece together the details of the game. He noticed that Merchant had laid a tape recorder, its little red light burning, at the edge of the bed.

"Wouldn't want to miss anything, would you?"

"Just make sure you don't leave nothing out," Oswalt said.

Merchant pointed to the bag the wig was in. "She carry that hairpiece down in a bag, or what?"

"In her purse."

"Along with the black dress?"

"Yes."

"She was wearing a white one?" Oswalt asked.

"Yes."

"But when they grabbed her off the street she was wearing the black one she carried down in her purse?"

"Yes. She put it back on when we went down."

"Why?" Merchant asked him.

"Because I asked her to. She . . . she looked good in it."

Oswalt snorted. "Yeah, it turned her into good bait. Was she wearing underwear?"

Stafford glared at him. "What the hell does *that* mean?"

"Nothing. I'm just trying to get the whole picture. We know what she was wearing on the outside—was she wearing *underwear*?"

"Goddamn it, you pervert."

Merchant held his hands up. "Easy now, easy. That might have been going a little far, Gary. Get on with it, Stafford. Forget about the underwear. It's just one of the things that guys get their ladies to do, walk around without underwear in a restaurant or bar or on the street, just because they're the only one who knows it besides her and it turns them on. Get on with the story."

Stafford winced and finished his summary, ending with the two of them coming into the room. He pointed to the tape recorder. "That's all you guys are getting—I've told you everything I know. The rest of it you'll have to piece together for yourself."

"Oh, I'm beginning to get the picture all right," Oswalt said. He flipped through his notebook. "Nobody else knew about this?"

"No, nobody knew about it. We don't know anybody here, and even if we did, we wouldn't let them in on our private games."

Merchant wagged his heavy head. "Dunno, Gary. Something's fishy." He looked at Stafford. "I don't mean what you and your wife did. Like you say, that was between y'all. I mean the whole scene. I got a gut feeling there's some connection between what went on here and what happened out there on the street. Just a feeling. Her going down to the lobby and all and changing clothes. Of course, if you're holding something back . . ."

"Hell," Oswalt said, getting off the bed, "I got the *full* picture now all right. The little woman got tired of his fucking games and took off back to Mississippi. He probably tried to get her to pull her dress up in an alley out there and screw him in front of God and the world. Let's go. If he wants to keep on with it, let the uniforms handle it. We got more important things to work on."

Stafford's eyes met Merchant's. "Man, I want my wife. I've told you everything. Those guys *took* her."

The big detective continued shaking his head. "Something's been left out here. Something ain't right. You didn't say nothing to anybody, your wife didn't say nothing?"

"No. I mean, a maid looked at her funny in the bathroom when she put on the wig and changed dresses, but—"

Oswalt was standing by the door. "Come on, Merch, this is a domestic thing is all."

"*What* maid?" Merchant asked.

"It was just a maid in the bathroom down there, a black woman, somebody cleaning the place. She saw Susie go in the stall wearing the white dress and come out with the black one on. And she saw her put the wig on, but I just figured she was curious. That's all. That's all Susie thought. Neither one of them said anything."

Merchant looked at Oswalt. "You make anything of that?"

The little detective shook his head. "Not a thing. Let's go."

"Did anybody else see her, speak to her, *anything*?"

"No." Stafford stood up and slipped into the chair where he'd been sitting earlier. He stared at his open hands.

"Anybody see y'all later, when you were leaving the hotel?" Merchant had put in a new tape and turned the recorder on again.

"The bartender. Harry. Harry somebody. I don't remember whether the last name was on his nameplate. I don't think so. I think it just said *Harry*. He saw us. When we got a drink after, you know, *after*."

Oswalt nodded. "Yeah, after y'all had recovered from that long trip from Biloxi. Come on, Merchant, there ain't nothing here."

"Did he say anything to you?"

Something turned in Stafford's mind at Merchant's question, something dark and down deep, and he hesitated before answering, as if somehow it had all been heading to this one crucial point, the whole crazy afternoon hinging on this answer.

"Stafford." Merchant reached out to touch him. "Did you say anything to this guy Harry? I mean, I guess you ordered drinks or something, but did you say anything else to him, or did he say anything to you? Did you—"

"Yes. He kept looking at her, you know, the way men do at my wife. We talked a little bit at the bar, and he said something about her being beautiful and all."

"And I guess you got off on that," Oswalt said.

Stafford ignored him and continued to speak to Merchant. "You know, just *stuff*. He asked if she was my wife or my girlfriend."

"*And*?" Merchant pushed. "What'd you say?"

Stafford swallowed hard. "I told him *no*."

"You told him *no*?" Merchant stood and looked down at him. "What the hell did you tell him that for? What else did you tell him?"

"Well, I—I told him—" He put his head in his hands.

"What the bloody fuck did you *say* to him?" Merchant's voice was rising. "Let it go, man!"

"I told him . . . ." Stafford swallowed hard. "I told him I was paying two thousand bucks a night for her."

Merchant looked at Oswalt, then back at Stafford. "You told him she was a damned *hooker*? A two-grand-a-night *hooker*? You incredibly dumb son-of-a-bitch! Don't you know what—" He snatched up the recorder and pocketed his notebook. Oswalt still stood at the door. "You call in, Oswalt," Merchant said. "I'll pick that bastard up and meet you in the car. Hope to hell he's still down there. Harry, huh?"

Stafford nodded.

"I'll call from the car." Oswalt closed the door behind him.

"But what—"

Merchant reached and patted Stafford on the shoulder. "You just hang loose till we get our man Harry wrapped up. We got some talking to do to him." He shook his massive head. "Man, I hate to say it, but you are one stupid sonofabitch, dumb as a housefly, if you'll forgive me for saying so. Innocent as a Goddamned baby! You and your fucking games. You ain't got the foggiest notion what you've done." He snorted. "A librarian!"

Stafford stood, weaving, and walked toward the window. He felt like a very old man. "God, what's happened here?"

Merchant shook his head slowly, looking past Stafford at the now dark curtain. "I don't know yet, but you stay right here until you hear from us. I 'spect ol' Harry will have some information for us, if and when we find him. We'll send somebody over for you when we need you downtown. We'll probably be back for you in a couple of hours. Sit tight. And stay off the Goddamned bottle."

Then he was gone and Stafford was left staring across the room at the window, where through the crack in the curtains he could see evening settling down on the city. Soon it would be full dark.

VI

Someone stood in the doorway behind him. "Are you busy?"

"No, uh, not terribly. Just a second while I finish this . . . ."

At work at a computer terminal on a small desk shoved against the back wall of his office, Stafford did not immediately turn his chair around to face the voice. He was, in fact, *very* busy. The director had him on a special project involving the procurement of some water colors and chalks and pen-and-ink sketches done out at the barrier islands by a local artist. Marvelous things they were, too, strikingly impressionistic, but better in color and shadow, he thought, than the highly publicized prints of Walter Anderson, whose island art had taken the South by storm.

"Been to Pompeii lately?"

At that he swiveled his chair and looked up into the eyes of Susie Clayburn.

"Uh, Susie, I'm sorry. I was just . . . . Hey, have a seat." He stood and gestured toward a chair across the desk from his.

She set her book bag on the floor beside the chair and sat down, the filmy dress—not unlike the one she was wearing the first time he saw her, only a different color—allowing him a glimpse of her legs before it settled across them.

"You looked at my legs again."

He blushed, but she was smiling.

"Yes, I guess so. You'll have to forgive me. As I told you the other night on the beach, I'm human. Worse, I'm male, and males are *supposed* to notice such things."

"Right. I understand that," she said, "but aren't they supposed to *sneak* a peek? I'm not really supposed to see you watching me, am I? Isn't that the way it goes?"

"Yeah, probably, but I'm not real good at that sort of thing." He shuffled some papers on his desk, trying to avoid her face. "Should I have dropped a book and glanced on the way down to pick it up? Or maybe taped a little mirror on my shoe? I keep one in the desk here." He slid open the drawer and pointed.

She laughed. "I don't know whether it would have been better, but that's the way it's usually done, from junior high on up to nursing home."

"Yeah, I guess so." He was mildly embarrassed, though the joke about having a mirror in his drawer had been clever.

"Why do guys do that?" she asked.

"What?"

"You know, try to look up girls' dresses?"

He shrugged and grinned. "I guess they think they'll *see* something. I was joking about the mirror, you know."

"I know that. What would they *see*? I've noticed guys just walking along looking at girls'—at their crotches, like they think suddenly the girl won't have anything on down there and they'll be looking right at the real thing."

"It's just guys doing what guys do, I guess. Maybe they like to pretend that they can see through clothes. Hell, I don't know, Susie. It's just part of being a male animal. Maybe it's better than running up and sniffing, like dogs."

"Do you do that?"

"What? Run up and sniff?"

She laughed. "You know what I mean. Do you look at girls' crotches?"

Stafford looked away from her. "I don't think that I look at girls' crotches. I don't think so. Hell, maybe I have, maybe I do. I don't *know*. If I do, it's nothing conscious."

"You are certainly interested in my *legs*."

"Sorry, but that's as far as I tried to look. Trust me."

Stafford was uncomfortable now, like he had been caught in some sort of lie. How could he explain why males acted like males? Because it's the law, he could say to her, the law of nature. The male stares at the female where he knows the entry point is. Or he tries to. That's his target, the one nature intended for him. And God knows, some of the girls on campus pulled their jeans on so tight that you could see the bullseye quite plainly.

"Drop the subject? Sorry to put you through it, but I've always wondered. I just seem to be comfortable talking to you." She smiled again. "I really don't mind."

He looked at her quizzically.

"That you looked at my legs. You've earned that, I think."

"How? What do you mean, earned it?"

"I got an *A* on the Pompeii report."

"Oh, all right, I get you. I wasn't sure."

"She said it was one of the best papers she'd ever gotten in her class."

"Well, I'm glad."

Things were smoother now. He was comfortable with her and she apparently was with him. She talked for a while about the Pompeii paper, summarizing its strengths and delighting in how well the slides and artifacts had gone over.

"They especially liked the shot of that guy with the huge erection." She looked away when she said it.

He had forgotten that it was in with the other slides: a little chap carved out of stone, two or three feet tall with a penis almost as big as he was angled toward the sun and carried like a heavy burden. There were perhaps sixty or seventy slides in a box and he had simply handed it to her in a larger box with chips of stone and pottery and a clear-glass container of volcanic ash.

"God, I am so sorry. I just forgot about it being in there. It's Priapus. Everybody photographs him. They used to put him in gardens. Served as a kind of scarecrow. I just forgot. The Pagan Penis, I call it."

"No, no, it's OK, really. They enjoyed it, especially the boys, who, of course, had all kinds of clever things to say about the 'little two-headed guy.' When I previewed them, I thought about taking him out, but I didn't really see anything wrong with it. I mean, it's not like we were looking at a shot of a naked person. He's hardly anatomically correct, and he's so *cute*."

"Jesus," Stafford sighed, "what a fool."

"I can see how he might keep birds out of a garden," she said.

Stafford squirmed in his chair.

"Mrs. Cooper wondered why I didn't just bring you in to talk about being there. That would have been a good touch, but I didn't think about it soon enough."

"I would have gone."

"I didn't know you well enough to ask. Besides, they would

have pushed you into talking about the little two-headed man, which is what all the boys were interested in."

"Say," Stafford changed the subject, "I'm working on an art project right now that might interest Matilda."

It was time to talk of other things. How incredibly stupid to have let Priapus slip through, how embarrassing it must have been for her. Then again, she didn't appear to the kind of person who embarrassed easily. Cool, level-headed. He turned back to the desktop behind him and picked up a stack of photographs.

"See what you think of these. They're just photos, of course, but you can tell a lot about this guy's work from them."

Susie leaned and took the photographs, laying them on her lap. Her fingers were long and perfectly shaped, her arms lusciously white, lightly downed below the elbow, and the dress fell open slightly when she bent her head forward to study the pictures, revealing the upper arch of her breasts. She contemplated the first one on the stack, a beach painting of dunes crowned with sea oats, above which two ospreys wheeled.

"What are they? Sorry—I *know* what they are. I mean, who did them?"

Stafford came from behind the desk and bent over her. His arm brushed across her shoulder as he tapped the top photograph. Her hair was exactly the color of the sea oats.

"There's a fellow over in Mobile by the name of Smithers who spends lots of time out on the barrier islands sketching and painting. Or *used* to." He swept his arm in an arc to the south, from east to west. "From Dolphin Island off the Alabama coast all the way over to the Chandeleurs off Louisiana. He does scenes like these, pen-and-inks too, splendid stuff, and we've got an opportunity to buy most of the collection for a display in the Commons—well, really, all across campus. We think he's at least as good as Walter Anderson. Students may think he's better."

"I've seen lots of Anderson's work. You go into a book store anywhere along the coast and you bump into his stuff. I find it too flat, stark, not much soul in it. He's all line and motion, too repetitious for me, but these . . . ." She held a handful of the photos out, spread like a fist of cards. "These are deep, so rich in color. Mr. Stafford, these are *great*."

She had shuffled through the stack and started going back through, more slowly, as he stood at her side, his arm still lightly touching her shoulder, her hair spilling down across her breasts. He eased his head back and to the right until the sea scenes and her hair flowed together. It looked so perfectly balanced, the sea and sand and sky and oats and her hair, all marvelously blended, as if she should have been there on the beach with the man who had done the painting, stretched out before him in the sun, one with the wind and water, someone to haunt his world as nothing else ever could again. It's the way Stafford would have wanted it, if he could have been that man.

"Call me Jack. Remember?"

She turned and looked at him, her face not three inches from his. He could feel the heat from her body.

"OK, *Jack*. I've never been out to the islands, but my opinion, for whatever it's worth, is that these are terrific."

"I'm glad you like them. We have a shot at rounding up a good three quarters of his whole collection for what I figure is a song. Smithers is getting on in years now, almost ninety, and doesn't go out there anymore, at least not to draw. The University of South Alabama has been trying to land the collection for years, but he had some sort of falling out with them and doesn't want his paintings there. He says they'd be closer to the islands here anyway, and that's where they belong, close to what inspired them. Damned Romantic, you know. USA could pay him five times what we can afford, but he wants *us* to have them. The only possible kink in the plan is with the family, who naturally want to go with the highest bid."

"That's the way it always goes, isn't it?"

"Yeah." Stafford slowly shook his head. "That's the nature of the beast."

She handed the photographs to him. "Well, I hope we get them here. I'd love to see them hanging over there, maybe some in the Fine Arts Building."

"Oh, there'll be plenty to hang all over campus. It'll be just perfect." He walked around the desk and laid the photos beside the computer. "We should know in another week or so whether we've got them. Soon as I get this paperwork done and we get his signature. I should have everything together and out of here by late this afternoon."

"In time to get to the beach before dark?"

He had heard her. There was no mistaking what she'd said, but when something you've been wanting to happen so badly suddenly does happen, you shake your head and look and listen again, to be certain that you haven't just willed it out of thin air.

"The beach?"

"Yes, the beach. The one we walked on the other night. I'd like to see it in the daylight. If you get your work finished in time, I mean. And if you want to."

"Well, I—"

"I'm sorry, Jack. I'm coming on too strong. That's not like me. You're supposed to ask *me* to go to the beach. It's just that I've been thinking about the other night and how much I enjoyed being with you. It's Friday and all, and I just thought we could maybe do it again. No paper due on Saturdays, you know, and I could stay a little longer."

"Jesus, Susie, if only you knew how I wanted to call you. I just didn't want to force the issue. I was afraid I'd spook you, after what you said about guys coming on to you."

"So we have a date?"

They did indeed have a date, and though it consisted only of a long hand-holding walk on the beach and dinner at a local restaurant, with several passionate kisses late in the evening as they sat on the porch watching ships inching along out in the Gulf, Stafford was satisfied that he had found the woman he had begun to think he would never find.

"What're you doing tomorrow?" he asked as he escorted her to her car. It was quite late. There was little traffic along the highway, which whizzed with cars most hours of the day and night. Damned if his heart wasn't pounding like a high schoolboy's.

"Nothing in particular," she answered. "Did you have something in mind?"

"Well, you said in my office today that you've never been to the islands."

"No. From the beach road in Pascagoula I can sometimes see the glow of them in the sun, so I can tell where they are, just a faint little lighter shade to the sky where the sun is bouncing off the sand out there, like the ghosts of islands, but I have never seen them."

"Like the *ghosts of islands*. You've got a good metaphorical mind, Susie."

She smiled.

"Would you like to? You know, go to the islands?"

"You mean tomorrow?"

Stafford pointed off to the Southeast. "Yes. I have a friend up the Pascagoula who owns a small sailboat that we can use—that is, if he's not going to be using it. If he is, he's got another boat we can borrow, one with an outboard motor. Not as romantic as sailing, but it'll get us there. We could go out and spend the day on Horn or Petit Bois. Horn would probably be better. That's more Smithers and Anderson country. Bigger island, lots more diversity in wildlife and vegetation. Got ponds on it. We can have a picnic, spend the day. The weather's still plenty warm and the water temp is holding in the mid-eighties, so we can swim and . . . ."

She held his hands in hers. "Well, if you promise we won't break down out there and have to spend the night, where you could take advantage of me, I'll go." She leaned and gave him a quick kiss. "Now I've got to run. It's late."

"Sure you don't want to spend the night here? I'll sleep downstairs—"

"All my stuff is at home. I'd just have to go by there in the morning and pack it, making us late. No, I'll go on in and pack tonight." She looked at her watch. "Heavens, it's almost morning anyway. What time?"

"Well, late as it is, probably not until nine or so. I can't call Jerry this late. I'll phone him first thing in the morning and line up the boat. I'll zip by your place and pick you up first. Around nine. And if you want to, bring something to sketch with. It's beautiful out there."

"What if you can't get a boat?"

"Then we'll do something else. But tomorrow's ours."

"Are you sure you know where the apartments are?" She had gotten into her car and rolled down the window.

"Yes, I know where the Buena Vista complex is. I know right where it is."

"Number eight. Do you want me to make sandwiches," she asked.

"No," Stafford said, leaning to kiss her good-night. "I'll have everything we'll need."

She rolled up her window and drove out of the yard. He stood watching her taillights blend into one in the distance.

Like the ghosts of islands. "Damn," Stafford whispered. "Damn."

VII

Oswalt was leaning back in his swivel chair, drawing deeply off a cigar, while Merchant sat beside him, chin in his hands. Stafford was across the desk, his eyes on the array of mug shots spread before him, ten or twelve to a sheet.

"Man, you are one dumb shit, if you don't mind me saying so."

Stafford sniffed and rubbed his nose. "I don't guess it matters whether I mind or not, does it?" He sniffed again. "Anymore than it matters whether I like breathing your cigar smoke or not. People don't smoke cigars much these days."

"Well, *I* do," Oswalt said. "And this is *my* fucking office. You don't like it, set your ass outside and look at them pictures."

The office was a dingy, cluttered little room like those in the movies, with a few certificates hung here and there on the walls, a calender, and odd photographs, some family shots. Stafford didn't look long at them—he didn't want to know about these people *or* their families. But it was good to be in the real world again.

A golf club was leaned in one corner, a little blue cup over the end of the handle. File cabinets lined a wall, two drawers half open with the corners of folders sticking out and pieces of paper taped all over the sides. Oswalt's desk was scattered with a sea of papers, broken only by a blue IBM Selectric. He didn't even have a computer terminal. Primitive, Stafford decided, and very untidy. Several different sizes and kinds of rock held clumps of paper down.

He looked up from the mug shots. "You collect rocks?"

Oswalt grunted. "What a eye. Yeah, everywhere I go I try to bring back a rock or two. Use'm as paperweights. You might have noticed that we don't have any real rocks down here. Just mud."

He reached and tapped a piece of red sandstone with his pencil. "That's from Palo Dura Canyon, out in Texas. Where Quanah Parker fought the U.S. Calvary. He was a Comanche chief, you know, momma was white." His eyes got dreamy. "Musta been easy in them days, everybody fighting for what they knew was right, whether white or red. Not so easy now." He motioned to the pictures Stafford was thumbing through. "Doing any good there?"

"Gary," Merchant said, "you know he ain't gon' find him in there. You know . . . ."

Oswalt shot a glance at him. "I know what I know and I know what *you* know. Let'm *look*."

"That lava?" Stafford was pointing to a piece of reddish-brown rock that looked like a sponge.

"Yeah. Got that in Hawaii. Had to go over there to pick up somebody being extradited back here."

Stafford returned to the mug shots and shook his head. "These are all the same damned face, picture after picture. Every one of them is black and featureless and has a sneer or a pout."

"They ain't exactly high school yearbook snapshots," Oswalt said. "Most of them guys wasn't real happy campers when they got their pictures took, wasn't looking forward to an afternoon screwing a girl on a beach somewhere."

"I told you that I didn't get much more than a glimpse before they pinned my face to the sidewalk. I didn't see enough of them long enough. And those boys. Well, they were just three boys, like—" He met Merchant's eyes. "Don't you understand?"

"Well," Merchant grunted, getting to his feet, "our boy Harry ought to be arriving pretty soon. We sent some uniforms out to pick him up. Seems like he had to leave work early for some reason. We'll find his ass, though. He'll narrow the field for us, I 'spect."

Stafford looked up from the photos. "What's this all about? What does Harry have to do with this?"

Oswalt smirked. "Let me try to explain it to you, Mister Librarian. Pardon me for being nasty, but I am Goddamned tired of the field-grade stupidity we have to clean up after."

"Mr. Stafford," Merchant broke in, "I'll just bet you that not two minutes after y'all were out the door our boy Harry made a call to a friend of his to tell him that some new flashy, high-priced, good-looking lady was working the turf. And that friend probably made a call too, to someone higher up. Or hell, Harry may know the Man himself. Don't you see—"

Oswalt sighed. "He don't see shit. He's as simple as one of them damned rocks."

"Let up on him a little, Gary," Merchant said. "Get back to your pictures, Mr. Stafford."

The two detectives had obviously been on station much longer than normal, but neither seemed ready to leave. They patiently sat at Oswalt's desk, he with his feet crossed on the blotter the typewriter sat on; across the green felt surface, where it showed through the layers of paper, Stafford could see telephone numbers and names, tic-tac-toe slashes, and doodles, the sea of paper dotted with stones.

"Can you think of anything else?" Merchant asked, leaning forward in his chair, chin in his hands. Oswalt took another cigar from his shirt pocket, slid the cellophane wrapper off, and licked its length. Without looking at Stafford he took out a little red lighter and held its flame to the end of the cigar and drew deeply.

"You don't have to bite the ends off those, do you?" Stafford asked him. It was strangely comforting to pick at Oswalt about his cigars.

Oswalt laughed. "You seem to be more interested in my cigars than you are them pictures." He wagged the cigar in his mouth and said out of one corner, "These here expensive kinds like I smoke already got holes poked in'm, go for around a quarter apiece by the box. Swisher Sweets. Soaked in syrup or rum or some kinda sweet shit." He licked his lips. "I like'm. Kinda like candy." He reached in a drawer, pulled out a box, and opened it. "Have one."

"No thanks," Stafford said.

"How about forgetting the damned cigars then?"

"Can you think of anything else?" Merchant repeated.

Stafford glanced up from the photographs. He had seen a thousand copies of the same face. "No. I can't think of anything else." He shoved the stacks of mugshots across the desk. "And I can't see any reason to go on with this. I did *not* see enough of the guy to identify him. It's that simple. Now, I have to get to air. These damned cigars are killing my sinuses."

Oswalt stood up and stretched. "Well look, it's damned late and I don't see that we're accomplishing anything here. The hook is out for our boy Harry, and sooner or later the uniforms will get him. He probably don't know nothing, but he might." He swept his coat off the file cabinet. "What say we take you back to the hotel for the night. Start this thing over in the morning?"

"Amen," Merchant muttered. His eyes were at half-mast.

"Guys," Stafford said, "I know you're worn out, but so am I. You gotta realize, though, that I got a wife—"

"I got a wife too," Oswalt grunted. "Ain't as young as yours, ain't as pretty, but I know where she's at and I know she's safe. And I know better than to go out and tell a stranger that she's a hooker, whatever she'd bring. Probably half a dollar in the dark."

"Come on, Gary. Let him alone." Merchant was on his feet now, with his jacket slung across his arm. He leaned over and put his hand on Stafford's shoulder.

"Jack—I guess I can call you Jack now, since we're family. Jack, it ain't going anywhere tonight. Wherever she is, she's in for the evening. If they've got her, whoever the hell *they* are, they'll keep her till daylight. Or till they find out they've made a mistake, that she ain't some kind of high-class competition. If they *don't* have her, she's probably got enough sense to lay low till sunup. More than likely she'll show up in the morning, maybe down at the Eighth, maybe at the hotel, wondering why the hell you ran off and left her. Could be hunkered down behind a dumpster somewhere or back in Mississippi. You never know about women."

Stafford stared at him.

"I mean, Jack, they're different from us. She might have got scared and caught a bus back home."

"Bullshit. She's here. I *know* she's here."

"Easy, son." Merchant reached and helped him to his feet. "Gary, I'm gon' take him back to the hotel. You leave word—"

"Got it covered, Merch. You take care of him." He looked at Stafford. "Count on it—in a few days all this will be just like a bad dream." He reached and shook Stafford's hand. "Man, I'm real sorry about all this, you know, about what we had to put you through and all, but you'll have your wife back tomorrow. I'd bet on it."

"Right," Stafford said as Merchant led him from the room. The clock, he noticed, was pushing ten.

There was little sleep for Jack Stafford that night. He undressed and crawled into the bed, soused with what was left of the Seagrams, entertained the notion once or twice of getting dressed and going out for more, then slipped off into a series of fitful naps, expecting any second for the phone to ring or a knock to come at the door.

He wasn't even sure that he had slept at all when he heard the first faint sounds of what he supposed was the coming dawn. A large boat out on the river blew its horn and a truck groaned by on the street, its brakes hissing twice, a siren wailed somewhere far off, a jet roared in the distance. Closer by he could hear water running in the pipes as someone showered. When he turned back the curtain, he was surprised to find how dark the city was, its lights thin and anemic below an impenetrable black sky. A darker space told him where the river was. The clock read 12:37.

"Jesus," he said aloud. "This is the day that wouldn't die." Then he regretted saying it, knowing that however miserable it had been for him, it had probably been a hell of a lot worse for her.

He thought briefly about phoning the station, but he knew that if anything had happened someone would have called. Instead he sat on the edge of the bed a few minutes trying to stabilize his whirring head, then rose and ran a bath, standing in the doorway while the tub filled so that he could hear the phone. He wanted a shower, but the noise of the water might drown out a call if it came.

He looked at himself in the bathroom mirror, smelled an armpit. He winced. "Good God, I've got to have a bath. If they find her, I can't pick her up looking and smelling like this." He stretched the cord as far as it would go and set the phone just outside the open door. Naked, he kneeled in the tub and soaped himself, lathering his hair with the little bar of hotel soap, then leaned forward and rinsed with a small stream of water from the faucet.

He had just finished flushing the soap from his hair when he heard a knock, two light knuckle taps.

"Just a second!" He scrambled out of the tub and wrapped a towel about himself, his wet hair slinging a trail of water to the door.

"Can you come with me?" the voice said even before Stafford got the door open.

It was Merchant, his wide face old looking and haggard, the bags under his eyes sagging far down on his cheeks. His breath was heavy with the smell of whiskey and cigarettes. He was not smiling.

"Yeah. Hey, come on in. What's up. What's happened?" Stafford backed into the bedroom and began rummaging in his bag for underwear.

"We got our boy Harry down there," Merchant said, leaning

against the wall. "Caught up with his white ass half an hour ago."

"And?" Stafford dropped the towel and put his shorts and socks on. He didn't really give a damn whether Merchant was watching or not.

"Won't say a Goddamned thing. Nothing. Hasn't asked for a lawyer. Nothing."

Stafford whipped his pants on and a sports shirt. "So what now?" He stuffed in his shirt and buckled his belt.

"Well, first thing is we want you to identify this guy as the one you talked to in the bar. From there, I don't know."

"Where'd they get him? Where'd they find him?"

"I snatched him when he got home a little while ago. Looked like he'd had a . . . ." Stafford couldn't hear the rest of what he said.

They left the room and entered the elevator.

"I thought the uniforms were going to get him," Stafford said. "You said you were going home."

The elevator stopped in the lobby.

"I got involved, let's say," Merchant muttered. When they got to the street, Oswalt was waiting with the engine running.

"Wasn't in a big hurry, were you?" he asked when Merchant and Stafford got into the car.

"He was taking a bath, Gary. Let's go."

"He can't see you," Merchant said.

The three of them were standing before a small plate-glass square that looked in on a very plain room with a table and two chairs, one occupied by Harry, who looked as if he had had a pretty rough night too. His hair was plastered flat against his skull, his mustache matted and askew, and his eyes were bright red. He had on a sport coat, whose right lapel was ripped half off, and a bright red spot on his cheek suggested that whoever brought him in had not done so gently. Behind him a clock ticked off its seconds. It was almost one.

"That *is* the son-of-a-bitch, ain't it?" Oswalt asked Stafford.

"Oh yeah, that's him, that's Harry." Stafford felt a fury rising in his throat. "He hasn't said anything?"

"Nary a word," Oswalt said. "He's screwed up and pretty stoned, but he's got his wits about him enough to keep his mouth shut."

"All right," Merchant said, pulling Stafford out into the hallway.

"Here's the deal. Now that you have confirmed that Harry's the guy you talked to, we're going to have another few words with him. I'm going to take you back to the hotel. You wait there until you hear from us. That's all. Just wait."

So again Stafford waited, lying flat on the bed fully dressed, his eyes on the ceiling. For long hours the morning dragged out while through his mind ran the long train of memories of his lovely wife, who might never be in his arms again, whose delicious body he might never feel beneath his again. He wept, and he tried to pray, though he could formulate nothing that did not sound trite and foolish.

Strange it was to realize that no matter how much a man doubted God, no matter how certain he was of himself and his deep resources, when conditions grew terrible enough, when desperation was the last sea to drown in, he always reached his hands up and tried to find what all along he had denied. It happens every time.

After a while he dozed off and slept until the phone rang.

VIII

At eleven-thirty that Saturday morning, the two of them were passing due east of Round Island in the Mississippi Sound off Pascagoula, humming along in a little sixteen-foot powerboat toward the south and the dark line of trees on Horn Island, which runs in a gentle curve sixteen miles east to west some ten miles off the mainland. Jerry Harmon's sailboat was out of service for a couple of weeks, but Stafford had no objection to taking the boat they were in. There was more room in it, for one thing, allowing him to stash fishing gear, a picnic basket, a roll of blankets, an extra cooler of ice, a five-gallon container of water, other odds and ends, and a pup-tent, which he liked to have along on his island trips for gear storage or for shelter if it rained, or perhaps for other things.

Susie was riding in the middle seat, just in front of him, leaning this way and that as swells tilted the boat. She pointed at landmarks as they made their way down the river and out into the Gulf and he shouted out what he knew of them: the Highway 90 bridge, Ingalls Shipbuilding, the causeway that curled out to the recently completed Naval base just south of Ingalls, now equipped with a cruiser and two frigates. Intrigued with Round Island and its stone lighthouse as it slid by on the left, she leaned back and asked whether they might tour it one day.

"Sure," he yelled over the engine noise. "It's small, but it's very pretty. Lots of trees, but not much beach. And the lighthouse, of course. We can come out anytime you'd like. Horn's much more interesting. Bigger. Lots of game on it. Inland pools with fish and oysters. Got everything."

She shouted something and turned back toward the long flat line of Horn. The wind billowed her white overshirt, tied by its tails around her waist. Beneath that she wore a red tee-shirt but, he noticed with no small degree of pleasure, no bra. Ribbons of her hair spilled out from under the little white cap she wore and streamed golden in the sun.

In a larger boat Stafford could have swung around to the east and gone through Horn Island Pass, which separates the larger island from Petit Bois, then headed west and anchored on a shoal, using a stern anchor buried in the sand on the beach for stability. The trip through the waist-deep water of the surf would be easy enough. That would be preferable to unloading all their gear on the inside beach and carrying it over dunes of deep sand a half mile to the Gulf side, where with the sea breeze they would have no concern for mosquitoes and gnats and where the water was crystal clear as it rolled in from the south. The view would be better and the swimming delightful on the outside.

He knew, though, that the pass, choppy at all times and heaving with ground swells, would hammer them pretty hard, perhaps even make Susie ill, so he elected to beach the small boat on the inside and carry everything across. It wouldn't take that long, and a lot of the gear he could wait to unload later, if they needed it at all.

When they ran out of dark water, he puttered slowly into the shallows, cut his engine, and allowed their momentum to carry them to shore. After unloading the equipment he wanted to take across, he dragged the boat as far up the beach as he could and stretched out the bow line and hitched it to a solid stump jutting from the sand. No matter what the tide or wind did, the boat would go nowhere.

Balancing one of the ice chests on his shoulder, he walked Susie over to find a good campsite. She carried a roll of blankets and towels under one arm and the pup-tent under the other, dangling from her right hand a bright red canvas travel bag.

"That was rough." She stepped in his footprints on the warming sand, which tapered up to the first line of dunes.

"Lots of open water. The sailboat would probably have been a little smoother, but we'd still be five miles out."

"You really think the tent's necessary, huh?" she asked him as they struggled to the top of a dune studded with palmettos. Before them lay a smaller line of dunes and beyond those a flat stretch of sand that led to the rolling blue-green waters of the Gulf.

"Well," he grunted, shifting the ice chest to his other shoulder, "it's a good storage building for all your stuff, keeps the blowing sand off of it, and if it rains, you can always crawl up inside it for shelter."

"And this roll of blankets?" They had started walking again.

He stopped and looked at her. "Uh, well, to spread out for our meal."

"You could cover a lot of sand with this roll. How many did you bring?"

"Enough, I guess. A couple. I told you, I like to be prepared."

"Uh-huh. That's what I'm worried about. Know what I forgot?"

"What?"

"A camera."

"Brought your sketchpad, didn't you?"

"Yes," she answered, swinging the red bag. "It's in here."

He shifted the ice chest to his other shoulder and they continued along the trail. "That's better than a camera."

"You think so?"

"Sure. A camera can't interpret, can't improve on what it sees. Do you think people would buy Andersons' or Smithers' stuff if they had just taken pictures? Maybe you'll find something nice out here, sketch it, or paint it."

Then they topped another dune and stood looking out onto the outer beach, beyond which the Gulf spread off to the skyline.

"Maybe so," she said.

They chose a spot on the sand well out of the upper reach of the surf, easily determined by the little swirled patterns formed by water action on the last high tide as the waves swept in, lost their momentum, and returned. Every way he turned there was trash from island visitors and jetsam from trolling fishing boats and freighters farther at sea: beer cans and plastic wrappers, jugs and bottles and buckets, pieces of nylon rope, limbs and trunks of trees from God only knew where and timbers of all sizes, some thick as a horse. *Smithers and Anderson simply blocked it out*, he thought, *didn't see it*. He hoped she was not put off by the panorama of trash.

If it weren't for the great storms that roared in off the Gulf every few years, flushing away the debris of ships and summer idlers, the trash would be intolerable. Nature had her way of cleansing, though, hurling massive storm surges against man's petty fouling and leaving the beaches pure and clean again. He had walked Horn after a hurricane and found not a single can or bottle or snarl of rope on the sand, just shells and sand dollars where the sea had emptied her pockets. Like in the beginning, like the sun rising on the first day of the spinning mottled world.

Stafford suggested to Susie that she walk along the beach while he brought the rest of their stuff across the island. The picnic basket and his fishing gear would pretty well do them for now. If he fished and caught anything, he could always go get the other ice chest.

"When you are out of sight, I'm going to change into my bathing suit, if you don't mind." She nodded toward the red bag beside the rolled-up tent. "You won't look?"

"No. But take care that you don't draw a bunch of boats in here and mess up the fishing."

She laughed. "I'll be quick." She unbuttoned her shorts even before he had gone.

When he returned with the fishing gear and picnic basket she was waist deep in the surf, her hands out flat on the surface of the water to either side, as if she were trying to lift herself by them. What an absolutely perfect figure she had, and how white and fine her skin was. He stripped down to his cutoffs and waded out to her.

"I don't want to be bossy, but did you put on sunscreen?" he asked.

"Yes. Can't you smell it?"

When he bent until his nose almost touched her shoulder he detected a faint coconut fragrance.

"Yes. Sorry. You're just so fair, I was—I just thought I'd warn you."

She turned and faced him. The bill of the little white cap was turned to the side. "How do you know I'm fair?"

"God, you're cute," he said, reaching out to take her hands. The top of her black two-piece was amazingly thin, so that her nipples stood out clearly in its wet sheen. "No, you're beautiful. No, you're *incredible*. No—"

"You don't have much body hair," she said, running her hand across his chest.

"I'm higher up the ladder of evolution. If I had hair all over my chest and back, I'd already have swept you up and lugged you back into the dunes and ravished you, perhaps eaten you for dinner."

"Wouldn't you have to club me first or something?"

"No. I like my women alert and kicking."

"Hmmmm." She reached and ran her hand over his right shoulder and down onto his biceps. "I guess you could do it." She laughed and kissed him lightly on the cheek. "Come on, let's go eat. I'm starving." She pulled him toward the sand.

"Can I kiss you first?" he asked, holding back.

"I just kissed you first. How can—"

He grasped her around the waist and pressed his body to hers, softly kissing at first, then kissing harder and deeper, until she gasped and pulled away.

"Jack, slow down, please. We've got the whole afternoon for things to run their course. You say you are a gentleman, and I believe you. Don't mess this up. I came out here with you to have fun on the island, but that doesn't necessarily mean the sort of fun that men usually have in mind. Slow it down." She started pulling him toward the beach again. "Come on, let's eat."

Stafford was surprised at how easily he backed off, allowing her to lead. He wasn't accustomed to this coyness. The older women he dated generally wanted sex as much as he did, and they had no reservations about it: one or the other led and the other responded. Everything was so spontaneous, almost as it had been in the seventies, when free love was sweeping college campuses, though he knew that the reason he was successful so often and so quickly was that he chose well whom to approach. He almost never messed around with anyone much younger than he was, and he had a keen eye for picking women who needed the deep, slow love of a capable man.

He was cautious about AIDS, far more common among the young; but much more important, he preferred older women because they knew how to make love, something he himself had only in recent years learned, and he had learned it from them, from lonely older women, women life had already wounded. They knew, and they taught him, that there were two people involved and that the outer boundaries of love-making were established by the limits of the imagination of the two people making it.

College girls couldn't mellow into a relationship. They played their silly little games, and their lovemaking was shallow, then afterwards they felt that you were obligated to them, bound to them, as if some sort of social contract had been formed from the physical union. He wanted women with a past, women who became someone other than themselves, or maybe became what they *really* were, for that brief period of love-making, who loved wildly, almost savagely, as if they never could quite satisfy their longing, and then closed the door softly when they left, their faces and clothes in order, and waited for *you* to call; or if they called you, they were discreet and—dare he say it?—*professional* about it. No entanglements, no complications.

The one sex partner he steadily turned to was Emily Miller. The other two were just now-and-then wham-bams, one who had endured a dreadful marriage to an arrogant husband, a superintendent at the shipyard who was a bastard in every respect and for whom he felt nothing but contempt as he made his wife writhe and moan, the other a widow five years his senior who worked for a drugstore in Ocean Springs. None of them pressured him, ever, and he felt comfortable with them. They would call or drop by, set a date and time, then show up ready for action.

They had lunch on the beach, using the ice chest as a table between them.

"Wow, the stuff you've got in here," she'd said when she took out their pimento cheese sandwiches. "Cokes and beer, a bottle of wine, milk, juice, bags of fruit . . . and salad makings? How many days did you say we're staying?"

"I told you, I like to come prepared," Stafford answered. "I might catch a redfish or two and we can cook them on the beach for dinner."

"Can you make that run across the Sound after dark, with those cork things everywhere—crab-trap markers, you called them? Will it be safe?"

"We can get into the river before dark. You don't have to be back early, do you?"

She had laid out one of the towels over the ice chest, putting a sandwich and sweating Coke at each end, with napkins.

"No, not really. I told Polly—my roomie, you remember—that I'd probably be in before eight, but it's no big deal. You wanted Coke, didn't you?"

"Beer, actually, but you've already got the Cokes out, so Coke'll be fine."

After lunch he put on his shirt and an old Aussie hat and she slipped on her white overshirt and cap, and after reapplying sunscreen—he wanted to ask her to let him rub hers on, but didn't—they headed west on the beach.

Stafford had strapped on his fishing knife, shoved a plastic box of lures into a back pocket of his cutoffs, and shouldered his rod. From mid-summer on into late fall redfish fed in the gullies that stretched out finger-like from the beach, sometimes singles or two or three, sometimes great schools of them appearing as red blobs in the crystal water as the mass of fish moved along, vague scarlet ghosts, sometimes with a big bull or female working the flanks. Catching one was a simple matter of easing to the edge of the water and flinging a lure out beyond the mass of fish and reeling it back through them. In their feeding frenzy one would snatch the bait and the fight to the beach began, sometimes lasting for several minutes as you cranked, pulled, cranked and pulled, until, exhausted, he rode a wave up onto the beach and you claimed him. Or the line snapped, which could easily happen using a fifteen-pound line against fish that could weigh well over twenty. Then you had to put another lure on as fast as you could and try to catch up with the red ghost, always moving, and cast again. Landing a big red should certainly impress Susie, but not as much as having fresh redfish fillets on the beach later. If things worked out the way he intended, this would be a memorable day for the exquisite blond woman whose footsteps he swallowed into his own as they walked in the heavy sand.

In one hand Susie carried her sketchbook, dangling from the other a green plastic bucket she'd found earlier, plunking little oddities into it: shells and sand dollars, an osprey feather. Like a child delirious with discovery, she stayed a few paces ahead of Stafford, turning around now and again to hold up to him some shell she'd found. He walked along watching her motion on the sand, convinced that of all the women walking the world's beaches at that moment, this was the one he wanted with him.

"You didn't set up the tent," she reminded him as the ice chest grew smaller and smaller in the distance. "I thought you were supposed to stash the gear in it."

"The weather's pretty. Wind's mild, no clouds threatening. Everything'll be fine till we get back there."

"OK," she said and returned to her search for shells.

Keeping even a remote corner of his mind on fishing was difficult, but when he saw at the edge of his vision a couple of large fish moving across a bright sandy shoal from one finger of dark water into another, he snapped back to the real world and lunged past Susie to take a position just ahead of where the fish had disappeared into the cut. He hurled the red-headed chartreuse lure at a point beyond where they had dropped off the shoal and just ahead of where he judged them to be.

Susie had stopped her beachcombing to watch as Stafford, standing in water just below his knees, twitched the rod, reeled a few feet in, and twitched again. He was reeling in the second run of slack, fearful that he had misjudged their position, when the fish struck, bowing the rod and stripping out line. With Susie squealing in the background, he tightened the drag ever so carefully, turned the fish, and began working him toward the beach.

Judging by the dogged straight pull, it was a sow or bull red, and he had to work it slowly as the stubborn shadowy fish moved to the right, then turned to deeper water, yielded when Stafford bowed back hard on him, then turned to the left and out to sea again.

But he tired quickly, rolled on the surface, and after one more feeble effort to head back out, began to move compliantly toward the beach. When the red approached the first breakers, Stafford backed out of the water and allowed a crest to ride the fish out onto the slick sand. In three strides he had it hoisted by the gills.

"Oh, Jack, he's beautiful, and you got him on the first cast." She was squinting at the redfish, nearly two feet long, now laid out on the beach beyond the edge of the water, his gills flaring for oxygen in the alien air. She stooped and ran her finger down the middle of his belly, flinching when he flapped his tail against the sand.

Stafford removed the hook with a twist. "Ten pounds, I'd guess, maybe a little more. Lotta good eating here."

"What'll we do with him now?" she asked.

"I probably ought to try to catch another one or two, some to take back, but I don't want a whole lot to clean, so I'll just lug him to the campsite and go across for the other ice chest. You walk on up the beach and when I've got him filleted and stashed on ice I'll join you. You should find something to sketch." He shaded his eyes toward the west. "I don't see anybody else, no boats anchored along there anywhere, so you should have it to yourself."

"What if I get lost?"

"You won't. Stay on the beach and you won't. But even if you leave it for something, I'll just follow your tracks. You won't get lost." He hoisted the fish and headed down the beach to the campsite.

When he joined her well over an hour later and perhaps two

miles up the beach, following her tracks where they dipped down onto the tide slick, then turned up into the white, loose sand of the upper beach, Susie was sitting on the top of a dune staring off toward the middle of the island, where even before he rose to her level Stafford could see a flock of buzzards massed in a sandy stretch of palmettos. Earlier he had seen some of them spiral down, so he knew something was dead over there. Decades before, buzzards had flown in great flocks out to the islands to roost in the evenings, but a cholera epidemic among hogs on the mainland had so reduced the scavengers' population that it was now uncommon to see many on the Horn. In fact, he could not recall ever having seen more than one or two circling out over the Gulf.

She had her sketchbook on her lap, beside her the green bucket.

"Jack, what do you suppose they've got?" she asked as he panted up.

"Dunno. Maybe a hog. There are wild pigs out here. Maybe an alligator. Whatever it is, it isn't feeling a thing, and they're having a hell of a meal. Too bad we've eaten."

"Yeah, too bad. Do you think maybe we ought to check it out, in case it's some*body*?" She was clutching her little green bucket of shells. She had been in the water—sand clung to her legs up to her bathing suit.

"I'll walk over there if you want me to and look , but it's just some animal they've got. Bet on it." He looked over her shoulder. "Whatcha drawing?"

She held the pad up. He could recognize trees and palmettos, some small clouds, and heaving shrub-studded dunes. She had blushed the trees and shrubs with pale chalk and swept the sky with blue. The gauzy little clouds seemed to follow each other obediently, like sheep. A pair of pelicans flew, wingtips nearly touching, just above her dunes.

"Where are the buzzards?" he asked her.

"I don't see them. I see past them, through them. I see trees and sky and dunes. And gulls."

"You've drawn the pelicans well." He tapped the page with his finger. "Brown pelicans. Beautiful birds."

"Is that what they are? I thought they were gulls."

"Oh, much rarer. Much nobler than common gulls. They'd be offended if they knew you thought they were gulls."

"Please don't tell them." She was so incredibly lovely sitting there atop the dune, her hair trailing out in the sea breeze, that Stafford had to keep reminding himself to go slow. Jesus, he wanted to kiss her.

He smiled. "Not a word to them. You've done a great job with this." He pointed to the cluster of buzzards. "Now I'm going over there to find out what the guys in the black suits are having for lunch."

He scrambled down from the dune and struck out through scattered palmettos and low-growing shrubs he could not identify toward the mass of dark birds, whose shuffling and clacking he could hear at some distance.

"Mind if I go along?" She had come up behind him, still wagging her green bucket. She had the pad clamped under her arm.

"It might not be pleasant," he warned.

Well before he reached the spot, the buzzards broke like a clap of thunder and rose in different directions to circle, the heavy wings whistling and buffeting. Their shadows rippled over the dunes. Some settled in the larger trees that ran down the middle of the island, others continued to ride down the wind, bank, and flap back into it.

"It's a deer," Stafford said as they approached the place the buzzards had risen from. "A small deer."

The carcass had been stretched out of shape and torn apart, the way wild dogs would have done it, but he could see no evidence in the agitated sand that anything other than buzzards had fed. The deer's swollen tongue lolled as if she were licking salt. Why hadn't the buzzards gone for *it*, he wondered. There was no evidence of a penis, so he assumed that it was a doe, though the entire anal and vaginal area had been eaten away. Upwind of it, he studied the scene, trying to determine what had killed the deer. An occasional crosscurrent swirled the smell in their direction. Susie was holding a hand over her mouth and nose.

"Oh, Jesus, Jack." She pinched her nose and backed up, turning toward the beach. "Let's go. We've seen it. Let's go.

"Too young to have died a natural death, I'd say," he suggested on their way to the beach. "Can't imagine what might have killed it out here. Shouldn't be any hunters around." Behind him he could hear the buzzards fluttering back down to their meal.

"I'm not that interested in knowing why it's dead," she said. "You'd never guess from Anderson's sketches and Smithers' paintings that stuff like that was going on out here, would you?"

"They were *selective*, Susie," Stafford answered, sweeping his eyes up and down the beach, "as artists must always be. They looked for the good, the beautiful."

They made their way slowly east again, hand in hand. Stafford had left his fishing tackle at the ice chest, so he carried the green bucket, holding it out to her whenever she found something she wanted to add to it.

"What'll you do with these?" he asked, shaking the shells around and looking at what she'd collected.

"Don't break my sand dollars, boy." She bumped him with her hip. "I don't know what I'll do with them. Sketch them, maybe. Make a display. Anybody living on the coast ought to have a shell display, don't you think?"

"Absolutely. And these can remind you of the day you spent on Horn Island with a librarian."

"Who doesn't look at all like a librarian." She reached over and pinched his forearm.

They lolled on the beach awhile, so afternoon was well on the wane when they reached camp. After some water and a beer Stafford suggested that they take a swim and then he'd start a fire to cook the fish. He had put cornmeal, a quart of cooking oil, salt and pepper, and a cast-iron frying pan in the bottom of the picnic basket, and there was plenty of wood along the beach to get a good fire going. Wine, a salad, and fried redfish so fresh that it might still be twitching when he dropped in the pink fillets ought to go a long way toward making Susie feel that this had been a special day. Then, after dinner . . . .

They swam for awhile out near the blue-green water of the deeper Gulf that lay a hundred yards or so off the beach. The tide was coming in, so there was no danger of their being carried out to sea, and there was nothing to fear from anything that swam in those waters, notwithstanding the remote possibility that some sort of predator fish might take a swipe at an arm or leg. He'd gotten scratches from bluefish and mackerel, but he had never heard of a shark attack off the islands.

Susie Clayburn swam as gracefully as she walked, taking long, even, balanced strokes, coupled with perfectly timed kicks that propelled her through the water with tireless ease. He swam alongside her, with greater effort to keep up than he had imagined he would need, sometimes passing her just to show that he could do it, then dropping behind again. She seemed not to fear the deeper water at all, at one time veering to her left and thrusting into the oncoming waves with such vigor that he lost sight of her momentarily and was on the verge of calling out when he saw her stroking toward him, face up, smiling.

She did not tire quickly enough for him, so after what seemed well over an hour he suggested that they go back to the beach and have another beer and he'd prepare dinner. The sun had slid far over in the western sky, and the wind, bearing the faintest trace of fall, picked up.

Susie sat on one of the ice chests watching him make the fire. "That water's wonderful." She was sipping on a beer, still dressed in her bathing suit, but with her shirt on. "I've been in the ocean only a few times in my life."

He grunted as he finished the little sand pit and began laying small strips of driftwood in the bottom, over which he would lace larger limbs as the fire progressed. He still wore only his cutoffs. "You looked at home out there to *me*. It was all I could do to keep up with you."

"Oh, I've done lots of swimming. Just not in salt water. It lifts you up so much that you seem to be *skimming* instead of swimming."

When the fire was going to his satisfaction, Stafford opened the second ice chest and removed half the redfish and, using the chest as his kitchen counter, cut the fillet into two-inch sections, which he dropped into a plastic bag of cornmeal, flavored with salt and pepper. This he shook vigorously until all the pieces were well coated.

"That's a lot of fish," she said.

"Susie, would you mind getting the oil and pan out of the picnic basket?" He thought it a good touch to involve her in making the meal. That way it would be *their* dinner and not *his*. "Pour a couple of inches of oil in the bottom of the skillet."

"You brought a pan and oil and cornmeal? Heavens, Jack Stafford, you really don't forget the tiniest thing, do you?"

He laughed. "I try not to."

He took the pan from her and set it across a piece of wire mesh he'd wrested from a tangle of timbers on his way back to camp after catching the fish and fashioned into a cradle that would keep the pan from sliding into the fire. As he waited for the oil to heat up, they spread one of the blankets and put the ice chest they had used for a table at lunch in the middle. Earlier he had taken out the wine and salad bag, whose contents, already drenched with oil and vinegar, he emptied into two bowls from the picnic basket. True, he *had* thought of everything.

When the oil in the skillet began to bubble and roll, he reached for the pieces of fish and carefully slid them in, noting with gratification that they immediately whined and sizzled. He winced at the heat on his face.

"Susie, hand me the tongs from the basket, please," he said as the fish began to float and tumble.

She rummaged about for a few seconds, finally setting the contents out onto the blanket.

"Better hurry. They're getting close. Gotta get'm out of that oil." The smoke from the skillet was blinding him. He hooked a stick through the hole in the handle and slid it to the edge of the fire.

"Jack, there're no tongs in here."

"Then a spatula! Hell, *anything*!"

She pointed to the empty basket. "No tongs, no spatula."

He looked over at the blanket, where everything that had been in the basket was neatly set out. Susie was shrugging, her eyes on the roiling fish.

"Holy shit!" Stafford grabbed the basket and inverted it. Nothing fell out. His eyes lit on the absurd little plastic forks lying alongside a stack of napkins. "Good God Almighty!"

"Your knife, Jack," she yelled, "use your *knife*."

He fumbled with his scabbard, realized the knife wasn't there, and scrambled to the ice chest he'd been using as his cooking table, swooped up the knife and tried to spear the pieces of smoking fish. He flipped the last fillet out onto a paper plate just before it turned completely black, then snatched up the skillet, using his tee-shirt to protect his hand, and set it down away from the fire. He slid the jumble of burned fish onto paper towels on top of the ice chest and sat back on the sand.

"So this is blackened redfish, huh?" she asked as she probed a piece with her plastic fork the way a woman might poke at a dead snake with a stick.

"No, *burned* redfish." He rose to his knees. "Hand me what's left of the oil."

"Please?"

"I'm sorry. Please. I'm sorry I lost my cool and yelled at you. Sorry for swearing."

"Like we'd been married five years," she said, laughing. She passed the bottle of oil to him.

The mood he'd been working on was dashed now. He flung the first pieces of fish out into the dark water and wiped away the black residue from the bottom of the skillet with paper towels.

"Too bad we don't have a dog to feed it to," he said.

She laughed. "No dog would eat it."

Then he laughed too and wrapped the handle with his tee-shirt again, and he poured the rest of the oil in the pan and slid it back onto the wire. As it began to bubble, he carefully dropped in another batch of battered pieces. This time he was ready: When the fish was done on one side, he skillfully trapped the fillets between two long narrow pieces of driftwood and flipped them, allowed them a few minutes on the other side, then scooped them up and out onto paper towels he'd laid out on the ice chest.

All this while neither of them had said anything, though he knew that she must be thinking what a fool he was not to have thought about tongs or a spatula if he was going to fry fish. A woman *would* have thought of it.

"That was a clever solution," she suggested as they laid the ice chest out with their dinner, "using the wood. Not as good as tongs, I guess, but it did the trick."

He blushed. "Well, I thought of just *about* everything." He poured the wine and held a stem out to her.

"Wine glasses he thought of, but not tongs for the fish." She rolled her eyes and laughed.

He held his glass out to her. "Here's to this glorious day."

She clinked hers against his. "Which, by the way, is slipping away pretty fast." She sipped from her glass and nodded toward the west. "We're going to be pushing this thing awfully close, aren't we?"

The sun, taking on a deep orange as it settled slowly, was still at least an hour away from dropping into the Gulf, but he knew that she was well aware of the time it would take to carry the gear back across the island and how long the trip was to the mainland and upriver to Jerry Harmon's dock.

"We've still got a lot of light," he reassured her, "we'll be all right."

They ate then, with the fire cracking and popping at their backs and the sun casting long shadows in the dunes. The tide was still inching up the sand toward them, though they were at least a dozen feet above the high line. She had two pieces of the fish, he had four, and they finished off the wine.

"Glad it was a big fish." She daintily wiped the corners of her mouth when she was through eating. "That would have been tough throwing away all we had because you burned it."

"Yeah," he said, "I planned it that way. Thought it would be entertaining for you."

"It *was*," she said.

When they had finished, she packed the picnic basket and rolled up the blanket while he buried their trash from dinner up in the dunes. Then they stood together on the slick tidal sand and stared out across the darkening water.

"I saw two books in the basket," she said. "How long did you plan for us to stay out here?"

"Oh, I always carry books along, just in case I get a chance to read."

"Mercy, those covers and titles—I wouldn't have figured . . ."

"They're just fun reading for me. Just escape." He kept his face turned from her. "They're a break from serious reading is all."

She looked back toward the coastline. "Jack, we'd better get a move on. The sun's almost gone."

He reached and touched her arm. "Susie, wait a minute."

"Jack, the sun's going down. We've got to get off this island."

"Come here." He sat down at the edge of the water and patted a place for her to sit. "Please."

She came and kneeled beside him. "Jack, what is going on here? It'll take two trips to get this stuff to the boat, and then we've got to run across the Sound. It'll be dark before we get there. All those crabtraps. I'm getting nervous."

He stared out over the Gulf and said quietly, "I could carry a load over to the boat and fiddle with the engine and tell you it wouldn't start, that I'd have to wait till morning to see well enough to fix it, could even yank a couple of wires loose so that it really *wouldn't* crank. But that would be lying. The engine's fine and it'll start first pull. I know that. Now *you* know that. But I also know that I want to spend the night out here with you, in that orange tent."

He worked his toes in the wet sand. "If you really do have to get back, I'll do my damnedest to dodge those crab traps and get into the river before it gets full dark. With the running lights and my big flashlight we'll make it just fine. But I really want us to stay out here."

She remained silent, her eyes in the same direction as his.

"I've brought along plenty of provisions for us—the fruit's for breakfast. Milk and orange juice too."

"You know," she said softly, "if you hadn't worked so hard setting all this up, which is in itself a form of lying, of course, and if I hadn't enjoyed this day so much with you, I'd say let's pack up and shoot for the river." She reached and hooked a hand in one of his. "But, frankly, I think I'd like to stay out here with you. I told Polly that if I didn't get back tonight, it would mean that I had stayed over with you."

He sighed and pulled her to him over the wet sand. "God, you are full of surprises."

"Jack, ground rules . . . ."

He released her. "Susie, I won't do anything that you don't want me to do. OK? You're in charge of that department. You've got my word on it."

"Jack Stafford," she said, rising and pulling him to his feet, "*you* are the one full of surprises. I never thought I'd run across a man like you. You intrigue the hell out of me. I'll spend the night out here with you in that little orange tent, which I haven't even seen unrolled yet, much less set up, and I'll sleep in it right beside you, but sleep is all it will be. Understood?"

"Hey," Stafford said, holding her hands, "it's your ballgame. I'll go as far as you want and no farther."

"Jack," she whispered, touching him on the cheek, "it's not that I don't want to make love to you. I *do*. But I don't need the complication right now, and for me that's what it would be, a complication. I am scared of you, frankly, scared of your experience, your intelligence. You've been to Pompeii, been all over the world, for God's sake. I've never been *anywhere*. The age difference is not a factor, but the experience is—you're a man of the world. If I made love to you on this beach tonight, it would just be too complicated for me. I'd feel like you were measuring me against all the women you've had, and apparently you've had plenty. I have played with you, eaten with you, shared several memorable hours with you, but I won't make love to you. In time, maybe, but not yet."

"Well, you're wrong about one thing. I wouldn't measure you against anybody. But it's your game, so to speak. I won't touch you unless you want me to. OK? You've got my word on it."

"Thanks, Jack. I just wanted to be clear about it."

"You have been," he said.

"It would be an honor to sleep with Pompeii Man in his orange tent." She kissed him lightly on the cheek. "I will tell you, though, if you had brought along tongs, I would not do this. You would be too much in control of things. Watching you flail around for something to pick that fish up with was worth the trip out here, you clumsy man. You had more trouble catching it the second time than the first."

They both laughed at that, the experienced man of almost forty who'd been to Pompeii, had been all over the world, who understood and reveled in life's great mysteries, who'd had more girls and women than he could even remember, and the young woman just out of her teens who had spent a couple of hours once just across the Mexican border and had perhaps never made love—and he was very glad to be with her on that beach, fading from day into starlit evening, to be sharing whatever it was that they had shared that day and would share that night, even if he could not have her.

When they had finished the last bit of tidying up from dinner, Stafford suggested that he pitch the tent in the dunes to take advantage of the wind, which he knew would shift in the night from south to north as the land mass cooled and the water kept its warmth. The breeze would keep them comfortable and drive away mosquitoes and gnats.

"Do you want me to help?" she asked. "Or is it a man thing?"

"You just enjoy yourself. I'll do it. I've set this thing up so much that I could do it one-handed, in the dark. It won't take ten minutes."

He selected a spot high above the beach in a valley between two dunes and built a large fire, then carried up the ice chests and picnic basket and finally the tent and blankets, leaving Susie walking on the beach until he had things the way he wanted. He was careful to erect the tent far enough away from the fire that an errant ember would not melt a hole through the nylon. After he had unrolled it and tapped in the stakes, he stretched the guy-lines tight and dug a small trench around the periphery to conduit off rain if it should storm.

When he was finished with the tent, he laid a couple of logs across the fire. There were bits of usable wood everywhere, sun-bleached logs and uprooted stumps abraded by the surf and mahogany and pine timbers used as stacking runners on freighters and jettisoned after offloading cargoes. In seconds the dry wood was wrapped in flame. Susie was waist-deep in the rising water when he returned to the beach.

She waded over to him. "I wish we'd have a full moon."

"Wrong time of month. We'll have nothing but stars."

"Out here I'll bet they light things up almost as much as the moon would, like thousands of little penlights beaming down on us."

"You're good with metaphors and similes, Susie Clayburn," Stafford said, taking her hand. A late-forming cloudbank had snuffed out the western glow that he had hoped they could enjoy, leaving the water before them a black bulge that stretched out to the horizon, where a few small lights of ships inched along. "I suspect that the sea is where metaphors first came from as some man topped a sandy rise somewhere and beheld a sight such as this, only I doubt that he'd have had much to compare it to."

"I'd figure the stars," she said.

"The stars?"

"Yes, when some woman looked up past the head of the hairy man that had her pinned to the ground, wondering whether any of those holes in the night sky could offer escape."

"Jesus, Susie, where'd you get that?"

"It just came to me. Sorry. Sounds like an indictment, doesn't it? I didn't mean anything by it. I'm minoring in English."

He stared at her face, lit by the faintest trace of light from the west, and shook his head. What an incredible woman he had with him. Twenty-one years old and primed to become whatever he wanted to mold her into. Beautiful, intelligent, clever, marvelous sense of humor. It was almost more than he could believe. And here he was alone on an island with her and would later share her bed. *You have got to be careful with this one, Jack, old boy, you can't let this one get away.*

"Do you want to swim?" he asked.

"Sure."

She removed her shirt, neatly folded it, and laid it on the sand. Stafford had put his shirt on a bit earlier. He removed it and laid it beside hers. He wished that he had brought swim-trunks. His cutoffs, great for walking along the beach and camping and fishing, were a hindrance in swimming—the pockets filled with water and created drag.

"Susie," he yelled as she moved into the surf, "would you mind if I swam in my undershorts? These cutoffs slow me down."

"No, of course not. You can swim naked, if you want to. It won't bother me."

Damnation, what a woman. What exactly did she have in mind to do with him? She seemed so loose and casual about sexual matters when they talked, but left no doubt where she stood on actually going to bed with him. She was inviting him to swim naked with her, but . . . .

"Do you want me to take *my* suit off?" she asked as she came back to the beach. He stood with his cutoffs unbuttoned and unzipped but still clinging to his hips.

"Susie, I just don't understand what is going on. What about the ground rules?"

"Jack, swimming naked with you is not the same as making love to you. I know you won't touch me unless I let you, so we can be naked out here all night and nothing will happen. Right?" She looked at him for a nod, which he gave. "I like swimming naked. I like *being* naked. Now, if you'll turn around and take your clothes off, I'll take my swimsuit off and we'll swim."

"How close can I get?" he asked over his shoulder as he dropped his cutoffs to the sand and slid off his jockeys.

"Jack, you won't be able to get close enough to see or touch *anything*." Her rolled-up swimsuit sailed over his head and landed high on the sand just as she swatted him on the buttocks and plunged into the surf, rising up on a wave, stroking toward deep water.

"Susie," he yelled over the tumbling water, "orient yourself on the camp." Behind them the fire burned brightly in the cut between the dunes.

He stood for a moment at the edge of the beach trying to figure out where she was in the darkness before him. Then he saw a flashing arm about twenty yards out and heard her laugh and she was gone.

He plunged toward the spot where he'd seen her and began pulling in long strokes, thrusting with his kicks, but she was not there, nor could he see anything of her when he stopped swimming and treaded water out near the edge of the shelf, beyond which the deep lay. Panic began stirring in his chest as he swam back toward the beach. How in God's name would he handle it if something happened to her out there?

Then the notion struck him that he might find her far out in the waves, exhausted, near drowning, dive and come up behind her, hook an arm around just under her shoulders and ease her back to shore, where he'd bring her back to life and spend the rest of the night making love to her in the tent.

He had just made a turn to the west and slowed to an easy stroke parallel with the beach, his head high out of the water so that he could hear her call, when he felt something brush past his feet, followed by a shrill "Pompeii Man!" And she was gone again, her arms flashing for an instant before she disappeared into the dark waves. Whatever notions he'd had about touching her, or even seeing her long enough to know what he was seeing, faded as he followed a zigzag course back to the east until he saw to his left the dwindling fire in the dunes. He wasn't swimming with her or after her—he was merely swimming in the same Gulf. Male or not, stronger or not, he was no match for her in that night sea.

After a few minutes, having seen nothing of her and heard nothing, he left the water and backed away from the edge of the surf and shouted for her. As good as she was in the water, he was still uneasy.

"Susie!" he yelled, first east, then to the south, then west.

Nothing. Nothing but the hiss and tumble of the surf. He turned and noticed that the fire was almost out so he gathered bits of driftwood along the way and climbed to the campsite and fed on increasingly larger limbs until flames leapt higher than his head. Earlier he had pulled up a couple of larger logs, which he laid across the fire to burn in two, giving him an even bigger fire at the moment and leaving the halves for later burning. Driftwood, as wonderful as it was for campfires, burned with fast heat and light and was done too soon.

The fire now cast a glow all the way to the beach. Stafford walked back down to the water's edge and yelled again, in all three directions, getting no reply but the steady beat of the surf. He knew nothing else to do, so he struck off to the west along the beach, realizing suddenly that he was still naked. All the while he was building up the fire he simply didn't notice.

"My God," he said quietly to himself, "how the hell can you not notice that you're buck-ass *naked*? What if I come up on somebody out here? They'll think I'm crazy." He was glad it was not dead summer, when other people would be camping along the eastern tip of Horn. A couple of hundred yards down the beach he turned toward the sea and yelled again and again got no reply but the mocking surf. *Swish, gone—swish, lost—swish, gone—swish.*

"Jesus," he said to the tumbling black water, "what in the name of all the gods of the sea am I going to do?" He cupped his hands to his mouth and shouted her name again and again, in all directions. Maybe she was off in the dunes relieving herself. He dropped his hands to his sides and stood staring out at the enormous Gulf. The dancing fire threw jags of light across the sand.

Or maybe she was playing with him. Stafford walked down the beach to the west and raised his face and shouted again, this time with as much force as he could muster and with an edge of anger to his voice.

"Susie! Susie, if you can hear me, answer me, please. This has gone on long enough. Susie!"

"Ja-a-a-a-ck."

The voice came low and ghostly from a higher ledge of sand to his right, and he spun and crouched back on his heels and raised his arms. He widened his eyes to draw in more light and swept them across the stretch of sand and then he saw her. She stood halfway between the water and first line of dunes, her body faintly outlined against the white background.

"Susie, what are—"

"You couldn't catch me in the water, Pompeii Man. Can you catch me in the *sand*?"

Then she was gone, bounding down to the beach and east toward camp, with Stafford in pursuit, but before he could gain on her, she cut up from the water again and ran toward the dunes, tantalizingly slow at first, then in a burst of speed, disappearing over a low hill of sand before he had done much more than glimpse her starlit body.

Hell, she could cut her feet on some of the trash strung out along the upper beach or slash her legs on palmettoes. Stafford struck out in the direction he had last seen her, keeping his eyes on the sand ahead, dodging cans and clumps of driftwood and whatever else seemed not to be sand, and as often as he dared he lifted his eyes to search for her. She flashed with dazzling speed across his line of vision between two dunes, rose as if by magic up the side of a farther mound of sand, then disappeared again.

"God . . . *damn*," he panted as he topped one of the dunes, "I am too fucking *old* for this." He dropped to his knees, chest heaving, and tried to catch his breath.

"Jaaack."

He could see her just across a sandy flat at the foot of a taller dune, perhaps fifty feet away, her hands cupped to her mouth.

"Yoooooo, Jaaaack."

"Shit," he hissed and scrambled to his feet and lunged down the slope toward her. Before he was halfway to the spot where she'd been, she had crossed over the dune, almost twice as high as the one he had just descended from and, silhouetted against the night sky for a starlit instant, plunged into the dark again. His heart was hammering away under his ribs, his legs weak and watery and heavy as lead, but he hurled himself with lunatic frenzy against the steep hill of sand, sliding back two feet for every three he took in stride, trying to remember that he was the male in pursuit here. He fell forward onto his hands briefly, used them to steady himself, and with one more heroic lunge in a flurry of sand crested the peak and stood there humped over, gasping, while his pulse drummed away in his temples. Above him the stars stared coldly down.

"God*damn*," he whimpered. Saliva strung from his mouth. "Is this my Golgotha?" He dropped to his knees and slumped forward until his forehead touched the sand. In that position he rested, trying to catch his breath.

"Hello, Pompeii Man."

He rose to his feet, hands on his knees, and squinted into the darkness before him. He wasn't sure where the voice had come from, only that it was close.

"Susie," he croaked.

"Right here, Pompeii Man."

He straightened. She was directly behind him, so close that he could feel her breath on the back of his neck. Her nipples touched him and the rest of her body closed on his as she wrapped her arms around his waist. The two stood in silence on the top of the dune, blended into one, then the wheezing man humped over again in dead knee-wobbling weariness, trying to recover his breath and focus his mind enough to think of what to make of the woman holding him.

"I've got sand all over me," he finally managed, straightening up again. "All over my—all over me."

"I've got it all over me too. Can't you feel it between us?"

He could. The tiny grains were all that separated him from the body he had craved for weeks now, and all he had to do was turn around and take her, sand and all, drive her hard against the dune until she screamed with pleasure, or *pain*—hell, at this point he didn't really care, wasn't sure there was a difference. But his penis was as useless as a piece of old leather, and he doubted that he had the strength to turn around and face her, much less summon the energy for love. He slumped forward again.

"Yes," he sighed, "I can feel the sand."

"Are you all right, Jack?" She was nuzzling the back of his neck.

"Yeah, yeah, I've got to get my breath back is all. I'm not used to chasing naked women in the dunes at night. Haven't done that in awhile." He was still struggling for breath, but his heart was calming down. "Been at least a month."

She turned him around and molded her body against the front of his and kissed him strongly on the mouth. "My God, you've even got sand on your forehead."

"I know. All over me."

"I'm sorry, but it *was* fun, you know. And it was the first time for me too."

Strangely, though she had kissed him with passion, her breasts against his chest, his penis nestled in her pubic hair, he felt nothing but gut-wrenching weariness. *In shape, shit*, he thought, *I'm as dead to my ass as an old man.*

She backed away from him. "You want to go wash this sand off?"

"Yeah . . . uh . . . I guess so." He was taking deep breaths now, but he could barely stand.

He followed her back to the beach, trying to stay up on his trembling legs. *What a crazy-ass night.* He watched her move gracefully over the sand. *Out here with the most beautiful woman I've ever seen and I can't even get a hard-on when she touches me with a full frontal. My dick's coated with sand like a fillet rolled in cornmeal.*

In the water again, he felt his spirits recover a bit, though he was still weak in the legs as he waded out to where she scrubbed her body in the surf. Beside her he squatted and rubbed his hands over his arms and legs and torso, then ducked under and rinsed his hair and face. Last, he swished his penis around and carefully inspected it with his fingers to be certain that no grains of sand remained. If by some miracle he did manage to make it with her, he didn't want to ruin things with that damned sand.

"Is there any fresh water on the island where we can rinse?" she asked as she returned to the beach. "I think I've got all the sand off, but I don't know whether I can sleep with salt all over me."

He squatted down and rinsed one last time for good measure. "Well, there's an artesian well at the Ranger Station on the inside beach, way over to the west, but we'd have a hell of a long walk over there, in the dark, and would probably get so sweaty and sandy that it wouldn't be worth it, not to mention the brush we'd have to get through. I have a five-gallon bucket of water in the boat. We can rinse off with that before we go to bed."

"There's my Pompeii Man again, thinking of everything."

"Yeah, well, your Pompeii Man is just about as dead as Pompeii itself right now."

She took his hand and they walked up the beach toward camp, naked as newborns, though Stafford gave little thought to the fact as his body slowly returned to normal. He thought only of the walk over to the boat and the weight of a five gallon bucket of water.

He had hoped she would not mention the fact that they were still nude—as exhausted as he was, he wanted to see her naked in the light—but when they reached the spot where their things lay, she picked up her bathing suit and walked out into the surf and put it on, then her shirt, and he followed her lead, hating the feel of clothing against his nakedness. Perversely, only now, with his cutoffs back on, did he feel himself begin to stir.

The Coke they had when they got to camp almost fully revived Stafford, and he shared a Butterfinger with Susie. At long last he felt like a man again, certainly strong enough to walk over to the boat and bring back the water, which in short order he did, returning to find her wrapped in a large towel and sitting between the tent and fire on one of the ice chests. His legs were still weak.

"I took my bathing suit off," she said, "so all I've got to do is rinse and dry off and slip on some clean clothes."

"You mean you don't have anything on under that towel?"

"Nothing. But why would that possibly interest you? You had me up against you naked out there in the dunes and nothing happened."

"Susie, you—"

"I'm teasing, Jack, you know that. Come on and rinse me off."

She walked to the edge of their little circle of light and draped the towel over a bush. In the glow from the languishing fire her form was golden, so exquisitely perfect in every proportion: calves, thighs, buttocks, her back flaring into shoulders that, though broad and firm, seemed so astonishingly matched to the rest of her, and falling across them her hair, which even wet was a rich straw color.

"God," he breathed to himself, "this is the finest chapter in youth's sweet-scented manuscript."

"Ready?" She dropped her head back so that her hair fell free of her shoulders. "Just pour when you're ready."

Stafford twisted off the spout cap and hoisted the bucket to his shoulder, tilted it so that a steady stream of water came out instead of gulping chugs, and let the water wash down across her face and hair and shoulders as she turned to direct the stream where she wanted it to go. She was careful not to turn enough to the side that he could see her breasts. After he had emptied perhaps a third of the bucket, she said that she was rinsed well enough and reached for the towel and draped it around herself again.

"Do you want me to rinse *you*?" she asked when she had turned to face him.

"Well, that bucket's still pretty heavy. I'll just go off there in the dark and wash down. Won't take but a minute."

She handed him a towel and Stafford lugged the bucket around one of the dunes and after draping the towel across a shrub lifted the bucket, allowing the water to cascade down over his head and shoulders and torso; then he splashed off his legs and carefully rinsed his penis. He dried himself off in the dark and carried what remained of the water back to camp.

Susie was dressed in a pair of clean shorts and tee-shirt when he set the bucket down beside the tent.

He squinted. "What does your tee-shirt say?"

She laughed. "SQUEEZE ME."

"That an invitation?"

"Could be."

He set the bucket down beside the tent. "Well, listen, there's enough water left for us to rinse down again, if we decide to take another swim."

"That what you want to do? Swim?" She was combing out her hair, wincing as she encountered knots.

"No, no," he said. "Just that *if* we decide to swim, we have water to rinse off again."

"What I'd really like to do, after you get some clothes on, is walk on the beach again, look at the stars awhile. Would you like to do that with me, Pompeii Man?"

"Absolutely. Give me a second."

Stafford rummaged around in the picnic basket until he found a small paper sack wrapped with a piece of twine, untied it, and pulled out a tee-shirt, some jockey shorts, and another pair of cut-offs.

"My, but you travel light," she observed as he pushed back the flaps of the tent and pulled himself up inside, cantilevering his legs outside through the flaps and rubbing his feet together to clean them of sand. He pivoted on his butt, swung his legs into the tent, removed the towel, and pulled on his clean dry clothes.

"Ready." He crawled out and spread the towel over the top of the tent, where she had already draped hers.

They walked west along the beach, noting the scattered lights at sea. He pointed out constellations to her, identifying some individual stars, and remarked that if they stood still for a bit they might see a satellite zipping along. So they stood then, still as the night itself, with him right behind her, pressing his body to hers, taking care not to touch her with his hardness.

In a few minutes, as he had predicted, something that to the casual eye might escape attention moved from north to south across the starry sky, appearing at times to feint and dodge. He brought his right arm up and pointed, leaning his head against hers.

"There. There's one."

She watched for a few seconds where he pointed, then nodded. "Yes, yes, I see it, like a moving star."

"Right, just like a moving star. And if we stayed here watching long enough, we'd see five, maybe ten, of them tonight. It's amazing how many are out there."

He had kept his face pressed against hers, his chin on her shoulder. She seemed to be pressing back.

"Susie, may I kiss you?"

For an answer she put an arm around his neck, pulling his lips down to hers, and this time he knew that she was feeling something, and he turned so that his hardness was against her.

"Enough, Jack," she said after a brief while. She pulled away from him. "The ground rules go for both of us." She dropped her right hand and formed it around the bulge. "There'll be another time for him. And her. They'll get together, sooner or later. As much as they'd like to tonight, we can't let it happen."

"Susie."

She lifted her hand and held it over his mouth. "No, Jack, not tonight. A lot rides on what happens tonight. If you let me control this . . . if you just leave me in charge of this part of it. Well, we'll both in time be glad, that's all."

Goddamn, he breathed to himself, *how I would like to be back on that dune top right now and you naked and against me.* He had never in his whole life been so turned on, so on the very edge of exploding. Was she on her period, or what? *You will be serviced tonight, my man, if it has to be done with the old right hand.*

Back at camp, he let her crawl into the tent and spread the blankets to suit herself. There would be one beneath them and one to cover them, with a third folded and laid across the open end of the tent to serve as a pillow. Once they were in for the evening he would zip up the mosquito flaps and nothing would pester them.

"Ready, I guess," she said, poking her head out. "I need to brush my teeth and make a little bathroom trip, and then we can turn in, if you want. It must be getting late."

Stafford, building up the fire for the night, shrugged. "Dunno. I didn't bring a watch." He looked up toward the stars, as if they would tell him anything. "I'd guess around nine or ten."

"Well," she said, standing up and stretching, "we're on Pompeii time, so doesn't matter."

He went behind one of the dunes while she made her trip in the opposite direction. When she came back to the fire, he was through brushing his teeth and standing there shirtless, wondering whether he should remove his cutoffs.

"You ready to go to bed?" she asked, shaking out her hair, which had now dried to its lighter natural shade.

"Guess so. You?"

"Do you sleep naked, Jack?" she asked.

"No. Undershorts. You?"

"Panties and a tee-shirt usually. I'm not sure out here. Should I wear bullhides?"

Stafford laughed. "Hey, I told you, you're in control here. I'll do whatever you let me do. If you'll sleep naked, that's the way I want it. I will too."

"Tee-shirt and panties, and you keep your shorts on."

"Yes'm."

"Really, Jack."

"Really," he said.

When the two of them were inside, Stafford zipped up the mosquito netting at the opening and they stretched out, facing the sea. The tent was pretty tight with two occupants, though he had spent several nights in it with a woman in Colorado—most of the time they had not been side-by-side. The evening was still fairly warm, so he suggested that they fold the top blanket back at their feet and pull it up if they needed it, as they probably would along toward morning, when the wind would switch and the late September sea breeze would have a bite to it.

They lay for a long while on their stomachs watching faraway lights move across the Gulf and talking freely about themselves, something they had not done much on their earlier dates. He learned that she was an only child of divorced parents and that her mother lived in Mobile, where she ran a small antique store just off Government Boulevard and lived comfortably enough off the trickle of income from the store and the beneficence of her husband, an attorney, who felt an obligation to maintain Susie and her mother in some style. Susie had chosen the community college in Gautier because she wanted to live somewhere other than the city her mother lived in and because she wanted to be near the Coast.

Stafford told her a bit about his childhood and education and travels, finally working the divorce into the conversation, though she seemed to have no reaction at all to it except to observe when he had finished talking about his former wife that he seemed to have had a fairly eventful life.

"You're a man of the world, Jack Stafford. You have been everywhere and done everything. I've never known a man who had any depth at all." She laughed. "Really, I've known nothing but boys."

"The world's a big place, Susie, and I haven't seen a sliver of it. Not nearly as much as I want to see."

"I haven't seen *any* of it," she said quietly.

He reached and placed his hand on her head and stroked her hair. "Maybe I can change that someday."

"I'm still kind of warm," she said. "I don't suppose you'd mind if I took off this tee-shirt?"

He laughed. "Let me think about it."

"These blankets aren't exactly as comfortable as sheets." Remaining on her stomach, she twisted and tugged until the tee-shirt was off. She tucked it into a corner of the tent.

The wind, he noticed, had swung around to the north, occasionally gusting and flinging sand against the foot of the tent, another reason he had chosen to face it seaward. She lay now with her hands still beneath her chin, looking out toward the Gulf, but she was speaking less frequently and more slowly.

"I guess it would be in keeping with the ground rules, wouldn't it, if I kissed you good-night." He ran his hand lightly across her shoulders.

She tilted her face to him and said, "Yes, I guess it would." She kissed him without passion on the lips and lowered her head to the pillow blanket, her face turned away from him. For a long time he lay propped up on an elbow gazing down on the beautiful woman stretched out beside him, even in starlight amazingly perfect in proportion. Her hair was swept back toward Stafford, trailing out to his end of the rolled blanket, and when he laid his face down, he touched the hair, and all the mingled smells of Susie Clayburn and the beach came through his nostrils and mouth and he had to fight the urge to roll over and take care of things for himself in a few easy strokes. In a while, lulled by her soft, even breathing, a kind of peace settled over him and he flattened out and slept, his face nuzzling her hair.

He awoke deep in the night. They were still lying on their stomachs, uncovered, their thighs touching. Dark as it was inside the tent, he could see that she was resting her chin on the rolled up blanket with her eyes wide open.

"You awake?" he asked softly.

"Yes. There's lightning off there." She pointed to the southeast. "It's running everywhere, great long streaks."

But there was no thunder coming across the water to them, so he assured her that it was probably just heat lightning and nothing to worry about.

"Besides, we're in a tent."

"It's awfully delicate," she whispered, turning over, her arm falling across the small of his back.

"Believe me, it'll take a beating. I've been through several storms in this little orange tent, and it'll keep us dry." He dared not look directly at her, but he could see in the corner of his eye her breasts and her panties.

"I wonder what time it is." Her fingers were delicately stroking the lower part of his back.

"Dunno. It's got to be somewhere in the early morning. Maybe around two or three. Should have brought a watch." Hell, he didn't have any idea at all what time it was. And he didn't care. He was trying to figure out what her hand on his back meant.

"Hasn't cooled off a whole lot yet, has it?" she asked.

He turned his face to hers. "Well, it's cooler than it was."

"When I woke up, my hair was all over your face."

"I know," Stafford said, rising on an elbow, his mouth only inches from hers. "It smells like the sea. I went to sleep smelling it. It was wonderful. It's the color of Smithers' sea oats, you know. Exactly the color of the sea oats. Every time I think of you, I think of the sea, of the islands. And it'll be even worse from now on."

"Why's that?"

"Because every time I'm out here, I'll think of this night, of you, of our lying here side by side."

"Maybe I'll be with you. Then you won't have to think about tonight."

He leaned and kissed her softly and she dropped her head back down on the blanket, arms spread. Her breasts were clearly visible to him in starlight from the tent opening. They were small, but absolutely perfect in shape. He rose to his knees and kissed the lobe of her ear, moved slowly to her neck, then shoulder, on to the inside of the arm that lay on his side of the blanket, inching along until his tongue touched her finger tips. He could feel tiny goose bumps springing up as his tongue moved.

She said nothing when he shifted his lips across to her left breast, where his tongue sought out and circled her nipple, and still said nothing when he delicately tongued the other nipple and eased his mouth toward her navel, where he tasted salt. He did not want to rush, to feverishly set upon her the way he knew any boys she'd had so far had probably done, making her defensive and nervous. His older women had taught him how to love slowly and methodically, savoring every inch of the body. As he moved lower, she moaned, and by the time he had gone past her navel and run his tongue along the top of her panties, he could feel a vague motion in her hips.

He worked down the inside of her thigh to her knee, shifted to the other thigh, and moved back up, all the while spreading her legs wider until by the time he had reached the spot, she was open to him, the only thing separating him from her was the thin panties, through which he could already feel her wetness.

"Susie," he leaned and whispered in her ear.

Still she said nothing. The only sound was the swishing of the water before them.

To his mild surprise he felt no urgency, only the slow realization that it was going to happen, that this woman was allowing him to do what she had already said that they would not do, that they were one with the night and the sea and consummation was near. He slipped her panties down and off, folded them carefully, and laid them in the corner of the tent.

"Unless you tell me not to, I've got to go out there and get something. Be right back." When still she did not speak, he crawled out of the tent and went to the picnic basket and removed his wallet, where he had stashed it earlier, and fished out a condom and crawled back in the tent. She was still on her back with her legs spread.

"I figured you had that base covered," she said.

He slipped off his shorts and removed the condom from its package. "You never know. Everything but tongs."

He dropped between her legs and began kissing her breasts as he probed until he slid effortlessly inside her and she took him completely.

And then there was only that timeless void, which a man and woman know when their passion has risen past all reasonable restraint, that instant when the earth stands still on its axis or spins wildly out of control, when reality is just that man and that woman, wherever they happen to be.

When the sun found them that Sunday morning, lightening up the little orange tent, Jack Stafford was still intertwined with Susie Clayburn, while before them the great Gulf rolled in and rushed up the sand, remembered itself, and drew back again.

IX

A month to the day after their Horn Island visit Jack and Susie, married the night before, were slicing through the placid sound off Pascagoula in Jerry Harmon's sailboat. The weather was perfect for such a trip, caught in that marvelous in-between time of the Deep South, after the savage heat of summer has subsided but before the onset of cold, a time of indefinable longing and tongueless promise.

Almost like spring, Stafford thought as he aimed the little boat toward the dark line of the island. Susie's hair trailed out its splendid gold only an arm's length away. To east and west the sea spread out like hammered lead, and a dome of pale blue sky sat upon it, the lean strip of island slicing between the two vast stretches like a knife. He pointed the boat toward the first outcropping of big dunes, to the west of which he could now make out the beginnings of individual trees. He noticed with relief that they had that end of the island to themselves.

Just before noon they established camp where they had that night. The wind had swept away all signs of their visit except for two blackened log ends that protruded from the sand. Stafford arranged the load of gear they brought over from the boat and went back for another, motioning to Susie that he could handle what was left.

When he returned, an ice chest on one shoulder, a jug of fresh water dangling from his opposite hand, she stood facing the Gulf where their little tent had been.

"Sad, isn't it?" she said.

Stafford set the water and ice chest down and placed his arms around her. "What's sad?"

"Just things, the way they change. This is where we were, where we first really came together, where we first made love, and there's nothing to tell that we've been here."

"I would have thought you'd be happy coming back," he said.

"I *am* happy. But this place . . . don't you think it's sad?"

"No. Now you're mine. You weren't before. Before you were just some wild woman I had to chase through that dark water and then run down in the dunes."

She smiled, taking his hand. "If I recall correctly, I caught *you*. You couldn't keep up with me. Remember?"

He kissed her on the cheek. "Yeah, I remember."

"There's nothing here to—you know what I mean, Jack—to commemorate our visit. The sand has covered everything over. I guess it's like a couple going back to a house where they first lived and finding other people's trash all over everything, other people's dust and hair. There's no sign of *them*, that they ever lived there, made love there."

"The lone and level sand," he said quietly.

"Jack, there ought to be something here."

"So you're saying that we should put up some sort of monument that we were here, something to commemorate our night out here?"

"Yes. There ought to be a marker or something."

Stafford kicked the log ends. "These are ours, I think."

"Before we leave this time I want to put up something to mark the spot, something that will last, at least awhile, to remind us about that night, to make others wonder what happened here."

"M'lady's become a Romantic."

"Don't you think we ought to—"

"We won't forget, Susie. You don't forget a night like that."

"Promise me we'll put something up. OK?"

"You got it. I'll find something to mark this spot. Ought to be something on the beach I could use." Then, "But remember that no matter what we put here, it'll eventually be washed away when the storms come across."

"But it will last awhile," she said.

Then he pitched the tent and they enjoyed its privacy while the great Gulf swished against the sand.

When they had dressed, hand in hand they retraced their steps of that first day, walking west up the beach, noting that now the sea breeze had an edge to it that it had not had before, a signal of approaching winter, which trees along the mainland and scattered low-growing hardwoods on the island had already declared in their sharp colors. Fall came on so abruptly on the islands: one trip out everything would be brazenly green, the beach and dunes shimmering with late September heat; the next, perhaps only a few days later, a keen wind would be white-capping the bay and flinging sheets of sand across the island, and in the wooded stretches yellow would start to show, sprinkled with the brilliant red of sumac.

They came at last to the high dune from which they had watched buzzards feeding off the deer. He walked ahead of her up the steep slope, holding her hand and helping her to the top. They could see where the deer had been, but there was no indication that anything remained of it, no skin or bones.

"You want to walk over there?" he asked her.

"No. Not really. I can see that it's all gone. The wind has covered what was left of her."

"I told you it would be different when we came here again," Stafford said, running his bare foot through the sand. All we'd find if we went over there would be the trails of crabs and raccoons."

"I feel sad again," she said.

"Don't. Think instead of China and Greece, Alexander in his tent, Montaigne in his tower, St. Theresa in her wild lament."

"What?"

"Nothing. Just recalling a poem about a dead groundhog. The poet finds it dead one day and watches its progress of decay over a year, from the time it begins what he calls 'its senseless change' until nothing is left but bleached bones."

"What do China, Greece, and St. Theresa have to do with it?"

"Just that even the great civilizations follow the same cycle of life and death as the insignificant little groundhog. The soldiers and philosophers and religious giants: all succumb, all fall and decay." He smiled tightly. "The Pompeiis. All cities great and small. Everything and everybody in their season. Nature comes and covers our little camps and our great civilizations, with sand or ashes or grass or water."

"And you don't think that's sad?" She clung to his arm.

"No." He shrugged. "It happens. You just accept it. Things change. That's the realistic attitude, a scientific one."

"You said we would be different when we came again." She clutched his hand. "And, like always, you were right. Everything *is* different."

"The next time we come, things will be even more different for us," he said. "That's just nature."

"But, Jack, change isn't always bad. It isn't for us. Tonight you won't have to chase me in the surf and the dunes."

"I'm glad. It's going to be lot cooler tonight than it was then, and that water's beginning to chill down pretty quick."

"That wasn't what I meant."

He pulled her close. "I know. I know what you meant."

"Now *you* sound sad."

"It's the little trace of the Romantic in *me*, I guess. The scientific side says one thing, the Romantic another. The Romantic in me says to pity the poor deer for the life she's lost. The scientific side says that she's been scattered all over this island and beyond. Her atoms ride the wind with the buzzards, prowl the island with the foxes and possums, scoot along the bottom of the Gulf with the crabs that surely found her up here. She's in the sand and the air and the water. She's all over." He swept his hand in a circle about his head.

"My poetic Pompeii Man," she said, kissing him.

"Yeah. Notice that it is the scientific side that spawns the poetry."

Much later, with a fierce silver moon shining down, they took a blanket to the top the dune where she had held him sandy and helpless that night, and they made love as the wind gently switched from south to north and the surf below them swished and sighed.

The next morning, just after the sun began to coax steam from the towels they had hung on the guy rope leading out from the front of the tent, they dressed and walked the beach again, hand in hand. She carried her pad and made a few sketchings as they walked, and he carried her green bucket for shells. They walked so far west that by the time they got back to camp it was almost noon.

After a quick sandwich he concluded that the closing weather from the northwest probably meant heavy seas, so they struck the tent and she helped him carry their gear back over to the boat. While she stayed on the inside beach he walked back over for the ice chest.

"Will you put up a marker?" she yelled at him as he topped a dune.

He smiled at her and nodded and dropped out of sight.

Stafford walked to the outside beach and scouted the drifts of the upper sand until he found something that suited him, two barkless limbs bleached almost white and sanded smooth by the surf. A few more feet and he found a piece of gnarled yellow nylon line from which he cut a short length.

When he returned to Susie, he took her hand and led her toward the outer beach until, high on a dune, they could look across at the campsite. In the side of one of the dunes that formed the depression where the tent had been, he had driven the longer stick, then lashed across it the shorter one.

"There's your marker," he said.

"It looks like where someone died in a wreck."

"Or where something religious happened. What happened there that night was almost religious, wasn't it?"

Susie clenched his arm. "Yes, I guess it was. Yes," she said softly, pulling him back toward the boat, "it will do just fine."

As their little boat moved slowly back toward the coastline, the wind picked up from the south, flinging sand up and through the dunes, smoothing out and leveling, filling in the tracks of the man and woman. Their marker cast a thin shadow on the sand.

X

A Sunday afternoon in early March, the first spring of their marriage, they had returned from a walk down the beach across the street and showered together, something they did often, after which he always swept her up and carried her to the bed and made love to her.

They had their pleasure and were lying spent with passion side by side, he with a leg thrown across one of hers, their hands still joined, staring at the ceiling. Neither of them spoke for some time as the Gulf breeze drifted in from the window and slowly spun the blades of the ceiling fan above their bed. His mind, being in no other fashion entertained, flew back over the months since that day he saw her legs for the first time and lit, almost as if directed by some dark finger, on a scene in his office with Emily Miller, who had dropped by for a chat only a day or so after his marriage and in leaving said simply, "Jack, you can stand just so much cream." He had turned the scene over and over in his mind several times since that day. There had been something very strange in the way Emily sat there across from him and had her say.

When Stafford and Susie married, breaking off with his old female companions had been simple enough for him. He had quietly called the two wives and the woman from Ocean Springs to tell them that he was now married, and each of them wished him well. It was with mild surprise, then, that he had looked up from his desk one afternoon and seen Emily standing in the doorway.

"Oh, hello, Emily. I didn't hear you knock."

"For good reason—I didn't."

"Well, come on in. He rose and offered her a chair. He could smell stale smoke as she slipped past him.

She sat down and opened her purse and removed an elaborately engraved silver case from which she shook a cigarette. She clamped the cigarette with her lips, slid the case back into her purse, and lit up with a small pearl lighter, her eyes on the *Thank You For Not Smoking* sign above Stafford's desk.

"Emily, if they catch you smoking in here . . ."

"Screw'm."

"How's Howard?" he asked.

"Howard who?" her throaty voice came back.

"Emily, come on."

"Knock, knock," she said.

Stafford shrugged. "You're already sitting in my office."

"It's a knock-knock joke, Jack. Remember them? Or have you lost your sense of humor along with your freedom and common sense? *Knock, knock.*"

He spread his hands and tried on a smile. "OK, Emily, who's there?"

"Howard."

"Howard who?"

"Howard you like to go fuck yourself?" Then she laughed her throaty laugh, but there was little mirth in it.

"Emily."

"Howard's fine. So glad you asked about him. He's in love again."

"Yeah?"

"With a boy just out of the Navy. Pensacola boy. He's in one of his classes. Pretty, all right, and Howard's thrilled with him."

"Emily, you know I don't—"

"Sure you do, Jack. Howard brought him home a few days after you called to advise me about your marriage, as a matter of fact. Good news, like bad, comes in herds, you know. Howard packed a few things and they drove off to some Goddamned where for the night. Got back just in time for class yesterday. Howard seemed refreshed. I felt like asking him whether he could spare the boy for about half an hour, but I figured that if he would go off somewhere with Howard for the night he probably didn't want what I had to offer."

"Emily, what are you doing here?"

"Mighty pretty little guy. I could have used him, Jack. Maybe used him *up*."

"Emily."

"Howard's my burden to bear, I guess."

Stafford cleared his throat and raised his hand like a man trying to stop traffic.

"Emily, enough. Why are you here? When we spoke on the phone, I thought you were all right about this. No complications. We agreed on that from the beginning. What's this about?"

She just looked at him.

Stafford said again, "What's this *about*, Emily? What's on your mind?"

"He has provided me with a nice place to live and with as much money as I need to get by in reasonable fashion. And he leaves me the hell alone to do what I want to do. I could bang a guy right on the couch beside him and he wouldn't care. He'd probably offer us cigarettes and a drink when we finished."

"Emily—"

"Sorry, Jack, but I need to talk a little. What really gets my blood going, though, is to find some guy's bright red jockey shorts hanging on my shower rod drying. Or his silky shirts tumbling in my drier. I mean, that's too damned *much*. It's like I have a son with a live-in lover and I'm doing the laundry for both of them. And I think that's what it's come down to—I'm Howard's *mother*."

"Ditch him if you don't like it."

"I can live with it," she said, drawing deep on her cigarette and billowing smoke toward the no-smoking sign. "Besides, one of these days he may bring in a guy that likes women too, and we can share him."

Stafford looked impatiently at his watch. "Em, I've got work to do."

"So, you've settled your affairs, have you?" she interrupted. "So to speak."

"I guess you could say so. I feel real good about it, frankly."

"I'm glad. I've seen quite a lot of her. I watched the two of you in the Commons yesterday at lunch. You did very, very well for yourself. And you appear to be marvelously in love. It must be nice to be in love."

"Emily, you're trying to spread gloom here."

"She's a world-class looker, Jack, and you must know that

every man she crosses the path of will notice it and fall in love with her. Pretty as a little songbird. Exactly like a little songbird. Lucky you." She held the cigarette between her teeth and wagged it back and forth with her tongue.

"What's the remark about the songbird? Something tacky?"

"Me *tacky*? Come on, Jack. She's just pretty, like a little songbird. Looks like she could break out in song any minute. She adds color and music to your world. That's all I mean. It's a compliment."

"Yeah, I'll bet."

"She as smart as she is pretty, or dumb as a duck?"

"I think she's damned smart," he said. "From all I can tell. Sharp, great with metaphors, Emily, fun to be with. She's wonderful."

Emily smiled. "Jack, there's not a sophomore girl on this campus who isn't giddy with metaphors. They learn that stuff in literature classes, as you well know, and if they think you like for them to use it, they will."

"Emily, are we a bit jealous?"

She shook it off. "How long's it been since you've been seriously involved with a shallow girl?"

"Susie's not shallow. I've told you. She's sharp. She calls me her Pompeii Man."

"Oooh, that *is* clever. Pompeii Man. Where'd she come up with that?"

"It's a longer story than I've got time to get into here, Emily."

"She may be a little witty, but that's mostly because she's cute. She's got no *depth*. She hasn't had time for life to roughen her up. That's why you haven't messed around with students, Jack. There's nothing to them. They're hollow vessels waiting to be filled. That's why they're *here*. They don't even know how to *fuck* yet. And judging from what I've observed, they won't learn how until they find some guy past forty who's capable of showing them how, some guy who's learned from an older woman. Jesus, Jack, you didn't know how to love a woman when we first started things up. You were like a high school boy, salivating and clawing at me—quick as a mink, as the saying goes."

He laughed. "Well, I'll admit that you taught me a few tricks."

"Bet your ass I did. And I learned from a man nearly sixty years old, a doctor, over thirty years older than I was."

"I didn't know that. I just figured that Howard—"

"Howard never taught me a damned thing about sex that was worth learning."

"Emily, I've got things to do."

"Take your little girl's daddy's money away from her, yank her scholarship, if she's got one, and throw her into a trailer with a shipyard worker for awhile. Then you'd have a *woman* with some depth to her. Living in a trailer with one of those sorry-ass sons-ofbitches for a couple of years would put *decades* on her, show her what hard sex is and love's not. Then she'd be primed to learn how to *make love* and you could teach her what you know, what I've taught you. You could teach her patience and gentleness and the magic of both your bodies. But you've got to see some Goddamned *clouds* in those sky-blue eyes. She's got to know the worst before she can appreciate the best. First the storm, then the sun and flowers."

"Come on, Em. You can't keep on with this."

She sat forward in her chair. "That girl," she said in her husky smoker's voice, "doesn't have the mileage you need, Jack, the experience. I know you. I know what you require. She hasn't been enough places, hasn't suffered enough. She's nothing but surface cream right now. It's all physical—surface friction. She nice and tight for you?"

"Emily, stop it."

"Right now she's so new and fine that you don't have to work at it, do you? You just satisfy yourself."

"You don't know anything about what goes on between us."

She took another deep drag on the cigarette, held the smoke while she thought, then exhaled. "You know, it'd be different if you had dew on you too, if you were fresh out of the nest. You could learn right along with her. But then, we both know she'd be ahead of you in a heartbeat. Goddamned American males. They mature at forty, if at all. Jack, you're a hell of a lot older. You've been through a bad marriage, you've been places, done things. You've known *women*." She smiled a bitter smile. "You've known *me*. And when the new wears off that pretty little thing, you're going to come looking for something deeper. And I might not be available."

He laughed. "Emily, you are so fucking *jealous*."

"You should have given her another five years, or ten, or six months with some abusive bastard from that shipyard. Or maybe with a fag." She drew on the cigarette again, exhaling through her nostrils. "You don't have the patience to wait for her to season,

Jack. Could be that when she *does* get the experience, when the silky little cocoon splits and the real Susie comes wriggling out, Mr. Pompeii Man, she'll smother your ass with hot black ashes. There are more things in heaven and earth, Horatio . . . ."

Stafford laughed. "I'll change her gradually, Em. I'll teach her what she needs to know. She'll be fun to mold."

Emily leaned toward him again. "Listen, my friend, you just remember that what she learns, she'll learn for good. Be certain what you want before you go trying to teach her anything."

He studied the details of Emily's face, hardened now to a hawklike finish. He could see the years of anguish and frustration woven in the tight wrinkles in her face and in her eyes the little flare of jealousy. As he watched, she ground the cigarette butt out against the bottom of her shoe and tossed it into the trashcan. He had never known a vicious woman in his life who had not been turned that way by some man who didn't know how to treat her.

"What'll *I* do now, Jack?" she asked quietly. "Where'll I go when I get so horny I can't stand it any more? To the first pickup load of pipe fitters from the shipyard I find stalled on the highway? To the jet in the jacuzzi?"

"Well," he laughed, "it's dependable. The jacuzzi'll always get up for you, and I hear those pipe fitters are aptly named."

Emily Miller did not laugh. She single-handedly fished out another cigarette and lit it, never taking her eyes off Stafford's face.

"Maybe I could re-teach Howard to enjoy sticking his pecker into something that doesn't have teeth or hemorrhoids. Little faggot sonofabitch. I really ought to walk in on him sometime when he's wrapped with one of his little beauties and blow his Goddamned brains all over the sheets, then take his boy and teach him what that thing's for. But they'd throw me in prison for it, where I'd have to learn about another kind of sex or go without. Wouldn't that be a Goddamned irony? I kill a fag, then end up being one."

She drew her small fists up into knots. Her skin seemed suddenly very old to him, washed out and yellow. She was pathetic.

"Come to think of it, though, no court would touch me," she said, sucking air past the cigarette between her teeth, "not after what that bastard has put me through."

"He's never assaulted you, has he?"

"Now, why in God's name would you finally come around to asking that, after all these years? It's like you don't know me at all and now you want to. No, he doesn't beat me. Never has. I think

I could take a beating better than what he's doing to me. And I know why women go back to men that abuse them. It's simple. They just figure every other man is probably at least as bad, maybe worse, than the one they're taking the shit from."

Stafford studied her face. "May I ask you something?"

"Sure," she said. "Ask away."

"Do you and Howard . . . you know, do y'all ever—"

"Do we ever *fuck* anymore? Is that what you're asking?"

"Yes."

She removed the cigarette from her lips and rolled it gently in her fingers. "The wonder is you never asked me that before. Strange, isn't it, given all the scare over HIV? Seems you would have wanted to know. You never wanted to know anything about me while we were together, did you?"

"I did. I just didn't ask." He fingered a pen.

"You always used a rubber," she said, "so what difference would it have made?"

"A man would be a fool not to, these days, with anybody."

"And a woman would be a fool not to insist on it."

"Well, do you? You and Howard?"

"Not in years and years, Jack. I can't even remember when. I'm more his mother than his wife, and he's not Oedipal. Closer to *pedopal*, I'd say, given the age of some of those boys . . . or maybe just *pit-i-ful*."

She stood to go, reached over and ground her cigarette out on one of his paperbacks and threw the stub beside the other one in his trashcan, leaving a black, powdery circle on the pale skin between the breasts of the woman on the cover, a scantily-dressed blonde embraced from behind by a sun-darkened male stripped to the waist, his lean body shadowy with muscles.

"I was clean for you, Jack. You didn't get anything from me that you could pass along to your little songbird. Even if you hadn't used a rubber, you wouldn't have gotten anything from me. But let me ask *you* something."

"Fire away."

"Why in hell did you have to *marry* her? You could have had her every Goddamned night without that complication. Why not just shack with her?"

Stafford shrugged and spread his hands wide in front of him. "I don't know, Emily. It seemed like the thing to do. I needed a wife. And she's the prettiest woman I've ever seen."

"She's a *girl*, Jack, still wet with dew, just cream."

"Emily, you are so fucking jealous of her."

She slammed her hand on the desk. "You don't know how I feel about her, you asshole! Maybe I am a little tired of losing to boys and girls, yeah. That hurts a little. Especially when I know what I've got to offer."

"Come on, Emily."

"Just remember that at least for the time being I'm out there, in case you tire of your voluptuous, creamy little milkmaid, Jack." She looked at the book. "Or is she the daughter of a Baron? What have you fantasized her into?"

He laughed. "This one has blue blood in her veins, Em, she's royalty through and through, and she is Susie Clayburn Stafford, the genuine article. No fantasy needed."

"Not yet. I hope she stays Susie Clayburn Stafford for you. Watch out, though, Jack, you can stand just so much cream." She stepped out, then leaned back inside his office. "You'll be looking for something stronger and darker before the dew dries off of her. Bet on it." She left, closing the door softly behind her.

Stafford stood at the window and watched until she appeared on the walkway behind the building and rounded the west wing, which joined the parking lot. She walked stiffly, her shoulders slightly stooped.

"Not much cream left of you, is there, Emily?" he whispered to the glass.

The perplexing thing was that except for her initial tackiness about Susie, Emily, in all her bitterness, had seldom said an unkind thing about anyone other than her homosexual husband. He could understand her outburst about the insensitive Howard, who had made her life miserable with his constant flings and small eunuch cruelties, and, really, her little caveat about Susie sounded like the way a mother would warn a child headed toward perceived danger or disappointment. It had to be because she was jealous. Maybe she was in love with him. There was something in her words now that kept bringing them back to mind, something more troubling, and he realized that Emily knew more than he knew, had used that intensely penetrating skill of understanding motivation that all women seemed to possess and seen through Susie's veneer of loveliness and found something, or, worse yet, *nothing*.

He removed his leg and released his hand from hers, rolling over until he could study the face of the sleeping woman beside him. How perfect her shape was, how excruciatingly and incredibly flawless her lines, from her hair, swept across her pillow as a photographer might have directed it done, to her face and shoulders and arms and breasts, all the way to her feet, whose toes, unlike those of most women—misshapen by the daily punishment of restrictive shoes—were as genuinely beautiful as any toes he had ever seen. She could have been a model for any magazine or painter. But for fear of waking her from her serene, childlike sleep, her breath sweet and slight, he would have leaned and kissed each of them. *Oh, Susie Clayburn Stafford, you* are *cream. You are almost more than a man should be allowed to possess and hold.*

His eyes lingered on her finely sculptured body until an uncomfortable realization settled on him like the awareness of mortality itself: *This woman is* too *perfect. That is the problem. She is every man's greatest desire and greatest fear.* It was like a light coming on. He now knew this, just as he knew that beneath the fine exterior there was nothing that could intrigue him for long. Like a creamy pearl shell on the beach, high above the tideline, there was nothing inside, nothing but a husk where one might hear only the whisper of the ocean in the empty coil.

It was the curse of youth that he was seeing before him, stretched out in her physical splendor, a body without the experience to make it interesting for long, a body without bruises and scars, without the wrinkles of anguish and age and deep hurt. Just a shell. Beautiful pearl, pink and white. And behind her lids lay blue pools of innocence, unshadowed by hurt or despair that gave depth to a woman's eyes. They were eyes that danced and sparkled with joy or clouded over with anger, but they had no depth, no *depth*, and as fast as they clouded, they cleared, like the eyes of a child who, disappointed by some trivial denial, brightens at the prospects of a piece of candy. Her eyes had never known real fear or hunger. So unlike Emily's eyes, where he could see layer upon layer of complicated emotion.

Her beauty was exquisite, without blemish, but wooden, lifeless, soulless, and in so many ways her innocence was like that of an infant. No mystery, no mystique. She had never been anywhere, had never read widely, had never known anything but security and comfort. Unless you could count two boys from high school, if she had told him the truth, she had never even had sex with another man.

As he lay there studying his wife's lovely form, he kept thinking of Poe's Ligeia, whose physical perfection was balanced with incredible learning and an element of the mysterious, especially in her eyes—that addition of strangeness that made her beauty complete. Susie's eyes had nothing in them below their pale, unruffled blue. She needed that added dimension of strangeness, like Ligeia—some darkness, some shadowy, faraway depth in her eyes.

That stud from Pompeii, Priapus or whoever he was, the little statue whose penis was almost as big as he was, had to have been thinking about some mysterious, unfathomable woman, maybe yet buried ashes. Only someone so profoundly beyond his reach could hold his attention that long, could harden him to stone and keep him erect for all these centuries, some dark lady whose soul he could not plunder.

That Sunday afternoon, with his beautiful wife still stretched out in blissful sleep on their bed, Stafford went downstairs and scanned his bookshelves until he located the American literature textbook he had used when he was an undergraduate. He looked up Poe's story.

"The 'strangeness,' however, which I found in the eyes," he read, "was of a nature distinct from the formation, or the color, or the brilliancy of the features, and must, after all, be referred to as the *expression*." And further: "The expression of the eyes of Ligeia! How for long hours have I pondered upon it!"

Those dark orbs of Ligeia, those black, enigmatic eyes. If only the woman upstairs, the fair-haired, blue-eyed Susie, could stir within him the same passion that Poe's narrator felt gazing into his woman's eyes. That madman saw correspondences for Ligeia's expression in the whole of nature: ". . . in the contemplation of a moth, a butterfly, a chrysalis, a stream of running water. I have felt it in the ocean, in the falling of a meteor . . . ." As he sat there with the book in his lap, he could think of nothing that Susie's eyes corresponded to except, in its forever curve from horizon to horizon out over the Gulf, the pale cold blue of the sky, beyond which lay the nothingness of space—the shallow, meaningless blue of the irises, which surrounded steady, small pupils that seemed never to vary much in size and which were themselves surrounded by a flat and snow-white tundra of innocence. He returned the book to its slot. It was absurd for him to feel that way about her eyes, and perhaps it was nothing more than the fact that his own eyes were a deep brown, almost black, with so much liquid depth to them that sometimes when he stared at them in the mirror he was almost frightened by the passion they held.

Stafford walked to the front door, where he slipped on his old sneakers and jogged across the street to the beach, leaving Susie to her sleep.

XI

He groped in the dark to answer the phone. His head was foggy and he had no idea what time it was.

"Stafford?"

"Yeah," he managed.

"Merchant here. I'm sending a uniform to get you."

His mind quickly focused. "What's happened? Have you found her?"

"Easy, man. Yeah, we found her. She's at the hospital. Over at Charity. She's all right. A uniform—"

"Goddamn, Merchant, tell me more. What did they do to her? Where's she *been*?" He had switched on the lamp and was trying to get his shoes on.

"Like I say, man, a uniform's on the way. Get down to the lobby and meet him. Your wife's all right. Banged up, but all right. He'll bring you down here and we'll take you to her. And, Stafford, bring your wife's bag and a clean dress. Hers is all messed up."

Stafford tied his shoes and snatched the white dress and Susie's bag out of the closet and slammed through the door, then remembered and went back into the room for her shoe. He noticed that the clock on the TV registered five-thirty.

Jesus, he thought as he unzipped the bag and slid the dress and shoe in, pushing past a couple waiting for the elevator, *she may not even have the other shoe.*

"Sorry," he said to the man and woman, "but I've got to get down to the street. The police are waiting for me." Where in bloody hell could *they* be going at that hour? He stepped into the elevator even before the doors had fully opened and slapped the *L* button time and again until the doors closed, sliding to before the astonished faces of the couple who, frozen in place, waited.

"I want to *see* her." It was the fifth time Stafford had said it. He was seated before Oswalt's desk and beside him Merchant sat silently twirling his thumbs, eyes straight ahead, not on Oswalt, who sat expressionless studying the contents of a file, but beyond, beyond the wall upon which hung the diplomas and certificates that established Oswalt's authority to do whatever it was that he did.

"Guys, please." Stafford was leaning forward, forearms on the desk.

Oswalt looked up from his reading. "Hey, your wife is all right. That's all that matters, ain't it? That she's all right, in one piece and all? And they are taking care of her. Still checking her out. Don't *rush* it."

"But why can't I *see* her?"

"You can, but not until we have talked this out."

"They not going to let you see her yet anyway, Jack," Merchant said. "They're still checking her out."

"What's there to talk about? I want to know what they *did* to her."

Oswalt closed the file and slid it aside. "Stafford, the problem is that your lady won't say nothing." He looked at Merchant, whose eyes were still fixed on, or beyond, the wall.

"So what's the—"

"She won't say *nothing*, man, she won't tell us what was done to her and by *who*. Don't you understand? We told that sonofabitch Harry, who never said nothing neither, we told him to go back to whoever it was he didn't know nothing about and wasn't telling us nothing about and tell them that the woman was somebody's *wife*, that she wasn't a Goddamned two-grand-a-night hooker, that her dumb-ass husband got off on spinning some sort of stupid tale about her hooking, is all. And to let her go. Told him we wouldn't follow him and we wouldn't hassle him, just to go and tell them to turn her loose and quick."

"And we figure he did," Merchant said. "We got a call from somebody saying that we could pick her up down at Jackson Square. Which a uniform did. Found her huddled up on a park bench near the statue and called an ambulance that carried her straight to the hospital. We ain't figured out yet how they got her down to the Square that fast. I mean—"

"She was pretty messed up," Oswalt broke in. "Not hurt real bad, just messed up."

Stafford raised up in his chair. "What do you mean *messed up*? What'd they *do* to her?"

"If she won't tell us," Merchant said, "how the hell can we *know* what all they did to her? She's been roughed up for sure, beat on and all, but she won't let anybody check her for evidence of rape. Won't let the doctors. She's just froze up and won't say a fucking *thing*. They wouldn't let us in with her but a few minutes, and she wouldn't tell us *nothing*.

"Which is why," he continued, "we brought you down here before taking you to see her. You gotta get her to talk to us, man, tell us what they did to her. And who did it. With descriptions and all, names if she picked up any. Otherwise, we ain't going to be able to do anything. *Nothing*. She don't talk, we can't do a thing. It's that simple."

Oswalt shifted in his seat. "See, the only thing we know for sure is that you told Harry your wife was a whore. We can't *prove* that he called anybody. Harry's like that rock there." He pointed to the piece of Palo Dura sandstone on the desk. "He's a Neanderthal to begin with, and scared shitless of the very people he called. And you can bet he did make a call. There'd have been money in it for him. But even if we can prove he made a phone call, that won't tie him directly to what happened to her. He's clammed up like a piece of rock 'cause he knows that his ass is deader'n that rock if he rats on these people."

"A phone call to *whom*?" Stafford asked. "Who are *these people*? Surely you've got some ideas."

Oswalt screwed up his face. "Yeah, we got it narrowed down to a few thousand *whoms*."

Stafford stood and leaned on the detective's desk. "Then why don't you start bringing them in?"

"It's not that easy," Merchant said.

Oswalt sighed. "Just be glad you've got your wife back."

"It's just not that easy," Merchant repeated. He had gotten up and straightened his tie in a small mirror on the wall at the end of Oswalt's desk. He looked as if he had not slept in ages. He turned to Stafford. "*She* don't talk, *she* don't point the finger, identify some people, we can't do a thing."

"*You* are not the one that was snatched off the street," Oswalt said. "And even if we *were* sure enough to bet our asses on who done it, as far as any DA would be concerned, we'd be just guessing. We can't pick people up on guesses. Street punks, maybe, but not everybody. And, Stafford, you ain't even convinced me yet that you're not the one that did it. Y'all coulda got in a fight—"

"That is preposterous! Now, let me go see my wife."

The little detective held him in a steady gaze. "OK, say you're telling the truth and by some miracle you did identify the one that beat you up. He could just say you gave him the finger or something, called him a nigger, and he was just straightening your ass out. He don't know nothing about yo' wife, who just happened to disappear about the same time at the same place. And you can bet your ass the three boys would show up then, right out of thin air, and testify that you *did* give him the finger and call him a nigger. They seen every bit of it. *Heard* it."

Stafford nodded. "I want to see my wife."

"We're just *guessing* what happened," he continued. "Besides, connecting the ones that actually grabbed her with the one that ordered her grabbed would be right at impossible. We coulda leaned on Harry a week and got nothing else from him. Not even threat of prison or a good beating would loosen his tongue. He probably got a good chunk of change for his call, or would have if she'd been what he thought she was—what *you* told him she was. Might get his ass kicked around a little bit for all the trouble he's caused. But he won't say nothing. Bet on it."

"It ain't a code we're talking about here, ain't no principle involved," Merchant said. "It's plain-ass *fear*. No honor among'm. They'd turn their own mommas over to us if the price was right. But gettin' your ass killed is a heap-big sacrifice to most people, and they ain't willing to make that trade. These animals *will* kill, Stafford, just like that." He snapped his finger. "Quicker'n a snake strikin'."

Stafford slumped back down into the chair. "Do you think she knows why she was grabbed?"

Oswalt leaned forward. "You mean does she know that her dumb-ass husband put her into what we'll call a state of jeopardy to feed a Goddamned *fantasy*?"

Stafford nodded glumly.

"Far's we know she don't. But we got no idea what they said to her. Or what she said to them. If you're real damned lucky, she don't know. If she does—or if she puts it all together later—she'll hate your ass, big-time. You can bet on that. Any woman would."

"Will y'all tell her?"

Merchant laid a hand on his shoulder. "Stafford, what would that gain us?"

"Yeah," Oswalt said quietly, "in a trial, of course, both of you'd have to tell everything about it."

Stafford stared across the desk at the wiry detective. "Trial?"

"Yeah, in a trial. You ever heard of'm? That's one of the steps we use now to put people in prison. Y'all identify them, we arrest them, the court system tries them, and they go to prison—sometimes. Surely you've heard of the process."

"You're such an asshole, Oswalt."

"May be, but I ain't stupid, which is what you are. You and your fucking games. And I can just imagine how hard you're gon' try to get her to talk to us."

"You figure I'd try to talk her out of telling you what she knows to protect myself?"

"I know Goddamned well you would," Oswalt answered, his cheeks in his hands. "I got you figgered out. You'd do anything to keep her from finding out how stupid you are." He nodded. "I guess I would too. Oh, yeah, you'd do *anything* to keep her in the dark about this. Let me tell you something, Mr. Librarian, if I had my way I would arrest *your* ass for what's happened here. For stupidity, if nothing else."

"Did she ask about me?"

"She ain't asked about nobody," Oswalt said.

"Please take me to her, now," Stafford said. He pointed to the door. "If you don't, I'll go and find her myself."

Merchant reached over and pulled him back down into the chair. "Easy, Jack. Just relax. I'll take you over there. We just want to line up some questions for you to ask her. Even if she doesn't want to talk, you may get some critical information out of her. Now, we want to go over these with you."

Stafford nodded. "All right. I'll help you anyway I can."

Oswalt gave him a look.

"I swear I will."

The little detective handed him a legal pad on which he had written a page of questions. "These are some specific items we'd like you to cover with her. Now, don't take this Goddamned page in there and read the questions off—just memorize'm and work'm into your conversation whenever you can."

Stafford took the pad and studied it a few seconds, then tore the sheet off and folded it and stuck it into his shirt pocket. "Now can we go?"

As they sat in the car in the parking lot before driving off, Merchant summarized for Stafford Susie's injuries as he had observed them and as they had been reported by the attending physician. She had been struck about the head repeatedly, and her lower jaw, though not broken and with no damaged teeth, was badly swollen, making it difficult for her to open her mouth. One eye was blackened, and there was evidence that a knife had been applied to different parts of her body, "like they were just pricking her," as Merchant put it. Her arms and legs were bruised in several places, and someone had cut a shallow cross, a small one, right in the middle of her chest.

"Not deep, not big," Merchant said, "just broke the skin. But he rubbed something into it, ink or dye or stove-black or something that wouldn't wash out, to make it a tattoo."

"What's that all about?" Stafford asked. "The cross? Is it some sort of satanic thing or what?"

"Well, we've got some ideas about it, but we're not sure. Got initials on it."

"Initials?" Stafford was staring straight ahead at the dilapidated houses in the lot across the street. Why in God's name would they have Police Headquarters in this squalid section? Then he knew why. You build the fort where the Indians are. You let them see it, live in the shadow of it.

"Yeah. *SG.*"

"And that doesn't mean anything to you guys? That doesn't help you narrow the field down?"

Merchant glanced at him. "Sure, it narrows the field, if somebody with the initials SG was the one that did it. What if the person doing it just wanted us to *believe* SG did it?"

"Merchant, how does she look?"

"She looks like I told you she looks. She's been beat up."

"They let you guys see the cross?"

The big detective flicked his eyes at Stafford. "Yeah, we seen the cross."

"What else did they let you see, Merchant?"

Merchant started the car. "Hey, does it bug you that a black man saw your wife's chest? Jack, you're mighty Goddamned protective about a woman you threw to the wolves. Now lighten up, man. They had her breasts covered, if that's what you're getting at. That's all we saw—her face and arms and legs and that cross. And she didn't seem to be terribly happy about us seeing what we saw. Now I want you to get your mind right or I'm taking your white ass right back to the hotel."

"Sorry, man. I'm sorry." He was squared around in the seat. "But I need to know—was she *raped*?"

"Put your seatbelt on." Merchant pulled into the street. "Like we told you, she wouldn't say so and she wouldn't let the doctor examine her for rape, but there was some blood in her panties, they said. No semen, though, that they could tell. Which suggests that maybe they messed with her but didn't rape her."

"Thank God. At least there's *something* positive here."

Merchant had his hand hooked casually over the wheel. "Now, I'm not saying this to scare you, only to keep you straight on things, but lots of rape victims these days don't have any semen on'm or in'm. The assholes out there are gettin' smarter or they're just more careful. Whatever, these guys coulda used condoms."

Thanks, Merchant, thanks a hell of a lot, Stafford thought as they drove along a back street. They turned onto Tulane.

"How far to the hospital?" Stafford asked.

"You can almost see it from here," Merchant said. "Hang on. We'll get there."

"Why Charity?"

"What?

"Why did they take her to *Charity* Hospital?"

"That's where we normally take crime victims," Merchant said. "Good trauma unit, you know. And it ain't but a few blocks from headquarters."

"But it's not just for, you know, for people who—"

"Jesus, man, for a librarian you just don't know shit, do you? Yeah, it's just for poor people and niggers, Stafford. You worried about—man, you ought to be on your knees in this damned car thanking whatever powers that be that we got her back for you."

Stafford stared at the slowly lightening New Orleans skyline, dingy and ominous rising out of the morning mist, and an overpowering gloom settled over him. There would be no sun this morning, heavy clouds from the south having gathered and pushed over the city, leaving the buildings dull and somber, their windows blank and passionless. Old motels glided past, tacky bars and houses, a brewing company. Even the palm trees seemed chastised, beaten into submission. He wondered how the Quarter would look at this hour, with its ornate wrought-iron balconies, which once seemed so quaint and storybook lovely, warm and appealing, then decided that even there he would see nothing but baroque shapes, dark vines abounding, gargoyle faces leering. He knew he didn't want to see it. The whole city was a horrid jungle to him.

"I *am* grateful, Merchant," Stafford said finally.

"When have you eaten, Jack?"

"I don't know. I don't know when I've even thought about food. I'm not hungry, if that's what you're asking."

"Just wondered," Merchant said. "Sorry."

"I can't even remember when I've been to the bathroom."

"You need to go?"

"No. Later maybe. It'll wait." He leaned and pulled Susie's bag into the front seat with him.

"What?" Merchant asked.

"Hope you won't charge me with littering." Stafford pulled out the wig and balled it into his fist and rolled down the window, then looked over at Merchant.

The detective thrust out an arm to stop him, but Stafford already had his hand out the window. "Man, that could be evidence." He pulled his arm back and turned his eyes to the street. "Maybe you should keep it as a reminder. Just don't you tell anybody I was around when you threw it out. Better yet, tell'm you flushed it down the commode at the hotel." He kept his eyes straight ahead. "It's *your* scalp."

Stafford flung the wig away from the car and it caught the air and spread like some winged thing come suddenly alive, sailed and landed finally at the edge of the street where it tumbled and balled up, then crouched, a dark lump in the gutter.

XII

The trip to New Orleans was one of those spur-of-the-moment things, though secretly Stafford had been wanting to get away with his new wife for months. Their first anniversary was approaching in the early fall, and but for a couple of professional trips he had taken her nowhere at all. Europe was on his mind, but funds were low—perhaps by the following summer, if he managed well. New Orleans was handy and cheap and gloriously suited to a couple newly married.

He awoke early that Thursday morning in August, long before the sun, and lay in the dark thinking about how wonderful she had been the night before, how dazzlingly beautiful and succulent right there in that very bed. The pillow and sheets still smelled of her. Rising onto one elbow, he stared at the curve of her shoulder, half obscured by the cascade of straw-colored hair that fell onto the sheet. Even in the subdued light of dawn from the cracked curtains her beauty was obvious. So incredibly desirable, so . . . .

He grinned as his eyes made out the shape of the straw hat on the dresser, half draped by the red-checkered blouse. Her jeans lay crumpled on the floor beside the bed, the lighter colored panties still inside them where she had stepped out. It had been a storybook night.

"Jesus, I'm sorry, Susie," was all he had managed to say that day a few weeks into their marriage when, during lovemaking, he had uttered another woman's name. Stafford was sitting slumped on his side of the bed, his heart still racing from passion, his mind whirling.

She had lain in silence awhile, staring off out through the filmy curtains toward the lights along the beach, then rolled over to face him. "Who's *Margot*, Jack?" Her eyes were cloudy with hurt.

He said nothing.

"Jack, you called me Margot while we were making love. Just when you were getting ready to come you called me Margot."

"You must have—"

"I didn't *must have* anything, Jack. You called me Margot just before you came. I didn't misunderstand anything. You called me *Margot*."

"Susie, I'm sorry," he said, reaching for her. "I didn't mean anything by it. I was just thinking about a character I've been reading about."

She pulled against him, straining toward her side of the bed.

"A character? In one of those damned paperbacks you read? You were thinking about one of those women from your cheap novels while you were making love to me?" Her face was red with rage.

"Susie, it's just something I do. My mind just needs some room to work. Sex is mostly psychological anyway. It's not just a coming together of flesh. If a guy just thinks about what is *physically* happening . . . ."

"God, Jack, I know it's not just physical. We're in it not with just our, our genitals. Animals engage in purely physical sex. But they mate out of instinct. I'd hope we're above that. A man that pays for a prostitute pays for something *physical*, something better than maybe his hand. She's nothing but a vessel to him. But Jack, we are *involved*. With each other. Physically and emotionally and—just every way there is to be. That's why we use the term *romantically involved*."

"Look, Susie, the bottom line is that I was *fantasizing*, something men *do*." He lowered his voice. "The guy who buys a prostitute, he fantasizes too. When he enters her, he's entering someone besides her, someone he's loved and lost or loved and never had, that untouchable girl from high school or college, his neighbor's wife or a movie star or maybe the woman who's left him. He uses his mind to help him reach back there to her, and the prostitute is simply the warm body beneath him. Just like the boy in the closet whose hand becomes the physical means of bringing his memory or his fantasy alive, and—more importantly—to consummation. Everybody fantasizes, Susie. Women too. It's a natural thing, healthy."

"Well, *I* don't. Do you think I transform you into a football player or movie star or big-time politician or some damned cable-puller from the shipyard when we're going at it? No. It's Jack, just Jack. Maybe I don't have enough imagination. Maybe I ought to try it, though, give you a little more height, some more muscles, give you a PhD, give you a bigger penis—have a go with someone besides a librarian."

"Susie, please. Lighten up." He was stroking her back the. "We don't want to go saying things that we'll regret."

She glared at him. "You're a fine one to say that."

"Just calm down. Let me try to explain things to you."

"Am I not good enough, Jack? Not pretty enough? Not as pretty as *Margot*?"

"Susie—"

"God knows how many times you've told me that I'm the prettiest woman you've ever seen. Are you tired of me already? Why is Margot so special?" She was sitting up with her knees drawn to her chest.

"Susie, I was just putting *you* into a scene I read not too long ago in a book called *The Heat of Summer*. You had Margot Trimmer's *name*. She's not real. She's a character in the book, the wife of a minister." He laughed. "She's somebody a middle-aged romance writer dreamed up."

"*The Heat of Summer*? Jesus, Jack, how do you stand those damned things?"

"*Quite* a minister's wife, actually. That's all. I imagined you with her name and in her clothes, but it was *you*. Margot's nothing but cold print on a page. Well, *hot* print on a page. My mind was just confusing her with you."

"Why do I have to have somebody else's name? Why can't I just be me?"

"Susie, everybody fantasizes. Anyone who tells you they don't is lying. Men, women, everybody. It's just part of making reality more exciting. For days after our first time on the island, every time I made love to you I was reliving that night. It wasn't that you weren't good enough as you were, not that you weren't pretty enough—it was just so incredibly exciting to recall that night, our first time. It'll always be exciting to me, and I'll relive that experience a thousand times, *ten* thousand times, before it fades. And if anything should happen to you, years hence when I make love to another woman it will be you I am making love to, on the beach, on this bed, wherever, and she will be merely the physical means . . . ."

She was resting her chin on her knees. "That I can understand. I think about that night at the beach sometimes too when we're making love. But I don't put somebody else's clothes on you, or take them off you, and rename you and pretend that you are married to someone else. You can't expect me to be happy about this, Jack. I'm not sure it's a healthy thing."

"Of course it's healthy, Susie, as healthy as anything we do mentally. It's daydreaming."

"We daydream," she shot back, "when we want something *better*. Or different. I *daydream* about a house of our own somewhere. I *daydream* about having children, which we'll never have. We both know it."

"Please, Susie, this is going too far. We don't need to talk anymore about this."

"Do you want someone better than me, Jack, or different?"

He had gotten up from the bed and was standing naked behind the curtains looking out at the Gulf, where far off two shrimpers were trawling slowly from east to west. He could see her reflection in one of the glass panels of the French door. She looked like a little girl, pouting, ready to take her doll and go home.

"Susie, haven't you ever—even when *we* were making love—thought back about the boy who first made love to you? Or about some man you thought especially attractive? I mean, I'm not the most handsome guy in the world. Haven't you ever thought about some Hollywood stud or—"

"In truth, no," she said. "As for the first boy, that's *all* he was, a boy, and he was on me like a dog, panting and snorting and humping. The first time he didn't even get in. He lost it before he even got in me. After that he at least knew where to go with it, but he wasn't making love, that's for sure. I don't think he knew *what* he was doing. I damned sure don't think of him. Or the one who came later, who acted just the same. Wham, bam, thank-you-ma'am. Some other man? Not yet. Not Hollywood type, not jock, not shipyard worker. And I hope that the day doesn't come. I just don't think you know women at all, Jack."

"Well, if you don't fantasize yet, you will. It's healthy. Normal. Susie, it's something I do when I make love to a woman, something I've always done since the plain beastly fervor of sex wore off for me years ago. It's got nothing to do with the way I feel about you. It's just a—it's just an enhancement, embellishment. It's *nothing.* And it's certainly no intimation that I don't love you or that I wish you were someone else. In my mind I can dress you anyway I wish, make you any age, make you younger than you are, marry you off to anyone. I can make you a wealthy baroness or a penniless wench, and I can make love to you in Mississippi or Rome or Moscow, in a barn or on a sand dune or in the stinking bilge of a shrimpboat. But it's still you, and I guess it always was you I was making love to. It seems that I have known your body and your face forever. You are so completely, so overwhelmingly beautiful," he said, approaching the bed, "that I could never, ever, hope to make love to anyone else. Can you understand this?"

She lifted her head and smiled. "Maybe. But I still think it's weird. Tell me more about it, Jack, if you can."

He moved back to the bed and sat down beside her, taking her face into his hands and kissing her. "All right," he said quietly, "I'll try."

It began, he said, at age nine when he discovered himself one Sunday morning in a closet while his parents were away at church. Left home alone with an upset stomach, he was rummaging around for a Monopoly game, kneeling in the musty dark, when the image of his teacher came to him, a woman he had gazed longingly at the two months he had known her, though he did not know why she made him feel the way he did in certain places, and in the shadowy closet she stood naked before him. At that age, never having had a sister nor seen his very modest mother nude, he could not imagine what a woman looked like without her clothes—he could remember only that Mrs. Scales was undressed, a glorifyingly white goddess, and that slowly she walked to him and kneeled and took him into her hands. And he remembered the throbbing dry joy that came to him when she had held him long enough. From that day forward he was a slave to the passions of his imagination and his glands, the two intertwined, pursuing.

"I'd gotten strange feelings around girls before, but they always passed quickly. I didn't understand them, didn't know what to do, but once I had had the *feeling*, once I knew what brought it on, I was hooked. I could recall Mrs. Scales anytime at all anywhere when I was alone, and it happened over and over. Or movie stars, women from church, girls I liked from school. But I don't guess there's anything unusual about it. All boys do it. *And* girls."

"Some, maybe," she said, "not all."

"Later, when I first made love to real girls, I was so overwhelmed by a joyous lust, so easily and quickly gratified, that I had no time and no need for the insubstantial stuff of fantasy. It was always over so quickly." He lay beside her, stroking her leg.

"Was it like what you had imagined?"

"Oh, God, no. It was nothing like what I had dreamed. And it felt so different. I mean, a hand is one thing, but—"

"Your fantasies came back?"

"Oh yeah, they came back, but only much later, after I had married my—married Jamie. Boy, I really did a lot of fantasizing when I was with her. She was a whole *cast* of characters."

"And they've been with you since?" She nuzzled his neck.

"Yes, except for a few times with you, in the beginning, when I was so taken with you and your body that my imagination was completely shut off. Just the sight of you, your smell and feel. That was my whole universe. Jesus," he sighed.

"And now it's never just me?"

"Of course. But seldom you just as you are right then. It's you, like I say, in the dunes, it's you in seat of the car that stormy evening in the parking lot at Wal-Mart, it's you on the floor of your mother's bathroom. It's always you."

"Even when I've got someone else's name?" She was kissing him softly about his mouth and eyes.

"Yes. You may have Margot Trimmer's name and be in the loft of some French farmer's barn, and it may be Margot's clothes I take off of you—and I may even be the farm worker taking them off—but it's your body and face I see. My imagination could never improve on that."

"I'm glad," she whispered.

"You wouldn't believe the places you've been and the clothes you've worn." He smiled, then told her, though he felt a little foolish, "You wouldn't believe all the different guys you've had making love to you—farmers, bikers, fishermen, field hands, a boy from some freshman English class."

"You mean you pretend you're someone else too?"

"Yeah, lots of times I do. I've even imagined I was the first boy to make love to you. And sometimes I pretend that I'm a little boy hiding in a closet watching you make love to someone else."

"God, Jack, this is sort of hard for me to handle." She was

looking at him as if he were a stranger sitting naked on her bed. "I mean, it's not like you're a pervert or anything, but I thought I knew you really well, and now I'm just not sure."

"Susie, nobody ever knows what anyone else is thinking. You can speculate after watching and listening, but there's no way you can *know*. Ever. That's just the way it is. When we're making love, you could be thinking about some football player you went with in high school and I'd never know it unless you told me. And I could be pretending you are a sheep. You just don't know."

She was laughing. "A sheep? Where in God's name did that come from?"

"That was a joke. But fantasizing is healthy, Susie. You might try it more often yourself. It's *innocent*."

She laughed, slipping her panties and bra on, then pulling on a tee-shirt that fell almost to her knees. "Maybe when you get a little bit older. And fatter. Or maybe when you've lost your hair."

"You got a long time to wait, little sister."

She turned around and thrust her butt toward him, twitching it. "Baaaaaaa."

He reached and pulled her back onto the bed. "The good thing is, though, that no matter who you are during the wrestling, sheep or woman, it's always Susie Clayburn I find when the passion is through."

In time he came to ask her to dress certain ways for him, to fix her hair differently. They went to lingerie shops together, where he would pick out panties and bras that he especially liked on her, oftentimes very daring sets so outrageous that she would wear them only in bed with him. He learned the size of everything she wore and secretly bought outfits that seized his imagination—skirts, dresses, blouses, nightgowns—and surprised her with them. His fantasies became a routine with them and he found it difficult sometimes to separate the real from the ideal and seldom really cared to.

Silence surrounded them, him in his awareness of her, her in the oblivion of sleep, silence hot and still and faintly foreign, almost frightening, the only sound in the room her breathing. He wanted to reach out and touch, hold her, roll her over and resume the exquisite mingling of bodies of the night before, but she was so far into sleep, so remote from him, that he dared not penetrate whatever world she was dreaming. He hoped only that he, wild and virile, was in it. He could not, would not yet break the stillness.

Instead, he slid quietly from the bed and walked to the kitchen, where he made coffee and sat a very long time at the table sipping from his cup and staring into the brightening room. He smiled finally and picked up the phone and dialed information for the number of a hotel in New Orleans that he knew. When he'd hung up, he called a colleague and explained that he would not be in, that he had been called out of town on an emergency and would be back to work Monday.

With the stealth of night itself he packed his travel bag and hers, glancing now and again to be certain that she still slept as he eased out drawers and found what he wanted, carefully folding and placing them in their proper order as he knew she would do. Then shuffling silently among the hanging clothes in her closet, whose atmosphere was a euphoric mixture of cedar fragrance and traces of perfume, he selected what he wanted her to wear that night and the night after. Her overnight and make-up cases and his shaving kit, kept in the bathroom closet, were always ready to go, except for toothpaste and brushes, which he would add after breakfast.

Before she was awake he had the car loaded and some blueberry muffins steaming on the kitchen table, beside them glasses of orange juice and milk. He had just split and buttered the muffins and poured his second cup of coffee when he heard her in the bathroom. His timing couldn't have been better. She walked through the kitchen doorway and into his arms.

She had not known where they were going until he followed I-10 to the south, while 12 went on west to Hammond. He'd told her only that they were going to take a day-trip over into Louisiana, for her to wear a white dress that she looked particularly enticing in.

"New Orleans?" she read off the green sign as they split off I-12. "Jack, are you taking me to *New Orleans*?"

He just drove, his eyes straight ahead, and for a long time both were silent.

"My *God*," she said as the first stretches of Lake Pontchartrain appeared, "you *are* taking me to New Orleans."

"That's the direction we're heading in."

"For the day?" Her dress had ridden up mid-thigh and it was all he could do to keep his eyes on the road.

"And night," he said. "Maybe longer."

She turned and looked into the back seat. "Where are—?"

"In a hotel, of course."

"No. Where are our clothes? Our overnight stuff?"

"In the trunk. Everything's in the trunk."

"You packed my bags?"

"I did." On either side of them Pontchartrain glittered in the sun.

She reached and squeezed his arm and giggled like a little girl. "There's one thing about you—you are ever full of surprises, you sneaky devil. New Orleans. Heavens, it's been forever since I've been there. What prompted this?"

"Nothing. I've been wanting to take you somewhere special, and New Orleans is as special as any place gets in this area of the country. In time we'll be able to afford to go to Europe, maybe in a year or two. Right now, New Orleans will have to do."

She leaned and kissed him. "New Orleans will do fine, my man, just fine."

In a short while the Big Easy rose out of the mist. What a wonderful old city it had been to him in the early years, when he would make pilgrimages from college to lie on the levee with a bottle of Boone's Farm apple wine, a muffaletto dripping with olive salad, and a fresh pineapple cut up right there on the spot. Usually with a girl along, sometimes by himself. A couple of times with his first wife. When the narrow, colorful, fragrant streets were thronged with revellers all hours, and no one walked in fear—lovers clasped to each other, older couples holding hands and laughing, families with children in tow, and even the aged shuffled along with glittering eyes.

New Orleans was an elixir then, when everything was so spontaneous, when shopowners smiled and left their doors open for anyone passing by and policemen, when you happened to see one, nodded and grinned. Mindless, wonderful days when a fellow could walk the streets with his girl and never have to worry about being snatched into a doorway and beaten senseless or stabbed for what little cash he carried or for his leather jacket or baseball cap or sneakers. When the only drug he knew anything about was the easy waft of marijuana smoke that came from doorways and windows. When sex was so easy and natural and mutually agreeable, on the levee or in some cheap hotel room or in the dark, plant-shadowed corner of a courtyard swarming with drinking people.

OK, maybe it wasn't as perfect as I remember it. But it was better. Stafford smiled as his mind wove back to those days and New Orleans began to take shape before him.

Now it was a place of fear, like any other big American city. A city whose streets, though they still filled with noisy people during the day and early evening hours, had about them an aura of distrust and dread, relieved only by the free-flowing liquor, and even that would not keep the sensible around long after midnight. And there were sections of the city where people would no longer go—even in the light of day, even in their automobiles—enclaves of violence and drugs where the police ventured with trepidation. Radiating out from downtown, narrow streets lined with once opulent homes were fast falling to ruin, their shops fewer each year and their houses tumbling. Now the sidewalks and streets, still teeming with shoppers and traffic during the daylight, emptied at night, and shopowners retreated to their fortress homes until the light came again and they could return to see whether they had a place left to sell their wares and wares to sell, leaving their doors shut and locked all day long and admitting only the people who knocked or rang their bells and then only if they perceived that the caller had good reason for coming in.

Except for irrepressible youth who still flocked to the city during school breaks, and partygoers of all ages who choked the city during special events and enjoyed the safety of numbers, the trolleys were now quiet inside when they clanked and clacked from stop to stop, people clutching tightly what was theirs, their eyes fixed straight ahead except to glance at whoever was getting on, to see whether they had anything to fear from the next passenger who weaved up the aisle. These green cars moved all night long through the dark streets, taking people from one point of light and safety to another as the passengers huddled and hoped.

The drive had taken them just over two hours, including a brief stop for a sandwich at a delicatessen on the outskirts of the city, so they arrived at the hotel just past noon. After a few minutes of negotiating the narrow streets off Canal, Stafford saw the sign jutting out from a towering wall of buildings. He had chosen a place where he had stayed many times, a bit farther from the center of the Quarter than he liked, but reasonably inexpensive and nice, with a fantastic bar and a view of the river from the upper floors. He parked at the front entrance and checked them in, leaving her in the car with the engine running and the air conditioner going, then came back out and drove around to the garage area at the rear. He took a ticket from the little red and white mailbox looking affair that stuck it out to him like a pale, thin tongue, and drove into the darkness of the massive concrete structure, following the yellow arrows the best he could with his sun-dazzled eyes until he found a spot next to a column, where he parked.

Susie unbuckled her seatbelt. "I guess it's safe to assume that you weren't joking about bringing me to New Orleans, huh?"

"That's right, Momma," Stafford answered, getting out of the car. "The truth ought to have settled in by now."

He shouldered their hanging bag and grabbed the other two with one hand, motioning for her to take her make-up kit and overnighter, leaving nothing in the car except his bottle of Seagrams, which he could come down for later. He'd probably have a couple of stiff ones just before bed—he slept poorly the first night out anywhere and needed something to numb him. If they wanted a drink before that, they'd just go to the bar. He liked that idea anyway, taking her to a bar. Few things got his blood going faster than the way men turned and looked at her when they walked in.

Struggling with the bags, he let her go ahead of him, through the automatic doors and over to the elevators. By the time he caught up she had the door open and had backed into a corner and set her two bags down.

"Going up?" she asked sweetly.

"Well, I'd like to go *down* on you," he answered, swinging the bags in, "but we'll go up first. Them that goes up will also go down."

The room was pleasant enough, though more expensive than he remembered, with a king-size bed and the usual institutional furniture scattered about. Cheap prints hung on the walls: an idyllic forest scene on one side of the mirror above the dresser, on the other a ship tossed high in heavy seas. As Susie removed the hanging clothes from their bag and sorted them in the closet, he sat on the bed, his back against the headboard, and watched her hips move inside the thin white shift. His eyes swept across the prints again. *The woods would do*, he thought, *on a blanket, naked, far from everybody and everything. Spring or summer or fall or a mild day in winter. Or, hell, slamming about in a ship, squeezed up in a berth, clinging to each other like death. Either would do nicely.*

"I cannot imagine why you chose these dresses," she said when she had removed the hanging bag from their clothes, her head deep in the closet. "I haven't worn this black one in—I haven't worn it since that afternoon you brought it in. God, do you remember? Whooo, what an afternoon. Kinda daring for a trip like this, don't you think? Where was it anyway?"

"In your closet, way in the back," he said. "I just reached in and got a couple of things. Did I mess up?"

"No, not really. I'll manage." She set the bags in the closet and stepped back. "What do we do now, Mr. Entertainment Chairman, now that you've got me in New Orleans with this oddball wardrobe and the bags have been put away?"

He grinned. "What would *you* like to do?"

"Do you mean before or after?"

She had walked to the window and parted the curtains. He leaned past her and opened the window a few inches, something you couldn't do in one of the newer hotels. Sounds from the street drifted in. Across the building rooftops, cluttered with air-conditioning towers and tubes, he could see way off in the distance barge traffic on the river.

"What makes you think I brought you all this way for that?"

She tossed her hair to one side and smiled. "I *know* you did, no thinking to it. You didn't come down here to read. By the way, where's your book. You always have a book." She walked to the bed and sat down.

He still stood by the window watching the river. "No time for books this trip. What I'd really like to do is . . . ." He hesitated.

She lifted her head. "What? What have you got in mind *this* time? Do you want to make love?"

"You'll think it's kinky."

"Jesus, Jack, *what*? If you think I'll think it's kinky, it's got to *be* kinky. *What*?"

For an answer he went to the closet, and pulled out his travel bag.

He removed something from the bag and clutched it behind his back. "Close your eyes," he said. "Keep them closed. Stick out your hands."

She did as he said.

"Where'd this wig come from?" She spread it like the wings of a bird.

"Actually, at a flea market near Ocean Springs. Bought it a

few weeks ago, but I wanted to save it for a special occasion, like this."

He took the wig and placed it on her head, tucking in strands of blond and awkwardly adjusting the auburn hairpiece until the woman sitting on the bed in front of him was a stranger with rich shoulder-length dark hair. Suddenly self-conscious, as if somehow his wife were not the same woman who had come in with him, as if by altering her hair he had altered her completely, body and soul, he lifted the wig off and laid it on the bed beside her.

She smoothed her hair back. "I hope you disinfected that thing."

"It's clean. I washed it. And dried it."

"You are something. So what do I do with it?"

"I, uh, I thought we might . . . ."

She smiled up at him. "You want to play a game, right?"

"Yes."

"Jack, do you realize how much of this stuff you have me do? It's almost like you don't want me unless I'm somebody else. How long's it been since you made love to *me*."

"Come on, Susie, we've been through this enough times. It's *always* you. You know that." He reached out and stroked her cheek. "I like the games, yes, but it's always you when the games are over. It's *you* I come back to. We've talked about this enough. You know how I am."

"OK." She picked up the wig and slipped it on her head. "What do you have in mind this time?"

Her agreeable tone emboldened him. He went back to the closet and took out the black dress, a filmy, low-cut evening affair whose slit ran well past mid-thigh. He held it out to her like a gift.

"Will you put this on?"

"Yes, of course."

She stood, pulling the dress she had on up around her shoulders.

"Wait. I want you to put the wig and dress in your purse and go downstairs and put them on in the lobby bathroom. When you're ready, call me on the house phone and I'll come down for you."

"What?"

"Just—I want you to take the dress and wig down in your purse. You know, just walk down there to the bathroom near the elevators, then change into these things there. Call me when you're ready."

"Jack, this may be *too* weird for me. I mean, we've played some games, but mostly in our own bedroom. We're in New Orleans, among strangers, and you're asking me to go down there and put on this ridiculous outfit and then call you to come down and get me? Who am I supposed to *be*?"

"My dark-haired beauty. That's who you'll be. A stranger from New Orleans. Do you want *me* to put something else on?"

"No," she said. "I like you just the way you are."

"Will you do it?" He was still holding the dress out to her.

"Yes. Give it here." She frowned and picked up the wig and dropped it on her head, then reached for the dress. "I'll wear it for you."

"Susie." He folded the dress and handed it to her. "You've got to follow the script. Put the wig and the dress in your purse and go downstairs and change in the lobby restroom. Then call me."

"Jack, I really don't like this . . . ." She stared at the dress in her hand. "We're in a strange place. Why don't I just change into the dress and wig and go outside that door and then knock, pretend that I've just come in off the street?"

"You'll be my two-grand-a-night lady, calling up to let me know you're here, here at the hotel for me."

"You want me to play a happy hooker?"

"At two thousand a day you ought to be happy."

"Don't you realize that people are going to *see* me?"

"Susie, that's the point . . ."

"From a farm girl in Mississippi to a big-time hooker in New Orleans in less than twenty-four hours. How's that for rising in the world? I hope you've got money, Jack—this'll cost you big."

"I've got plastic, and my wife never looks at the bills."

She shook her head and dumped the contents of her purse on the dresser. After folding the dress and stuffing it into the purse and squeezing the wig in on top of it, she kissed him and started for the door. "God, and a few hours ago I was lying beside my husband in my own bed having pleasant dreams."

"Susie." He sat back on the bed. "Take off your panties and bra before you go."

"*Jack*!"

"Please."

"Jack, I'm liking this less and less."

"Please. When we're through, we'll go out on the town."

She sighed and looked past him out the window, laid the purse down on the dresser, and removed her underthings while he watched. "Tell you what, buddy, you had better come quick when I call." She smoothed out her dress and slipped through the door.

The phone rang and Stafford rolled over and looked at the clock on the table. Jesus, it had been forever since she went downstairs. He could have read fifty pages if he'd brought along the novel he'd been reading. He snatched up the receiver.

"Hello, Susie? Where the hell have you *been*?"

He nodded, drumming his fingers on the table while she talked.

"Just settle down, I'll be right there." He put down the phone and slipped his shoes on.

What man in his right mind, he thought as he waited for the elevator, would send a beautiful wife like her down into the lobby of a strange hotel in a strange town among God only knew what kind of people, and her with nothing in her purse but a black dress and wig and nothing on her body but a white shift that anyone could see through, no matter the light? God . . . .

She was standing in front of the door when it opened, her face starkly white between the dark wig and black dress.

"Tell me about it." He pulled her into the elevator and punched the button for their floor. They were alone.

"Like I said, there was a woman in the bathroom when I was fixing my hair," she said. "A black woman. She kept staring at me. She wouldn't leave."

"So what? Who was she?"

"So nothing, I guess, and I don't know who she was. Maid maybe, or something," she said. She looked straight ahead into the highly polished brass plate that the buttons were mounted on and readjusted the wig. "It's just that she kept watching me, like she knew me or something, like she wanted to say something to me."

"Did she?"

"No. She just watched me go into the stall in the white dress and come out in the black, then stand at the mirror adjusting the wig, and she studied me when I tucked the ends under. She didn't say anything. And when I met her eyes, she looked back to what she was doing. But she was *studying* me. I got so nervous I went back into the stall and waited and waited, but she wouldn't leave. She just kept humming and—"

"So what was she doing?" The elevator had stopped on their

floor, but he held the Door Close button down.

"Hell, Jack, I don't know. She was cleaning or something, wiping down the doors or scrubbing toilets. I don't know. And humming like—humming religious music or something. She had a rag in one hand and a bottle of something that smelled like cleaner in the other. But she kept cleaning the same lavatory, so I know she was watching me." She looked at the door, then at his thumb on the button. "Are you ready to get off?"

He let the opportunity for a cute reply slide—he wasn't in the mood for it. The door opened and they stepped out. "I don't see how she could have been much interest to you or you to her, if she was just a cleaning lady." He spoke quietly as they walked down the hall toward their room.

"Well, Jesus, Jack, it must have seemed pretty weird to her. A blond woman goes into a stall wearing a white dress and comes out brunette and wearing a black dress . . . ." She reached out and grabbed his hand. "It's just that she kept looking at me like she knew me. Or *wanted* to know me. And she kept cleaning the same lavatory. She was stalling for some reason. I don't know what it was all about. It was just one of those weird things that get you to wondering is all. You and your damned fantasies have got my imagination working overtime too, I guess."

"It was probably just the wig," he said as he slipped the card into its slot. "I'll bet she hasn't seen anyone put on a wig like that in there before. Or," he whispered as he opened the door, ushering her ahead of him, "she was interested in this sleek dress and slice of thigh." He ran his hand up her leg as she passed. "Maybe she's from Beruit."

"Beruit? What does that mean?"

"Lesbanese," he said, laughing, in a good mood again. "*Les-ban-ese*. Get it?"

"Well, whatever, she made me nervous as hell," she said to his back as he closed the door behind them. "I dropped the same hair-pin four times while she was staring at me."

He opened the door and looked both ways down the corridor, then closed it. "She's probably never seen a two-grand-a-night girl before." He held his arms out to her and smiled. "Now come here and earn your money."

Afterwards they dressed and went down to the hotel bar for

a drink before venturing out onto the street. He had proposed nothing in particular and she had suggested nothing, so the plan was simply to walk and look and do whatever they wished, whatever looked like fun. This was a serendipitous day anyway, snatched out of nowhere, and August or not, to Stafford it was like one of those days in early spring after the sogginess and chill of winter but before the sear of summer, when the earth rekindles and all the juices are up and going, an exactly perfect moment full of unfocused expectancy, when tiny hooves can be heard in the woods and the sap is running full.

He asked that she wear the black dress and go braless, which she agreed to, though she refused to wear the wig and go without her panties. Sitting in a dark corner of the hotel bar, she was simply the loveliest woman he had ever seen, anywhere, real or on screen or in his mind's eye, and her face still held the radiance of lovemaking. He held her hand beneath the table and slipped a foot between her legs.

"God, I love it here with you," he whispered. "I love it *anywhere* with you."

"You're just in heat." She grinned and clamped his foot with hers. "I like it here too. We ought to do this more often. And by the way, why are you not working?"

"I had an emergency, told them I'd be back Monday. Between now and then I've got to figure out what that emergency was." He looked at his watch. "Tell you what, why don't we have a drink and then hit the town? We can make up our day as we go. What would *you* like to do?"

"Oh, Jack, I don't know." She smiled demurely, like a little girl. "What *should* we do? How long are we going to be here?"

"Well, we'll spend the night, of course, go home late tomorrow. Hell, we may even spend another night."

She reached and squeezed his hand. "You're in charge here. What do *you* propose?"

"Commander's Palace or Court of Two Sisters for dinner?"

"Wow, either would be great. I—"

"Brennan's for breakfast in the morning."

"Accepted," she said. "What about later tonight?"

Stafford studied her face. "Thought we'd make a few bars, maybe go down on the river for awhile. Oh, I'd like to have muffalettos on the river for lunch tomorrow."

"Great!" she said. "What about this afternoon?"

"Well," he said, "it's ours and free. We'll have a drink, then talk about it, drift along wherever the spirit moves us."

"I'm with you," she said.

"And I'm glad," he said.

They sat quietly for awhile. He slowly scanned the bar. "Nice place. Now what about a drink?"

"Fine. Just one, though, OK? It's hot out there. I'll get sick in this heat."

"OK. Just one. Whiskey sour?"

"A daiquiri, any kind of fruit. Something slushy and cold."

"Yes'm."

The bartender seemed very much aware that they were there. Though he had his back to them, he was looking their way through the mirror with his dark, quick eyes every time Stafford turned around, and even in his periphery he was aware that they were being examined. He supposed that any man would keep his eyes on a woman like Susie. He enjoyed it. It reminded him of an evening in Birmingham, not long after they were married.

He had taken her with him to a meeting . . . .

"Jack, this is *too* kinky," she had said after re-reading the note he passed to her under the table. They were seated in a restaurant perched on a ridge above the town, where Stafford was attending a librarians' conference. He had had a few drinks at an earlier reception and, giddy and self-assured, felt like pressing his luck with her.

He smiled secretively and said, "Look, this is our first long trip together. We're in a distant town where nobody knows us. Everybody else is at that goofy banquet. Let's get wicked." Over her shoulder he could see through the large plate-glass window the lights of the city fanning out from the foot of the mountain. He had kicked off his shoes and was rubbing his socked feet over her calves.

"Jack, I don't know—" She held the piece of paper lightly in her hand. "It's one thing to wear all those outfits, but *this*?"

He ran a foot high up her leg, but she clamped her thighs.

"Susie, come on. Let's *do* it." He pointed to the note.

"What do you mean *let's*, white boy? It'll be me taking my clothes off."

"Nobody will ever know but you and me."

"Jack. Oh, Jack." It was an exasperated tone, but she reached and picked up her purse and left the table. "Be back soon."

As she crossed the crowded floor of the restaurant and disappeared, he watched her reflection in the stretch of glass, through which the lights of Birmingham spread out like a great stretch of starlit sea. With quickened pulse he noticed that his were not the only eyes that followed her. Two men sitting a couple of tables over pivoted and watched her, whispering to each other and grinning.

Stafford knew what they were saying: "Boy, how'd you like to take that home with you?" or "Man, I'd love to hammer that."

In a few minutes she reappeared in the glass and he turned to watch her, her legs outlined through the thin dress by the lighted hallway where the restrooms were, and even in the diminished light of the restaurant he could detect a faint blush on her face. She handed him the purse and slipped into her chair.

"You did it, didn't you?" he asked.

"Go ahead. See for yourself." She was not smiling.

"Everything?" His temples were pounding.

"See for yourself."

He held the purse down on his lap and unsnapped it. Her pantyhose were neatly folded on top of her bra and half-slip. He closed the purse and handed it back to her.

"I feel absolutely naked, Jack," she whispered.

"You *are* absolutely naked under that flimsy dress."

"If I walk between a bright light and any of those guys—" She gestured to three tables of college-age males wearing the same kind of jerseys. "They'll see everything I've got. If they were paying any attention when I walked across there, they'd have noticed that my legs didn't shine on the way back."

"Oh, Honey, you are shining all over." He could feel himself getting harder and harder as he thought about the woman across from him, dressed now in only a thin dress, her underthings in the purse. The two men who had watched her were studying the scene out of the corners of their eyes. They knew what was going on. Had to. He wanted to lift his foot and thrust it up between her thighs and into the secret spot—he wanted the men to see him do it—but he knew that she would never allow it. She had been accommodating enough. In fact, he never thought she'd do it.

"I'm so uptight right now," she said as they waited for their steaks, "that I'm not hungry anymore." She nervously ticked her knife against the edge of her salad plate.

"Just relax, Susie. When the tenderloins get here you'll be

hungry enough. You'd better build your strength for what's coming later, after I get you back to the motel, if I manage to leave you alone until we get off the mountain."

She flashed a quick grin. "If there's a wind blowing out there, or if I have to walk across a ventilation grate . . . ." She giggled.

"What?"

"I was thinking what my mother would say. You know how moms worry about your wearing dirty underwear? That what-if-you-were-in-a-wreck stuff, you know."

They laughed at that together.

Her appetite and humor returned, as he knew they would, and after their sumptuous dinner they returned to the hotel, where he removed the last bit of clothing remaining on his lovely wife and laid her gently on the bed.

He kneeled before her and pulled her into a sitting position. She was so incredibly beautiful that he was panting like a junior high kid.

"Now," he said quietly, "I want you to say, 'Fuck me, Jack.'"

"Jack, come on. You *know* I don't use that word."

"I want to see the word on your lips. Say it, Susie. Say *fuck*."

"*Jack*."

"No, no," he said firmly. Put *fuck me* before my name."

Her face clouded over. "Why do you want me to say it?"

"Simply because I've never heard you say it. It's like—I don't know, I just want you to say it. I want to see it on your lips. For me."

She threw her hands out and fell back on the bed, her legs splayed. "All right. Jesus, Jack. *Fuck me*!"

"Susie, Susie, easy." He lay down beside her and, stroking her hair gently, tried to calm her.

"I don't understand some of this stuff you're doing to me. I really don't." She stared at the ceiling, and her eyes were rimmed with tears.

"Oh, hell, Susie, don't cry. I just wanted to hear you say it."

"You've heard it. OK? Can we get on with this? I'm tired."

They made love, or rather *he* did, after which she curled into a ball far on her side of the king-size bed and said good-night and nothing else.

It would be better to forget about the last part of that night, he thought as he walked over to order their drinks.

The bartender glanced in the direction of Stafford's wife and said, "I would of come over to the table. Didn't know you'd made up your minds. Thought y'all was just talking, keeping cool."

"I'd like a Jack and water, double please, and the lady would like a daiquiri. Something cold and slushy, she says."

"Do you suppose she would mind pineapple? That'd be quickest, since I already got some made up." He was a fairly young man, robust, with short-cropped dark hair carefully waxed in almost 50's style, with an equally well-waxed mustache, thick and very, very dark. His arms were covered with coarse black hair, and it sprouted out of his shirt at the collar. He looked like a former football player, lineman probably, heavily muscled, his neck thick, and his brown eyes were quick and sharp, moving constantly from Stafford's face to the woman in the corner, to the highly polished surface of the bar. The name Harry was stitched in red above the pocket of his white shirt. *Appropriate enough*, Stafford thought.

"I'm sure pineapple will be fine. Anything fruity and cold, she says. Matter of fact, give me the same. Ought to be better for the weather."

The bartender looked past Stafford's shoulder again at Susie. "Whatever the lady wants, huh?"

Stafford studied the strong shoulders and arms as the man made their drinks. He could see Susie through the mirror, and he noticed that Harry was watching her too in quick little glances. His eyes were dark and penetrating.

"Nice, huh?" he found himself saying.

The bartender met his eyes through the mirror. "Sir?"

"The girl. She's pretty, isn't she?"

Harry seemed to blush at that, averting his eyes from Stafford's to his drink-making. He mumbled something that Stafford couldn't make out.

When he set the drinks down, with logo napkins, he acknowledged, "Yessir, she is indeed pretty. More than that, I'd say. If you'll excuse me for the observation, I'd call her *ravishing*."

Stafford grinned and nodded and looked at the drinks.

"Charge it to your room?"

"Yeah," Stafford said. "Number, uh, 1242." He fished a little card out of his pocket to make certain. "Yeah, 1242. Just charge it to the room'll be fine." He picked the drinks up and started to turn back toward their corner.

"Say." The bartender motioned subtly with his head. "Say," he continued, his eyes on the corner where Stafford's wife was sitting, "if you don't mind, let me ask you something."

"Sure." Stafford set the drinks down and moved his face toward the bartender's. It was obvious that Harry wanted to be discreet. "What?"

The man lowered his eyes to the polished walnut surface of the bar and whispered, "That your *wife*?" He raised his eyes and glanced toward Susie, shyly, like a little boy who's seen a girl almost too pretty to imagine and stumbles around trying to find the words to talk about her.

Stafford turned slowly and looked where Harry's eyes had gone. He stared for several seconds at his wife's lovely face, then turned back to the bartender. "I *wish*," he said softly.

"God-damn, she's *fine*," Harry sighed. "Girlfriend, huh?"

Stafford cleared his throat and lowered his face toward the bartender's. "For tonight she is," he whispered.

The bartender gave him a long look. "You mean—it's none of my business here, but what do you mean, for *tonight*?"

"What do you figure a woman like her would be worth for a night?"

Harry turned and glanced in the mirror at Susie, then faced Stafford again. "Do you mean? You—" He cleared his throat. "Got no idea. She'd bring a lot, though. I mean, that's a prime cut there."

"What would you guess?" Stafford asked. "You know, if you had to come up with a figure?"

"Shiii—man, I don't know. One like that. *I* couldn't afford her. Where's she from?"

"She's from around here, but that doesn't matter. She's with me. That's what matters. Now what do you figure she's costing me?"

"She's from New Orleans?" The bartender glanced in the mirror again, then stared into the polished surface of the bar.

"I didn't say that. I said she's from around here. Hell, I don't know exactly where she lives. I mean, I haven't been home to meet her folks."

"I sure ain't seen her before." He shook his head and sighed. "And I'd remember *that*. But it's a big town. I wouldn't know what she'd be worth. That ain't my field of expertise. Maybe five hundred for all night. Maybe more."

"Way cold," Stafford said, sliding the drinks around. Susie was watching him through the mirror. She smiled.

"More than five . . . . Eight?"

"Still cold."

"A *thousand*?" Harry turned and glanced at the woman through the mirror.

"Still a long way off, but you're moving in the right direction."

"Holy shit," Harry sighed. "Don't no woman in this town bring much over thousand for a night, no matter what she looks like or what she does, or not that *I* know anything about. We talking a night or a *week*?"

Stafford laughed. "One day and night."

"Man, a thousand bucks will get you just about anything this town has to offer for just one day and night. For a thousand dollars I'd give up my girlfriend and mother and both sisters for a *week*."

Stafford jerked his thumb toward Susie. "A thousand won't buy that one."

The bartender looked at him. "More'n a thousand, huh?"

"Yeah, a lot more."

"Hell, I give up. You're talking about a league I don't know nothing about, ain't even *heard* about."

Stafford winked and picked up the drinks. "Try *two* thousand," he said.

"You're bullshittin' me."

"No, I'm not. Until noon tomorrow she's costing me two thousand bucks. But it'll be worth every penny."

Harry shook his head and sighed again. "Hot-*damn*, man, I don't know whether I envy you more for the money you gotta have to afford something like that or for having that particular woman for the night. If I had to choose between a bundle of cold cash and a hot woman like that for a night it'd be a damn hard choice. But two thousand is un-Goddamn-believable." He glanced back into the corner. "What all does she do?"

"Well now, that's for me to find out, isn't it? She's already done enough to make me believe she's worth the money."

"God-*damn*. What do you do for a living, own a bank?"

"I—well, let's just say that I'm not hurting for money."

"That is some kinda woman."

Stafford just grinned and picked up the drinks. "I appreciate the second opinion. See you later, Harry."

The bartender glanced self-consciously at his nametag. "Yessir. Enjoy your stay in New Orleans."

Stafford turned back to him. "Oh, by the way, did anybody ever tell you you look like Mike Ditka?"

The bartender seemed to be less interested in Susie after that, though Stafford did catch him looking their way a couple of times, quick little glimpses as if he had forgotten some little detail of her appearance that he wanted to be certain of. Stafford could imagine how hard it would be not to watch her as she delicately sipped her daiquiri. He was not doing a very good job keeping his own eyes off her.

"What was all that about?" Susie had asked him when he set the drinks down.

Stafford grinned. "Oh, just about what New Orleans has to offer in the way of fun these days. Just stuff."

"He kept looking at me."

"Yeah, I kept looking at you too. Actually, he was telling me what a fine looking woman he thinks you are. I was just confirming his appraisal." He lifted his drink and reached over and clinked it against hers.

"Don't you think that's sort of disgusting, a guy talking about your wife like that?"

"No. It's flattering," Stafford said.

"It's like y'all were discussing a horse or a car you were trying to sell."

"Aw, lighten up, Susie. Besides, *I* brought it up. He didn't start anything."

"Well, I feel funny about it. Jesus."

"You ought not be so beautiful." Stafford removed a ten from his wallet and laid it on the table.

"Isn't that an awfully big tip for a couple of drinks?" she asked. "Or is that for the drinks too?"

"It's a tip. I put the drinks on the room tab."

"Mr. Big Spender," she said, smiling.

"Susie. Come on. Let's toast." He held his drink out again, at eye level, and she raised hers and clinked it against his. "Here's to a good time in New Orleans," he said, finishing off his daiquiri and reaching for her arm.

XIII

But for the fact that his wife was there, somewhere behind its walls and windows, the hospital would have been nothing more to Stafford than any other brick building, still blazing with lights though daylight had come, with little trails of steam coming out of pipes on the roof. Merchant drove to the Emergency Room entrance and passed it and parked in a spot reserved for ministers.

The big detective pointed to the *reserved* sign. "Fuck'm." He straightened his tie. "I probably spread the gospel better than they do, and I never get to pass the plate. And they don't have to worry about gettin' their asses shot off."

Stafford didn't answer.

"At least the ones I convert from sin don't generally get a chance to backslide for a year or two." He grunted getting out of the car. "Come on, Jack, you're getting your woman back. Try to get in a better mood."

"Fuck you," Stafford said as they walked up the wheelchair ramp into the building. "Fuck you and this damned town."

"Back off that self-righteousness and self-pity, motherfucker—you the one that put her here."

When they were inside Merchant led him past the reception desk to an elevator and they went up one floor.

"Do you know where she is?" Stafford asked him as they stepped off.

"We can't go directly to her room. We got to talk to the doctor first." He nudged Stafford and kept his hand on his back as he steered him down a long hallway.

"Why?" Stafford tried to shake the hand off his back. "Why do we have to talk to a doctor? Have y'all been holding stuff back?"

"We doing it this way because this is the way it is done. And you watch your attitude with this man, Stafford, because he controls things right now." He grabbed Stafford by the arm and stopped him at the last office on the left. "Here we are." He knocked on the door.

The young doctor who opened it looked like a college sophomore, short and wiry, with only a light blush of whiskers on his chin and across his upper lip. He had traces of precocious gray in his almost black hair, cut short and slicked straight back, and he wore bifocals, which had slid down so far on his nose that when he looked at the two men standing in his doorway he peered over the steel frames the way an elfin clock repairman might greet a visitor, only in his eyes there was no warmth, no mirth and no twinkle, only high seriousness and the steady calm of a man who worked on broken things.

He introduced himself and motioned for Merchant and Stafford to sit in the two chairs across from his desk. The room was lined with shelves filled with dark, heavy books, their monotony broken only by a small plastic skeleton affixed to a straight rod rising from a base. Its head was slumped over and slightly to the side, like some abandoned, crucified man whose bones the birds had picked clean. The desktop had nothing on it but a small lamp and an open book from which he had apparently been reading.

Stafford stood in the doorway. "If you don't mind, I'd rather go—"

"I do mind," the doctor said, without great feeling. He motioned toward the chair beside Merchant, who was already seated.

"Set the bag down and take a seat, Jack," Merchant said. "He's got to brief you first."

"*Brief* me?"

"I want to discuss your wife's condition with you, let you know what to expect," the doctor said. "There are considerations. It won't take long."

"Considerations?"

"Considerations. Just be patient. I'll explain."

Stafford set Susie's bag on the floor and slipped into the chair beside Merchant, and the doctor sat down behind his desk.

"So what *is* her condition?" Stafford asked.

For an answer the physician opened a drawer and pulled from

a folder the faint sketch of a woman's face, like the early stages of a portrait, made by someone with a pencil. He spun it around and slid it across the desk until it rested in front of Stafford. He pointed with the pencil.

"Her face is bruised pretty badly and swollen here and here."

The sketch looked nothing like Susie. Someone had divided the generic woman's face into sections and given each section a letter, shading in the bruised areas and approximating the swelling in her cheek and lower jaw. *Da Vinci*, Stafford thought, *this is like something Da Vinci would have drawn.* A second sketch, underneath the first, was of her body, again divided into sections and shaded where there were injuries. He touched his pencil point to each of the areas and described the damage there.

"How *is* she?" Stafford asked.

The young doctor flicked his eyes up, then pointed back to the sketch. "Pretty large hematomas here, here, and here. Bruises, that is. Where someone hit her or kicked her." He put the facial sketch beside the other one and indicated a dark spot above her right eye. "Large *knot* there, where she was hit with something probably harder than a fist, but it's difficult to tell. Fists can do a lot of damage. People don't realize that when someone's hit with a fist, they're usually hit with all the upper body mass of whoever's doing the hitting. It's a lot of force."

"*I* realize it," Stafford said.

The doctor went on. "Some little scratches here and there. Knife pricks, very small ones."

He seemed so cool to Stafford as he moved his pencil back and forth between the sketches, like he was talking about just the face and body on the paper and not a real woman. "No bones broken anywhere so far as we can tell, but she refused to go in for X-rays or let us do much more than give her a surface going over. Her limbs flex like nothing's broken, and her breathing's fine, no indication of ribs damaged, anything like that. Jaw's awfully sore, judging from her reaction to our probing, but we can't spot anything broken or dislocated. Opens OK, closes without apparent pain. No grating or popping or grinding, nothing to suggest a fracture. Teeth are OK too, the best we can determine, but we didn't really check them closely. She wasn't a very accommodating patient. Besides, we were more interested in bones. I'd have a dentist give her a good examination, just in case there are some cracked teeth or loose ones."

Stafford stood up. "I want to see her."

The doctor motioned him down. "Let me finish, please. She's got lots of bandages on. We found no need for the gauze on her face and head, but she wanted it so we put it on. It makes her feel more comfortable. So her face is wrapped. Again, no need for it, so don't be startled. If it makes her feel better, we'll leave it on."

"Has she said anything?" Merchant asked.

The doctor shook his head. "Well, she's been awfully traumatized, but I'm pretty sure she can talk, but no, she hasn't said a word. At least not to me. She just clamped her teeth together and shook her head *no* when we tried to examine her more fully. The nurses haven't mentioned anything about her talking."

"So how do you know she wanted the gauze on her face?"

The doctor shrugged. "She grabbed a roll off a tray and started winding it around her head herself, and we got the message." He tapped the pencil on the sketch. "Something else I would suggest you do is get her some counseling back home. Maybe professional, maybe a minister or priest. Somebody to talk through all this with her."

"Was she raped?" Stafford was leaning forward on the desk.

The doctor peered at him over the rims of his glasses with his clock repairman's eyes. "Look, Mr. Stafford, she refused to let us examine her fully. We did manage to get those clothes off her and there was evidence of anal and vaginal bleeding in her undergarment, but we can't force an examination. Not unless you tell us to go ahead and do it anyway. As out of it as she was when she came in, she had her wits about her enough to resist a lot of probing. We can go in and sedate her and do it. You give me the word and I'll get the paperwork together and go in and do it. But we won't just force it on her."

Stafford sighed and sat back in his chair. "No, I don't think so. If she doesn't want you to do it, I don't think you should. If she were unconscious or something or her life was in danger, maybe."

"It's your decision."

"But what do you *think*? Did they—"

"Hey," the young physician said, his face suddenly animated, "that blood came from somewhere. They put something in her, and you and I can pretty well figure what it was, can't we? Like I told you guys . . . ." He nodded to Merchant. "There was no visible semen on her or her clothes, but over half the rape victims we get in these days don't have semen in or on them. Sometimes the guys don't get that far, sometimes they use condoms, sometimes they use—well, things, objects. We simply cannot establish proof of rape without a thorough examination. There are things we look for. Certain damage. Upon closer examination we'd be able to tell."

"But you're pretty sure—"

"Mr. Stafford, I can't see that it makes any difference here. If it meant enough to you, you'd tell us to go ahead and examine her. We could put her under in a flash and check her out. Since you won't, I don't guess you really want to know. I'm not sure I would, if she were my wife. They did everything they could to her. I'd bet my diploma that she's been raped and sodomized repeatedly, but without a direct examination I can't prove it. The blood came from somewhere."

"If you think the bleeding's serious enough, I'll sign for you to examine her."

"I think you should do it, Jack," Merchant said.

The doctor looked at Merchant, then at Stafford. "There's no bleeding now. The blood on her legs and clothes was consistent with the kind of surface bleeding associated with tissue and membrane damage incurred during rape. That I can verify. Beyond that, what can I say? There's no bleeding now." He tapped his pencil on the blotter before him. "I'd be glad for the lack of semen. It probably means that they used condoms or objects and there's a much better chance that they didn't infect her with anything."

Stafford studied the sketch a few seconds. "Did they do anything else to her?"

"Just what I showed you. Legs are bruised where they probably held them open, around her lower thighs and calves and ankles, but that's all I could see. Little bruises all over her body where they manhandled her. But, as I say, nothing's broken, the best I could tell." He breathed deeply and settled back in his chair, locking his hands behind his head. "And they etched a symbol on her chest, a plus sign or something, pigmented it with some sort of carbon substance, maybe ink or graphite, made a tattoo out of it. That's about it, the best we can tell."

Stafford sat forward in his chair. "This cross, or plus sign, or whatever the hell it is. What's that all about? Some kind of satanic shit?"

The doctor shrugged. "It looks like a plus sign to me, the kind kids put on walls with the guy's initials or name above, the girl's below. This one just has some initials above the horizontal arm.

Maybe it is a cross. Jesus, man, we don't know what it is. People come in here with all kinds of things carved into'm, usually a hell of a lot deeper than your wife's tattoo and a lot bigger and in every color in the rainbow. At least it's just a *cross*, if that's what it is."

"What in hell is this cross all about, Merchant?"

Merchant shrugged. "Jack, New Orleans is voo-doo heaven. All kinds of shit happens here. Your wife got caught up in something bad is all. They *could* have carved a New Orleans street map on her, so I'd be happy that's all they put on her and let it slide."

"Let it slide, hell," Stafford said, standing again. "I want to see my wife. You crazy sonsofbitches aren't helping me come to terms with this at all."

"Sit down, Jack." Merchant reached over and yanked him by the arm and slammed him hard into the chair. "And shut the hell up until the doctor's ready for you to go down there." He removed his hand. "Man," he said quietly, "the tattoo can be removed. The tattoo ain't *anything*. Believe me. It's the least of your worries."

Stafford stared coldly at him. "Not anything, my ass. What if it were *your* wife branded like a cow."

"It *ain't*," Merchant said. "I got more sense than to go around telling folks that my wife is a two-thousand-dollar-a-night hooker."

The doctor spun his head at him. "*What*?"

"Forget it," Merchant said. He pointed to the physician's desk. "Get on with the Goddamned report." Then to Stafford: "And you keep your mouth shut until he's through."

The doctor scanned the clipboard again. "That's all they did physically."

Stafford jerked his head up from the sketch. "What does that mean, *physically*?"

"Well, they traumatized her quite badly. She's been through a lot." He cleared his throat. "And they shot her up with something."

"Shot her up? *Drugged* her?"

"With something. We'd have to get a blood or urine sample to tell for sure, but she won't let us. She was pretty well out of it when she got here, but she was aware enough to refuse to give us blood or let us X-ray her or do more than that cursory examination."

"Shot her up?" Stafford looked at Merchant. "Why didn't you say anything about this?"

Merchant said to the doctor, "You didn't say anything about drugs when we talked to you."

"We found the mark just after you guys saw her. We weren't

looking for that. There was too much else to look for. We just overlooked it the first time, thought she was in shock. They were clever with it, shot her inside the arm."

"Hell," Merchant said, "I thought she was just in shock."

"Can you get anything from the blood in her panties?" Stafford asked. "Can you tell anything from that?"

The physician looked at Merchant, then back at Stafford. "We can't find them."

"What do you mean?" Stafford asked.

"Her panties have disappeared. That was the one article of clothing we might have been able to get something from, but . . ."

"How the hell could they *disappear*?"

The doctor shrugged. "They were there with her other things—an ER nurse took them off of her—but they're not anymore. I saw them myself. Any evidence from her attackers would more likely be on them than on anything else, but they're gone. Bra too."

Merchant looked at Stafford, then at the doctor. "She wasn't wearing a bra."

"What the hell could have happened to her panties?"

"I don't know," Merchant said. "We saw them earlier too, but nobody can find them now."

"Well, this just beats all." Stafford got up and paced in the little office. "You've lost the one piece of clothing that might have had evidence—"

"Might," the doctor said, "might not. It doesn't matter, though, because nobody can find them. We can get something out of the stains on the dress, unless they're all *her* blood, and I'll bet they are. My sense is that these guys used packing tape and lifted every hair off her that wasn't rooted, and they probably washed her down, maybe vacuumed her, and I'll just bet you that not a single stain on the dress came from one of them. I doubt that she had the dress on when they were doing whatever they did to her."

"Listen to him, Jack. The man's probably right."

Stafford sat down and leaned forward in his chair. "What do you think they gave her, and how much?" He looked at Merchant again. "I mean, could they hook her?"

The physician shook his head. "No, I don't think you've got to worry about that. Probably some kind of sedative, a tranquilizer. No telling really, without lab work. But she wouldn't know what she was craving even if her body did demand it."

"One good thing about the drugs," Merchant said, "she probably suffered a hell of a lot less from what they did to her."

"True," the doctor said. "The trauma could have been a lot worse without the fix."

"But why would they give her drugs anyway?" Stafford asked, moving his eyes from the doctor to Merchant.

The detective shifted in his seat. "Well, she wouldn't be nearly as likely to remember those guys, for one thing, and if the case got to trial, her testimony would be at best shaky, since she was doped up, and you can bet your ass those guys would argue that she asked for the drugs or had taken'm before they got their hands on her. And for another thing, she—now you got to take this the right way, Stafford—she'd have been more fun for'm stoned."

"You chaps are a really sensitive lot, aren't you?" the doctor said to Merchant.

Merchant glared at him. "You want to trade jobs? We'll see just how Goddamned well *you* handle it."

The doctor held up his hands. "Sorry. I'm sorry. This has been stressful for all of us."

"Stressful? *Stressful*? How the hell can you—look, can I go see her now?" Stafford has risen in his chair and stepped toward the door. Merchant remained seated.

"You can see her. But she's not going to be the woman you knew. And I doubt that she will be for a while. She's badly traumatized, still a little stoned too. Just go easy. Oh, one other thing—they cut her hair."

Stafford met Merchant's eyes, then said to the doctor, "What do you mean?"

"They cropped her hair, cut it with scissors or something. I can say for a fact that whoever abducted her wasn't a hairdresser."

"That's probably the funniest thing you've said in your life," Merchant told him.

"Merchant, you didn't say anything about her hair being cut. What the hell else? You keep adding shit as we go here." He swung his eyes back and forth between the detective and doctor. "Before I walk out that door, is there anything else you want to add? Like maybe they cut her nose off and gouged her eyes out? Took off a leg? Jesus Christ!"

"I suspect that her hair is the least of your worries, Jack. I never saw her before, so I didn't know how long her hair was supposed to be. It was short in the license picture."

Stafford snorted. "I thought the cross was the least of my

worries. You guys are great at deciding what my worry priorities ought to be. I cannot *wait* till this damned nightmare is over. When can I take her home?"

"That's kinda up to you, and to these guys. We'd like to keep her in for a couple of days of observation, try again for X-rays, do some blood work, but we won't try to stop you if you want to move her back home." He turned back to Stafford. "I would suggest that you make contact with your physician, tell him what's happened. You know, just to play it safe." He looked very serious now. "He'll know what to do. Get her some counseling, and have a dentist check her teeth."

"I want to see her," Stafford said.

"All right," the doctor said, picking up the phone, "but again, don't go in there expecting to find the same woman you came down here with. You'll have to give her some time. She's gone through a lot." He dialed two digits.

"Bounds here. Mr. Stafford will be up in a few minutes to see his wife. Let him in. Then show him where to go to fill out paperwork. Oh, tell the officer he's coming."

"What officer?" Stafford had opened the door but not stepped through.

"Jack," Merchant said, "somebody took the panties, so something weird's going on. We don't want strangers going in the room. That's all. Don't try to make any more of it than that. I mean, suppose the guys that did it decided they'd made a mistake cutting her loose, that she might remember something that could identify them? They might send somebody after her. It's better to play it safe."

"And after what she's been through," the doctor said, "we thought it best that she not be disturbed by anyone without our approval."

"I think that's reasonable." Stafford sniffed. "I hope that means unwanted detectives too."

Merchant pivoted in his seat. "Jack, I know how you feel about all this."

"You don't know *jack shit* about how I feel."

"All you want to do is get your lady and beat it the hell out of New Orleans back to your sanctuary up there. But you need to talk her into letting the doctor examine her for whatever they can find, do a blood test. And I'd like to get a female specialist on rape to talk with her too. Got a real good one in the department—name's Bonny Wells, and she'll coax her into talking and into permitting a full examination. Bonny's damned good. We just can't do anything until she talks and let somebody exam her."

He stood and placed a hand on Stafford's shoulder. "And, Jack, try to get her to tell *you* something about those guys. She might tell you. Anything at all that'll help us nail their asses. Otherwise we got nothing. Even if we know who done it."

"Go to the elevators at the end of the hall," the doctor said. "Go to the third-floor nurse's station, on your right when you step out of the elevator. It's Room 312. A nurse will show you."

Stafford picked up Susie's bag, nodded to the two men, and closed the door behind him.

He saw no nurse at the station when he passed it, and there was no officer sitting in a chair outside Room 312. Whoever was watching didn't want to be seen. He turned and looked back at the nurse's station again, then opened the door.

At first he could only stand in the doorway and look at what had been the loveliest woman he had ever known, her face now swathed in bandages, with tufts of blond hair jutting out through gaps in the wrapping of gauze. Her mouth was uncovered, a swollen red welt in that tundra of gauze, as if something fierce and angry had broken through the snow, and they had left openings for her nose and eyes, which he noticed were closed. For that he gave silent thanks. He didn't want her to know he was there. Not now. Not just yet. It would be better later, after he'd had a little better chance to decide what to say to her. Now he would only stand there and look at her, stretched out beneath a sheet, that slim form indistinct except for the slight rises of her breasts.

On a table by the bed was a little plastic bag that he knew must contain the black dress, or what was left of it. He was afraid to look.

After a while he reached over and picked up a chair and set it beside her bed and slumped back into it to wait for her eyes to open. While he waited, he would decide what to say.

What *could* he say? Now it took all his fantasy could muster to imagine what she looked like before, what she looked like lying naked in his bed, perfect in every detail. The cream, the cream! God, what he wouldn't give to erase the last twenty-four hours, pretend that they had never ticked round, assign them to some hell of oblivion for all eternity. They belonged in a Breughel painting of unicorn evils, shrieking with scarlet demons, second after second—

one New Orleans, two New Orleans, three New Orleans, hell New Orleans, hell New Orleans, hell, hell, *hell*!

In time sleep overtook him.

How long he lay there inert, his body and mind so exhausted that he didn't even dream, he could not have told anyone. But for the gradual brightening of the blinds as the sun slid over the top of the building across the street, he would not even have known that it was time for the sun again. Time languished in another world, the one he had come from a few hours ago, a world of schedules and appointments, of regular meals, of a job, of blessed routine, of waking up at a certain time and rising and showering and doing all the things one did to get his world going again, then falling smoothly into a groove, a pleasant, well-oiled groove that led him through the day and home again. Oh, blessed rage for order, as some poet had put it.

He could barely remember leaving his house that morning, yesterday or two days or an eternity ago, his lovely wife beside him, off on a lark to New Orleans. Even the details of the bedroom, where the bed still lay unmade from their last night in it, would not come. It was as if time had been sprung, twisted too tightly until it leapt in a snarl, the way he had seen the mainsprings in old clocks do. He hadn't eaten in, in—he couldn't remember when. He could not even remember when he had used the bathroom last. His bodily functions seemed to have been forgotten, lost in the phantasmagorical maze he was floating through. His face hurt, his eyes, his head, his side, his legs. He felt like a very old man as he lay stretched out in the chair beside his wife's bed. God, what he wouldn't give for a bottle of whiskey. He thought briefly of going out and trying to buy one, turning it up somewhere in a dark corner of the parking lot, slugging it raw and searing until he could remember nothing again, but his car was back at the hotel, and he wouldn't have known where to drive to find a bottle anyway. And it was too early.

"What a Goddamned mess," he said quietly to the woman who lay beneath the sheet before him. But he might as well have been speaking to a field of snow, silent and distant and cold.

And then he slept again, or lay there with his eyes closed, aware only of an occasional noise in the hall or the swish of the door opening and a nurse silently padding around the bed, doing whatever it was she did, then the door swishing to again. Once he heard somewhere far off the wail of a siren, but for him it was of no concern. For a very long time he heard and felt nothing at all.

It was no discernible noise that woke him, no spoken word, not even the whisper of the door or rubber-soled shoes across the tiles, nor the light of the morning sun cutting through slats in the blinds. He was not even aware that he *was* awake until his eyes traveled up the sheet beneath which his wife lay and fastened on the hollows in the gauze wrapping. Far back he could see, like distant smoky fires, the eyes of his wife.

"Hi" was all he could manage, uncertain whether to reach out and touch her or remain stiff in his chair, where once again he could feel the pain coming on, through his limbs and face, through his hammered side.

Her lips did not move. They were puffy and red, sealed tight, and no sound came.

"Susie, can you hear me?"

The eyes did not blink, the lips did not move.

"Can you *hear* me?" He had slid to his knees and now knelt before her, his chin resting on the mattress, his eyes level with hers.

"Please let me know whether you can hear me. Just nod. Do something. Please, Susie, please give me a sign."

"We gave her something," a voice came from the door, which Stafford had not heard open. "To help her rest."

It was a young nurse, starched and official, looking over her glasses at him. She had obviously been up a long time.

"*Gave* her something? Can she hear me?"

"I don't know," the nurse replied, stepping into the room and easing the door to behind her. "Maybe. But maybe not."

"She won't answer me," Stafford said.

"She wasn't talking anyway, pretty well out of it, but we didn't know what with, so we just gave her a sedative. A mild one. That's all. When she comes around she won't be quite so agitated."

Stafford winced and hoisted himself back into the chair. He turned to the nurse, who was behind him, leaning against the door frame. "Did you—were you here when they brought her in?"

"I was here. I helped undress her. Her dress is in that bag. And her shoe." She nodded to the sack on the nightstand. "There was no bra."

"She wasn't wearing one. Was she able to walk?"

"I don't know whether she was able to or not. They wouldn't let her. She was in that wheelchair when she got up here to us." She motioned to a wheelchair in the corner of the room. "She was holding the shoe like a baby, singing to it. Do you have a child?"

"No," Stafford said. "No child. They must not have kept her long in the ER"

"Apparently not." the nurse said. "It wasn't a busy night. *Morning*," she corrected herself.

"Was she in bad shape?"

"She was pretty well beat up, if that's what you mean."

Stafford turned back and looked at the shape of his wife. "Do you think she was raped?" he asked quietly.

The nurse shrugged. She was brunette and pretty, her features soft, like something molded from warm white clay. "Looked like they did everything else to her. I wouldn't know about rape." There was no gentleness in her eyes, as if she knew how the woman under the sheet ended up there.

"The doctor said there was blood in her panties."

"There was blood all over her." The nurse pointed to the plastic bag again. "On her dress, on her panties. Like I said, the dress is in that bag."

"Where *are* her panties?"

The nurse shrugged. "Nobody knows." She stifled a yawn. "Sorry, but I've been here a long time." She looked at her watch. "My shift's almost over. Sorry."

"Were you here when they were taken off? The panties, I mean."

"No. I think they took them off in the ER."

"And nobody knows what happened to them?"

"No," she said. "They were in the bag with the shoe when she got up here, and then they were gone. Maybe the lab's got'm."

"Do you think she was raped?"

He felt suddenly foolish, not knowing whether Susie might be lying there listening to him. The eye hollows were still toward him, but he saw no points of light.

"Look," the nurse said, opening the door, "I've already said more than I should have said. This is a police matter and I don't feel comfortable talking about it. If you need anything that you think *we* can provide, give that string a tug." She pointed to a string that hung from a little box on the wall at the head of the bed. "I gotta go."

"Shit," Stafford said when the door had swished to. He stood and stretched and went into the bathroom, where he peed, then studied his face in the mirror.

"Look like I've been in a full-scale boxing match," he said to the battered image that looked back at him. "Like someone who's just waking up from a merciless beating." He splashed cold water on his face. It stung like pin pricks. "You stupid sonofabitch." He closed his eyes and tried to imagine what he had looked like before, what Susie had looked like before. There was no focus, so he turned off the light and closed the door.

He sat down again and shifted forward until by stretching out his left arm he could just reach the bag on the table. His fingers closed on it and he pulled it to him, clutching it to his chest as he slid back deep into the chair. Susie's face was still turned toward him, but he had no reason to believe that she was watching him.

Stafford slowly opened the bag until he could make out the folded black dress, beside it the shoe with the heel snapped off. A smell rose, a sharp, metallic smell like blood or fear or both, or something in between, something more animal than human, and he inverted the bag into his lap and the shoe rolled out, followed by her dress. And that was all. There were dark stains on the dress, which had been ripped in two places.

"Where in the hell are the panties?" he whispered, stuffing the shoe and dress back into the bag. He reached and put it back onto the table.

"The little guy."

Her voice was so strange, thick and deep, and it seemed to come from so far away that at first Stafford was not even certain it was Susie who had spoken. He sat looking at the gauze winding that covered her face.

"The little guy took my panties."

"Susie!" He slid to his knees and thrust his face up to hers. "Susie, thank God you can talk. We were afraid—I was afraid they had done something to you, that you couldn't talk."

"The little red-headed guy."

"It's OK, Susie, it's OK. I guess you're talking about the detective. Oswalt. He probably took them. It's all right." Or maybe it was the doctor, who was small in stature. But he wasn't red-headed. What difference did it make who took the panties? The main thing was that she was talking.

"The little guy. The little guy took them. They took my dress."

"It's all right, Baby. It's all right. Your dress is in the bag."

"There was blood. They hurt me, Jack. There was blood. I saw it. And they cut my hair, they cut my hair. You always said it looked like sea oats." Her lips were barely moving, and he could not see that her eyes were open. "The little guy has them."

Stafford was kneeling beside her holding her hand. "It's all right. They'll take care of them. They had to check them out."

"The little guy. With hair the color of blood."

"Oh, Susie, let's not worry about the panties. Or the dress. Your dress is in this bag." He picked up the plastic bag and held it before her face, but she made no motion to take it. "In the bag here. And here's your shoe." He held up the broken shoe. "I've got the other one. And your purse. They're in your overnight bag." He pointed to the green bag in the corner, where he had set it. "Clean clothes and underwear, everything you'll need when you're ready to go home."

"Blood everywhere."

"It's all right, Susie."

"Blood on my legs and my stomach, blood in my hair. Blood on the sheets. Blood everywhere. Beautiful bright-red blood, just everywhere. I never knew—I never saw blood such a bright red."

"Susie."

He didn't know what to do or say. He was afraid to touch her. Nurses were just beyond the door, but he wasn't sure that he wanted them hearing what she was saying. He stroked her arm and whispered softly that he loved her.

"They made me say it, Jack. Made me say it over and over." She shuddered.

"Shhh, shhh." He dropped his head against hers. "You don't have to say anything else, Susie. Just rest."

"They made me say it, Jack. They made me say it over and over. They made me say and do everything, Jack."

Stafford still could not tell whether her eyes were open. Only her lips were visible, her swollen lips that labored at the words.

He laid his arm across her chest. "It's OK, Baby, OK. Just be quiet. Rest."

"They did it to me every way there was. Front and back. Mouth. Every way." She was shivering, though the room was dreadfully hot to Stafford.

"I know they hurt you, Baby. Just relax. Just don't think about it."

She was now looking at him. He could see the points of light again. A heavy silence fell on the room. He could hear the vent blowing, and far away the sounds of doors opening and closing.

"They gave me something. They stuck me with a needle and gave me something that made me feel all warm and—"

"Susie, please. Just rest, Love, just rest. Shhhh." He reached and placed his fingers over her lips, but she turned her head aside and continued to speak in a muffled voice.

"There was blood, so I know they hurt me, but it didn't hurt. God, Jack, it—"

Stafford rose then and went to the door, summoning a nurse from the station. She came quickly to him.

"I want to take my wife home," he said.

"But I don't think . . ."

"I don't care what you or anyone else thinks. I want to take her home now. The doctor, whoever the hell he is, said I could. Please get the paperwork together and call for a taxi right now. I want him waiting. I am going to take her home."

"I'll have to clear it." Stafford watched as she went back to the station and used the phone. When she had hung up he returned to his wife's side.

Susie was still mumbling and making little whimpering sounds, but Stafford could make nothing of it. He kept stroking her exposed arm. Little bruises had appeared down around the wrists, where someone had apparently held her, and there were two larger ones on her upper arm and all up and down her forearms.

"Mr. Stafford." The nurse had her head thrust through the doorway.

Stafford covered Susie's arm. "What did he say?"

"Dr. Bounds says he has no reason to hold her, except she may be too woozy to walk. But the detective in his office wants to talk to you before you leave."

"Where's the cop that's been watching the room?"

"I don't know anything about that," she said. "I just know about the detective in Dr. Bounds' office. He says he wants to talk to you."

"Can you get the paperwork for me? Bring it here? I don't want to have to fool with the business office. I've got my insurance card and everything."

"I don't know. I doubt it, but I'll get it if I can. It'll take a few minutes."

"Let me know when everything's ready. Don't say anything to

the detective. What about the taxi?"

"He should be here any minute—he was just down the block —but it may take longer for me to get everything together. If they'll let me do it this way. It's unusual."

"Yeah, well, what's happened here is not exactly routine, you know. When the paperwork comes, just bring it in here, if you will."

"Yessir."

"And here," he said, reaching for the bag on the nightstand and handing it to her. "Throw this stuff away."

"But—"

"Throw it the hell away."

"I'll take it out of here," she said, "but I can't just throw it away without permission."

"As long as it's out of my sight," Stafford said. "One other thing. Where'll the taxi be?"

"Well, they generally pull up out front. I didn't tell him—"

"Please call him back and tell him to meet us at the ER exit. Isn't that out back?"

"Well, it's actually around the side. I'll tell him to meet you there."

"Which way is it?"

The nurse pointed down the hall to her left. "Go on the elevator to the bottom floor and turn left when you come out. It'll take you right outside to where he'll be."

"Thanks. And please don't say anything to anybody. This is all embarrassing as hell, you understand, and the quieter we can leave, the better."

"Yessir. I'll be right back with the paperwork, if they'll let me." She closed the door.

He was halfway down the hallway with Susie in the wheelchair, still in her hospital gown and with a sheet wrapped tightly about her, the overnight bag on her lap, when Merchant panted up behind.

"Dammit, Jack, I sent word I wanted to talk with you before you left. We need to talk to her too. Besides," he said, bent over hacking, "besides, you ain't checked her out. You didn't fill out any of the paperwork yet. Insurance stuff and all that. None of that's been done. You got to follow procedures, Jack."

Stafford stopped but continued to look straight ahead. "You can tell'm my phone number and where I live. I'm not trying to get out of paying for anything, and I've got good insurance. I want to get my wife home." He looked at the detective. "There's nothing left to say, Merchant. I just want to get Susie out of here, out of this Goddamned city."

"What'd she say, Jack? What does she remember?"

Susie's head was lolled back against Stafford's abdomen. Her hands gripped the wheelchair arms so tightly that her knuckles looked like something carved of the purest marble. Her bare right foot was tapping against the footrest.

"Merchant, she didn't say anything. She doesn't remember anything at all about it. She was too stoned, and too scared."

"Jack, she's got to remember something. Does she remember that gorilla Harry being there? Were the other guys black or white or what? Let me talk to her, Jack."

Stafford began pushing the wheelchair again. "She doesn't remember anything, Merchant. Nothing. And I've got nothing else to say. There's a taxi coming for us. Stay the hell out of the way and leave us alone."

Susie was mumbling something, but he did not slow down.

When they were before the elevators and Stafford had squared the wheelchair around to roll it onboard, Merchant, in one amazingly swift move for such a large man, swung in front of Susie and kneeled before her. She stiffened when she saw him, thrusting with her legs until her body was almost straight in the chair.

"Mrs. Stafford, please, what can you tell me?"

Stafford stepped from behind the wheelchair and grasped Merchant by his lapel, but before he could pull him to the side, Susie mumbled something. Merchant flung the hand away and leaned toward her.

"Back off, Jack," he said. He was down on both knees, as if in supplication. "Now, Mrs. Stafford, what can you tell me about those guys?"

"No, Goddamn it," Stafford seethed, "*you* back off! You're scaring her. Get the hell out of our way."

"It ain't *me* she's got to be afraid of." Merchant was breathing hard, his eyes fixed on Susie's.

The gauzed-wrapped head slowly turned toward Merchant's face and she mumbled something again.

"What?" the detective asked. "Ma'am? Say again."

"I fell," she said, louder.

"Wha—"

"Merchant, that's it." Stafford had pulled him to his feet and pressed him against the wall between the elevators. "That is fucking *it*. She can't tell you anything. Now, let us go."

"What does she mean, she *fell*?"

Stafford fixed him with a cold stare. "What do you *think* she means? She is trying to tell you what happened to her. Now leave us the hell alone."

The elevator door opened and Stafford pushed Susie past Merchant, leaving the wheelchair facing the back wall.

"What you are doing is *criminal*, Stafford. You got to carry this on your conscience, man. If you let those sonsabitches get away with this, they'll still be out on the street hurting people. You got to help us, man. Stafford—"

The door jerked to and the elevator started down.

In a dreamy sequence he wheeled his wife past the astonished face of a receptionist at the ER desk, through the automatic doors, and out into the parking lot, where a taxi was idling. The driver hopped out and opened the door and Stafford hefted his sheet-wrapped wife out of the chair and set her in the back seat, flung the bag to the floor, and slid onto the seat beside her.

"Go," he said, motioning the driver.

"Them folks trying to get your attention," the driver said. He pointed to a nurse and Merchant, who were running down the ramp. The nurse was holding papers in her uplifted hand.

"Just drive," Stafford said. And he told him where to go. When he looked back, the nurse was walking away from Merchant toward the hospital entrance, and the detective was simply standing there, growing smaller and smaller until they turned out onto the street.

Stafford left Susie in the taxi at the side of the hotel while he loaded their luggage and drove around from the parking garage, and then he had his wife in the car beside him and they were driving north out of the city. It was far up in the morning, though he had not thought to consult his watch. He had not even checked out of the hotel.

Afraid to risk being stopped for a traffic violation, Stafford drove very carefully through the now bustling streets. Thank God nobody knew what he was driving. "Shit," he said out loud, "they're probably glad we're gone. Now they can forget about all this." He glanced at his wife. "I just hope *we* can forget about it."

"Fuck it," he said to himself after a while. "Fuck that hotel and hospital and the police department, all the little hoods and pimps and niggers and spics and white trash thugs and New Orleans in general.

Forever." He kept his eyes straight ahead, focused on traffic and signal lights and stop signs. New Orleans, the city of charm and grace, had settled now into a filthy, stinking slime of a swamp and all he wanted was to see it disappear into his rearview mirror. Time was a distant concern, or no concern at all, as irrelevant as the jet he saw banking off to his left, headed off to somewhere. "And fuck all you alligators out there."

When they had cleared the heavier traffic of downtown and were zipping along on I-10, he reached over and clasped her hand. She was still wound in the sheet and her head wrapped with gauze. Dear God, what must the people who saw them have thought? She looked like a mummy.

"Can we take that gauze off now?" he asked.

She said nothing, so Stafford reached over and tried to find with his fingers the end of the wrap, where it was tucked or taped or whatever, but she pulled her head away and grabbed his hand and held it.

"Why are you leaving it on?" he asked.

She continued to stare straight ahead, deeply silent.

"Are you hungry?" Jesus, he just remembered that he hadn't eaten in, hell, he couldn't even remember how long it had been. Since the sandwich on the way in. His stomach was reminding him that he had biological needs. She probably hadn't eaten either. At least he had pissed at the hospital.

"Did they feed you? Do you need to go to the bathroom or anything?"

There was no response, so he drove on in silence as the glittering expanse of Pontchartrain loomed, then stretched away out on both sides of them and the ribbon of highway led them toward the north and home.

XIV

They arrived in Biloxi just after noon, and Stafford drove through the trees past the end of the shell drive to the back door, hoping that no one he knew saw them. Susie refused his arm and walked unsteadily from the car to the house and went to the bathroom immediately. She closed and locked the door and in a few seconds he heard the shower start, so he unloaded the car while she was in the bathroom and stood watching as she came out wearing a robe. Her head was swathed in fresh gauze.

"Susie," he said as she walked slowly past him toward the bedroom, "the doctor said you didn't have to wear that stuff. You're home now. It's just me. I don't mind. Take the bandages off. Please."

He followed her in to the bedroom and watched as she slid into bed, still unmade from that morning that seemed now to Stafford like a decade ago, and eased her head down on the pillow on her side. She kept the robe on.

He sat on the bed beside her. "Do you want me to call your mother?" He laid a hand on her shoulder, but there was no indication that she cared one way or another that it was there. "Would you feel better if she were here?"

A muffled "No" came back. Then more emphatically: "Don't call *anybody*!"

"Shouldn't you eat something?"

"No."

Stafford left the room and, ravenous, went to the kitchen and fixed two Spam sandwiches and devoured them, following with a

Coke. Only now did he realize how completely he had been separated from his body. It was almost as if it had not even been a part of him since the confrontation on the street, except for the sharp pain he felt in his side when he breathed deeply. And even the pain seemed remote, unreal, like it was part of someone else's suffering. Like he was reading about it.

Sitting at the table where they had eaten their blueberry muffins before the trip to New Orleans, he rubbed his hand across his face and felt the abrasions again and the knots along his jaw and at his temple and behind his ear. He had taken a pretty good beating. He slid the plate back and stared at the table top. There were the crumbs they had left, even the coffee cups, with a little dark liquid still in the bottom of one of them. Their milk and juice glasses sat by the sink.

He got up and pulled a new bottle of Seagrams from a lower cabinet, twisted off the top, and poured half full one of the glasses they had used for juice. After a few shots he felt the numbness returning, and when he had finished his third glass he could feel nothing of the pain in his side. He slumped his head forward until it touched the cool glass top and wept like a child, then slept.

When finally he awoke, he rose and checked on Susie, who had not moved. She was in heavy sleep, her breathing deep and regular. Stafford stood a long time looking down at the unmoving white shape of his wife, a silent stranger in his bed, stretched out like something covered with snow, something encased in ice which at length he might thaw out and find warmth in again. Beyond her form he could see through the thin curtains of the window that faced the beach road a lone shrimper returning to port, full and riding low in the brilliant blue-green water. He shook his head sadly and went back to the kitchen and his bottle, and there he stayed, eyes on nothing, drinking and trying to forget, as the sun slid across the sky, shifted low in the west, and bathed the kitchen in gold. At some point he fell into the blessed dark of sleep.

Stafford woke late in the night lying beside the table, the side of his face wet and cold against the kitchen tiles. He sat up and wiped his face off with his shirt sleeve and went to the bathroom, after which he looked in on Susie again, but she had not changed positions, so he checked the kitchen clock—1:30—and took another deep drag directly from the bottle, now almost empty. He left the house and staggered across the road to the beach. Twice he stumbled and fell at the edge of the sand. He was glad there was little traffic. All he needed now was to be hauled off to jail as a common drunk.

At the edge of the water he took off his shoes and removed his trousers and shirt, flung them behind him, no matter where they landed—if the tide took them, too Goddamned bad.

For one brief moment, as the sandy water encircled his ankles, he thought of dressing and going to a phone booth somewhere and calling Emily Miller. He needed a woman. But he shook off the notion and waded out toward the horizon, where the lights of two ships danced far off.

His head whirled and the stars made a grand circuitous parade of pinpoints in the dark as he waded out and out, until the water rose to his knees, then to his waist and chest, and finally to his chin, and he lunged forward into the dark, stroking toward nothing. Above, the constellations wheeled, unconcerned about him or his lovely, desecrated wife, who lay in whatever dreamless or ghost-haunted sleep she was in, while he threw a hand forward and pulled out into the black water, then another, farther and farther, his mind on neither the land behind him nor the vast Gulf beyond, his mind on nothing at all, his eyes fixed on the star-clotted southern sky.

All that long early morning he swam, keeping the glow of shore lights to his back, then transcribing a great circle back toward the glow until he saw the red lights of towers rise out of the sea, and finally the lights along the beach road. He circled again and again, with no fear, like some elemental creature driven by an urgency in the blood and brain-stem, unnamed and unknown but there and real, like the black water through which he moved, like the universe itself, purposeless and mindless, perhaps, but there and moving by some unknown principle, always moving. At the first suggestion of light in the eastern sky he drifted slowly toward the sand.

Sometime later a red sun woke him where he sprawled at the edge of the surf nearly a mile east of his house wearing nothing but his shorts. He looked up and down the beach. People were walking toward him. Jesus, the wonder was that no one had called the cops about a body on the beach.

Where he had swum, how far out he had gone, he could have told no one. He remembered the lights at sea and the lights he was swimming away from, the dark rush of the water past his sweeping arms, some phosphorescent streaks around him, and the night sky swirling with stars.

He wasn't even sure what day it was until he noticed that even with the sun swelling up out of the Gulf there was little traffic. *Has to be Saturday*, he thought, trying to rise to his feet. He dropped back down on all fours and breathed deeply, then rose to his unsteady feet. *God-damn*. He was still drunk as the wind and with nothing on but his jockeys. Easing back out into the water, he waded slowly up the beach, the water just past his crotch, searching the sand ahead for some sign of his clothes and shoes.

At last he came upon his pants—he had flung them far enough up on the beach that the tide had not taken them—though his shoes and shirt were gone.

"Fuck it," he said, tugging the damp, sandy pants over his legs. He heard his keys jingle and felt the lump of his wallet.

He scanned the sand one more time for his shoes, then squinted into the sun to see whether his shirt might be floating in the surf, but he saw nothing that looked like it, so he turned toward his house and, careful to avoid a staring couple, started home.

Susie was sitting at the kitchen table when he came in. She was wearing one of her housecoats. The gauze was gone and he saw for the first time what they had done to her face, though he said nothing, simply slid into a chair beside her and dropped his chin into his hands, eyes fixed on hers.

"I'm glad you took it off," he said.

She nodded.

"Do you hurt anywhere?"

"A little. Down there. My head hurts, cheek's sore." When she spoke, her mouth barely opened. She worked her jaw from side to side. "Jaw hurts some."

"Do you want to talk about it?" he asked her.

"When the time comes," she said.

"I don't guess there's much we *can* say right now, is there?" he said. "Except that I'm glad we're alive and back home and that I don't intend to go near New Orleans again."

She nodded, unsmiling. Her face was a combination of blues and purples, her eyes all but swollen shut, and when she spoke, her lips, still dreadfully puffy, barely moved. "Where have you been?"

He gestured toward the beach. "Swimming."

She nodded.

"I'm glad you're finally up and talking. Did you sleep OK?"

She nodded. "Still feel like hell. Like I'm having one gigantic hangover."

He sucked his lips in between his teeth and stared at the table. "Well, we've been through a lot."

"*We*, white boy?" She had apparently just come from the shower, and her hair, undried, was slicked back like oily flax.

"Sorry. I just—"

"I know what you meant," she said through barely parted teeth. "Like my new haircut?"

"Your hair'll grow back. Did you eat anything?"

She pointed to the sink. "Had some coffee. Milk."

"That's the first food you've had—"

She said nothing.

"Since the sandwich we had going down? Is this the first—"

"No. What the hell difference does it make?"

"When did you eat? Did someone feed you something?"

"Yes."

"Who fed you? The police? Or did you have something at the hospital?"

"If you must know, *he* fed me."

"At the hospital? Someone at the hospital?"

"No. *He* fed me."

Stafford stared at her.

"Who's *he*?"

"A man," she said flatly. Her lips barely moved.

Stafford rubbed his eyes and ran his hand across his mouth. "Susie, what are you saying? *What* man?"

"*The* man."

"Stop being cryptic. It's hard enough for me to think. What man are you talking about?"

"Satan," she said.

"Satan? Now, what the hell does that mean? Who's Satan?"

"That's what they called him." She was opening her mouth farther now, with effort.

"Who? The guys that grabbed you?"

"It's what they called him. When he finally came. The *man*."

"Satan was the name of one of the guys?"

"He was the *man*," she said.

"*What* man?" Stafford asked. "Was he one of the guys that grabbed you?"

"No. He came later. He was in charge. He was top dog."

"Was he black?"

"No, not black. He was big and he was dark but not black."

She reached and unfastened the waist tie and opened her housecoat, slid it over her shoulders and dropped it until all that Stafford could see of her was nude. Her breasts had small bruises all around them, her nipples were swollen, and right in the center of her chest, just below the mid-line of her breasts, a small dark cross was etched, a very simple one, made apparently with a needle or knife-blade and ink. The perpendicular slash was an inch and a half high or so, the crossarm perhaps a bit more than an inch and on the crossarm sat the initials *SG*, split by the upright. The flesh about the cross was slightly red and welted. She pointed to the cross.

"They told me about it," Stafford said. "He do that to you?"

She nodded. "Yes, *he* did it."

His eyes had had tears since he came into the kitchen and found her, now they flowed fully down his face. "It's all right. We'll have it removed. Nothing will show."

"*SG*," she said.

"Yes," he whispered softly. "Tell me about it. Who is SG?"

"SG is me." Her eyes were like stone.

"Your last initial isn't *G*."

"Satan's Girl," she said. "I'm Satan's Girl."

Stafford looked at her. "That's what the SG means?"

"Yes. Satan's Girl."

"We'll have it removed," he said.

She pulled the housecoat back over her shoulders and fastened the strap. "No."

Stafford leaned and opened the cabinet door beneath the sink and spun off a handful of paper towels and wiped his face. "You'll never even know it was there. They can do it so there won't even be a trace." He was snuffling like a child.

"It *stays*," she repeated.

"Susie."

"He said I must wear it, forever."

"Who? Satan?"

"The man they called Satan, yes."

"Susie," he said quietly, struggling for control, "this has been hellish enough. We'll be years getting over this. One of the first things we'll have to do is get it removed. We can't—that's a *brand*, a symbol of that night of terror. We can't go through the rest of our lives looking at that Goddamned thing!"

She was crying now. "I have to keep it, Jack."

She was having great difficulty speaking, so he reached and took her bruised face into his hands. "It's all right, Baby, you don't have to talk about it anymore right now. Let's wait until later. I've got to go clean up."

She nodded and went back into the bedroom, and Stafford peeled off his clothes and stumbled to the shower.

Late that afternoon, after she had slept most of the day, he asked her whether she would like to walk on the beach a while, but she declined. She did agree to share a pizza with him for dinner, so he had one delivered. With no small relief he noticed that she could open her mouth wide enough to eat it if she cut the wedges into very small pieces. After two slices with him at the table, she returned to the bedroom.

Her sleep that night was fitful, with much moaning and twisting, which could as easily be her coming out from under the drug that they had given her as anything else. Once she flung an arm across the bed and struck him on the shoulder, but he could not tell that she had awakened. When he jolted awake and sat up, her breathing was even and deep.

Sunday there was a dreadful silence in the house. Susie got up late, long after Stafford had finished the papers and taken an early walk by the water. She said little to him, ate her breakfast alone, then went back to bed and slept through the rest of the morning, while he sat on the porch and watched the beach fill up—families with their children and dogs, young couples and some not so young, and solitary souls walking quietly along the sand. Gaily colored floats dotted the light surf, and even before noon sailboats were tacking along, headed out to darker water, fishing boats trolled farther offshore, and beyond them commercial vessels shone in the sun. Stafford sat and watched.

After a sandwich for lunch he went into the bedroom to see whether Susie might like something to eat, but she either did not hear him or would not respond to his voice, so he opened a beer and walked down to the beach and settled against a pier piling and watched the people.

He tried to think of nothing as he sat there, buzzed about by throngs of beachgoers, blanked his mind as one would obliterate his sight staring at the sun. It would do no good to think about what had happened, anymore than it would change a single second of the whole nightmare. He willed his mind to behave like the dark water he looked off at—when the hull of some great ship rushed through it, propellers churning, the water closed behind it, healed in closing, and in minutes it was as if nothing had passed there at all. Only when the sun had dropped low in the sky and Stafford became aware of the beach thinning of people did he rouse himself and, quite sunburned on his face, arms, and legs, return to the house.

He called in the next morning and said the two of them had a stomach virus and he wouldn't be at work for a day or so.

"You hadn't planned to go to school today, had you?" he asked when she came to the breakfast table on up in the morning. She was dressed in jeans and a blouse. Her face was still swollen, though the bruises seemed not to be as distinctive as before and her lips were not as puffy.

"You have to be kidding." She sat down and accepted the coffee he held over to her.

"I'm not going in either. I thought we might try to talk this thing out a bit more today, decide what we're going to tell people. You know . . ."

"What's to tell? I fell down some stairs." She gripped her jaw with both hands and worked it from side to side. "Still sore as hell."

"Susie."

She looked at his face. "Looks like you might have fallen too." She had never asked a thing about what had happened to him after she was taken. "What a clumsy couple."

"Susie, nobody's going to buy that."

"I don't give a good—"

"Here's what I think we should do . . . ."

She shot him a hard look. "*Your* fall wasn't as bad as mine, Jack, so maybe I'm the one who ought to cook up the story, if we have to. I say it's nobody's business and we don't owe any explanations." She was forceful.

"Susie . . . ."

She pointed to his face. "They do that to you when they grabbed me?"

"Yes."

"All I saw was the one big guy land on top of you. He was hitting you with his fists. Then they had me in the car."

"Susie, nobody's going to believe—"

"We got the bloody *fuck* beat out of us in New Orleans, Jack. That's what happened."

"I thought you didn't like that word."

"I still don't like it, but, my man, I can say it now without hesitation. I heard it enough and felt it enough and had to say it enough during that eternal night that it's a part of my popular vocabulary now. Thought you liked it. Fuck, fuck, *fuck*!"

"Susie, we can't just hide what happened."

"Sure we can, Jack. You got the hell beat out of you and I got the hell beat out of me, and I got *fucked* front and back, up and down for the better part of an afternoon and night, by what seemed like every damned nigger in New Orleans and at least one white guy."

She smashed her hand down on the top of the table and sloshed coffee over the front of her blouse and jeans but she didn't seem to notice. He handed her some napkins. She brushed his hand away and kept talking.

"You and I are the only ones who know what happened, and you don't know the half of it. It's going to stay that way. Do you understand me?" She leaned forward and thrust her face into his. "Nobody else up here, not the New Orleans Police Department. Nobody. Do you *understand* me, Jack?"

He nodded.

She eased back into her chair. "I mean it. I'll leave you the very minute I find out that you've told anybody about what happened down there."

He studied her face. "You'd *leave* me?"

"If you tell anybody, I will." She reached and laid a hand on his arm, then withdrew it. "Don't make me, Jack."

"I won't say a word, if that's the way you want it."

"That's the way it is going to be." She hesitated and took a deep breath. "Do you want to know about it?"

He looked at her quizzically.

"Do you want me to tell you what happened to me? I mean, sooner or later you've got to know about it. Do you want to know now?"

Stafford nodded. "Yes. I guess I do . . . ."

"All right. I don't remember all of it. I was so scared at first that I couldn't have told them my name, if they'd asked. When they got me in the car they pulled me across the hump on the back floor and kept me pinned with their feet. I was bowed face-down over that damned hump. One of them covered my head with a blanket or sheet or something and they drove somewhere with me. There were lots of turns and twists."

"What did they say to you?" Stafford asked.

"Well, at first this one kept saying, 'Be quiet, Bitch, or we'll cut you up and feed you to the alligators. Just be still and you'll be all right.' He kept saying stuff like that over and over. That was the one that had his feet on my back. He didn't have to keep reminding me—I was too scared to say anything. The other one, the one that had my legs pinned down, was saying something I couldn't understand, and he kept trying to run his hand up my dress, but the other one said he'd better leave me alone until we got there, wherever the hell that was. Then the driver said something to them and they didn't say anything else but jive bullshit until we got to the place where we parked.

"They took me to a parking garage or warehouse or something and took the blanket off of me and put something over my head—a pillowcase, I found out later—and strapped my arms behind me. God, that hurt. They used those plastic strips that the police use and strapped my wrists behind me and then pulled my elbows together in the back, and that hurt like hell, but they took that one off. And I took an elevator ride that seemed to go up forever, but it was probably just slow, and then they led me into a room where there were some other guys—they were laughing and drinking and smoking and talking loud and they really got loud and nasty when they saw me—and then into another room where they threw me on a bed. They kept the tie on my wrists, but when I heard them leave the room I slung the pillowcase off my head and I just sat on the bed staring at the walls and ceiling of that room. I didn't know where I was or how I got there or who those guys were or anything. It was like I had been taken to another world or was another person or something, like I was in another zone.

"There was just a table with a simple little shadeless lamp, which they'd left on, and a couple of chairs and the bed. Like a small bedroom anywhere, with wallpaper that had little chains running through the design. Pink and gold and green wallpaper with little roses and chains, but they might have been vines. Roses don't really go with chains, do they? There was nothing hanging on the walls. No pictures. Nothing. But at least it was air-conditioned."

"Susie, we can talk about this later." He poured each of them another cup or coffee and added Kahlua to his.

"No. I need to talk about it, Jack, and you need to know what I went through. I lay in that bed all day yesterday thinking about it, and I decided that I need to talk. But let me tell you this." She pointed her finger at him. "You'd better not tell a soul. Not the police, for sure. Because I'll deny everything, *everything*. I'll even tell them that *you* beat me up, if I have to, that you assaulted me in an alley. Whatever. What happened to me *happened*. Past tense."

"I told you I wouldn't tell anybody. You would really tell them that *I* beat you up?"

"If you mess with me I will, yes. If it takes that. What I am saying, Jack, is that what happened is nobody's business but mine and whoever I decide to tell about it. And I have decided to tell *you*. And *just* you. Do you understand me?"

He nodded, not looking at her.

She drank some coffee, then shuddered. "Put some Kahlua in this, will you?"

He glanced at her, then took the cap off the little brown bottle and reached over and poured a thick stream into her coffee until she nodded. He added another shot to his cup and drank deeply.

"Thanks," she said, taking a swallow.

"Didn't know you liked Kahlua in your coffee."

"Never tried it before," she answered. "Thought I might like it. I've tried lots of new things lately."

Stafford sat back down.

"As I was saying, all that's past tense. It's done. It happened and we can't go back and undo a minute of it."

"Susie, have you got any idea why they did it, why they grabbed you?"

"Well, it wasn't random," she said.

He could read nothing in her eyes, but he felt his stomach knotting. "What do you mean?"

"They thought they had somebody else."

"What do you mean?" he asked.

"When they came back into the room after a while—I could hear them talking on the phone and talking loud among themselves in the other room, that damned jive that they do—there were three of them and they started asking me who I was, and who *you* were.

And I kept telling them who I was and who you were. They asked me over and over and I told them over and over." She slugged the Kahlua-laden coffee. "'I shoulda got the purse, man,' one of them kept saying. Then another one pulled me to my knees on the bed. He took out a pocket knife and turned me around and cut the tie off my wrists and forced me back on the bed and pressed the knife tip to my throat and told me I'd better level with them, and, Jack, I just froze up and couldn't say anything. I couldn't even remember . . ."

"What did they do then?"

She drained the rest of her coffee and motioned for him to pour in straight Kahlua. He poured the cup half full.

"One of them grabbed me by the ankles and held me while one of the others pulled my dress off. And then they took off my panties and told me to sit in the middle of the bed and not move till they got back. They all left the room and then one at a time they'd come in and ask me questions, the same questions, like they were trying to see if I would slip up. Like they were cops and I was being questioned for some kind of crime and they wanted to see if I could keep my story straight. Who was I and where did I come from and who were you and who was my *man* and on and on. Like I was a hooker or something." She sipped from her cup, her eyes on him. "And they kept staring at me, at—you know—but at that point they hadn't touched me.

"And they kept telling me I was lying and then they started slapping me and hitting me, with open hands at first and then their fists, and pulling my hair and pinching me and acting like they were going to cut me with a knife. They kept pricking me with a God-damned knife. And they started touching me, rubbing my breasts, touching me, you know." She sniffed and rubbed her nose. But she went on. "Then one of'm grabbed a handful of hair and yanked my head back and cut the hair off. He *sawed* it with his knife.

"One of the others said something about my hair being all fucked up then, and he got in behind me with a really sharp knife and just started cutting my hair off, like razor cutting. My hair was all over the bed. Then they left me alone and all I could hear was them talking in that other room. And they got on the phone again.

"Finally one of them brought in a syringe and one climbed on the bed on top of me and sat on me and held my arms above my head while the one with the syringe shot me inside my upper arm. At first I didn't feel anything—just a sting like any other kind of shot—but then everything got warm and soft and I felt sort of woozy."

"Susie," Stafford broke in, "why don't we talk about this later, if you want to?" She was getting more and more agitated as she talked.

"No. I don't know how much you need or want to hear it, but I need to get it out. But I mean it," she said, looking hard at him, "you'd better not tell anybody any of this."

"I won't," he said.

"I just kind of mellowed out and lay back, looking up at that shadowy ceiling while they sat on the edge of the bed watching me. I had a hand over my crotch, I remember, and an arm across my breasts. They didn't touch me or anything then, just sat there, not talking, looking at me. Then one of them said something like 'Ain't she fine?' and he turned off the light by the bed but turned on another lamp in the corner of the room, one I didn't even know was there, and I just lay there staring up at the ceiling while they sat around me like buzzards or something waiting for me to die. The drapes were so heavy that I couldn't even tell whether it was still light outside. I had lost total track of time, like it just didn't count anymore.

"Then, all at once, like they had done it on cue, they left the room and everything got real quiet, except I could hear them talking low and fast, and I got more and more relaxed and kept seeing strange designs in the wallpaper and on the ceilings and the room would warp this way and that and I was lying on my cut hair, and it was tickling me. And for a long time I lay there, naked, staring up at the ceiling and back and forth at the walls. And, Jack, all I could think about was wondering whether I looked cute lying there naked on that bed with my hair cut short. I felt like a little girl."

"You didn't try to cover yourself up with a sheet or anything?" Stafford asked.

"I might have. I don't remember. I remember at one time having both hands over my crotch is all."

"Then what happened?"

"After a while—I don't know how long—the talking got louder in the next room, and then the door opened and I turned my head and there was this black guy standing there taking his clothes off. He rolled a pink rubber on and came over and pulled me to the edge of the bed and started rubbing himself over my lips and he told me to suck him, and I did. God, it tasted awful—that lubricant, I guess. After a while he crawled on the bed beside me and started kissing me and whispering things in my ear, then he spread my legs and kissed me all along the inside of my thighs and worked his lips all over me down there and up to my breasts, and then he went in."

Stafford stared at the bottom of his cup. "Did you fight him?"

"I might have pushed back at him. I don't know. All I know is that he was big and strong and he kept on until he was through, which was quick, then he slapped me hard on the side of the head and left, and then another one came in, black too, only smaller, and he did it and then another, only the third one made me suck him first, like the first one, then he screwed me, and on and on this went. There must have been eight or nine, or the same ones taking turn, and they were all so rough, kissing me as hard as they could, then hitting and slapping, and calling me names and making me say things, then pounding away until they had finished with me."

"Susie, you don't have to go on." Stafford had poured his cup half full of Kahlua now and was drinking it like coffee.

"I don't care. I'd just as soon talk about it. Maybe it'll help." She held her cup out for more Kahlua.

Stafford nodded and poured her cup half full.

"Every one of them used a pink rubber. Like that was the color they had all decided I might like. Or it was the color of the day. Or they just had a big crate of'm. Whatever. Bright pink, the color of a pacifier."

Stafford drank in deep gulps.

"And this went on for God knows how long, like half the black guys in New Orleans had been summoned to enjoy this white woman. But it was probably three or four of them taking turns. I just don't know. I don't know. After a while one felt about the same as the others, and their faces just swam together."

Stafford shook his head slowly. "Oh, Baby, I know how they must have hurt you."

She looked away from him out toward the Gulf and took a deep swallow of her drink. "Don't start the pity stuff, Jack. You don't know anything at all about how it felt."

He reached and turned her face back toward him.

"And Jack," she said, "it didn't hurt much at all."

"What do you mean? You had blood—"

"Didn't hurt much, Jack. I was too stoned. She reached and poured the rest of the Kahlua into her cup. "Fact is, most of it didn't hurt at all. I'd have to say that it wasn't at all unpleasant until they did perverted things or hit me. I saw stars when they hit me. But even that didn't really hurt. It was just like something solid but soft hit me, like a big wave. No pain, just a jolt and stars and lightning.

There were times when the other part felt . . ."

"Susie."

"You remember the old advice about rape, 'If you know it's going to happen anyway, just lie back and enjoy it'? Well, I was so stoned that I wasn't sure I was being raped."

For a few seconds he was silent. Then: "Did they all use condoms?" The Kahlua was beginning to make his head swim.

"Yes. They were afraid they were going to get *AIDS* or something from *me*!"

He rubbed the back of his neck. "Thank God for that," he said softly.

"It went on and on and on, for—I guess it was for hours. I just lost track of time."

"All black?"

"They were all black guys except for one white. I never got to see the white guy's face—he had a Mardi Gras mask on, a red one, a devil's face, appropriate enough. He was completely naked too, like the others. He was stocky and had lots of heavy black hair all over his body. He kept saying things to me. He just kept saying what a fine woman I was, what a fine *piece*, and kissing me all over. At first it was almost like he was really making love to me, instead of just pounding me the way the others did. But then he got rough. Oh God, Jack, now *he* hurt me. He was so rough. He was big anyway and he was taking long hard strokes, and he slipped out and then, when he, he almost went all the way into my . . . ." She took a deep breath. "He almost went all the way in back there. Back *there*. And then he flipped me over and went in on purpose, and he kept going deeper and harder." She had tears in her eyes.

Stafford didn't have to wonder who the white man was. Susie had been just another little fringe for Harry. He gritted his teeth and said nothing.

"And I screamed it hurt so bad, and he kept slapping the back of my head until I hushed. And finally he was finished with me."

"Susie, why don't we wait until later? Why don't you rest?"

"Well, at that point the worst was over, Jack. Like I said, this went on for what seemed like hours, one guy after another." She was talking softly now. "But time was somewhere else for me. I was outside time. It could have been days, for all I knew. I was smothered in that dismal room by one man after another." She sighed. "And then *he* came."

"He?" Stafford had stood and moved to the window, through

which he could see the sky above the Gulf, where little puffs of white were sliding along against the deep blue. He came back to the table.

"Yes. *He* came. And it was like some god had descended. The others had apparently had their fill of me and were playing cards or doping or something in another room, next to the one I was in, making all kinds of noise, jiving and laughing and all, and they were saying all kinds of stuff about me. One of'm had come back in with some scissors and cut on my hair some more, trying to even it out. He scooped up all the hair he could from the bed and floor, and I heard him yell out to the others, 'Satan ain't gon' like this. He ain't gon' like this a-tall. Y'all better help me clean this place up.' But the others stayed where they were. I just huddled up under a sheet trying to make some sense of what was going on, which was pretty much impossible with everything that had happened and from whatever that dope was . . . ."

"You said *he* came. Do you mean the one they called Satan?"

"Yes. The one who'd cut my hair and tried to clean the mess up went back to where the others were, and suddenly everything just shut up in that next room, like they had all been whisked away to someplace else. There was no sound at all. You could have heard a pin drop. I don't know for sure, but I think that he opened the door to the room they were in and just stood there. And nobody said anything until I heard this voice say 'Where's she at?' Then somebody mumbled, 'She in there,' and the door to the room I was in opened and this tall dark guy was standing there looking at me. I was curled up in the sheet.

"He stepped in and pulled the sheet back and turned the lamp on beside the bed. He looked me over, almost like he was a doctor examining me, then walked back out of the room and I heard him say to the others, 'Aw, Goddamn. You sonofabitches! You wasn't supposed to do that. You done messed her up bad. You was supposed to bring her here, get her to talk. That's all! Get y'all's asses out of here. I'll deal with y'all later.' Pretty much those exact words. Oh, he was *mad*. Then I heard chairs squawking and a lot of mumbling and the others left, and then it was just me and him."

"This was Satan?"

"Yes. I told you, it was Satan." Her face took on a strange look then, almost a longing.

"You said he was dark. But he wasn't black?"

"No. I don't know what he was, but he didn't look black, and he didn't talk black."

"Was he cajun?"

"He didn't talk cajun."

"How old was he?"

She shook her head from side to side. "I have no idea. Might have been in his late twenties or early thirties. Not real old."

"What did he do?"

"He sat down on the bed and just looked at me for a few minutes—he had left the lamp on—then he said, 'Pretty rough on you, wasn't they?' I just nodded. And he said, 'They wasn't supposed to do this. They got carried away is all. Sonofabitches sure can't cut hair. They'll catch hell for this, bet on it.'

"Then he lay down beside me, with his clothes still on, and started stroking my arms and body and legs, but he didn't touch me—you know. He just caressed me, loved me, held me like a child until I was clinging to him and crying. He kept saying 'Poor beautiful baby, poor beautiful baby.' He took out a handkerchief and wiped my eyes and nose and mouth, and he kissed me all over my face, which must have looked like hell, the way they had been beating on me. And, Jack, he didn't smell like the others. They smelled like smoke and beer and sweat, all but the white one. And he had doused himself with some kind of cologne that I could smell on me even at the hospital. This man, he smelled nice. Nice is the best word for it, like he had showered and shaved and not put on any cologne at all. It was a clean smell.

"He looked down at the blood on the sheets. 'Goddamned animals,' he said, 'they'll pay for this. They'll *pay*.' He picked me up off the bed and held me beside him while he reached down and yanked the bloody sheet off, then threw the top sheet—which had been wadded up at the foot of the bed—over the mattress and laid me back down. Then he went into the bathroom and wet some bathcloths and came back and bathed me. All over. My whole body. And, Jack, he was so gentle. I just lay there like a child and let him bathe me."

"Then what happened?" Stafford wasn't sure he really wanted to know, but what he felt was almost like a thirst, a deep, compelling thirst to know what she had been through.

"He gave me some pizza from a box in the other room, and a soft drink, and then he wiped my face off again. He asked me whether I would like to take a shower, and I told him that I would."

"You were still *naked*?" Stafford asked.

"Yes. Jesus, Jack, I was *stoned*. I didn't even pull the sheet over me. I just—I just didn't feel uncomfortable with him. Hell, Jack, I can't explain it. Maybe if they hadn't shot me up or the others hadn't been so rough with me. He was just so easy . . . so gentle."

"You just sat there in the bed naked and ate pizza with him?"

"Yes," she said.

"And you remember all this, even though you were stoned?"

"Very clearly." She studied the rim of her cup.

"So what did he do with you then?"

"We took a shower."

"You went into the shower with him?"

"Yes. After we finished eating he led me to the bathroom and helped me into the shower. I was so woozy that I could barely walk, and he took off his clothes and got into the shower with me and bathed me, my body and my hair, and then he held me under the warm water, held me and kissed me gently, not like the others had done. They *crushed* my lips. They were brutal. But he didn't try to go in me. He just held himself against me, up between us and it was almost like we were dancing in a warm rain, and, oh Jack, I've got to tell you, I felt so clean, so wonderfully warm and clean, like a little girl in a warm rain, and I *wanted* him to touch me."

Stafford could only stare into the bottom of his cup. The Kahlua was gone, so he stumbled from the table and rummaged in the cabinet for a bottle of something, *anything*, while she went on.

"Then he dried me off and took me back into the bedroom and laid me on the bed. 'I will make love to you if you want me to,' he said, 'but only if you want me to.' And, Jack, I said yes, because I didn't want him to leave. I didn't want the others to come back. And he took a condom out of his pants pocket and put it on, and he made love to me, Jack. He was so gentle, not like the others."

Stafford sat there at the kitchen table, a bottle of rum in his right hand, listening to his wife without knowing what to say or feel. It was as if his world had been wrenched out of its old orbit and sent off into cold, dark outer space where he could not breathe, could not think, and though the commerce of the day went on as before outside the walls of his house, the sun coursing through the deep sky, and the waters of the Gulf lay in blue splendor only a few hundred feet from him, Jack Stafford felt that he no longer belonged to anyone or anything, belonged nowhere in the vast universe. He felt smothered in some dark, cold ash.

"And when we were through, he cleaned me up and then

himself and turned off the lights and we lay on our backs talking. He asked me where I was from, where I grew up and went to school. When I made love the first time. When I came to New Orleans and why. And then he asked who my man was, and when I told him that *you* were my husband, the same man who brought me to New Orleans, he said not to lie to him anymore—he meant who my *man* was, whose girl was I, who I worked for, not who the guy was I was with on the street. And I told him again why I was in New Orleans, that I had come with you, my husband, on a whim or something, and that I didn't work for anybody, that I was a college student and your wife. And he rose up on an elbow and said that he wasn't sure that he believed me, and I swore to him that it was the truth.

"And he said that it really didn't matter, that I was his girl now, and he asked me how I felt about that, and I said, all right, if he wanted it that way, and he said he did. Jack, I didn't know what else *to* say. I just didn't want him to leave and the others come back. Then he turned the bedside light on again and reached over and got a knife out of his pants or jacket pocket and then he straddled me and said that it might hurt just a little, but he had to do it, and he opened it and as gently as he could he cut the cross in my chest and made the initials, then inked it with a felt-tip pen. It just stung a little. Then he went to the bathroom and brought back some alcohol and a cotton ball and swabbed it and it stung some more.

"When he was finished, he sat back and smiled at me. 'OK, whether you're telling the truth about all this or not, anybody that goes to bed with you now will see my brand and know he better not mess with my woman without my blessing. You're Satan's Girl now. He tithes to anybody, it better be me. And you remember this—anytime you need me, I'll be here for you.' It's funny, but I can remember just about everything he said to me, like it's recorded in my head. And he gave me a telephone number . . . ."

"A telephone number?"

"Yes. Just a number where I could reach him. But I don't remember what it was. It doesn't matter."

Stafford slowly shook his head. "And that was it?"

She looked at him a long time, unblinking, then continued: "No. He pulled me off the bed and danced with me in that dark room, with no music, just danced with me, up close, kissing me on my hair and face and lips, and before I knew what was happening we were on the bed again."

"Did you *do* it again?"

She closed her eyes and held her head back as if she were looking through her lids at the ceiling. "No. He just lay there holding me for a few minutes, then we showered and he put on his clothes. He said, 'I gotta go now, but I'll be back to see you in the morning and we'll talk some more.' Then he kissed me and went into the other room and a couple of the guys came back in where he was and he talked to them. They were quiet and I couldn't hear what they were saying, but they didn't bother me again.

"I went to sleep after he left and sometime during the night I woke up with somebody injecting me again under the arm. I didn't know what was going on, but they were in a big hurry. They kept whispering real fast, like they had to get me somewhere quick. They made me shower again and dress, and they put a pillowcase over my head and put the shoe in my hands and the next thing I knew I was on a park bench somewhere in the dark. By myself. I was in and out of it most of the time, mostly out. There were lights and then it got dark again."

"And that's it?" Stafford was now drinking straight rum and chasing it with orange juice. Susie was slowly sipping the last of her Kahlua. He was hunched over in his chair, staring at this woman who was now not the wife he'd known, whose eyes, though still blue, had a frightening depth to them.

"Don't you figure that's enough?" Her voice was hard. "But, Jack, this is all between you and me. I don't want to go back down there and talk to the police. It is *ended.* Right here at this table. I've said all I intend to say and I want it ended right here. Do you understand? You say anything to anybody about this and I'll—well, I've already told you what I'd do."

"And you can't figure out why they did it?"

"Jack, I've said all I've got to say."

"I've got to take you to the doctor to have you checked over. To do a blood test."

"I'm not going to see a doctor. And I'm not going out of this house until I look right again. Now, you tell them at the library anything you want to about what's happened to your face. Tell them you got in a fight. Whatever. But nobody sees me until my face is clear. Do you understand?"

"What about a blood test, Susie? At least we need to get a blood test."

"What for, Jack? If I got something, I've got it. And I don't want to know about it. If you want to stay with me, it's your business, but I don't want to know. I told you, they wore rubbers, every one of them, even Satan, and that's that. If you're scared of me, you wear a rubber too, if we ever get around to sex again. And if you still want me after this."

"Oh, Honey, this isn't going to change things between us, but, Susie, we need—common sense tells me that we ought to get you checked out. They may have done something to you that the doctors didn't find down there. You may need some, some therapy. You know, to help you get over it. And we need to get your teeth checked."

"No. All I need is a little *time*. My doctor's not going to know anything. And I'm not going to a dentist—my teeth are fine. Nobody knows anything, Jack." She stared hard at him. "Nobody knows *anything*. Do you understand me?"

"What about your mother?" he asked.

"Same. She doesn't see me until my face has cleared up. And you don't tell her *anything*."

"Susie, people will know something happened. They're not fools."

"Jack, most people *are* fools and they will *think* they know something. They won't *know* unless you tell them." She fixed her eyes on his. "And if you tell them, I will be history for you. I don't want to have to keep saying this. Do you understand me?"

Stafford wasn't sure whether she was looking at him or through him. He nodded and reached to touch her hand. "Susie, you told me in the hospital that the 'little guy' took your panties. Who were you talking about?"

"I was stoned, Jack. I don't know. Some little guy came into the hospital room and took them out of the bag and left with them. He had red hair, thin red hair, and freckles all over his arms. I think. Or I might have dreamed it. What difference does it make who took them? I damned sure don't want them back."

"Oswalt," Stafford said. "That Goddamned Oswalt."

"I don't know his name. I don't *care*. What does it matter?"

Stafford laid his hand on hers. "Nothing. It's nothing." He stood and walked to the kitchen window and looked out across the street, then at her. "Will you walk on the beach with me tonight?"

She tried a smile, but it was a very weak one, almost a smirk. "Yes. On the beach in the dark. But that's it."

The sun was way up in the sky now and the sand across the road threw back its glare. He suddenly felt very old and sick, and before he knew what was happening, the coffee and Kahlua and vodka and rum, along with scalding orange juice and bits of cereal came gushing out and into the sink and he heaved until he felt like his insides had been squeezed out by some giant fist.

When he was through rinsing out the sink and his mouth and washing off his face, he turned to speak to Susie, but she was gone from the table, so he walked outside and around to the back porch, where he sat slumped against one of the posts as the afternoon wore on toward night. Off and on he dozed.

That night, well after the sun had faded in the west, leaving a scarlet swath as if some bloody thing had died at the edge of the world, they walked quietly on the beach, side by side. They did not speak as they padded along above the surf, shoes in their hands. Susie was wearing a pair of shorts and flimsy blouse with no bra. He could see bruises up and down her legs.

Stafford's head still pounded from the heavy drinking earlier that day, but at least he was thinking clearly again.

"What will we do about all this?" he asked her.

"What is there *to* do? It's done. It's finished and over, I guess. It happened, and we can't take any of it back. We can't go back to that day and sleep in late or turn the car around on the interstate and not go to New Orleans. We went and it happened, and that's that. It's history, and you can't rewrite it. At least we survived it. Bruised and scarred, in more ways than one. But we *survived* it. I could be dead, you know."

"Susie, I'd feel better if you saw a doctor."

"Jack." She stopped and faced him. "If I got something from one of those animals, then I've got it. I told you, they used condoms, every one of them. If I've got it, I just don't want to know about it. Your choice is to determine whether you want to take the chance making love with me again, when I get to the point where I feel like *I* want to make love again." She turned and walked on, then said over her shoulder, "Or *fuck*."

He caught up to her, and after a few minutes of walking, neither speaking, he asked whether she would like to swim. He could see boats out on the horizon, but she seemed not to notice. Behind them their footprints trailed out, side by side, his the larger and firmer, hers the delicate impressions that the sea obliterated in one gentle swish.

"No. I'd just like to walk right now."

They continued along the edge of the surf in silence as the evening settled softly about them, the man and his woman, no longer at ease in their world, a world that only a few days earlier had been one of simple stars overhead and sand and almost soundless water at their feet and far out on the Gulf the twinkling lights of shrimpboats dragging their nets in the dark.

XV

One afternoon several days later Stafford arrived home from work to find a strange car parked at the edge of his driveway, the driver still in it, a black man, his head laid back on the headrest, eyes closed. After parking, he went through the back door and yelled for Susie, but he heard no answer, so he passed on through to the front, opened the door onto the porch, and stepped out. Whoever was in the car—a nondescript sedan, pale blue with Louisiana plates—still slouched in the front seat, his head thrown back and his mouth open. He had his window down and an arm rested on the sill.

Stafford descended the steps and started toward the car, then stopped.

"Aw, shit," he said, and turned around.

"Whoa, hey," a voice came from the car. "Hang on, Stafford."

He turned around and faced the man, who had opened the door and swung his feet out onto the edge of the lawn.

"What the hell are you doing here, Merchant? I've paid my Goddamned hotel bill and the hospital."

"Easy, Stafford. Take it easy, man. It ain't nothing like that."

He turned back to the house and stopped at the door, squaring himself across the opening.

"Mind if I come in?"

"I damned sure do."

The big detective had his hand on the screen door handle. Stafford stood looking at him.

"Glad I caught you home. I came by earlier, but the car was gone, so I went down on the beach and waited awhile, then came up and took a nap." He wiped his face. "Been at the library?"

"Yeah," Stafford said. "I've been at work. Why?"

Merchant shrugged. "Mind if I come in?" He pulled at the handle.

"We don't have anything to talk about, Merchant. Just go on back to New Orleans and leave us alone."

"Your wife here?"

"We don't want to talk to you. Leave us alone." Stafford remained squared away across the door opening. He was almost as tall as the detective, but he kept remembering how Oswalt had slung him against the wall like a rag doll. He'd hate like hell to have Merchant grab him. "We have nothing to say to you. Please leave."

"You never returned any of my calls—do you guys ever just pick up and answer the phone, you know, like some people do?"

"Not since the trip down there, no. We screen everything that comes in, answer the ones we want to answer."

"I guess you didn't want to talk to me. You just threw away the letters too?" Merchant had retreated to the edge of the porch, where he leaned against one of the rails.

"Yes," Stafford said. "But apparently you didn't get the message that we don't want to talk to you."

"Well, I thought maybe a personal visit might work."

"It won't."

Merchant pivoted and swept his eyes up and down the beach. "Mighty pretty place you got here. Must be great to look out on that water day and night. You rent this place or own it?" He had taken off his coat and draped it across one of the porch rails. His sleeves were already rolled up nearly to his elbows as if he had had the coat off earlier. The big man's arms and hands looked more like those of a farmer or mechanic, someone used to handling heavy tools, or maybe a boxer.

"Merchant, if you were interested in the status of the house, you'd already know that we rent it. Exactly what do you want?" Stafford was relaxed in the doorway now, but his body refused entrance.

"You seem to have healed up pretty well," the detective said. "What about your wife? She get over everything all right?"

Stafford watched a shrimper on the blue-green water. "We're fine. Write that down in your little book and let us alone. Or have you got your recorder running? Want to hear about our love life?"

"I was hoping we could talk some about the guys that grabbed her." Merchant dropped down into one of the chairs on the porch.

Stafford pointed to the chair. "They're chalky," he said. "You'll get that chalky paint all over your clothes."

Merchant smiled up at him. "It'll wash out. Nothing permanent about that stuff. Most stains wash right out, you know. My veranda chairs used to do that too, back before we went plastic." He folded his arms and settled back, looking across the street to the Gulf. "Why don't you sit down and talk with me a little bit, Jack?"

Stafford remained in the doorway. "I don't have anything to say to you, Merchant."

"Maybe your wife does. She know I'm here?"

"I don't know. I haven't talked to her. But I'm sure she does. She doesn't want to talk to you either."

"What is it?" He looked up at Stafford. "Y'all just ashamed about all this, afraid to let us go after those guys? Scared? What?"

Convinced now that Merchant was not going to bolt into the house and confront Susie, Stafford relaxed, stepped from the doorway, and sat down in a chair beside him. He turned it to face the detective.

"Look, man, we're just beginning to get our lives back together. New Orleans was a nightmare that we just want to forget. We don't want to have to relive any of it, and we sure as hell don't want to go back down there to help you indict those thugs. I mean, that is what you are up here for, isn't it, to get us to go back down there with you?"

"Well, I was sort of hoping you might come back down for a day or two and help us identify some of them, give us a little more information. You know, shit that's come to you that you didn't think of down there. We're pretty sure who did it, and we sure as hell know why, don't we?"

"There's no way—"

"I brought along some pictures that might help some." He reached for his coat and removed a small brown envelope from a pocket. "A stack for you and your wife to look through. It might help."

Stafford shook his head. "You don't get it, do you, Merchant? She doesn't want to see pictures of those guys or be reminded of them, and I didn't see enough of any of them to do you any good. Besides, even if I did recognize one of them, I wouldn't tell you. We want to forget them, forget New Orleans. You might as well put them back in your pocket."

"You're the one that don't get it, Stafford." He swatted at a fly. "You just don't get it at all."

"Get what? What the fuck are you talking about, Merchant?" He tried to keep his voice down, but it kept rising until it was a shrill whisper. "Who *are* you, man, and what the hell kind of perverse interest do you have in this?"

"I am somebody trying to make a blind man see. You don't have enough sense to realize that what those sonsabitches did down there was *murder your wife*." He gestured with his thumb. "That ain't your wife in there, Stafford, that woman hunkered down refusing to talk to me. And I know Goddamned well that she knows I'm out here. I may not be a fucking librarian with a bunch of degrees, but I got plenty of common sense, and I can see. She knows I'm out here. That woman in there—she might have been a girl when you took her down there, but by God she's a woman now, bet your ass—is *somebody else*. Your wife, the little college girl you took down there, died in New Orleans, man, and unless you're luckier than I think you are, she ain't coming back to life again in that body. They *killed* her!"

He put his face right in Stafford's. "Now you tell me, Goddamn it, is that woman in there the same one you took to New Orleans?"

"Merchant, keep your voice down."

"*Is* she?" His face was filled with passion.

"What the hell are you trying to do to me . . . to *us*?"

"What I'm trying to tell you, fool, is that those guys snuffed out your wife and put that woman in there in her place. Your wife is not with you anymore, and you gon' be damned lucky to get her back. I know, man, I've seen it before. They pulled her across a threshold that will be hell to come back across. They still got a hold on her. Do you understand what I'm saying to you? They killed what was in the shell and stuffed something else in there. You got to get it out or she'll never be the same."

Stafford simply looked at him. He imagined a marvelous pearl shell in whose depths a grotesque dark thing coiled.

"There's an old woman in a nursing home in Baton Rouge, Stafford. She used to be my mother, but she's not anymore. Time and disease killed what was in the shell and left an old woman who can still feed herself and get about, but she don't know me from Adam when I drive up to see her. Calls me Teddy, some name she's heard somewhere that stuck, and accuses me, whoever I am to her, of stealing all her money and selling her home, puttin' her in that horrible place. Now, Stafford, if I could go after whatever it was that did this to her, if I could nail that dark force that killed my momma, I'd do it—I'd turn myself aloose on the case and go after it, all guns blazing, but it ain't as simple as picking some guys' faces outta a bunch of pictures. You can't see or put your finger on what did it. I can't do a damned thing about whatever killed my mother and left a stranger in that body. I would if I could, but I know I can't. Some*body* killed your wife, snatched away that blond kid you took down there and sent you home with a strange woman. Body may be the same, but the rest ain't. But you don't need me to tell you that, do you? I bet you think about it every waking hour, and you damned sure think about it when you crawl in bed with her at night, don't you?"

"Why the hell don't you get off my porch and *leave*?" Stafford pointed to the southwest. "Get on back down to that Godforsaken swamp you call New Orleans and you and Oswalt deal with your alligators. Leave us alone."

"And, Stafford, I didn't have a damned thing to do with what happened to my momma."

"Merchant, do you want me to call—"

"Who, the *po*-lice? You ain't calling nobody," he said. "The sad part of this for you is that you and me and her know that you sacrificed your wife to fulfill a fantasy. Not for any kind of cause at all, but for a damned *fantasy*."

Stafford rose in his chair. "Would you for God's sake keep your voice down!"

"You mean she don't know yet it was you that got her in all that shit?"

"No," Stafford said, settling back in the chair. "As far as I know she doesn't."

Merchant went on, more softly, "Sacrificed that good-looking girl to feed your stupid-ass fantasy. It's just like you pulled her clothes off of her and threw her spread-eagle across a rock and yelled out to the sky for those big ol' buzzards to come down and tear the meat right off of her bones. Which they did, only they picked clean the *inside*."

Head in his hands, Stafford rocked back and forth. "Man, just leave me alone, please."

The detective sat with the envelope in his lap. "If you don't help with this, you can bet your ass that them sonsabitches will get some other woman somewhere sometime and do the same thing to her. We can't try them for murder, but that's what they did to your wife, *killed* her, just as sure as if they had put a gun to her head and pulled the trigger. But we just might be able to lock some of'm up, Stafford, maybe for a long time. Bust up the ring. All you got to do is finger one of them. Just one."

Stafford shook his head slowly. "We can't do it. We're not fingering anybody and we're not going back down there. She won't talk about it. She won't even let *me* talk about it."

Merchant stared out over the Gulf. "So you guys are simply dropping it . . . ."

Stafford studied the gray porch boards. "Look, Merchant, you told me that you had a pretty good idea who ordered it, and you told me that there wasn't anything—"

"What I told you was that we couldn't do a Goddamned thing unless you or her *identified* one of them. There's a big difference between knowing that somebody's done something and getting someone to finger him for doing it." He patted the envelope on his lap. "If she can pick out just one of the guys that raped her, I'll have something solid that will let me twist his dick so tight that he'll turn on the *man*. Or the man *hisself* might be in that stack. Don't you see? Identify *one*—I swear that's all it'll take."

"Bullshit," Stafford snorted. "You also said that they wouldn't rat on each other. I mean, you *know* that guy Harry was involved."

"Man, you're making this difficult. Harry, the best we can tell, didn't do anything but make a phone call, which ain't against the law. And we can't even prove that. Harry ain't who we're after."

"Harry was—" But he caught himself and rose and pointed southwest. "You might as well head on back down there, Merchant, because I'm not letting her see those pictures."

"You started to say something about Harry. What about him?"

"Nothing about Harry. My wife has made it clear enough that what she wants to do is forget about all this."

"That's what that woman in there told you, yeah, but she ain't your wife. You got to get *that* woman to help us out, and it won't be easy. Just get her to look at the photographs, talk to me, help me . . ."

"She won't do it." Stafford propped his arms on the porch railing and looked off over the Gulf. It was hard to remember what that view of the beach and water use to do to him.

"You know, it's all over for you guys. Her innocence is lost,

Stafford. You ain't likely to get it back. She'll never be the girl she was on the way down that day. They even *branded* her, man, put a cross on her. She is a dark angel now, not the one you took down there with you, the one with blond hair and innocent eyes. Tell me how she looks at you now, Stafford—what do you see in her eyes?

"I know you're thinking that given time and enough love from you she'll soften up and become the pretty, innocent little thing she was, but the fact is that the girl you married has vanished from the earth itself, man, and the very best thing you can do right now is help us keep them sonsabitches from messing up anybody else's life. If I can get that bastard—if I can get him and have his ass put away, at least for a little while, it'll bring this thing to what they call closure, and that might help get your lady back."

"Closure, my ass."

"It would help."

"The guy you're wanting is Satan, right?" Stafford hissed the name. On the far horizon of the Gulf he could see a sailboat with gaily colored sails tacking into the wind.

"Satan?"

"That's who you want, isn't it?"

"Satan, huh? She did talk to you then. Will you help us?" Merchant, who had been looking very tired, was suddenly animated. "As far's I'm concerned, it would be like nailing the very Devil. Ain't nobody ever had a more appropriate nickname. Drugs and prostitution and murder and all kinds of heavy shit—man, you wouldn't believe what that guy's into, but he fucked up bad when he grabbed your wife. Little does he know that the stupidity of a God-damned college librarian can bring him down. We can get him for it, Stafford. We got him lined up for a big fall, but we got to have *her* say he was one of'm. Conspiracy, abduction, battery, sexual assault, denial of civil rights—man, you name it and we'll tag it on him."

"If you know he directed it, then you have to know some of the others who were in on it. Lean on them. Make *them* talk."

Merchant laughed harshly. "Without someone identifying them you could lay'm on the railroad track and the wheels would come across and lop off their heads and feet before they'd say a word. They'll call your bluff unless you got something solid. What we could do to'm don't begin to compare with what *he* would do to'm. Unless she identifies one, gives us some solid ammunition to use, they are not going to talk, period."

"Well, neither is she."

The detective sighed. "Yeah, I can see that. I sure would like to talk to her, though."

"No," Stafford said quietly. He was watching a couple walking along the beach, hand in hand, scuffing their feet at the edge of the surf. "Merchant, tell me something."

"What?"

"What *is* all this to you? Why are you so damned concerned with us? We're white, and blacks—mostly blacks—did this to us. Why are you so—"

"Why should you *care*?" Merchant asked. "You ought to be glad. And it wasn't blacks that did this, my man, it was *animals*, animals that might now and again hurt one of your people when they get in the way, but they *feed* off my people. They ruinin' more lives than you can imagine. And you better remember that animals come in all colors."

"Does Oswalt know you're here?"

Merchant shot him a quick look. "No, and you'd better not tell him."

"Why?"

"You'd better not tell anybody I was here, Jack." He bored into Stafford's eyes. "Nobody. Do you understand? Swear that you won't. Not Oswalt, not nobody. This is real important."

Stafford swallowed and shrugged. "OK. I won't say anything. Hell, I'm having to carry more Goddamned secrets—"

"It's important, Jack," Merchant said. "You don't tell *nobody*."

"Fine, you have my word." He sat quietly a minute, then asked, "Merchant, is he black or not?"

"Satan? Naw. He's dark, got some Indian or something in him, so we hear, but mostly he's as white as you. From somewhere out in the country around Shreveport. Cajun, maybe, but I don't know his pedigree. All I know is he is mean, and he probably come from mean."

"What else do you know about him?"

"Not much," Merchant said. "We know that he rides tight herd on his girls. *That* we've heard from a bunch of sources. We've never had a single one of them turn on him, though. He pays well, protects'm. They'd *die* for him. That's been one of the problems. Every fucking one of them is loyal to him. Like he's some sort of god. But mainly it's because they're scared to death of him. See, he lets them see his tender side at first, but then he shows them how mean he can be. 'See how good I can be to you if you treat me nice and behave yourself,' he says, 'and see how bad I can be if you don't.' I'm gon' tell you, Stafford, it'll be a high old time when we bring this sonofabitch down. That'll be *big-time* news."

"What's the bit about the cross he cut on her?"

Merchant nodded. "So ol' Satan himself did the cuttin'. I figured as much."

"What's—"

"Every woman he's got has got a cross or a plus sign or something on her chest. Every one we know about. It's something he does. It's his brand."

"And the SG?"

"There's an SG on every one I ever saw or heard tell of. Been a couple of'm turned up dead that I saw, only he didn't have anything to do with it, or at least that we could prove." Merchant pulled out a pen and drew a cross on the back of the envelope he was holding, then put an *S* on one side of the crossarm, a *G* on the other. "That's what he put on your wife, and I've seen that same sign four or five times. I don't know exactly what it means—it ain't his initials—but it's there."

"It means *Satan's Girl*," Stafford said. "So you knew when you saw her in the hospital who'd done it, didn't you?" Stafford felt his anger mounting.

"Satan's Girl. I'll be damned. Well, anybody can imitate that cross, Stafford. We had a pretty good idea it was his work, but we weren't sure. We aren't really sure yet, not unless y'all can pick out somebody that'll lead to him. Or unless she'll pick *him* out, testify against him. I'd bet my ass . . . ."

Stafford pointed. "Is he in there?"

Merchant patted the envelope. "Yeah, his picture's in there. Along with about fifty, sixty others." He looked hard at Stafford. "Uh-huh. You'd like to see what he looks like, wouldn't you? You'd like to see who's laid claim to your lady."

Stafford cleared his throat and spoke softly. "If you—would you mind? I mean—"

"I know what you mean. And the answer is *no*."

"Please, Merchant, please let me see him. After all we've been through, surely I've got the right to see a picture of the man who did that to my wife."

"No way, man. Not just for you to gratify your curiosity."

"Well, can I at least look at the pictures, see whether I recognize the one who jumped me?"

Merchant smiled. "I thought you didn't want to look at the pictures. My, my. You know you're not gon' pick out anybody. It's your wife who needs to look at'm now."

"Please." He held a hand out to the detective.

When Merchant passed the envelope to him, Stafford thought he saw one of the curtains move at a porch window, but when he turned no one was there and the curtain was still. He opened the flap and pulled out a stack of photographs, small black-and-whites, ten or so shots to a page, and he began to study them.

As traffic whizzed along the highway and early evening walkers began to arrive at the beach, Stafford slowly scanned the faces. They looked like the same ones he had gone through in Oswalt's office. He was three sheets into the stack before he ran across a white face, but this man was middle-aged with very fair skin and light hair and nothing about his visage to suggest violence or aggression. On the fifth sheet there were two whites, one bald with ponderous jaws, the other a gaunt man of twenty or so whose face declared nothing but stupidity.

Stafford tapped the picture of the skinny one. "I would bet money that this one went to prison for drugs. Right?"

Merchant leaned and looked. "Naw, not drugs. I don't know most of those guys, but that one I do. He stole about a dozen BMW's, before he was caught. He liked BMW's. Not as dumb, by the way, as he looks. If he hadn't tried to steal one that was occupied, he might still be operating. A guy was parked at a rest stop and was asleep on the back seat under a couple of coats, and ol' Jimmy thought them was clothes piled up back there and the guy was in the building taking a leak, so he popped the door and jumped in and was already hard at work on the wires before the owner hit him in the back of the head with one of them heavy, three-cell aluminum flashlights. Knocked him out, stone cold."

Stafford pointed to the fat one. "What about him? "

The detective shook his head. "I don't know him. Coulda been anything from rape to shoplifting." He grinned. "I know what you're doing, Stafford. It ain't gon' work. I'm not fingerin' the guy for you."

"You don't have to," Stafford said when he tucked that sheet behind the others and his eyes fastened on the face in the upper right corner of the next page.

Staring back at him was a pair of eyes set like ball bearings in a malevolent face, the irises intense points of black, above them heavy eyebrows, and the face was like something savaged from steel or stone: wide, squared off chin, hard-sculpted line of jaw, lips full but tightly drawn, cheeks high and bold, and a tall forehead with dark hair slicked straight back from it. There was some sort of small tattoo on his right cheek, but Stafford couldn't make it out.

"It's him, isn't it?" Stafford asked, placing the tip of his finger on the picture.

"Maybe," Merchant said, reaching for the photographs. "Maybe not. Would you feel any better if you knew it was?"

Stafford said nothing and slid the photos back into the envelope and handed it to the detective.

"It's the sonofabitch. I know . . . ."

Merchant gave him a weary look and rose to his feet. He picked up his coat and pocketed the envelope of photographs. "Still hot, ain't it?" He took a card from his wallet and scribbled something on the back and handed it to Stafford. "You got my home number there too. Call me if you can get her to change her mind," he said over his shoulder.

"Merchant." Stafford was right behind him. "Why did Oswalt take her panties?"

The detective stopped and turned. His eyes were hard. "Who says he *did*?"

Stafford swallowed. "She—Susie said that he took them from the bag. Not that it would have made any difference. They took them off of her before they raped her, and they all used rubbers. And they showered her several times. There wouldn't have been anything . . . ."

Merchant stared out over the Gulf toward the Southwest. "Oswalt," he said quietly, "well, well." Saying nothing else, he got in the car and drove away.

XVI

He awoke, not with a start, sharp and focused on the sound that penetrated his sleep, but with a thick fog of oblivion still hanging over him, pressing down with smothering weight until he gasped like a man on the very edge of drowning, his eyes fixed on the black cross of the ceiling fan blades, faintly lit by a diffused shaft of street-light from the curtains. In that twilight zone between sleep and awareness he tried to tune his mind to what had awakened him—the central system cycling, the refrigerator filling its icemaker, a sound from outside, from traffic on the street?

Then he heard the moan, deep and insistent, and he knew.

He had heard it so many times over the past few nights that at first he could not even decide which night it was: the one he was waking into or the one before or the one he might be dreaming. But there it was again, beginning as a faint whimper, then rising from far back in her throat and sliding along her tongue until it broke free into a sigh and a final hiss. They always came slowly at first, sometimes minutes apart, as if they gradually gathered strength within her until she could no longer restrain them, like steam building until it forces an outlet. He lay there unmoving, eyes on the ceiling, wondering if this time would be any different.

But it never was. In the dark he could hear her breathing soft and even between the moans, like some delicate forest creature wrapped in its nest for the night, high above the ground or deep within it, warm and oriented and secure. Then the almost inaudible whimpers would begin, sweetly infantile, and the moan would rise, fierce and throaty, and subside. After a while the cycle repeated, each shorter than the one before until one moan hardly ceased before another began. When her body heaved and twisted and her legs flailed, he knew that it was nearly over, so he simply slid over to his edge of the bed and let her wrestle with her ghost until the spell broke and she awakened or subsided into sleep.

It would do no good to roll over and clutch her, to wake her, to try to comfort or free her from her dark angel—it was simply something that he would have to lie beside her and wait out, just as she must endure it until it was over or she woke. So, like a man quivering as some great storm passed over him, he lay and waited, helpless against its fury.

Finally she was still again, breathing quietly, but this was not the deep, even breathing of sleep. He knew that she was not sleeping. She was sitting upright, her back against the headboard, staring out into the dark room. He didn't bother to turn and look, nor did he reach out and touch her filmy night shirt, which he knew would be drenched with perspiration. He knew. After nearly two weeks of the same thing he knew.

After Stafford returned to work, no one said anything about his bruises or about his absence, but, then, librarians were famous for their privacy. It was as if no one noticed that he was different, or perhaps no one cared. He did not resume his daily coffee breaks at the Commons, preferring to sit alone in his office and read, drinking coffee from a thermos.

One morning he heard a knock at the door and turned from his computer to see Emily Miller leaning in, smiling. Her smile vanished when she saw his face.

"What in the world happened to you?" she asked. "Where've you been? I've dropped by a couple of times, but you weren't in your office or at your coffee and nobody seemed to know where you were. Mercy, your face is a mess. Did you get beat up? Howard came in like that one time when he got hold of a rough sailor boy from Bulgaria. They spent the weekend over at Gulf Shores in a little honeymoon cabin. The guy nearly killed him. I loved it. Howard would have gone out with him again if the chap's ship hadn't left."

"I had an emergency, a family emergency."

"You must have been part of it."

He flashed her a look. "Yeah. I had an accident while I was over there. At my mother's house."

"Was your little songbird with you?"

"No, just me. I was moving some boxes on a shelf in the attic—for my mother, you know—and they were heavy with books and stuff and I lost my balance and they fell on me. That's all."

"Looks like they got you good." She leaned across the desk and gripped Stafford's chin, turning his face first one way, then the other, the way a mother would do to be certain that a child had properly washed his face. "Sure looks like somebody beat you up." She touched one of the bruises. "Matter of fact, Howard's looked like that more than once when he's latched onto one of his rougher boys. Those fags can be so brutal, you know. Or careless. God, the ways they get off. But he keeps going back for more."

Stafford winced and pulled his face free of her hands. "Just books, Emily. An avalanche of books."

"Well, I always told you books would kill you." She settled back in her seat and opened her purse. "I was just by here to drop off something of yours I thought you might like to have back." She held toward him her closed hand and let roll onto the desk a bullet-shaped shell of very pink pearl, through whose narrow end a small gold chain had been threaded.

"I just thought you might like to have it. You know, since we've broken up housekeeping and all. And since it appears to be final." She studied the shell a few seconds. "I believe it's the only thing you ever gave me in the way of a gift. It was awfully sweet of you, but I really think your wife ought to have it."

He spun the shell with his finger. "You don't have to do this."

"Yes, I think I do."

"Emily."

"It looks a little like a suppository, doesn't it?"

She rose and started through the door, then turned: "You know, Jack, I never said this before, but I was in love with you, you rotten sonofabitch. Some days and lots of nights I get the idea that I still am. And it wasn't just the sex and conversation. But that's all we could let it be, wasn't it, sex and talk?" She closed the door quietly behind her.

When she was gone, Stafford sat turning the shell over and over in his hand.

Jack and Susie sat on the porch late in the day watching the people on the beach and, far beyond them, fishing boats and shrimpers, an occasional freighter. Neither had said anything for a very long time. They didn't speak much anymore. Susie still moved through what seemed to him like a dream world, mechanically doing what needed to be done around the house, smiling seldom and grudgingly taking short walks with him on the beach. They had their meals in and never went anywhere at all.

She had shaped her hair herself with scissors and a razor cutter. From the rear and sides it looked like Emily Miller's hairdo, and her face had a hawklike profile that it had not had before. Sometimes when she turned to look at him, her head pivoted like a bird searching for prey, and her eyes were sharp and cold.

When he did something now, it was with conscious awareness that she wanted it done, and he was uncertain whether what he was doing was based on logic or not, but what he did know was that the old dominion had vanished, his cool scientific judgment now subjugated by an authority he saw as much in her eyes as he heard in her voice. And this he understood but little, her new-found power to command him—he knew only that what he had done to her entitled her to something, some exercise of power whose source and direction he could neither control nor comprehend.

"There's nothing you can do here," she had said the Thursday after their return from New Orleans. "I'll be fine. I'm just not going out until my face heals and my hair grows out a little. Go by in the morning and drop me from my courses."

This he had done, citing family complications. When finally someone asked about her not coming by the library, he said simply that she was working on her paintings at home.

She was barefoot and seated in a rocker, dressed in a light shift. The sun was settling red and lingering a very long time.

"New Orleans," Susie whispered, looking toward the glow.

"What?" Stafford had been fiddling with his fishing reel. He had invited her to go fishing with him that weekend. They'd camp out on Horn, if she liked. He had pieces of the reel scattered out over a newspaper on the floor.

"That red glow is over New Orleans."

"You reckon, huh? Looks like hell itself."

"More like blood," she said softly.

"You want to walk on the beach?" he asked. "I'm ready to put this thing back together. Be through in just a minute or two."

"I guess not. Not until it gets darker anyway. We might run into someone we know."

"Susie, your face looks fine. There weren't that many bruises to begin with, and they're just not that bad. And your hair looks great."

"After the sun's down," she said, and went in.

They walked to the beach barefooted when night had settled on the Gulf. Stafford commented about the fact that there didn't seem to be as many shrimpers working the sound, but Susie said nothing. She kept her eyes on the sand ahead, occasionally sweeping them out toward the darkening water. After wading in the surf until they were nearly a mile east of the house, one of the longest walks they had had since New Orleans, she stopped and turned him to her. He leaned to kiss her, but she gently pushed him away.

"Jack, please. I'm not in the mood for that."

"Sorry," he said. "You can't blame a guy for trying."

"Let's swim," she said. The breeze was billowing her dress.

"Fine with me. Race you back to the house."

"No. We don't need suits." She slipped the dress over her shoulders. Her panties glowed in the faint light of the globes on poles along the highway, and she had on no bra. She threw the dress high on the sand and lunged out into the surf, taking great strides to reach the deeper water.

Stafford stood dumbfounded a few seconds, then turned both ways to see who was on the sand with them. He could see a couple several hundred feet up the beach but could not tell whether they were walking toward him or away, so he checked his cut-offs to make certain that he did not have his wallet, then yanked off his shirt and flung it up near her dress and splashed out into the dark water where his wife had disappeared.

When the water approached his waist and he still had not seen her, he yelled out. There was no sound but the soft swish of light surf and the noise of traffic along the highway.

"Susie!" he yelled louder, cupping his hands toward the Gulf. Behind him he could see the other couple, stopped now and dark against the sand, looking out toward where he stood. *Jesus, go the hell on.*

"Susie!" He turned and yelled out her name to the east, south, then west.

No answer came, so he plunged forward and began stroking slowly straight out from shore, his face lifted high out of the water so that he could listen and watch. Every few strokes he stopped and treaded water, calling out her name.

When he had reached a point that he judged to be nearly a quarter of a mile out, he turned west and swam until he could see clearly the streetlight that stood near the corner of his yard, then reversed directions and swam until he knew he was well past the point where he had entered the water. Every hundred feet or so he called out.

A number of people had gathered now where the couple were standing. Stafford could see their dark shapes against the white sand and beyond them cars moving along the highway. He turned toward shore and swam until he was close enough that he thought they could hear.

"We're just swimming," he yelled out. "You can go on. My wife and I are swimming. Just *swimming*. There's no problem here." *Go on, mind your own fucking business!*

They waved and shouted something back, but he couldn't make out what they had said. They seemed to be dispersing, so he turned back to the east and swam on, calling her name.

After swimming parallel to the beach awhile, east and west, he tired and drifted slowly back to shore, dog-paddling and treading water, using the lights as his guides until he came to rest at the spot where he had entered the water, or very near it. His legs and arms were stinging where he'd brushed against hot jellies. He scrubbed the spots with sand and walked back in and rinsed off.

Everyone was gone from the beach, so he waded out and found their clothes.

"I just hope to hell she hasn't come out," he said finally to himself. He could make nothing of the tracks in the sand.

He walked slowly along westward, turning around now and again to call out for his wife. The traffic along the beach road had died away and he could hear nothing but the gentle surf.

"J-a-a-a-c-k." The voice came from the water.

Stafford stopped and stood and listened. "Susie!" he called. "Susie, where are you?"

"J-a-a-a-a-c-k."

He waded out and squinted, but his eyes found nothing in the dark but the heave of the Gulf against the lighter sky, both surfaces ablaze with stars, those above steady as stones, the others dancing.

"Susie! Susie, please . . . ."

Then, from somewhere out of the dark water, she was in front of him, surfacing without sound like a pale goddess knifing up from the deep, grasping him with both arms and pressing herself to him until he stumbled backwards toward the beach and fell and the water closed over his face, his eyes still wide open, and he saw the sharp stars blur and whirl and disappear when he finally blinked, eyes burning with salt and sand. And as he crabbed back toward shore, using his feet and hands, all the while his mind held the image of her against the backdrop of shattered stars as she rose naked from the black water. With one hand she pulled his head up out of the surf and clamped her lips on his, and with the other she yanked his shorts down onto his thighs and straddled him, forcing herself onto him. She ground against him, head thrown back.

"This is what you wanted, isn't it? Come on, Jack. *Fuck* me!" She arched over him and held her lips to his ear. "Pretend it's Aphrodite rising from the foam. Come on and fuck Aphrodite, *homeboy*!"

Stafford struggled onto his elbows and twisted his face from hers, gasping. His belly and groin and thighs were stinging.

Then she stopped moving and lifted her head and lay atop him, hands braced against the sand, staring down. Past her head Stafford could see the stars again, little holes in the black canopy of space.

"Maybe some other time." She stood, still straddling him.

She dipped and rinsed herself, waded from the water, and walked up the beach. He saw her bend over and pick her dress up and slip it on.

He lay for a few minutes, propped on his elbows, staring up at the same constellations he'd known all his life, those friendly little figures in the sky, so unchanging, so predictable in their nightly course. The black water rippled in and up onto his chest, pulled back, then rolled in again, the sand swirling about his buttocks and legs and feet and settling gently on his stomach and groin. He turned over and rose to his knees, then to his feet. Something bright tumbled in the surf. He waded out and picked up her panties.

Susie was sitting on the front steps with her legs crossed when he got home. The wet dress clung to her thighs.

"Where'd you go, Ja-a-a-ck?" she sang softly.

"The better question is, where did *you* go?" He plopped down beside her and held out his hand. "Here are your panties."

"You got'm back," she said.

"Susie, those people thought we were in trouble out there. They thought you were drowning."

"Let them think what they want," she said. "Even strangers ought to know that I can swim better than you."

He was angry as hell, but at the same time it was wonderful to see some life come back into her, a flaring of the old vigor. She was *talking* to him. "Where'd you *go*?" he asked.

"I went swimming. Isn't that what we agreed to do?"

"Susie, come on."

"I swam down that way." She pointed to the east. "Then I swam back up that way." She pointed in the opposite direction. "You came by me so close three or four times that I could have reached out and touched you. I just figured I'd scare you to death if I did."

"Jesus, Susie . . . ."

"Sorry, Jack."

"And what was that all about in the surf there? I feel like I've been sandpapered. What the hell—"

"I got horny. The sea did that to me, I guess. Thought we'd have a go of it. I thought you *wanted* to fuck me."

"Jesus, Susie—"

"But you couldn't get it up." She slipped an arm around him. "It's OK. You seem to have trouble at night in the sand. Come on inside and let's get cleaned up."

She pulled him to his feet and led him into the house and upstairs to their bathroom, where she removed her dress and his shorts, tee-shirt, and underwear. He just stood there, his eyes taking her body in.

"Where are your panties?" he asked.

"The little red-headed guy took them, remember?"

He just stared at her.

"I left them on the porch," she said. "They're wet and sandy."

"I can't believe you came out of the water naked."

"Well, what did you want me to do, holler and ask someone to bring my dress?"

"What if one of them had taken your dress? What then?"

"Then I'd have walked home naked," she said. "It's not that big a deal."

He sat on the commode, lid down, studying her body. There were almost no bruises left, just slightly discolored places on her arms and chest and thighs where bruises had been. The little black cross blazed out at him.

She reached, pulled him to his feet, and steered him into the shower, and turned the water on with her foot. As he watched, she bathed herself. Then she soaped him, head to feet, letting the almost intolerably hot water cascade over them until the room was thick with steam. His stomach and thighs still stung, but he felt his passion rising. He began kissing her all over her face and along her neck, pressing himself to her, and when he met no resistance, he boldly began probing for an entry.

Before Stafford knew what was happening she had buckled his legs and pinned him to the bottom of the tub, the water splattering over her head and back, and she drove herself down onto him, her knees wedging him tightly in the tub while she rose and twisted and slammed herself against him, whimpering and moaning, then threw her head back into the stream of water. Stafford could see nothing in the steamy air but pale glimpses of his wife's slicked-back hair, beneath it her bruised face with a grimace or a smile—he couldn't tell which—and then with one great thrust she ground down on him and shrieked with pain or pleasure or both and fell forward onto his chest. He was almost suffocating from the steam and her weight, and his passion was completely gone.

He finally managed to lift a leg and with his foot flip the shower lever. He spun each valve off with his toes and lay there in wet, weary silence as she pinned him to the bottom of the tub.

"I've got to get out of here," he grunted finally, "I can hardly breathe."

Without looking at him, she rose to her knees, then stood and got out of the tub and quietly dried off while Stafford lay propped up on his elbows watching her in silence as she wrapped a towel around herself and went to the bedroom. When he went in a few minutes later, the room was dark and still.

XVII

His eyes played around the bright kitchen, wallpapered in a pale blue with lattice and sunflowers, so unlike what he had expected, everything neat and orderly, the windows hard rubbed recently to the point that they literally shone in the morning sun. The table they sat at was a rich golden oak, deeply waxed, with matching chairs. No disarray, no sense of impermanence, confusion, the sorts of things you'd anticipate in the kitchen of a couple no longer in love. All the food put away, except for fruit and onions and potatoes, which hung in an inverted pyramid of wire baskets, and the sink carefully wiped free of water spots, a scrub pad in its little niche and a dry dish towel neatly folded beside it.

"This place doesn't look like you, Em," Stafford said, settling back and sipping his coffee.

"How's it supposed to look, Jack? Supposed to look old and worn out, desperate, what?"

Emily was dressed in a gauzy print blouse, apparently with no bra. Stafford could see the edges of her breasts through the opening at the top, where she'd carelessly or carefully left two little pearl buttons undone. She had looked very slender in her red skirt when she opened the door for him and escorted him into the kitchen.

"I don't know." He shook his head. "I don't know what I expected." He carefully adjusted his tee-shirt so that the sleeves rode up over his biceps when he rested his elbows on the table. His eyes took in Emily's face, which in the morning light seemed not so old now, as if she had softened and smoothed out since he last saw her. She smiled and sipped her coffee.

"Do you like it?" she asked.

"Oh, yes, yes. The kitchen. The house. Your yard. Everything. I feel like I've been here before—you've talked about all of it. I just, I don't know what I expected. It just looks different from what I thought it would."

"Well," she said, smiling again, "I'll take that as a compliment."

"Things going OK with you, Em?" he asked pleasantly.

She sighed. "Yeah, OK. I get lonely now and again, but I'm adjusting to my new life. I'm into aerobics big now—you may have noticed I've slimmed down. And I met a new guy."

"Really?" He didn't mean to sound surprised, but he was.

"Yes. A realtor. Out of Mobile. He's nice."

"Does Howard know?"

"Who gives a damn what Howard knows?"

"Married?" Stafford asked.

"Yes, I'm still married."

"Come on, Em, you know what I mean. Does he come here?"

"Jack, this visit, whatever it's about, isn't about me or my love life. Suffice to say that I'm getting over what we had. And for whatever business it is of yours, he's divorced. And he's been here, yes."

She reached and opened a drawer and removed a pack of cigarettes, shook one out and lit it, and blew smoke toward the window.

"Well, there's something you haven't gotten over."

She smiled. "Not quite. But I've cut way back. This is my first one for today. I'll take a few puffs off one every hour or so. Funny, but they tend to remind me of you."

"You look good," he said.

She smiled again and nodded. "I'm taking better care of myself."

Stafford allowed his gaze to leave her face and sweep around the room. Suspended from a gold wire above the door were two bluebirds that gently turned in the ribbon of air from the air conditioning vent, clicking together first beaks, then tails. On every ledge and shelf a pair of brightly colored birds sat, beaks touching—cardinals and mockingbirds and canaries, some he couldn't name. He slowly looked from couple to couple.

"Those are Howard's birds," Emily said. "He watches birds. Takes photographs of them. Tries to sketch them." She coughed and blew smoke toward the bluebirds above the door. "But he doesn't draw worth a damn."

"I don't remember you ever mentioning the birds."

"Maybe not. When we were together, Jack, I don't recall that the subject of birds came up very often."

"We never went anywhere, did we?" He slid a hand across the table to take her free one. The other dangled the cigarette.

"No," she said. "We were at your place screwing or sitting at the Commons or in your office. But we never went anywhere real, no."

"I should have taken you places. We should have done things together. I could have had fun with you, Em."

She stubbed out her cigarette and watched the sky through the window. "We did have fun, Jack, but that's over."

His eyes returned to the birds. "They're all paired—they're couples."

"Oh yes. They're in love, each pair," she said.

"Well, what . . ."

"Oh, they're not me and Howard, if that's what you're wondering about. Or me and you. They're Howard and other people. One of each pair just *looks* like a female. Even when it's two guys, one's got to play the female. You know, Inny and Outty. Gracious, Jack, I haven't been a songbird for a long time."

He studied her face.

"I was a songbird once," she said, "sat where some of these are sitting." She leaned and opened a drawer and shoved her hand beneath some dish towels. She withdrew four birds, all different, and set them down in a line before Stafford. One was a bluebird, another a thrush, one maybe a mockingbird, and one he couldn't identify. All had little chips and scratches and one, the base broken off, lay on its side.

"These are me," she said, drawing deeply on her second cigarette. "See how dull the female colors are. Howard was brighter, but he got broke. The Howard that went with these." She exhaled. "*Shattered* might be a better word."

"I don't follow."

"Back when we were first married and Howard seemed to like women as well as he liked birds, I bought a pair of songbirds for him our first Christmas together—the two of us, you see—and he liked the idea, so every Christmas I bought a new pair."

She stood and opened a cabinet door and took down a bottle of bourbon. "Want some sweetener in your coffee?" She poured a generous portion into her cup.

"Awfully early, but yes—I'll take a bit." He slid his cup toward her and she tilted the bottle.

"There are four birds here, so you can surmise that for at least four years I thought enough about him and us to buy a pair of birds each Christmas. Actually it was six years, but I smashed two of me before I decided to save what was left."

"You broke all of the Howards?"

"When I came home one day and found him in the shower with a student—Howard thought I was staying over in New Orleans—I ran the boy off and came into the kitchen to get a bottle and saw the birds hanging there and I just went into a rage and smashed all six Howards and two Emilys on the floor here. He shattered beautifully. Millions of little pieces of bright-colored porcelain, all over the tiles. The real Howard was standing in the doorway there with his fingers to his mouth like a little old lady watching puppies being slaughtered. Then I got to thinking about how absurd it was to smash all the Emilys, so I put what was left of me in the drawer there and told him he'd better not touch them. That's where I stay."

"Then—"

"These are all gifts from his boyfriends. Every new one gives him a set. Well, most of them." She swept her arm about the kitchen. "Tradition, you know. And when one doesn't get around to thinking about it, Howard buys a pair himself. You can see how many lovers he's had, and not all of them ranked a bird."

"How many years?"

"Howard's been a *declared* fag for five years or so." She drank from her spiked coffee. "He gets far more than a pair a year. Monogamy is not his strong suit when it comes to the *boyzzz*."

"And they don't bother you?" he asked.

"The birds, or the boys?"

"Both."

She smiled and cleared her throat. "No, not really. I'm used to them now. I'd miss them, I think, if they weren't around. The birds *and* the boys."

"Do they—do they, you know, mess around when you're in the house?"

"Sometimes. He tries to bring'm in when I'm not here, but there've been times when I went right on with what I was doing while they did whatever the hell they do back in his bedroom. Lots of times they stay over. Hell, I've even cooked for'm a few times."

"Jesus, I just don't see how you can stand it."

"Jack, you stand it when you have to. You'd be surprised what you can endure when you have to. What am I going to do, leave? No way. This is where I *live*. This is as much *my* fucking house as it is his. And if I kicked him out, the way I've threatened to do a thousand times, where in the world would he go? As I've told you before, it's more like I'm Howard's mommy now, putting up with little boys. Besides, it's just not that bad once you get used to it."

Stafford stared at her. "Emily."

"Jack, why are you here? You didn't just drop by to talk about me and Howard."

"I needed to talk to you—about something that's happened."

"Things not going well with you and the milkmaid, or has she evolved into the Baron's daughter?"

He shook his head. "There are problems, yes. I just needed someone to talk to."

"And you came to tell *me* about it," she said. "How sweet. I'm flattered."

"Emily, there's more to it than things not just going well . . . ."

"It's about what happened in New Orleans, isn't it?" She put the single birds back into their drawer.

"How do you—"

"Never mind about how I know."

"Em, how much do you know about what happened to us in New Orleans?"

She shrugged. "Enough to know that I probably don't need to know anymore."

"How? I didn't say anything, and I know Susie—"

"A cop came to visit me," she said.

"*What* cop?"

"A detective. From New Orleans."

"Came here?"

"Sat right where you're sitting," she said. "He asked about the birds too. Maybe anybody would."

"He give you his name?" Stafford asked.

"Of course he gave me his name. Do you think I would have let him in if he hadn't identified himself? Saw his badge, saw his pistol. He gave me his card."

"Who was he?" Stafford was standing now, looking out the window. "Not that I really have to ask."

"His name was—hell, I don't remember his name, Jack. Like

I say, I've got a card. I can get it." She lit another cigarette, took a deep drag, and blew smoke toward a pair of birds.

"A big black guy, right?"

"Big? Black? Hardly. Pushy little white guy."

Stafford jerked his head around. "He was *white*?"

"Yes, white. Red-headed, freckled—"

"A short, wiry little red-headed detective?"

"Yes, but what—"

"Oswalt," Stafford said. "You don't have to get the card. It was Oswalt. I figured it was Merchant. What the hell did *Oswalt* want with you?"

"All he wanted from me was information about *you*, Jack. And Susie. He wanted to know what I knew about what happened in New Orleans. Whether you'd said anything to me about what went on down there."

"Why did he come here, Emily?" Stafford sat back slowly in the chair.

"I told you, because he wanted to see what I knew about the New Orleans thing, Jack."

"Why would he come to see *you*?"

"Because you and I were lovers. Why do you think? We were lovers and everybody along the Coast who knows us knew it. He asked around and found out about *us*. That's simple enough. And I'll bet it didn't take long. He just figured that if anybody knew what happened in your private life, *I* would. He thought I might have something useful to him."

Stafford motioned for her to pour whiskey into his coffee. "Useful for what?"

"For whatever. Hell, I don't know, Jack. He said that something happened to the two of you in New Orleans and he wanted to know what I knew about it."

"What did you tell the little redheaded sonofabitch?"

Emily dashed liquor into their cups and set the bottle down. She smiled. "What *could* I tell him, Jack? I didn't know anything *to* tell him. I confirmed that you and I had had our little flourishes, shall we say, but that was it. Oh, and I told him that you said you got banged up by a bunch of boxes that fell on you at your mother's place."

"What did he tell you about New Orleans, Em?"

She drank from her cup. Then: "Only what he said at the beginning, that something happened to the two of you down there and he wanted to know what I knew about it. I didn't know anything about it, so I didn't tell him anything. When I told him what you said about the boxes falling on you, he seemed satisfied."

"Why didn't you call and tell me he came by here?"

"Because he told me *not* to, Jack. He didn't exactly threaten me, but he told me *not* to." She sipped slowly, the way a person drinks very hot coffee. "So I didn't. I don't figure I owe you anything. Besides, I got the idea after a few minutes that he probably isn't the kind of man you want to mess with, little or not. The guy's eyes—Jesus. He's one mean little bastard, you can bet on that. When he told me not to say anything to anybody, I took it to heart. It was a threat. Not in words, but it was a threat.

"We were sitting at this very table, and he leaned back and let his jacket fall open so that I could see a little black pistol in a holster under his armpit. That didn't just happen. He was telling me something. As a matter of fact, I feel uncomfortable talking to you about it now. I don't know what went on down there, and I'm not sure I *want* to know."

Stafford was really beginning to feel the whiskey. He shook his head. "Oswalt. That sonofabitching Oswalt."

"Jack, what's going on?" she asked. "One part of me says I don't want to know anything about it, but another part is dying to know."

He shook his head again. "I don't know myself, Emily, I honest to God don't have the foggiest notion what's going on."

"Are you getting on with your lives, Jack? Or are you letting this eat you up?"

His eyes swept across the birds again, those that he could see without turning around in his chair. "No, I'm not exactly getting on with my life. No need to give us a pair of songbirds for Christmas for damned sure."

She just looked at him.

"Did he say anything else, Emily?"

She shrugged. "No, not that I remember. He said that he wanted to know what you'd told me about what went on down there, and the box story seemed to sit well with him."

"Just wondered," he said, relieved.

"Goddamn it, Jack, what *did* happen in New Orleans?" She had emptied the cup and filled it again, half and half, with coffee and whiskey. "Can you talk about it?"

He dropped his head and stared at his hands. "No. Not

really. Susie says no. She doesn't want anybody to know about it. And her threat was very clear."

"Something bad happened down there," Emily said. "That much I'm convinced of. And you ran into something more than a box of books. That's still apparent from your face. Was there more to it than that? Did y'all get y'all's asses beat or have a run-in with the Law?"

"No."

"What happened to Susie, Jack?"

"You sure Oswalt didn't tell you?"

"He didn't tell me *anything*. He was trying to get information from me, not the other way around."

"She was raped," he finally said. "And beat up." He studied the two birds above the door. They spun slowly, clinked their beaks together, then swung back the other way until their tails touched. Then back the other way.

"Was it bad?"

"Bad," he said.

"What else did he do to her?"

"Not he—*they*."

"Who?"

"Just . . . just a bunch of guys."

"Oh, my lord, Jack. What else did they do to her?"

Stafford slid back from the table and stood, unsteadily, then leaned over the sink and squinted into the morning-bright sky. He turned and reached for the bottle. Emily slid it into his hand.

"What else, Jack? You came to talk, and I'll listen, although I probably ought not to. Jesus, that guy looked like he could kill me without blinking an eye."

"He probably could, so what I tell you, you'd better forget."

"I will. I promise."

"They brutalized her, Emily. They raped her repeatedly, sodomized her, beat on her for hours. Shot her up with drugs. She got a hell of an education in one night."

"Oh, my God, Jack. I'm so sorry. I had no idea what went on down there, only that something very bad happened to the two of you. How did *you* get in on it?"

He sighed. "I was with her when they snatched her. They beat me up." He could still feel a dull ache in his temple and the lump on his jaw, though smaller, was discernible yet. He knew the bruises still showed. "Beat the hell out of me."

"Where were you?"

"Walking down the street in the middle of the afternoon. Not three blocks from the Quarter."

Emily lit another cigarette and blew smoke through her nostrils.

"Why'd it happen, Jack?"

"Because I was there. In the way. I had her purse."

"No. Why did they grab *her*? I mean, if she'd been by herself I could see some guys grabbing her off the street, but . . . ."

Stafford took a slug directly from the bottle. "I'm—I'll be Goddamned if I know, Em, Goddamned if I know." His eyes were on the pair of cardinals on the window ledge before him, their beaks touching. "I don't know."

"Jack, why in God's name would they grab a woman off the street with her husband along? This doesn't make any sense. Did they take her purse? Maybe they were after money and and jewelry and assaulted her when they didn't get what they wanted."

"I hung onto the purse. And *nothing* makes much sense anymore." Stafford picked the bottle up again and tilted it back, letting the burning liquor surge in and down. His eyes watered. He set the bottle on the edge of the sink, where it balanced briefly, then tumbled over, gurgling whiskey down the drain. He snatched it up and steadied it far back on the counter against the backsplash.

"Where's the top?" he asked her. He was looking out the window again. "I've got to stop this."

Emily dropped the cigarette into her coffee cup, where it extinguished with a sharp hiss, and rose to her feet. With one hand on the table to steady herself she stepped over and capped the bottle, then moved in behind Stafford and wrapped her arms around him.

"My poor darling," she whispered, holding her face against the back of his neck. "My poor Jack. Looks like you're in one of your cheap novels now. I just hope it ends well for you."

"Oh, Emily," he tried, but the more he tried to talk, the more he blubbered. He suddenly wanted her, naked, in her bed, in her kitchen, anywhere at all. He wanted a woman. With a clumsy sweep of his arm he turned around and kissed her. He could feel hot tears on his face. His hands worked at the buttons on her blouse as he pressed himself against her.

She pushed away from him. "Jack, no, no—this is not a homecoming here. I can't do this."

He spun her around against the cabinet and with fumbling

fingers tried again to undo the tiny buttons, then gave up on them and yanked the lapel of the blouse to the side. Buttons popped and sprang and danced across the cabinet top and floor as she tried to twist away from him.

"Em, please, please."

"God-damn it, Jack, *no*. This is not going to happen!" She pushed him away far enough to duck down and out of his arms. He held onto her blouse as she spun free of him, then stood there with it in his hand, ripped halfway down the back, while she retreated slowly from the kitchen, her hands across her breasts. She pointed to the blouse dangling in his open hand. "Look at what you did! Goddamn it, Jack. Get out of my house!"

He lurched forward as she backed out of the room. "Em, please. I need you, Em."

"What you need is your *wife*, Jack," she said from the end of the dim hallway.

He had his pants at his feet and his shorts almost to his knees. He sat down on the hallway floor and kicked his shoes off, yanked his pants and shorts off, and whipped his shirt over his head. Naked, he rose to his knees and stared unsteadily at her where she trembled in the doorway of her bedroom, her eyes fixed on the crazy man weaving on the floor like an enchanted snake.

"Jack," she whispered harshly, "you are a pitiful sight. Put your clothes back on. Don't make me call someone."

He stood and stumbled to her and gathered her into his arms. She remained ramrod straight in the doorway with her arms at her sides as he fumbled with her breasts and thrust himself at her crotch.

"God, I need you, Emily," he panted. "I *need* you."

She tried to push him away. "You're acting like a damned animal, Jack. Please get yourself together and leave. This is not going to *happen*."

He shoved her across the room onto the bed and grabbed her skirt with both hands and snatched it downward and off with one rough motion. She looked at the ceiling and dropped her hands to her sides and stared straight up as he removed her panties and spread her legs and forced himself into her. He grunted and slammed against her.

"Jack, please stop. I don't want this. This is not *you*."

For an answer he rose on his hands and drove harder into her.

Suddenly Emily's hands shot up and he felt as if giant talons had seized him. She fixed her eyes on his. He stopped moving.

"Do you want me to tear your face completely off? I will do it, then I will charge you with rape. I'll have a yard of your skin under my fingernails, and your face will look like a plowed field—" She relaxed her grip a little. "Just stop a minute, Jack. Think about what you are doing. Listen to me."

Stafford loomed over her but he did not move.

"Now, you're doing to me exactly what they did to her. I don't *want* you, Jack. I've been through my withdrawal phase and I'm over you. You are *raping* me." She clenched his face again until he winced. "You are like them now. An animal, grunting and snorting like a pig. What you need is a whore, a fifty-dollar whore, or just go jerk off somewhere."

He stared down at her as she loosened her hands from his face. He could feel the sting of her fingernails on his cheeks.

"Now," she said, sliding up onto the bed away from him and closing her legs, "you put your clothes on and leave. I do not want you in me. I do not want you in my house. If you can't afford the fifty dollars, I'll give it to you, but you go and find yourself another woman. Or whip yourself off. I don't care what you do to satisfy your need, but I will not do that for you. Not anymore."

She put on her panties and rolled off the bed, took a robe from the closet and pulled it on and tied it. "Now," she said, her back to him, "I'm sorry about your face, but it'll clear up in a little bit. There may be some small scratches. You can just tell your wife that you did it trimming bushes or something. You're lucky I didn't really hurt you. And as long as we're talking about scratches, what happened to your belly and legs? That's too fresh to have happened in New Orleans. You look like you've been dragged across a beach."

"That's pretty close." Still nude, he curled up on the bed and held his head in his hands. Emily slowly turned and looked down at him, then knelt beside him, holding him the way a woman would comfort a frightened child.

"My poor abused little boy. Go home, Jack. You need your wife, and she needs you. Everything heals in time." She stroked his hair and held him in silence a very long while. There, there," she said, nuzzling him, "there, there."

XVIII

For Jack Stafford time passed slowly over the final weeks of summer and crept into autumn, drily ticking away as he and his wife distanced themselves from their dreadful trip to New Orleans. Her face healed, and his, and the pain in his side went away, but the great gulf between them had widened and deepened, so that they rarely spoke to each other, and when they did the conversation was terse and focused. What would she like for dinner? Did she need anything from the store? Would it be better to use bleach or not with the load he was washing. She was insulated and isolated from him by a wall that was impenetrable, as palpable as brick.

Susie ate very little now, and Stafford could not determine whether she got any decent sleep at all. He went to sleep each night after a brisk kiss with her light burning, though her eyes seemed to be looking through the pages of the book she was reading from rather than at them. Sometimes he would wake well into the night and find her, book still in hand, lying there with her eyes closed, and when he reached and switched off the light she would rouse and turn it back on and fix her eyes on the book again. And then there were those dreadful nights when she awakened him, twisting and moaning. Each morning when he got out of bed she was already up—usually dressed in a tee-shirt and shorts, or, now that cooler weather was approaching, in a sweatshirt and jogging pants—sitting at the kitchen table, thumbing through the newspaper and drinking coffee.

He would say good morning and lean and kiss her and she would meet his lips like a bird stabbing at an insect, quick, cold, lips firm and lifeless, almost like a beak. Then he would sit across from her and have his coffee and read sections of the paper she had finished. If it were a school day, he would silently prepare a simple breakfast and kiss her goodbye, go to the library and put in his hours, then come home to find her still at the table or lying in bed reading. On weekends he would piddle around the house, buy groceries, and read his novels.

What she did during the day he had no way of knowing. There was never any evidence that she went anywhere. It was obvious that she read a great deal, judging from the stack of books and magazines by the bed, but there had been no change in what she was reading. There were the same light romances she had read before and *Redbook* and *Southern Living*. When he tried to talk to her about how her day had gone, she had very little to say—*pretty dull, same as usual, all right, about average*, etc.

When he got in from work, he would sometimes walk around and go in through the back door so that he could pass close to her car and feel the hood, but it was always cool to his touch, and there was never any indication that the engine had been run. One day he went out and cranked it up just to keep it limber and mentally noted the mileage. Two weeks later the mileage had not changed.

If Stafford asked her whether she'd like to go out for dinner, her answer was always "Not now, Jack, I need more time. More time," the same response she gave when he asked her for sex. There had been no more sex since that night in the tub. She turned from him every time he tried to bring the subject up, and when he touched her, except for the quick, dry good-night or good-bye pecks in the mornings, she pulled away, not coyly, but abruptly, leaving him without words to address her. She refused to talk about it. Consulting with a counselor was out of the question—this Susie was emphatic about—and Stafford knew, after weighing and analyzing the problem from every angle, that he had no answers, no solutions. He had said nothing to her about Merchant's visit, though he was certain that she had seen the big detective on the porch. It was best, he concluded, to let time work whatever miracle it could. All he could do was wait.

Whatever notions he had of their lives returning to that innocent age they had known were slowly disappearing. There was no open animosity between them, simply a distance, a gulf, a coldness that neither seemed terribly eager to address, he because he had no notion how to approach her now and she for a reason that he could not fully fathom, though surely the savagery of her experience would take much time to get over. This he understood, and more. If ever he could retrieve his girl-wife from the shadowy woman she had become, it would take every resource he could call on, and greater strength than he was sure that he could summon.

Now they were on Horn Island, mid-afternoon on a Friday, this the first day of what he planned to be a full weekend trip out. It was something that he proposed and she had, to his great surprise, agreed to. It was not exactly agreement—she simply did not object. She said that since she had nothing else to do she would go. It was something to do. At least no one would see them on the island.

He borrowed Jerry Harmon's small powerboat and met her at the old Coast Guard station near the mouth of the Pascagoula. She sat in the car until he tied up at the dock and walked over and opened the door for her.

"Ready?" he asked.

"I guess so." She swept her eyes around the parking lot, studied the faces of the people near the dock. "Do you have everything in the boat?"

"Everything except your bag." He pointed at the blue overnighter she had brought with her.

She reached and got the bag and her drawing equipment, which she had wedged behind the seat.

"You're going to paint, I see," he said.

"Maybe. Depends." She clamped a white beach hat on her head and adjusted her sunshades. She wore a white jumpsuit, and a thin white scarf curled around her neck and rose to the chin. She was white from head to foot

"People are going to wonder who I'm taking to sea," he said.

"Let'm wonder."

She walked in silence beside him and allowed him to help her into the boat. She took a seat forward and stared straight ahead as he eased the boat out of the estuary and into the Gulf. She kept her face into the wind all the way to the island.

He crouched in their old camping spot, the ice chest and rolled-up tent and sacks of provisions surrounding him like a man who has circled wagons for the night to guard against whatever threat might be arrayed in the dunes or in the darkening trees beyond.

Between him and the beach, just outside the circle, Susie sat, her legs drawn up tight to her chest, eyes fixed on the vast Gulf that stretched out before her. When they reached the camp site she had taken off her scarf and hat and jumpsuit, beneath which she wore a pair of cut-off jeans and an old denim shirt. On the back of the shirt at some time she had drawn in acrylics a clump of sea oats.

There was no sign of the marker they had left. In a way he was glad—one of the last things he wanted to see again was a cross. He felt so dreadfully alone, as if a universe of cold stars separated them and not just a few feet of still-warm sand.

He rose and walked down to her. "I'm glad you came," he said as the surf rolled in and swished and rolled back out again.

"Me too." She pulled her legs beneath her on the sand. "It's good to be away from the house, and you couldn't have chosen better weather."

Faint bruises still ran along her upper arm, but they were fading like distant rained-out storm clouds, yellowish-purple and vague, and her face had recovered its youthful perfection.

With quickened pulse he reached and took her hand, though he did not look at her, nor she at him. She did not try to pull her hand away. In the corner of his eye he could see her hair loose in the breeze and brilliantly blond in the late sun, which was at least two hours from touching the Gulf to the west. It was all he could do to keep from pulling her to him, but he knew that patience was the key now, a slow, careful reknitting of the fabric that had been torn. This would be the night, he hoped, when they could renew their faith and come together as they had that other night in this spot, when they blended their bodies for the first time.

"Do you want to walk down the beach?" he asked her. "We can set up the tent later. I'll light the Coleman if I have to."

She stood and brushed the sand off her legs. "Just leave everything like it is, Jack. I'm not sure I want to spend the night out here. Let me think about it. I would like to go and sketch some. You come and get me later, before dark." She said it in a tone that left no room for argument.

"Would you like to swim first? It's not too cool."

"Not really," she said.

"So where'll I find you?"

"Over there." She pointed down the beach toward the falling sun. "In the dunes. Follow my tracks. You'll find me."

He shrugged. "If that's what you want."

"Yes." She walked up past him and removed her sketchpad and handful of chalks from one of the bags. She slipped the pieces of chalk into her shirt pocket and clamped the pad under her arm.

"I'll be along to get you in an hour or so," he said. "I think I'll cast a little."

She did not answer. He watched her walk slowly toward the surf, then west, keeping just at the edge of the water. *Dear God, will it ever come right again*?

He sat on the ice chest and had a beer, then walked down to the surf and cast awhile, working up and down the beach from the campsite. The sun fell relentlessly toward the water, squatting finally, an angry ball of molten fire that seemed to intensify as it sank, then sliding perceptibly into a sea that seemed to dissolve the fire and spread it across the whole horizon. Halfway expecting to hear it hiss out, he was amazed at how quickly it dropped until nothing but afterglow remained.

He carried his rod back up to the campsite, opened another beer, and drank it as he walked along the tideline, following the tracks his wife had made, the sand lit by the glow of the western sky stretched out like one vast smear of blood.

He followed her tracks just outside the slick sand of the tidal beach, a damp mantle dotted with fresh shells left by the the falling water, and soon he found her. She had deliberately kept just inside the white sand above the tideline, like a child afraid of water, and he could see where she had stepped up on the shelf where the water could not reach, but as far as he could tell she had not paused anywhere to look at anything, to study driftwood or a shell. She had kept to her purpose, walking westward on the beach toward the falling sun, which sank somewhere beyond that eyeball of water that stared off into space.

She sat on top of the dune where she had sat that day that seemed now so very long ago, her back to him, and for an instant he fancied that nothing had changed, that she was the girl she had been when with her sketchpad she had recorded in chalk pastels what she saw in the sky and trees and soft stretch of island in front of her, that day when her sketch showed green trees and palmettos and pelicans, which she thought were gulls, flying across a pale blue sky with puffy little clouds like ghosts.

She was twisted down in an uncomfortable looking hunch, legs folded under, the sketchpad on the sand beside her, staring out toward the distant line of trees, or beyond. A lone storm cloud skirted the coast, nearing the shipyard, whose lights were now blazing bright across the darkening water. All along the shore, lights stretched out as far as he could see.

He climbed the dune and eased down beside her. "I didn't know you had come so far."

She turned and looked at him or past him into the red smear where the sun had been. Her face was expressionless, as if it held nothing for him, as if it were merely there like anything else that had washed up on the beach and tumbled in the wind to lodge on the high dune. He wasn't even sure that she could focus on him anymore.

"I thought you were coming sooner. I have decided that I want to go back tonight."

"But all the stuff—"

"I never did agree to spend the night out here, Jack. You reached that conclusion on your own. I want to go back. I'll help you load the boat."

"It'll be way after dark by the time we get in the river. Those crabtrap markers are going to be hard to spot."

"You can do it. You've done it before. I can hold a light."

"OK. If that's the way you want it." He pointed at the sketchpad. "Have you drawn anything?"

She nodded and picked the pad up and held it out to him. She did not speak.

He kneeled before her and accepted it and lifted the heavy cardboard lid, turning it under. But there was only a blank page.

She reached and flipped the page and in the twilight a panorama of savage color leapt at him. She gripped the corner of the pad and twisted it until it was horizontal on his lap. Then he saw shapes rise out of surrealistic slashes of red and orange, black and green. This time the sky was the color of a bruise, and towering clouds with anvils swirling out from their tops trundled across it. Beneath the ominous sky the trees were stark, their arms flung out, with here and there an osprey nest wedged in their crotches, pale chrysalises with cruelly curved beaks thrust out of them, like some hellish scene out of Breughel or Bosche, but what caught his eye much more than the sky and the trees was the thick spiral of vultures at whose base an animal lay splayed, a confusion of red and black, unidentifiable organs spilling out on the sand, its visage grotesquely twisted by pain as if the animal still felt the fierce lacerating beaks. And in the foreground the beach was clotted with cans and jars, lumps of tar, snarls of rope, and rusty wire mesh. Horrid shapes of driftwood, like sun-bleached bones of the shattered dead, jutted from the sand.

He shook his head. "You drew this?"

"Yes."

"While you've been here? You did all this this afternoon?"

"It's not finished," she said. "I've been working on it for days. It's one reason I wanted to come back out here. To get the colors right."

Stafford looked toward the trees. "I don't see these colors, these shapes. There are no buzzards out there. I've never seen your sketches with so much color, and with such violence."

She shrugged and stared off away from him. "What do you know about it?"

"I don't understand, Susie. What is all this? You haven't sketched what's out here. This isn't you."

"You don't know what's me and what isn't, Jack. Not anymore. And you don't know *what* I see." She was looking toward the line of dark trees. "And I'm not sure I do either. I sketched what my mind saw, and it was like something or someone was guiding my hand." She pointed to the drawing. "It was almost like I didn't have any control over what my hand drew there. I am so damned *confused.*"

"Susie," he tried.

"Jack, listen to me." She reached and clutched his arm with surprising strength.

"What? What, Susie. Talk to me."

"I didn't tell you everything he said." She still was not looking at him.

"Everything *who* said?" He held the pad out to her and she loosened her grip on his arm and took it.

"The man."

"What man, Susie?"

"*The* man, Jack. Satan."

Stafford leaned toward her and placed his hand on her shoulder, but she withdrew from his touch. "What else did he say?"

"He told me, Jack."

Stafford held his breath. "Told you *what*? *What* did he tell you?"

"He told me—he told me why they took me." Then she turned to face him. The red evening was reflected in her eyes.

"He—"

"He told me, Jack. He told me what you told that bartender. And, by the way, *he* was the white guy who raped me. I remembered the rings he wore. And those ghastly hairy arms."

"But, Susie, you said—"

"I guess I didn't want to believe it at first. And then, once I did start believing it . . . I mean, how could he have made that up, or *why* would he? Once I did start believing it, I wasn't certain I wanted to hurt you." She held the pad in her lap. "Not that you didn't deserve being hurt."

"But now you've decided to?"

"I decided that if we are ever going to get on with our lives I've got to tell you everything."

"Susie, I just don't know what to say to you."

"And he told me that it didn't matter who I was or who I belong to, that if I wanted to be with him I could be. He'll take me. No matter who I am. Any time I want to go." She turned her face back toward the trees. "Jack, I'm not sure who I belong with or to anymore. He was so gentle . . . ."

Stafford just stared at the woman before him. "Susie—" He clenched his eyes and still he saw her face against the sky, the image reversed, the sky a pure white, her face and hair dark.

"My life is a ruin, Jack, hollow and senseless, and I can't get a focus on it anymore. I don't know who to trust, who to turn to. It's like my head has been emptied out and filled up with things I never knew before. It's like I've seen through to the other side of something, but I don't know what, and I can't make out the shapes." She closed the sketchpad and scooped up her things. "Come on, now. I want to go back."

Stafford watched as his wife descended the dune and walked toward the slick tideline. His eyes swept the darkening landscape once more and settled on the red-gold spread of sun-emblazened sky beyond the great eyeball of water that stared off into nothing. Now Jack Stafford understood about Pompeii and China and Greece and the immense energy of the sun, the boiling fountains of light of the stars, the cold barren loneliness of timeless space, and man's ridiculous folly and puny, tragic insignificance in it all, a creature that found substance and meaning and value only through the wild dreams he conjured in his haunted head. As he knelt there on the hill of sand watching in the afterglow of the western sky the shadows of evening settle on the island like black ashes, or dust or sand, swallowing everything into a suffocating wordless dark, Jack Stafford finally understood.

XIX

The knock was soft at first, then urgent and loud. Hair still damp from a shower, she rose from the bed and clenched her robe around her and descended the stairs. Against the thin curtain of the kitchen door was the shadow of a man's head. The knock came again.

"I know you're in there," a voice said quietly. "I'm here for you."

She stood silently in the sunlit kitchen a few seconds, then cracked the door the distance the security chain would allow.

"You ready to go?" he asked.

"Who *are* you?"

"You called and he sent me."

"*He* sent you?"

"Yeah," the man said. "You told him you wanted to see him, didn't you?"

"Yes," she said. "But I thought *he* would come."

"He's a busy man. You can't expect him to come up here just because you want to talk with him. You got to go to *him*. Open the door."

"But who *are* you?" she asked.

"Look, lady, he sent me to get you. You called and said you wanted to talk to him, and I'm here to take you back down. It don't matter who I am."

"I don't want to go to New Orleans with you. I just want to talk to him. I thought *he* would come."

"Mrs. Stafford," the man said, his mouth at the door opening,

"I don't know what your problem is, but you can't leave me out here on the steps like this. I'd like to do this quiet and quick. If you want to talk about it, open the damned door and let me in."

"But I don't know you."

"You don't have to know me. You called the number and said you needed to speak to him and he sent me to get you."

"Why couldn't he talk to me on the phone?"

"He don't do things that way," the impatient voice came back. "Look, just let me come in the kitchen and sit down and we can decide what to do."

"But what's your name?" she asked.

"Jones," he said. "Just call me Jones. Bill Jones. Or Sam Slade or Jim Smith. I don't care what you call me—just let me in."

She pulled the robe tighter and leaned against the door, which he had blocked open with his shoe. "I think I made a mistake," she said. "Please go away. Just tell him to forget about the call."

"Lady," the voice came with force, "you done opened one door too many already, so you might as well open this one."

Then his shadow rose and filled the curtain and the door sprang open, the two little brass screws that had held the security plate skittered across the kitchen floor, and the man was standing before her as she pressed against the refrigerator. He aimed a small black pistol at her face.

"You had better not scream, lady. You had better not make a single Goddamned sound." He was a short man, sinewy, with red hair, hands and arms splotched with freckles. A downy hair covered his arms.

"Do I know you?" Her voice was a mere squeak.

"I doubt it," he said. He reached and closed the door with his foot. "Look, lady, I'm here to take you down there. That's all. I don't want no trouble." He motioned at the robe. "That what you plan to wear?"

"No," she said, backing away from him. "I don't want to go to New Orleans. I wanted him to talk to me—up here or on the phone. I just need to talk to him."

"Lady, you ain't got a fix on this thing. Satan ain't going to talk to you on the phone. And he damned sure ain't coming up *here.* You called, he sent me to get you. Now, get yourself ready. I ain't got all day. I told him I'd be back by noon."

"I know I remember you. From somewhere."

"I doubt it," he said. "And I don't give a shit whether you do or not. Now go get dressed in whatever you're going to wear."

She studied him a few seconds, her face twisted in thought. "I know I know you."

He pressed the gun to her chest. "It ain't likely. You're confusing me with somebody else. Now go on and get dressed. You are going to New Orleans."

She continued to study him.

"Quit looking at me and get ready," he said impatiently. "I don't want to get spotted here." He looked past the kitchen door curtain onto the back yard, where his car was parked. He had pulled it as far forward as the little yard would allow, but it was still visible from the beach road.

"I told you, I don't want to go to New Orleans." She had backed into the corner formed by two stretches of counter.

The man one-handedly pulled a cigar from his shirt pocket, unwrapped it, licked its length, and lit it with a small red lighter. He stuffed the wrapper in his pants pocket and continued to stare at her. "And I told you that you *are* going. You shouldn't of called. He shouldn't of give you the number, but you shouldn't of called. You shoulda let it rest and everything would've been fine. Like I say, you done opened a door . . ."

"I just want to *talk* to him. He—"

"He said he'd see you. That's why I'm here."

"Why didn't *he* come?"

"I told you, he's busy. He's a big man. You're just lucky he's willing to see you."

"But he . . ."

"Look, Mrs. Stafford, I can't mess around here all day talking to you about this. Now, you get the hell ready and let's get out of here."

"I'm not going with you." She edged toward the door opening that led to the hallway.

He moved to intercept her. "Jesus, lady, why don't you make it tough? Can't you see this gun?" He held it up in his palm. "This is a *pistol*. I can shoot you with it. I have shot people with it before." He pointed to the counter. "I can wrap one of them dishrags around it and won't nobody hear a sound. Now, you got to do what I say."

She backed into the corner again. "Please don't touch me."

In a move so sudden that she had time enough only to jerk her head back, striking a cabinet door, he was on her, spinning her around and pinning her forward on the counter, hands behind her back. He slipped the pistol into his belt holster and held her wrists with one hand while with the other he stuffed a damp dish towel into her mouth so that the scream could not come. Then she was on the floor on her stomach, the little man astraddle her. He pulled her arms around and handcuffed her and rolled her over onto her back. "Jesus," he gasped, settling against a cabinet door and looking at her between his knees, "it's hard to wrestle a woman and smoke a damn cigar."

He pulled the pistol out and held it to her head. "Now, I'm gon' take that rag out of your mouth, but you'd better keep quiet. You understand? I'll beat the bloody hell out of you if you yell."

She nodded and he removed the dishrag and tossed it onto the counter. "Not a fucking sound."

"You're hurting me," she said quietly. "My hand is folded back." She had kept her legs clamped together but her robe had fallen open and the man was staring at her panties.

"Oh, sweet Jesus." He breathed deeply. "If I thought that sonofabitch wouldn't notice it, I'd sample you myself, you sweet little piece of cream." He snatched her to her feet. "Now, one way or another you are going to get dressed and we're going to New Orleans. And I ain't taking any chances on you yelling." He twisted her around and wedged the rag back into her mouth.

"Hate to waste this thing, but the social visit is over." The pistol still trained on her, he leaned and snuffed his cigar at the sink and one handedly shredded it, washed it down the drain, then pushed her before him into the hallway. There he turned her around to face him. "Where are your clothes at?"

She nodded up the stairway.

"Let's *go*. And stop that damn sniffling."

In the bedroom she motioned toward a closet with her head. He had forced the rag so tightly in her mouth that she could barely breathe, and when the tears came her nose stopped up. She was struggling for air.

He uncuffed her and yanked off the robe, keeping one strong hand on her shoulder, and a finger and thumb held her in some sort of dreadful clench that made it almost impossible for her to move. "God-*damn*." He held her before him and stared at her body. "I reckon I can see why he wants you back down there. Too bad you ain't like a bag of candy, where I could just get one little bitty piece and nobody would miss it."

He pulled her over to the closet and reached in and got a dress, then threw her on the bed and straddled her, pinning her arms to her sides with his legs. "Now, I'm going to stand you up and get a dress on you, and I'm going to take out that rag so that you can breathe better, but I got to give you a little something first. It'll help you relax."

She struggled at that, but the man's strength was too great, and she could do little more than roll her head and toss her body against him as he removed from his rear pocket a flask-sized case from which he took a syringe.

He slapped her hard across the head. "Now, you be still. I don't want to break this Goddamned needle off in you." She quieted and he inserted the needle on the inside of her upper arm. Her body flowed back on the bed as the little man astride her smiled and pulled the rag from her mouth. He whispered and ran his hands over her breasts, then removed her panties. Her eyes flared, then dulled.

Stafford drove home for lunch, as he had every day since going back to work after what he came to think of as the Return from Hell. He parked in the driveway and checked the mail out by the street before going in. Susie never even went for the mail anymore. He had mentioned that morning that he might be in for lunch but not to fix anything—he'd just make a hotdog or something. He wasn't sure she cared whether he came in or not. She never ate anything with him at any meal, just watched him across the table as he took one small bite at a time. He wasn't sure when she ate, *if* she ate, though gradually they went through the little sacks of groceries he brought in. It was easy enough to determine from the liquor bill that she was drinking a hell of a lot.

"Susie," he yelled as he went through the front door, "it's me."

No answer came back, so he pulled off his jacket and draped it across a chair, washed his hands in the downstairs bath, and went into the kitchen. There was a vague smell of cigar smoke. Stafford stood with his hands on the table and looked around the room. Something wasn't right. The kitchen door was ajar, and Susie almost never went outside in the daylight. He went to the foot of the stairs and called for her, but the only sound he heard was the swish of traffic from the street. When he looked back toward the kitchen door, he saw the deadbolt keeper lying on the floor next to the doorway to the hall.

"Shit," he said and bounded up the stairs. But there was no sign of Susie, only that smell of a cigar. He looked out on the porch and down onto the lawn, then went back inside. "What in hell is going on?" he asked out loud. His eyes played over the room again and he saw in a corner one of the rags from the kitchen. "What the hell!" He picked it up and started for the door, but something at the edge of the bed skirt caught his eye. He leaned down and picked up a little blue piece of foil.

It was the top strip of a condom package. He ran his finger along the inside and sniffed the lubricant, still fresh.

"Oh, sweet Jesus."

His head reeled as he sat down on the bed. He held in one hand the dishrag, in the other the little piece of foil. "Oh, my God." He stood and looked around the room again.

Her purse was on the bedroom dresser, and her make-up case was in the bathroom closet. Stafford sat down on the bed and looked out over the Gulf. Where? Where the hell could she be? Somebody had broken through the kitchen door and something had happened in the bedroom. Somebody had recently used a condom there, and it hadn't been him.

After a few minutes he went down to the kitchen and poured himself a stiff drink and shot it down. It scalded his throat, but within seconds he could feel the warmth pooling in his stomach, then radiating over his body. He poured another one and turned and leaned against the counter. There had to be some explanation.

The lingering faint smell of the cigar slowly began to stir in the dark of his mind. A cheap cigar. Where had he smelled precisely that smell before? He slugged the second drink and studied the table and kitchen floor. Someone smoking a cheap cigar had sat at or stood beside the table sometime that morning, leaving a little trace of ash by one of the legs and over by the sink. Part of a rubber package, the dishrag, the smell of a cheap cigar. It just didn't fit. Had the guy come and they sat in the kitchen talking and then moved upstairs to the bed? But why the broken safety latch?

Stafford walked onto the front porch and shaded his eyes toward the beach. He came back in and sat down at the table with his third drink. "I just don't—" He noticed the cigar smell again. "Something bad's happened here."

He picked up the phone and started to dial 911, then hesitated. He took out his billfold and removed a little white card and called a number on it.

XX

Through the rearview mirror he watched the thin man park his car off to the side of the road, get out and look around, then start down the rutted lane, leaping from one high spot to another to avoid patches of thick dark mud. A morning mist was clearing. Once he stopped to scrape something off his shoe with a stick. His face was red with agitation.

When the thin man was beside the car, he motioned with his head. "Get in."

The man walked around the rear and opened the door and slid onto the front seat. He looked down at his shoes.

"Don't worry about the car," Merchant said. "It'll clean up."

"I'm not worried about your Goddamned car. I'm worried about my shoes. I'll never get this shit off. Damned gumbo. Couldn't you have picked a better spot for this? Whatever the hell this *is*."

"I'm not worried about your shoes, Oswalt. And *this* is what is known as a meeting."

"OK, now that we've decided that neither one of us is too worried about the mud on me, what the hell is this *meeting* all about?"

Merchant glanced through the mirror again. "Didn't Jimmy tell you?"

"That little fart was babbling about Satan and drugs and whores. I couldn't make much of anything out of what he was saying. Stoned as a Goddamned rock. Why don't *you* tell me."

"He managed to tell you that we needed to talk, didn't he?"

"Yeah," Oswalt said, "I got that much sense out of the little dumb-ass. Otherwise I wouldn't be here. Now what's this about?"

"What'd you do with her?" Merchant asked. He had his left hand down beside his seat, his right one between his legs.

"What did I do with—"

"Don't *fuck* with me, Oswalt. What did you do with the girl?"

The detective giggled like a nervous little boy and sniffed. "So that's what this is about. Jesus, that never crossed my mind. Hell I was hoping—never mind. The girl? The Stafford girl? Well, whatever it is to you, I screwed her, for one thing." He giggled again and shook his head.

"Oswalt—"

"Right there on the librarian's bed, out cold as a cucumber, but I just had to sample it." His fingers were tapping furiously on his thigh. "She didn't resist—guess you'd call it consent."

"Oswalt . . ."

"Sweet Jesus, that is one fine woman. Even when she's out cold."

"I don't want to hear about that. Where'd you take her to?"

"What the hell is this to you, Merchant? And how'd you know it was me?"

"None of your business what this is to me. Stafford called me. He smelled your cheap-ass cigar smoke. That give me a pretty good idea who did it. And you left part of one of your rubber packages by the bed. I assume you still carry the blue ones you're always raving about. What do you call'm? Blue what?"

"Blue Angels. They're expensive. So thin you can read the newspaper through'm, but tough as a bullhide. Cost a lot more than my cigars." He sighed. "He deduced it from the cigar smoke. Ain't them Goddamned librarians *somethin'*? Real Sherlock there."

"Naw, I'm the one did the deducing. Of course anybody could be using rubbers with blue packages, but you been up there snoopin' around too. I know about that."

"Damn, you're acting like a detective too, Merch. Why don't you go and try to find some bad guys and stay out of this?"

"Why'd you take her, Oswalt?"

"Smelled my cigar, found part of a rubber package. Looks like I got a little careless. Shit. What *is* this, Merchant?" He was looking at the bayou ahead. "She made a call, called Koontz. Said she wanted to talk to him."

"Why?" Merchant asked. "Why would she call that bastard?"

"Aw, man, she's confused is all, life's bad fucked up. Got it in her head she needed to talk to him. He was hoping he'd never hear from her again. Course, he was stuck enough on her to give'r that private number of his. Y-O-S-A-T-A-N. That's his number—YOSATAN. Can you *believe* this shit? It's a wonder that dumb bastard's lasted as long as he has."

"And he sent you up there to get her?"

The little detective nodded. "Yeah. When she called, he had to send somebody. Long as he didn't hear anything else, he figured it was a closed issue. *I* thought it was over. Didn't nobody up there know a thing. They hadn't told anybody. The librarian told everybody a box of books had fell on his head. When she called, though, he got nervous, and when Satan gets nervous, folks jump. I was the safest one to send. Glad I got to go. Or *come*, I should say." He did his nervous laugh again, like a high school kid. "Lord, what a fine piece of woman. Even out cold."

"He's gon' kill her, ain't he?"

"Well, that depends on her, don't it? If she's willing to forget about being a Goddamned librarian's wife and go to work for him, he might not. I think he wants to play with her, too. The way a cat plays with a mouse. Depends on her. But, yeah, I 'spect he'll end up dumping her in a bayou somewhere. Let's say that he ain't gon' like her present attitude."

"Where *is* she, Oswalt?"

"Now, Detective Merchant, you know I'm not at liberty to discuss Mr. Koontz's business with you."

"How long have you been dirty, Oswalt?"

The detective pointed to his shoes. "Just got this mud on me."

"You've been dirty for so long you don't even remember when you started down. Did you have anything to do with them picking her up off the street?"

He shook his head. "Naw. No, no, no. That was just Stafford's dumb-shit fantasy that got her snatched. *Way* dumb. Ol' Harry believed him is all. Like there's ever been a two-thousand-buck-a-night hooker in New Orleans. Course, he just figgered Stafford was exaggerating the figure, but that maybe he *was* paying five hundred or a thousand. Whatever, he couldn't let it slide. Called Koontz, and it was the kinda thing he had to get checked out. You know, to make sure. If some good-looking broad was working his turf, he was ready to go to war, whatever she was making, and he had to find out whose stable she was in."

"You took her panties, didn't you?"

"Her panties?"

"At the hospital."

"How'd you figure that one out?"

"She told Stafford."

"*Had* to take'm. Too much they might could have learned from them panties. They could have been critical evidence if one of them dumb bastards left a trace of somethin', hair or juice or whatever. Do you know they went to the trouble of showering her down before dumping her on the street and then put her old clothes back on her, not just the dress but the panties. They shoulda just dropped her off naked or wrapped in a clean sheet. Dumb. Which is why they rarely live to be thirty. Too fuckin' *dumb*."

"Let me ask you again, politely—where did you take her?"

Oswalt squared around in the seat and leveled his eyes at the black detective. "Let me tell you, politely, you big black asshole, this ain't business that involves you, and I am not—"

Merchant's arm came around so fast that the little man had no chance to fend off the blow that sent his head against the door frame, his body flailing. The great gloved fist came down again and again until Oswalt was folded up on the floorboard like a rag doll. Merchant grabbed him by the collar and pulled him onto the seat, spun his body around as if it weighed nothing, and handcuffed his hands behind his back.

"Talk about it, you sonofabitch, or I'll kill you right here." He turned Oswalt back around and grabbed him by the ears and pulled his head up until his face was level with his own. His eyes were fierce. "You tell me or I swear to God I'll beat your scrawny white ass to a pulp right here in the seat of this car."

The man's lips moved, but no sound came.

"Speak up, Goddamn it. I'll rip your ears right off of your head. Snakes ain't supposed to have ears anyhow."

The lips moved again, but without sound.

Merchant shook him by his ears. His body hung like something dead, desiccated, its strength and passion gone, a bony husk.

"Let's try it this way—did you take her back to where he had her before? Just nod. You ain't got to talk."

Oswalt nodded.

"Anybody know about her besides you and Koontz?"

The little detective worked his head from side to side. Blood was seeping out of the corners of his mouth.

"Where is it? Where's the place? And you better not lie to me, Oswalt. What building is it?"

The little detective muttered something and Merchant shook him again. "Speak up, man!"

". . . old bindery," he managed. His lips barely moved.

"The old bindery building?"

Oswalt nodded. "Down—"

"I know where it's at," Merchant said. "Back to the room where they had her that night?"

Oswalt nodded.

"What floor? Top?"

Oswalt shook his head.

"Third?"

"No," he mumbled.

"Second?"

"Uh huh."

"You took her straight there? And nobody knows but you'n Koontz?"

He nodded.

"All right, you took her in there yesterday, early afternoon. Has he been there yet?"

"I don't know. I don't think so." His voice was stronger now, but his eyes had not opened. "I left her cuffed to the bed."

"Is she OK? Is she doped, or what?" Merchant eased him down into the seat and relaxed his grip, but he kept a big fist cocked.

"Yeah. She's all right. I give her some food last night and took her to the bathroom. Went by early this morning and took her to the bathroom again. Wouldn't eat anything. Then I shot her up enough to last awhile. He said he'd get by there today. Later."

"When later?"

"This afternoon is all I know. He had some kind of meeting last night and it went on this morning too." He shook his head slowly. "God-*damn*, you hit me hard, nigger."

Merchant smiled. "You call me that again and I'll break your fucking neck, you white-trash turd. You sure nobody else knows about her?"

"I don't think so."

"You telling me the truth, you little sonofabitch?"

"Yes." He was barely audible.

"All right, Goddamn it. But if I find out you're lying to me, I'll kill your ass. I'll blow your head off. Do you understand me?"

Oswalt nodded. "Can I go? Please?"

"You ain't going anywhere but into a car trunk until I get this checked out. You want to change your story at all? This is your last chance. You lie to me and I'll drag you out and kill you and feed you to the alligators."

"No," Oswalt said. "It's the truth."

"Good. By the way, asshole, I bet you didn't know cigars was so bad for your health." Merchant struck the little man a savage blow that knocked him against the door, then crooked his finger toward the thick brush that grew right up to the edge of the lane.

A slender black youth emerged from the wall of brush like a ghost and got into the back seat of the car. He stared at Oswalt, whose head rested against the window. The detective was moaning softly, his eyes closed.

"He don't look near as tough as he did the last time I seen'm," the boy said. "He ain't no bigger'n me."

"You know what they say about dynamite."

"What they say about dynamite?"

"It comes in—never mind. You know what to do." Merchant handed back a roll of duct tape. "Got your gloves on?"

The boy nodded and held up his hands. "What they say about dynamite?"

"I told you never mind about that." He grinned big. "You look like a doctor. Now, tape his mouth first, then his arms and legs, and do what I told you to do. You sure you got in here without anybody seeing you?"

"Yassuh."

"All right. Where's your car?"

"Back in yonder where you told me to leave it at."

"Can you handle him by yourself? Can you get him through the bushes?"

"He ain't big as me," the boy said. "I can't believe how skinny he is. Look like a red-headed snake, don't he?

"He *is* a snake. And he's got bad poison in him. Remember what they say about snakes, even when you think they're dead."

"What they say . . ."

"Jesus, never mind."

"You ain't got to worry. I rekkin I can handle this."

"No reckoning to it. The reckoning part is over. Now, I don't care what you do with his car, but get it the hell off the road. Drive it down this lane and hide it till tonight, way late, then get somebody to take it somewhere far off, up in the country somewhere, and strip it down. Keep what you want, sell what you can, and throw the rest—look, I don't give a shit what you do with it as long as it disappears. And I mean for good. Better not nothing surface."

"I know what to do," he said. "You ain't got to worry."

"OK." Merchant handed him a clutch of bills. "Here's a coupla hundred. The rest'll come when I know you done the job."

The boy nodded. "Since I got gloves on like a doctor and got my knife, be all right if I operate on him? Maybe cut his nuts off? You know what he done one time to—"

"I know lots of things he's done. I don't care what you do to him, as long as you do it later and finish the job you've agreed to. But watch that you keep that little sonofabitch taped up good, because he's mean as hell and if he gets a chance he'll kill you with his hands. Now get him out of here and do what you're supposed to do. And keep your mouth shut about it. Don't you tell nobody. Not *nobody*. Remember, I got enough on you that I can send your ass upriver—or down *under* it—anytime I want to. You know what I can have done to you." He stared stonily at the youth. "Jimmy, you don't want to fuck with me, do you?"

"Nawsuh, I don't. I do what you say and keep my mouf shut."

"See Oscar next week, Wednesday, seven in the evening. You know where at. He'll have the rest of your money."

"Oscar?"

"God*damn*," Merchant said, throwing his hands up. "Who'd I tell you to meet next Wednesday?"

"Yo' nephew."

"And what did I tell you his name is?"

The boy studied a second. "Name Oscar."

"That's right. Oscar. My nephew, Oscar. And where'd I tell you to meet him?"

"I 'member now. Oscar. Yo' nephew. At the bus station bafroom. I got it."

"You sure you got it straight?"

"Yassuh. I got it." The boy put his hand on the handle, then stopped. "What about his gun and money?"

"Take the money, but burn everything else in his wallet. Don't you keep none of them credit cards." Merchant said. "And burn anything you find in his pockets. When you're through with his keys, throw'm in a bayou or bury'm. I'll take care of the gun myself."

"How come I can't—"

"Because it would surface again, sure as shit, is how come." He reached and removed Oswalt's pistol from its holster and put it in his glovebox. "And Jimmy . . . ."

"Yassuh?"

"Don't you touch a single drop of liquor or drugs until this is done. You understand me? Not one drop or pinch of anything. You got to keep your head on right till this is done."

"Yassuh."

"Do everything just like I told you."

"Yassuh, jes' like you tol' me."

"Arright. Then get him taped up before he comes alive again. Be sure'n tape his mouth too."

"Yassuh." He got out, opened the passenger's door, and pulled the moaning Oswalt from the car onto the ground, where he taped the detective's mouth, then his arms and legs.

Merchant leaned over and held a key out to the boy. "Take them cuffs off of him and give'm here. And take a few more wraps. Be sure."

The boy removed the handcuffs and handed them and the key through the window, ran the roll of tape around Oswalt's legs and arms again, then grabbed him beneath the arms and disappeared into the brush. The rest of the thin body slithered in behind him and the foliage closed. Merchant shook his head and backed out of the lane. As he drove slowly past the other car, it began to sprinkle. Before he had reached the highway that would lead him back to New Orleans, it was pouring.

XXI

The two men in an old Ford truck were inching along the beach road in mid-afternoon traffic, headed west on 90 toward the highway that would take them north to Interstate 10.

"It wasn't necessary for you to come and pick me up. I could have driven down."

Merchant reached over and patted his arm. "It's OK, Jack, no problem. I'm just glad you didn't call the police here. I wish I could have got to you sooner. It just took a little more time to set things up than I thought it would."

"Set what up? You've got a plan? You know where she is? You didn't tell me shit when you called."

"Didn't have time to go into details. And yeah, I got a plan. I figure I know where she is. At least I know she's in New Orleans."

"But *why* is she in New Orleans is my question?" Stafford looked around the tattered interior again. "Is this all part of your plan?" The headliner was soiled and scratched and hanging loose above the driver's door, and the vinyl seat was split at every seam. At least fifteen years old, maybe twenty. He could smell exhaust fumes through his open window. "I don't understand all this fucking intrigue. Why's she down there? Why pick me up at school? And in this old truck?"

"You'll understand before it's all over. The bottom line is I didn't want anybody paying any attention to the vehicle or to us. Somebody might be watching the house, watching for you. We're supposed to look like average guys in a pickup, shipyard or oilfield workers—you know, salt and pepper trash."

"That why you're making me wear this?" He spread the front of the old green tee-shirt out before him and read *Oil Field Trash and Proud of It* upside down for the third time. Merchant had insisted that he put on the tee-shirt as soon as he got in the truck.

The detective adjusted the bill of his soiled Exxon cap down almost to his nose and smiled over at Stafford. "At's right, pardner. And if you'll look under your seat you'll find a cap for you."

Stafford reached down and felt around until he found the cap. He held it before him and read the label—New Orleans Saints. He put it on and turned the bill to the rear.

"That's the spirit," Merchant said, laughing, "but you'd better turn it back around and pull the bill down so nobody'll recognize you. Sorry I didn't pick you up sooner, but I've been one busy guy since your call. Now suppose while we drive down there you run over all that stuff you told me last night about what happened between your wife and those guys. I want to make certain I didn't miss anything."

"Jesus, Merchant, all this may be for nothing. For all you know, she may be way down on the beach somewhere." Stafford shrugged and slumped in his seat. "I just don't know."

"And I told *you*–she's in New Orleans. You let *me* do the figgering," the big detective said. "You just tell me again everything that she told you."

The sun was halfway across the sky to the west as they drove over the Pontchartrain Bridge. As he talked, Stafford studied the homes along the shore, wonderfully peaceful looking houses radiant in the sun, and before them, as if in a painting, brilliantly colored sailboats dancing on the bay.

After a long while he said, "Merchant, I've been doing all the talking. You talk awhile. What do you think's happened to her? If she's down here, where do you think she'll be?"

The big detective shrugged. "Ain't no way to be sure yet where she's at. Got some ideas. And I'm pretty sure I know what's happened to her. I wish you could have got through to me earlier."

"Tell me what you know. And I tried to get to you sooner. When I couldn't get you at work, I left that message at your house."

"I know. I just wish it could have been sooner. Man, I had one busy morning setting all this up."

"If she *is* in New Orleans, why would she come back?"

"Well, this much I can tell you—she didn't come on her own. Somebody brought her. And you know who they brought her to."

"But why? I told you everything she said about the whole thing. Twice. What would they come and get her for? She hasn't said a word to anybody about it."

"Jack, she made a phone call."

Stafford jerked upright in his seat. "What do you mean, a phone call?"

"She called the guy. She called Satan."

"Bullshit, Merchant. Why the hell would she do that? Where would she get *his* number? She look in the Yellow Pages under *pimp*?"

"He gave her the phone number when he had her. His private number. It was a very simple number for her to remember. You ain't gon' believe it. Y-O-S-A-T-A-N."

"Jesus. But why—"

"Man, he was *nice* to her is why, after them Goddamned thugs brutalized her. It's the way those sonsabitches work. It's the way they get the girls' confidence. They order their boys to beat and rape and sodomize these women, some of them just kids off the street, then they come in and treat them like they're in love with them, and most of the time it works. You know, like him showering with her and dancing and shit. Like he was in love with her. All he wanted to do was get her confidence. They fall for that shit. Only this time that bastard must have been shaking his head in disbelief. A young white blond, beautiful . . ."

"I can't believe that Susie would fall for it."

"Bullshit, Stafford. After what she'd been through. Like I told you up there that day I came by to visit, that woman you live with ain't the same one you brought down here that day. If you could be in her head for one Goddamned minute and know the jumble that's got to be up there, especially since she knows that you throwed her to the dogs, you'd understand why she wanted to talk to him. She had to talk to *somebody*. She had to try to make some sense of it all, and you wasn't much help. There just wasn't anybody else she could talk to. Man, you shoulda just broke down and throwed yourself at her feet, told her you were sorry for being such a stupid ass—"

"It wouldn't have done any good, Merchant."

"Maybe not, but it couldn't have hurt anything. She called to talk to the one man that seemed to understand her, that treated her with gentleness and respect, cleaned her up and fed her, that saved her from that pack of wild dogs her husband threw her to."

"Jesus, Merchant, lighten up."

"No, no, Jack, there ain't no lightening up, man. It gets heavier all the time, heavier from here on. Believe me, white boy." Merchant shook his finger at Stafford. "You know what she's going to go through now?"

Stafford watched the water. "What?"

"Satan has showed her the good side. Now he's got her back down there, he's gon' show her the bad side. He's gon' work her over hisself now. He'll beat the very hell out of her and screw her from stem to stern. Then he's gon' go sweet on her again. And he's gon' tell her how it'll be: 'Do right and you see my good side. Do wrong and you see the other.' And, Stafford, you gon' lose your wife for good. He's gon' shoot her up again and get her on the stuff, and she's gon' be hookin' for that sonofabitch at five hundred or a thousand bucks a night for ten or fifteen years, if she lasts that long, if she don't get killed or come down with AIDS or something. And if she don't agree . . . ."

Stafford swung his head from side to side. "My God . . ."

"Leave God out of it, boy, 'cause He ain't had a *thing* to do with it. You done it yourself, and it's up to you and me to get her out of there."

"Merchant, they've had her over twenty-four hours already."

"Well, again, if I got the straight scoop on what's happening, he's got her locked away somewhere until he can get around to her. That sonofabitch is a lot more interested in making money than he is talking to your wife, so he ain't in any damned hurry. And he sure ain't worried about problems from your end, because you're not supposed to have any idea where she's got off to. He's probably got it figured that don't nobody know where she's at." Merchant leaned forward and felt under the seat, then straightened back out.

"Do you think we've got a chance of finding her?"

The big detective grinned and nodded. "I do, my man, I do."

"Where do you think she is?"

He tapped his temple. "Jack, I'd bet my pension that I know where she is, but—"

"Then tell me."

Merchant studied the road ahead a few seconds, then glanced over at Stafford. "You remember the big building she said they took her to, where all the physical stuff took place?"

"There? They took her there again?"

"That's the word I got. It's a ol' textbook bindery near the river. Not much going on down that way, so they took the place over to do whatever the hell they do there. Run their drug and prostitution operations—sorta corporate headquarters, I guess you'd call it."

"How did you find out so fast?" Stafford asked.

Merchant remained silent awhile, then said, "A little red-headed guy told me."

"That Goddamned Oswalt?"

The detective nodded. "That Goddamned Oswalt."

"Was it Oswalt who came and got her?"

Merchant nodded again.

"I knew that smell was from his cheap cigars, that sonofabitch. So you're telling me that he was in on it?"

The big detective glanced in the rearview mirror, then returned his eyes to the road. "Well, he didn't have nothing to do with what happened to her the first time, if that's what you mean, but that little bastard's been crooked for years, only nobody's been able to prove it—or been willing to try. Hell, Stafford, ain't no way of knowing who's dirty anymore."

"But how'd—"

"Well, I got a good nose, as they say, I can smell these things, and Oswalt's been stinking for a few years now, and I ain't talking about them cheap-ass cigars. Just little things. Things that didn't look right, feel right, things he said. See, when your wife turned up missing off the street, I couldn't understand why whoever called from the Eighth insisted on talking to Oswalt, since any number of people could have gotten the call, and why a *detective* was put on it, and especially why one was put on it so quick. I mean, if you had been some kind of VIP, maybe, but not a librarian. Not that librarians ain't important, Jack—they just don't command that much attention.

"Ordinarily things would have rocked on until morning with the beat cops keeping an eye out for her, since shit like this happens occasionally and usually comes out OK the next day. I think your description of the big flashy car and the black guys with rings all over their hands and stuff got somebody down at the Eighth thinking it might be better to put a *friendly* in the loop, just in case Satan's boys were the ones that picked her up. Hell, for me the whole thing was one big cloud until you admitted that business about telling

Harry she was a hooker. Oswalt was just playing dumb, just trying to make sure what the real scoop was. I didn't put anything together *then* about Oswalt, but I felt kinda funny about it. Then when we got a call from Satan's people telling us we could pick up your wife before Harry even walked out that station door or used the phone, I knew somebody had to have tipped him off that Satan had something on his hands different from what he thought he had. I think Oswalt called him a lot earlier, probably right after you told us about Harry, but Koontz—that's Satan's real name, Sam Koontz—was intrigued enough, or worried enough, to try check things out for himself before he let her go. And he probably wanted to play with her a little, maybe see whether he could enlist her, so to speak, or just have fun with her, if you'll forgive me for saying so.

"I mean, it didn't make any difference at that point anyway—she'd already been put through hell. He had to either kill her or mess with her awhile and let her go. He washed her down to get any evidence off of her, made her think he was bein' gentle when all he was doing was taking care of himself. The panties were an oversight that Koontz didn't learn about until they'd already let her go. I guarantee you that if he'd been the one that took her out of there she'd have been naked or had a clean sheet wrapped around her. Oswalt probably found the screw-up first and took the panties. I don't know why he didn't take the dress too, unless he figured that since she didn't have the dress on during the assaults there wouldn't be much of anything on it. And the dress would have been missed quicker. The panties, though . . ."

"That little sonofabitch Oswalt—"

"When you told me that he was the one she said took her panties, it all clicked in and I knew for sure that he was covering Koontz's ass. He took the only article of clothing that they could possibly have gotten body fluids or pubic hair off of without actually examining her physically. By the way, I kinda doubt that they could have got anything off of'm. They usually take strips of packing tape and go over everything. Or a vacuum cleaner. They ain't even any lint left usually, if they know what they're doing. Your wife say anything about tape?"

"No. But she might have been too much out of it to recall."

"And then there was that trip up to talk to your friend . . . ."

"Yeah," Stafford said, "what was that all about?"

"Well, I'm pretty sure Koontz sent Oswalt up there to nose around to find out how much talking y'all had been doing. To find out whether y'all needed to be shut up. If anybody was to ask what it was to him, he could flash his badge and tell them it was official business and none of theirs. Or he could just say that he was trying to see whether the case was worth pursuing. And Koontz sent him up to get your wife, since if anybody stopped him for any reason, again he could flash that badge and tell them he was taking her back as a material witness—had to sedate her—and they could fuck off."

"I still can't believe she'd come down with him," Stafford said.

"Oh, well, she didn't come on her own. I told you, he doped her, loaded her in the car, and brought her down."

"How do you know that? That little sonofabitch. How'd you get him to tell you all this?"

Mercant grinned, one hand hooked casually over the steering wheel. "Wasn't easy. When I got off the phone with you—hell, that was around ten, wasn't it?"

"Yeah, around ten, I'd say, but I was out of my fucking mind. By the way, I owe you for about an hour and a half of phone time."

"Don't none of that matter. I called you as soon as I got in and my wife told me you'd phoned, and that would have been somewhere around eight-thirty. At any rate, when you mentioned the cigar smell and that strip from a blue rubber package and the fact that he'd been talking to your friend, that was all I needed to convince me. Oswalt was off duty and wasn't home, and there wasn't anything I could do that late, so I just laid there in bed all night thinking about how to go about it.

"This morning real early I got a nephew of mine—this is his truck, by the way—to call and leave a message for Oswalt to meet him down by the cemetery, that he had something to tell him about Satan. I knew that would get his ass in gear fast. He wasn't at the office, but somebody knew where to find him—he was in fact over at the building with your wife, or in transit to or from there—so they called and passed on the message, and he showed up about nine."

"Your nephew met him?"

"Naw, I wouldn't risk Oscar. I dropped off a snitch to meet him. A little sorry sonofabitch good for nothing else, somebody Oswalt had had a run-in with once. I figured he wouldn't pick up anybody he didn't know. They drove around a little while with this ol' boy jabbering about knowing all about Satan and his sins and going on and on about what God was going to do to him. Just pure horseshit. And he told Oswalt I wanted to talk to him. I gave him a hell of a good script." Merchant smiled broadly.

"So . . . ."

The skyline of New Orleans was visible now, rising out of a light blue haze. Merchant continued, "I tailed them around long enough that I knew Oswalt would be convinced that this little turd didn't know anything more than fifty thousand other blacks in New Orleans know about Koontz and was probably crazy as a loon, then headed off to an old bayou road where the boy was supposed to bring Oswalt to meet me. I just hoped that he wouldn't take the kid down there and blow his brains out and roll him in a ditch somewhere, maybe decide to go ahead and kill me too. I mean, he had to suspect that something was up.

"He took the boy down and let him out, then drove out to where he was instructed to meet me. I wasn't sure he'd come, but I knew his curiosity would be gnawing the hell out of him. Whatever, he came."

"How did you get him to tell you?"

"I got ways, Stafford, I got ways," Merchant said as New Orleans loomed before them.

"Great God Almighty, you guys," Stafford said. "Where's Oswalt now?"

"Don't worry about any of that. You can bet your ass nobody's going to be bothered with him again, though. My snitch had some business with him after our meeting."

"And you think she's there, in that building?"

"Yeah, I 'spect she is. Koontz owns that place and a dozen others scattered around. They look like they're abandoned from the outside, but inside he's got all kinds of shit going on, drugs and prostitution, contraband of every type imaginable. Got computers and shit. That's where Oswalt said he took'r."

"Why wouldn't he take her to Satan's house?"

Merchant looked over and smiled. "Hey, this sonofabitch has a *mansion* out in Gretna. More than one probably. And he's got a wife and kids, if you can believe that. He come from trash, but now he's got a social life completely separate from this low-life shit that he makes his living from. This is what you'd call his day job, and he's got it so refined now that all he does is make an appearance now and then, pick up the money, interview girls. He ain't taking no girls out there. He's married to—well, the name wouldn't mean anything to you, and I don't want you to know it anyway, but his wife's old man is big in oil and politics, used to be in state government, rich as God."

"Jesus, Merchant, does he know Satan is running this operation?"

"Oh hell yeah, my man," Merchant said, "he set him up to begin with. The high-end prostitution, at any rate. I don't know about the drugs and whatever else he may be mixed up in. Koontz probably got into all that on his own. But that thing with your wife must have scared the shit out of the senator. You can bet that's the reason Oswalt went up there to see your old girlfriend—they wanted to be sure wasn't nobody talking about it."

He cleared his throat. "Koontz has been nothing but trouble for him over the years—got a pretty good sheet—but he racks up the profits, and I guess that's what matters most. Eventually he'll have to kill him off, though. Koontz is still trash and too fucking arrogant to keep around forever. He's trying too hard to be independent and losing that high-end image, and the senator don't like it. Thing that worries me now is what he'll do to your wife. Koontz had probably wrote this little fuck-up off, but now that she's back on the scene, he may figure that she's just too risky and he's got to kill her and be done with it. All your wife wanted to do was talk things out with him. Only trouble was, once she called, he knew that things wasn't over. He assumed that he'd never hear from her again, but then that call came. He's probably kicking his own ass that they didn't dump her in a bayou somewhere before. Or, like I said, ol' Koontz might shoot her up and start working her. She'd be good for the stable. There ain't no telling."

"You really know how to cheer a guy up, Merchant."

"Just telling you like it is, my man, telling you like it is."

"Jesus," Stafford breathed, "Jesus."

"I told you, save that. Him and His Daddy ain't got nothing to do with this."

In a little while Merchant turned off the interstate and wove around through back streets until they were well to the west of the Quarter. Finally he pulled over and parked behind two pickups near a building under construction. Behind the walls saws were shrieking and hammers and nail guns were banging away.

He shut off the engine. "Won't nobody pay attention to us here. We got to kill a couple of hours." Merchant reached behind the seat and brought out a crushed paper bag. "Got some sandwiches here, pimento cheese, and some root beer in that ice chest in the bed." He fished out a flattened plastic-wrapped sandwich and held it out to Stafford.

"No thanks. I'm not hungry. My stomach's in knots."

"I can understand that, Jack, mine too. But it could be a very long stakeout and later on we may not have a chance to eat. Ain't nothing gon' happen for awhile. Why don't you try to get this down?" He pitched the sandwich onto Stafford's lap and got out and took two Barqs Root Beers from the ice chest in the bed, got back in, and handed one to Stafford.

"All right," Stafford said. "I'll try." He opened the sandwich and nibbled at it. "Are we near where she is?"

Merchant nodded. "Just down the street. You see that old brick building with the tall fence around it? In the middle of the next block. Over on the left."

Stafford squinted. He could see a big building, but it looked abandoned, with some of the windows broken out, others painted white. Clumps of knee-high grass grew between the fence and the sidewalk. "You're talking about that old building up there?" He pointed.

"Don't point, fool." Merchant yanked his arm down. "Yeah, that one."

"Good Lord. Looks like nobody's been in there in years."

"They want it to look that way. Watch for traffic, my man. You might be surprised at what goes in and out of there."

"Merchant, I'm beginning to believe I'll never see my wife alive again."

"Look, Jack, if things are laid out the way I see them, and if we're fast enough, we'll have the two of you back in Mississippi before midnight."

"Who's helping us? The police?"

"*Shiiit* no." He took a long gulp of root beer. "I don't know who to trust down there anymore. It may be that there ain't but two crooked cops in the whole place, but figgering out which two is the bitch part. No sir. I trust myself and I trust my nephew, and I trusted that little snitch Jimmy to believe that I'd be mighty rough on his ass if he messed things up. Now, though I ain't got any idea how much help you'll be when the shit gets going, at least you've got enough at stake here that I can trust *you*." He looked over at Stafford. "Can't I?"

"Yes," Stafford said, worrying down a lump of dry sandwich. "Yes."

"I got a problem, though," the detective said, finishing the last of his sandwich and drink. He pulled a zip-lock bag from his pocket and removed a pair of surgical gloves and put them on.

"What's that?" Stafford asked.

"The only librarians I ever knew looked like they'd shit if they saw a gun."

"What?"

"You ever been in the military?"

"No."

"You ever hunted?"

"No."

"You ever owned a gun?"

"No."

"Could you use a gun if you had to?"

"Oh, hell, Merchant, I don't know."

"At least you didn't just automatically say no. I mean, if you *had* to, man. Like if your life or your wife's life, or *mine*, was on the line, could you do it?"

"A fucking *gun*?"

"Look, Jack," Merchant said softly, paternally, "you got to get yourself psyched up for this. Before y'all's trip down here, you were living in a Goddamned dream world with all your books and your pretty wife. But you've had a taste of the real world, and this is *real* shit here, Jack, this is as real as it gets. This is the jungle, the bayou, and here you got to be willing to kill to keep from being killed. You didn't expect that we'd go in there grinning and making the peace sign and talking sweet to those guys, did you? Say, 'Hey, Satan, if you're finished with my wife, wonder if I could take'r on back home? Maybe next time you're up our way you could drop by for dinner and y'all can talk some more.' You figure we can do it that way, let's go try."

Stafford twisted uncomfortably in his seat. "I don't know what I thought, but I certainly never envisioned carrying a gun."

"So you figured a baseball bat or shovel or something?"

"I just never envisioned a *gun*."

"Well *envision* it, man. Will you use a gun if I give you one?"

Stafford swallowed and stared off toward a line of vacant, boarded up buildings. "I guess so, if I have to. If—"

He handed the zip-lock bag to Stafford. "Put a pair of these gloves on before we handle anything. In case we drop something. I don't want prints left on anything. Nothing."

Stafford removed the gloves from the bag and pulled them on.

"Now wipe your hands with this rag." He held out an oily rag.

"This looks like a diaper."

"It *was* a diaper. My nephew's kid's. Wipe your hands with it."

"What—"

"That's just oil on the Goddamned thing. Not baby piss. I don't even want to risk a transfer print. Just wipe your hands."

Stafford wiped his hands with the oily rag and handed it back to Merchant. "Now what?"

"Take another couple of pairs of these gloves and put'm in your pocket, in case you rip the ones you got on." When Stafford had taken two more sets of gloves, the detective slid the bag back in his pocket.

"Jesus, you're careful."

"Careful people stay alive down here, Stafford. Careful people don't go around telling bartenders their wife is an expensive whore."

"That was uncalled for, damn it."

"Sorry. You need to be reminded, damn it."

"I *am* reminded—every breath I take."

Merchant reached beneath his seat and pulled out something wrapped in a dingy towel, which he slowly unrolled until a short, malevolent looking shotgun lay across his lap. The barrel was sawed off even with the end of the forearm, and the stock had been replaced with a hand-grip.

"A Browning A5," Merchant said, "loaded with buckshot, with one in the chamber. All you got to do is switch this here safety off—" He moved his finger past the trigger guard and pressed a little metal bar until it clicked into position, then pushed it back until it clicked again. "Move your finger straight out to the front of the trigger guard and push the safety across, like I just done, to the left, drop your finger inside the guard and pull straight back and it'll shoot as fast as you pull the trigger until the gun's empty. But don't put your finger inside the trigger guard until you're ready to start mowing down that building."

"The bullets are in it?" Stafford asked.

Merchant shook his head. "*Shells*, Stafford. The shells are in it, yes, five of them. Number-One buck. Five shots at sixteen pellets a shell is the same as me shooting eighty times with this." Holding the shotgun across his lap, he slipped a black pistol from beneath the seat and slid it into a holster on his belt. "Point is, though, you don't have to do much aiming, Stafford. You can lay down a wall of lead with this thing in a couple of seconds." He tapped the shotgun with his finger.

Stafford slumped down into the seat until his head was barely above the sill of the window. "So you and your nephew and I are going up against an army whose commander-in-chief is a wealthy former state senator and whose field general is Satan himself?"

"Well, I hope we're just going up against Satan, but at this point ain't no way of knowing."

"This is shit, Merchant. I'd rather take my chances with the police."

"Too late," Merchant said wearily. "Things are in motion, Jack. We got to go through with it. Besides, I *am* the police."

"Merchant, I can't use a gun."

The big man's hand shot out and slammed him into the chest and knocked him breathless so fast that Stafford saw it only as a blur. Merchant's eyes were terrible.

"Goddamn you, boy, I have put my fucking life on the line for you and your wife. My profession, at the very least. And you ain't backing down on me. You can just forget about that shit. This shotgun ain't nothing but steel and wood, and you'll be shooting at animals, if you get to shoot it at all. You take it and you put your finger on that safety and work it until you feel comfortable with it, but keep your finger away from that trigger. You pull that trigger with the safety off and you'll blow a hole in this truck and let everybody in town know we're here and we won't hear anything again for months. Now take this gun!"

He thrust the shotgun into Stafford's hands. "All you got's them shells in the gun. Won't be no time to reload. You ain't got to aim, but you got to point in the general direction, and I mean toward *him*, not your wife, and at his *head*—that sonofabitch could be wearing a vest. If you can't take him out with eighty pellets, he *deserves* to kill your ass and take your wife. And, Stafford, hang onto the gun. It's my duck gun, with a replacement butt stock and barrel."

Stafford slouched in his seat with the shotgun aimed down his left leg toward the floorboard, and with an urgency in his bowels he clicked the safety off and on, off and on.

XXII

The New Orleans day was fading fast. A block and a half away from the old warehouse, Merchant and Stafford could study goings and comings, of which there were plenty, without arousing suspicion. In the time that they had been sitting there two long, low sedans, one white, one silver, had already passed through the gate of the chain-link fence, someone had swung two big doors open for them, and they disappeared into the warehouse. A smaller car had left another opening almost immediately and exited the compound, and another small car, sleek and expensive looking, went in.

"Awful lot of traffic for an abandoned building, ain't it?" Merchant observed.

"You really think she's in there?"

"Ain't no way to know for sure till we go in ourselves. What you seein' there is his henchmen bringing in daily collections probably. Drugs maybe. Shit, ain't no way of knowing. But one went out and three went in. When at least two of them leave, we gon' have to take our chances."

"I wish I'd brought a book."

"Book, my ass," Merchant said. "You got to be kidding. With your wife in there?"

"It would just make the time pass faster. It would calm me down."

"Do you mean to say to me that you seriously think you could get into a book—"

"No," Stafford said. "Probably not. How long do you figure we'll have to wait?"

"I hope not much longer," Merchant said. He motioned toward the building beside them. "When these guys shut down for the day and drive off, we're gon' stick out here like a sober person at mardis gras."

"Do you have any tools in the truck?" Stafford asked.

"What say?"

"Hammers and stuff. You know, *tools*?"

Merchant just looked at him.

"When these guys leave, we can get out and go in and start hammering around, try to watch the warehouse through a crack or something. It'll be a hell of a lot more convincing than sitting in the truck. And if we can't get in, we can bang around on the plywood out front. We'll make it look like we're securing things, you know. *Working*. If we're making a lot of noise, they won't suspect anything. Our noise'll just pick up after the others leave."

Merchant reached and patted a black bag behind his feet. "Well, what I got in *my* tool bag won't do, but—" He opened the door and got out and reached behind the seat. He pulled out a flat black-plastic toolbox. "Hmm," he said, flipping open the top, "yeah, a ball peen hammer and some wrenches and shit."

"OK, then," Stafford said, "when these guys leave, we go to work."

Merchant laughed and pounded the seat. "Man, you're getting into this thing now. I *like* that."

In a short while the workers who had been inside piled into their trucks and drove off and the two men got out with their tools, Merchant with the hammer and Stafford with a large crescent wrench. The doors were locked, so they began walking along the front of the building, tapping and hammering, keeping one eye on the warehouse down the street.

"I sure hope they ain't watching us," Merchant said. "This wouldn't fool a five-year-old for long."

"May be," Stafford panted, reaching and slamming home an unseated nail with his wrench, "but it's still more convincing than sitting in that damned truck. At this distance they can't tell what we're doing."

They did not have to pretend very long. The door where the smaller car had gone through opened and the white and silver sedans came out and pulled up to the gate, and a lean black man got out and unlocked and opened it, closed and locked it behind them, and got into the second car. They drove away in the opposite direction.

"Whew," Merchant said. "I was afraid they would come this way."

"What do you mean?" Stafford asked.

"I was afraid they might drive past here and eyeball us. Hell, I don't know who's in them cars. Could be somebody who knows me."

"Like maybe Oswalt?"

"Nope," Merchant said. "Not Oswalt. That I'll put money on."

"Was that the same two that went in?"

"I think so," Merchant said.

"They came out a different way."

"Yeah, but that bottom floor is probably just a garage area. They went in one and just drove down and out that other."

"There's still another car in there."

"I can count, Stafford. At least to three. Even a Goddamn *real* crow can do that."

"What do you mean by that?"

"Don't worry about it. It's a private joke. A black thing."

"What do we do now?"

Merchant stood by the truck a few seconds watching the building. Then he turned and looked down the street behind him and motioned to someone.

"What's happening?" Stafford asked.

"It's now or never," Merchant said with a tight grin. "Operation Satan Bash is underway. Get in the truck and hold onto that gun."

A red Camaro idled in behind them and stopped, and Merchant leaned and spoke to the driver. Stafford sat in the truck, his finger stuck straight out past the trigger guard, working the safety back and forth, back and forth. Merchant got back in, cranked up, and drove down to an alley next to the building they had been watching. He backed into the alley.

"I want to be headed out when the shit hits."

"Who's that in the car? Your nephew?"

"Yep. Oscar. Works for the UPS."

"Jesus, I was hoping he was a cop."

"Nope. One detective, one UPS driver, and—"

"And a Goddamned librarian," Stafford finished it for him.

"—a Goddamn librarian. Got to be the weirdest assault force ever assembled. I just hope to hell nobody else shows up."

Stafford breathed deeply. "So how do we go about this?"

"Just follow my instructions."

When he reached the end of the alley, Merchant stopped the truck between a brick wall and the cyclone fence that surrounded the warehouse.

"Where's Oscar?"

"He's down the street with one of these." Merchant held up a walkie-talkie. "When I give him the word, he's supposed to burn rubber and meet us here, where I hope we'll be waiting with a little blond package for the UPS man to deliver in Biloxi."

"What if she's not in there?"

Merchant adjusted his cap and sighed. "Then I guess Operation Satan Bash will be a flop, my man. Just hope she is."

"What do we do if she's not?"

"Look, Jack, now ain't the time to talk about what can go wrong. We got to move. I don't know how long them guys'll be gone or how many more are on the way or who's left in the building. It might be *full* of alligators for all I know, and we might get our asses shot off going through the first door. A lot depends on whether what Oswalt told me was the truth or not. He was all I had to work with."

"I don't know why you'd believe him," Stafford said, still working the safety. He knew that he'd be flicking that safety in his sleep for years to come.

"Like I say, Jack, now ain't the time to worry about it. Now's the time for *action*."

"Give me some more bullets—shells."

Merchant looked at him. "What the hell for? You probably won't have time to shoot what you've got."

"Please."

Merchant reached into the glovebox and pulled out two little flat boxes. He held them out to Stafford. "OK, cowboy, two boxes of five, plus five in the gun and that's all I got. You planning an extended engagement with these guys?"

Stafford opened the boxes. "You never know." He turned on his left side and dumped the boxes onto the seat, then stuffed his right-hand front pocket full of bright-green shells.

"Put that other pair of gloves on," Merchant said. "We're gon' double-rubber, take no chances. And hang on to them, no matter what, and burn'm when you get home. You understand? We don't want to leave a trace. And if you shoot that Goddamned gun, you got to pick up the shells, even if it slings them all the way across the room, which it might. Keep count of how many times you shoot and pick up them shells. We don't leave *nothing* to chance."

"Yessir." He leaned over and shook Merchant's hand.

"You ready, white boy?"

"Yessir."

"Let's go then." He slid from the seat, crouched, and motioned for Stafford to follow.

"Goddamn, this place stinks." Stafford was easing along the side of the warehouse in Merchant's shadow. He looked back toward the truck, where he could see the almost perfectly round hole the detective had made in the fence with some cutters he took from the black bag he carried. A rank growth of weeds lined the fence. "Smells like shit."

"It *is* shit, but this ain't a health inspection, Jack. And it ain't the kind of shit we need to worry about. Shit on your shoe sole ain't the same as shit on your other soul, if you get my drift. Just watch where you step and keep quiet and stay with me."

They tried a side door but found it locked from the inside. "No need to fuck with this one," Merchant said. "We'd make enough racket to wake up half of New Orleans."

"Jesus, we can't go around front. It's still too light. Anybody from the street might see us here."

"I know *that*. Keep your voice down. Let's try the back." He grabbed Stafford's shoulders and turned him around and they made their way to the corner of the building and eased along the back wall. "If there's any doors back here." Merchant squinted down the back of the long building. "Yeah, there's at least one ahead. Stay close, now. And quit aimin' that Goddamned shotgun at me." He reached and pushed the gun barrel until it pointed toward the ground. Stafford's finger worked the safety with the rhythm of a metronome.

They found the door padlocked on the outside. Merchant cradled the massive lock in his hand and smiled. "This is what I wanted," he said.

"Can you pick it?" Stafford asked.

"Shiiiit yeah, clean as a whistle. Got get out my little picks." He set down his bag and removed the bolt cutters.

"What else do you have in that bag?" Stafford asked.

"Nothing much. *You* got the heavy artillery."

Stafford looked down at the short, heavy shotgun. "You just got that pistol?"

"Yep. But don't you worry about me. You keep your eyes on that back fence, in case somebody comes along. They do, we gon' drop down and act like we're passin' a bottle. Act like we're drunk. You just lay that shotgun flat on the ground, but keep it handy." He reached in the bag and removed a small paper sack from which the neck of a brown bottle stuck. He passed it to Stafford.

"Damned if you haven't thought of everything," Stafford said.

"Yeah, but there's always the unexpected." The big detective slid the jaws of the cutters over the ring of the lock and slowly squeezed the handles together. "Now I got to pick this lock."

He clenched hard and thrust his jaw out as his massive hands moved closer to each other. Against the far blue sky an airliner seemed to leap from one building top to another. Its belly and the underside of the wings glowed with late sun.

Merchant stopped and took a deep breath. "God-*damn*," he gasped, "these are just too short for a lock this heavy. The handles are givin'. I need leverage."

"Why don't you—"

"I'm doing this, Stafford."

"Let me try."

Merchant looked at him. "Man, if I can't do it with my two hundred and fifty pounds, you sure as hell can't do it. You ain't exactly a weenie, Stafford, but . . ."

"I have more at stake. Let me try." He held out his hand.

Merchant handed the cutters to him and inspected the lock. "Man, I didn't even make an impression on it. Ain't no way we gon' do it with these. Let's try another door."

"Let me try," Stafford insisted.

"Have at it, then, damn it. But whatever you do, do it quiet."

Stafford handed the shotgun to Merchant and slipped the jaws of the tool over the steel staple through which the lock ran and put all his upper strength into the handles, squeezed and the jaws came together in one muted snap. He lowered the jaws half an inch below the first cut, and when they came together this time a piece of the staple sprang out. He lifted the lock through the gap and handed it to Merchant.

"Holy shit, Stafford," Merchant said quietly. "Maybe there *is* some advantage to bringing a librarian along. Librarians cut the hasp, not the lock."

"Actually," Stafford said, "that's referred to as the staple, which is made of softer material. The hasp is—"

"I don't give a rat's ass what you call the thing or what it's made out of. It's cut, the lock is out, and we can go in. God-*damn*, what has this world come to? People's lives at stake, and a librarian is standing here instructing a detective on the parts of a lock . . . ." He mumbled something else that Stafford couldn't hear.

"Two easy cuts are better than one impossible one," Stafford said. He reached for the shotgun. "It's an application of Occam's Razor."

Poised to push the door open, Merchant whispered, "I don't even want to know who you're talking about or what his razor could possibly have to do with cutting a lock. Are you ready, or do you want to go on talking about some asshole's razor?"

"What if they've got a security system?" Stafford asked.

"Then we'll just have to move fast, won't we?" Merchant opened the door.

There was no alarm. When the door had finished its raspy swing, creaking and grating, there was only the deep, resonant quiet of old empty buildings. They could hear themselves breathing. And with all the doors closed in front, the only light that fell into the garage area was the feeble glow of the twilight sky behind the two men who stood there in the doorway, one with a pistol held high, the other with a sawed-off shotgun, his finger sliding the safety back and forth. There was nothing down the entire length of the bottom floor but a string of columns and at the far end a car draped with a pale cover.

"There's your third car." Merchant eased the door to and nudged Stafford. "He's got it covered so birds won't shit on it. I ought to go over there and scratch a cross on the Goddamned thing."

"Merchant!" Stafford whispered.

"Sorry. Let's go." He stepped farther in. "We can't use the elevator. Got to find the stairs. She say how high they might have gone up?"

"Only that it seemed forever. Maybe the top floor?"

"These old elevators are slow. Could be the one above. Ain't but four floors altogether. Oswalt said it was the second she was on, and I noticed that there were window units on the second floor. You said she mentioned that the room she was in was air-conditioned."

"Yeah. That's right."

"Then she's probably on the second floor, like Oswalt said. But I say we go to the top and start down, make sure there's nobody above us that can come down on us when we try to get out of here."

"You the general?" Stafford asked him.

"You want to lead? I mean, just because you figured out the lock thing—"

"No. I don't want to lead."

"Where would *you* start?"

"I say top floor too. Makes sense. If I had to fight some sort of pitched battle in here, I'd want to be able to get onto the roof. I'd say top floor."

"Pitched battle? Man, you are fucking *into* this, ain't you?" He laughed low. "*Pitched battle.* Man, you somethin'. Librarian's gettin' primed for a pitched battle, a firefight." He tapped Stafford on the shoulder. "Top floor's where we're headed then. But we ain't using no elevator. We're going up the stairs."

Finding the stairway was easy enough, though opening the seldom-used heavy steel door without noise was not. It creaked and groaned and squawked across the concrete floor. Merchant winced and pulled, winced and pulled, until at last he could ease his large body between the door and frame. Stafford trained the shotgun on the long, empty garage area and backed through behind him.

"You might know it would be black as pitch in here," Merchant said, his hand on Stafford's shoulder. "We got to be real careful. If they got any sense at all, this stairway will be booby-trapped, but I figure they're too arrogant to worry about it."

"Should we use a light?" Stafford asked.

"Why, hell yes, if we had one that would work." Merchant was tapping a flashlight against his thigh. "This sonofabitch worked this morning. I checked it out. Goddamn it. Wal-Mart special. Probably got *Made in America* stamped on it."

Stafford flicked on the penlight he had taken from his pocket. "Mine's not much, but it'll help. It came from Sears. Sometime I'll teach you how to value shop."

"Well, I'll be damned," Merchant said, "the librarian comes through again."

Slowly they ascended, staying one step below the tiny beam—past the second floor, then the third, until finally they arrived at the last landing. Stafford trained the penlight across Merchant's shoulder until it weaved on the number stenciled on the gray door.

"OK, soldier, fourth floor." Merchant raised his pistol. "Here we leave the trenches. You ready?"

Stafford slid the safety across and left it, though his finger wanted to reach around the trigger guard and push it back, the way it had been doing for hours. "Ready," he said.

The floor was empty, with only scattered columns breaking the long expanse of wooden flooring. It had apparently been used only for storage, though Stafford could see in the glow of twilight from a row of windows that ran the entire length of the building tracks on the dusty boards where someone had recently walked. He tapped Merchant, who shrugged and motioned *down* with his finger.

The hallway on the third floor was long and narrow and dimly lit with a single lightbulb hanging from the ceiling at either end. Directly across from the stairwell there was a large room through whose doorless opening Stafford could see the evening sky framed by three high windows.

"Jack," Merchant whispered. "Try to step on the seams between the boards—they ain't as likely to creak that way."

Merchant eased down the hallway, Stafford right behind him, and looked into the room. Empty. There was nothing in it at all. He held his ear against the door of the next room, then slowly tried the knob, pushed the door open, and eased his head through. He pulled back, shook his head, and moved to the next one. Stafford walked backwards behind him, shotgun trained on the stairway opening. Noting the elevator door at the other end, he began pivoting every couple of steps, front to rear, front to rear. Twice a board chirped.

Merchant reached the last door, listened, and opened it, stepped back and shook his head. "Nothing," he mouthed. He pointed down.

Stafford nodded. It was like Russian Roulette, with all the chambers clicked but one.

XXIII

The woman was groggy, her face puffy and distorted, and she was wincing from the lamp on the table beside the bed. The only sound was the loud hum of the air conditioner mounted in a window.

"How long have I been here?" she asked the man in the dark suit who had just turned on the lamp and now sat beside her.

"Since yesterday afternoon, my sweet," he said. "You've had a nice long nap."

Her hands were cuffed to a steel rail that ran between the wooden posts of the headboard. "How long have *you* been here?"

"Been sittin' at that table over there for a couple of hours waiting for you to wake up. Just doin' some paperwork. Didn't want to disturb your beauty rest."

She strained against the steel bracelets. "Why am I like this?"

"To keep you from walking out of here," the man said.

"I've got to go to the bathroom," she said. "I haven't been to the bathroom since last night, when—when the redheaded guy fed me. No, this morning. I got to go this morning. But I need to go again."

"You remember that much, huh?"

"Yes. I remember he came to the house to get me, and he gave me something, and I remember . . ."

The man nodded. "You probably done enough remembering." He unlocked the cuff from her right wrist and pulled her to her feet. She weaved and fell against him, then righted herself. He did not remove the cuff from her left wrist. "You remember where the bathroom's at?"

She nodded and made her way slowly to the door.

"Leave the door open," he said. "And don't be long."

She went in and closed the door behind her anyway and in a few seconds opened it and stood looking at him. Her legs were unsteady. She still wore the pale-blue dress that the little red-headed man had put on her.

"Where's the man who brought me here?"

"I 'spect he's off protecting the City from people like me," the man said and laughed loudly. "Get back on the bed."

She looked about the room, as if she were really seeing it for the first time. "What *is* this place?"

"It's where I do a lot of my work is all. And it's your home away from home."

"I just want to go back to my real home," she said. "I'm sick."

He pointed. "I think you'd better get back on that bed. You don't look well."

"All right," she said. "I need to talk to you. And then I want to go home." She returned to the bed and held out the wrist from which the handcuffs dangled. "Can you take these off?"

"Will you behave?" he asked, and laughed.

She nodded and he removed the cuffs from her arm and pitched them onto a chair. He pulled her onto the bed. She slid up and sat with her back against the headboard.

"All I wanted was to talk to you." Her speech was vaguely slurred, and she was still woozy. "You seemed so understanding, so gentle. Why didn't you call me?"

"And so I am understanding and gentle, but I got more important things to do than talk on the phone with women." He was sitting on the edge of the bed, his hand moving casually over her legs, stroking her shins. He smiled. "What did you want to talk to me about?"

"About—I wanted to talk to you about . . . I don't know. I just wanted to talk to you."

"I'm here," he said, rising from the bed and removing his heavy jacket, which he draped across the chair he had been sitting in. He then took off a shoulder holster that held a huge black pistol, kicked off his shoes and removed his tie, and sat back down, extending his exploring hands to her upper thigh. She pulled her legs up.

"Don't do that," she said. "Please."

"Been settin' here watchin' you sleep, thinking about what kind of money you can make the two of us," he said. "You are one fine woman." He pushed her dress up past her waist and when she tried to stop him he lifted a finger in warning. "When Satan wants to take your panties off, he takes them off. You want me to handcuff you to the bed again?" She relented and he removed her panties. "Oh, my love, you will please many a man." He rose and forced her thighs apart with his knees and with his thumb slowly massaged her.

"Please, no, I don't want this," she pleaded. "I'd better go home. My husband must be worrying about me."

"This is all there *is*, Love, what civilizations were built on, what wars were fought for—the worship of this small thing, this shrine before which all men kneel and tremble. This is what men will pay for and kill for and go to prison for. This is what life is all about. Men come from it and they go back to it time and time again, as often as they can. It's the universal church. You may never have noticed it, but the opening is shaped like the doorway of some ancient cathedral."

She tried to pull away from him.

"You have a choice now, sweet Susie. You can take advantage of this gift you have here and work for me or I can throw you to the boys. You remember them, don't you? They'll work on you until they tire of you, and then they'll cut your throat and throw you in a bayou somewhere and the alligators and fish will feed off your creamy flesh."

"Oh, my God," she whispered to the ceiling. "Please just let me go back home."

"I *am* your God, my sweet. And you *are* home. You should have kept quiet. You should have borne your bruises and scars and memories of your trip down here and kept your mouth shut. Why I gave you that number, I can't imagine, except that for a brief moment I was taken with your beauty myself, swept up the way my customers are with fine women. I guess what I really wanted was to have you in my fold." He moved and leaned over her. "And I still do."

She twisted to the side and balled up and clamped her legs together. "I just want to go home," she said.

He sat up and glared down at her. "Like I said, you *are* home now, my girl. Satan's girl. You're here, and you'll work for me or you'll die. It's that simple. You work for me, I'll protect you and treat you well and pay you more money than you ever dreamed of."

Her eyes flashed at that. "I don't want to work for you, and I don't want your filthy money. I wanted to talk to you because I thought you were an understanding man, and I find out that you are just a *pimp*. One minute you talk and act like a sophisticated man, the next you talk and act like a street pimp, like those other guys. You're just a common pimp."

"No, not common, my angel. I'm too wealthy and powerful to be called *common*." He threw his head back and laughed. "You are the one who's common. I got dozens of good-looking women working for me, just as pretty as you." He reached and pulled her legs down until she was flat on the bed and pried them apart again.

His voice rose. "You think that what you got there is *special*? Every woman walking around has one of these things. Every fat cow of a woman, every wore-out, diseased, skinny whore in the gutter or out there on the bayou—*every* woman's got one of them things, shaped just about the same as yours. Line a thousand women up with their legs spread and nothing but one of these showing, and one looks pretty much like another. It's just a snatch, a cunt, a pussy, whatever you call it, and *every* woman has one. It's just that you've got a young, beautiful body and face to go with it and that makes it a valuable commodity. But it damned sure ain't indispensable. Dozens of women like you work for me, *dozens*." Then his voice softened. "But I hate to let someone pretty and young like you go to waste. Oh, baby, men will tithe heavy to worship here."

"Please, just let me go home and you'll never hear from me again." She pulled her legs up beneath her dress.

"Honey, if you hadn't of called, you could have stayed home. You could have lived out your life with your little ol' husband up there on the Mississippi Coast, your *librarian* husband, and never heard another word from me. Had kids and got fat and old and ugly and never heard from Satan again. But, *no*—you had to call. You had to remember that fucking number and *call*."

"I promise, I'll never call again." She was crying hard now.

"Oh, I ain't worried about that. I can fix it so I never hear from you again, if that's what you want. That ain't what I *want*, but I'm not going to sit here and keep messing with you. I got things to do. You've got the offer. You work for me—here in New Orleans or over in Miami or in Houston—and you ain't goin' back to Mississippi and your sweet librarian husband." He laughed. "Is he really a fuckin' *librarian*?"

"Yes," she whimpered. She remained balled up at the head of the bed.

"Oh, I bet he's lots of fun, ain't he?"

"He's my husband and I love him."

"Problem is, you remember too much. It's on your mind. You was supposed to forget about your trip down here. The only reason I let you go the other time was I figured you wouldn't remember nothin'. Or if you did remember, you'd be too scared and ashamed to talk about it. But you did remember—and worse yet, you *called*—so your choice is to work for me or die. It's that simple."

"Swine," she hissed. "You are just like those sweaty, filthy swine you put on me."

"No, no. I have the power and they have none. I got money and I got power, and I can put you to work or I can kill you, but *they* can't do *anything* unless I say so."

"All I wanted was to *talk* to you," she said, the color raging in her cheeks. "You told me I could call. You seemed decent before. Now I see what you really are. You are just like them."

He had risen from the bed and removed the rest of his clothes. Then he got back on the bed, saying nothing, but he was doing strange things with his hands, weaving them through the air as if they were birds, casting jagged shadows on the wall. He opened the drawer of the small table beside the bed and removed a package of condoms, opened it, and rolled on a bright pink one.

"I told you," she said defiantly, "I just wanted to talk to you about what happened, about what—"

"You came because you *had* to," he said.

"I *came* because some man drugged me and brought me down here." Then she dropped her hands onto her face and sobbed. "I just wanted to talk . . ."

"You are mine, in my power" he said. "You will do what I say." He reached and tilted her chin back and jerked her dress apart at the top. He tapped with a hard finger the little cross between her breasts. "Mine," he said.

"All I want, all I want is to go back home to my husband. You *had* some power over me. But you don't anymore. I know what you are now. But I'll forget all this happened—all of it—if you'll just let me go home."

He dropped back onto his legs and laughed. "Oh no, my lovely little pussy, you came back because you wanted to be with me, because you bear my mark. And because you *can't* forget. Now, whether you choose to work for me or to die, I intend to have a little fun with you."

"No," she said.

Then he rose on his knees and yanked her arms up, pinning her hands behind her neck and pulling her body forward and her head down. "This is what you have come for."

She arched her head back. "Please, no," she grunted.

He slammed her head down with his left hand, his right swooping under and grasping her jaw and squeezing until she had to open her mouth. He jammed himself up and in, so deep that she coughed and gagged and tried to pull back, her hands flailing against him, but he held her down. "This is the body," he said, "the body and the blood."

"Oh, God," she tried to say past the thing that choked her, but what came was a moan, followed by a pale gush across his thighs.

The shadow on the wall rose and thrashed. "You Goddamned bitch," he screeched. He slung her against the headboard. "You God—"

She turned and rolled off the bed and scrambled across the floor into a corner of the room, where she curled into a tight ball. She held her hands across her face while he rose on the bed like some great dark thing from the sea, towering over her, then descending, pulling her up by her hair and flinging her back onto the bed and striking her head and body with his open hand, slapping and slamming her with all his fury while she coiled and whimpered.

"You are mine, Goddamn you, and you will not throw up on me. Ain't no woman ever throwed up on me." He slung her against the headboard and stepped off the bed. He took a long, slender black knife from his pants pocket, flicked open the blade, then stretched her flat again and rose over her.

"I'm gon' carve your ass up, bitch, then I'm gon' make a fuckin' cross on your face and I'm gon' call the boys over and let them have you until they're tired of it and then throw your ass in the bayou, where I should have throwed you before, you Goddamned housewife librarian's pussy! Ain't no woman ever throwed up on me. I'm gon'—"

They were cast in this manner, as if in stone—the sinister man reared high, knife poised, every muscle sharply defined, and the delicate pale woman, lips clenched, eyes fixed on the fury hovering over her—when the door burst open and an enormous black man fell forward onto his knees, a pistol pointed at the man on the bed, and behind him five roaring flashes, and the man rising on the bed twisted and leapt toward the chair where his clothes were scattered and the room roared and roared.

XXIV

They were so busy watching to be certain they were not followed that the truck was on the interstate headed north before either of them spoke. "When we get to the state line," Merchant said, alternating his eyes between the rearview mirror and the road, "we'll pull over at the Mississippi rest stop and you'll get in the car with Oscar and your wife. He'll take you on home."

Stafford's heart was still hammering away. "You certain she's in there? You sure let them get away from us awfully fast."

"Hell, man, *you* give her to Oscar. If that was her rolled up in that Goddamned sheet you give to Oscar, she's in there. And I *meant* to let them get away from us."

"Well, where *are* they, then?"

"Probably up ahead somewhere, or somewhere behind us. Oscar knows the way. UPS don't ever let you down, do they?" He reached and patted Stafford on the leg. "Just relax, man, this particular battle's over."

"I don't understand why I couldn't go with them," Stafford said. "With her."

"Because if somebody was to follow us out of there, they'd have to keep up with two vehicles, and unless they saw us put your wife in with Oscar and saw you get in with me, they wouldn't know who was in which one. You know, confuse'm a little bit. I really think, though, that we got out of there without anybody seeing us. That place looked dead to me."

"Goddamn, what a day." Stafford stretched his legs out and dropped his head back on the seat. The stream of air from the window felt wonderful, and his heart was beginning to settle.

"Oh yeah, man, we probably got the hell out of there just in time. If them guys had come back and blocked that damned alley on us . . . ."

"I heard you shoot a couple of times as we were coming out. Who were you shooting at?"

Merchant roared. "Nobody, man, I just put a couple of rounds into that car we saw covered up, for good measure, you know. I just felt like it. I was revved up."

"Jesus Christ, you shot his car?"

Merchant looked over at him. "Well, now, don't you rekkin that's the least of his worries, Jack?"

Stafford laughed. "Yeah, I guess so. That's funny as hell, you shooting his car like that."

"It was probably stupid, but I felt like it."

"Merchant, will they try to find us?"

"No, no. I don't think so. Now that we're away from there, we're free, free as the fucking wind. They won't know what went down, and the senator won't care. He'll just be glad that somebody knocked that sonofabitch off. Hey, how many shells you got left?"

Stafford twisted in the seat and pulled the green shells from his pocket and counted them. "Got six here, all unfired."

Merchant handed some shells to Stafford, reached in his pocket again, and handed him some more. "Should be four empties there. Count the loaded ones."

"Can I pull these gloves off?"

"No, not yet. When you get home you can. And don't forget to burn'm."

Stafford spread the shells out on the seat between them. "I count four empties and five loaded ones, plus what I've got--fourteen altogether."

"We done pretty good with the brass, we didn't leave fingerprints, and they can't tell shit about a shotgun pellet—"

"What about the shells from your pistol?"

"Nine millimeters are awfully common, but I'll change out the barrel and firing pin when I get home, just to be safe. Yassuh, Mr. Shotgun Jack, we came out slick."

Stafford smiled and shook his head. "You *have* thought of everything."

"All but how to cut a lock hasp." Merchant patted the shells.

"Staple," Stafford said and laughed.

"Yeah. Staple." Merchant tapped him on the leg. "Throw them empties out, one by one, over in the lake, out as far as you can. Make sure you get'm over the rail. One at a time, a few seconds between."

"And you're sure Oswalt's out of the picture?" Stafford asked. He picked up a shell and leaned out the window and flung it as far as he could. He could smell a faint saltiness in the air, the way he used to at home in his bed, with Susie beside him.

Merchant put a hand on his shoulder and left it there. "Jack, there's a bayou way off to the west, between New Orleans and Baton Rouge . . . ." He squeezed Stafford's shoulder.

"Oh, sweet Jesus, Merchant. You *killed* him."

"I beat the shit out of him, but I didn't kill him. If I did, would it matter?" Merchant said. "Didn't you kill Koontz?"

Stafford threw out another shell but said nothing. He looked out across the wide stretch of Pontchartrain where the vast belly of stars overhead blended with the dancing stars below. The water had a million seams of silver.

"Jack."

"Yeah?"

"Just to make you feel better, you fired eighty Goddamn pellets across the wall above the bed and just two hit the bastard, both in the hand that was holding the knife. One went through the back of his hand and one tore a finger almost off. At least that's all I could see in the time I had to inspect him."

"You mean I *didn't* kill him?"

"No," Merchant said. "Half a pound of lead smeared across that wall and all you did was nick him. It was like one of them westerns, where the guy shoots a gun out of somebody's hand. You blew the knife right out of his Goddamned hand. But *I* killed him."

"I didn't hear you shoot."

"I emptied most of a clip at him when he went for his gun and I know I hit him at least twice. My ears were ringing so bad from that shotgun that even *I* couldn't hear the pistol."

"I was afraid I'd hit her," Stafford said.

"I know. I was hoping we'd catch him away from her. When we busted in and I saw him on the bed with her, I knew that even if you did get the nerve to shoot you'd shoot too high to keep from hitting her. The pistol did the trick."

"You're not just telling me this to make me feel better?"

"Hell, Stafford, there ain't no way you can feel better anyway.

You got your wife back and you're a fucking hero and didn't none of us get killed."

"Well, I don't feel like I've got her back yet," Stafford said, flinging a shell out over the rail. "I damned sure *tried* to kill him. If he'd gotten to that chair . . ."

"We'd be dead, one or both. He had a pistol, even had a hand on it, but he didn't get it out. He'd have killed all three of us in a heartbeat."

"Jesus, I can't believe we got out of there without getting hurt," Stafford said.

"Well, so far we did everything right and Oscar did what he was supposed to. I'm glad we didn't need those extra shells, though."

Stafford tried to smile, but his lips would not conform. He could only vaguely remember the interminable wait, with Merchant's ear pressed to the door, then the big detective stepping back and throwing his body against it, then the smoke-filled room, still reverberating from shotgun blasts, green shells cascading onto the floor, fumbling to feed shells into the gun while Merchant crouched down beside the man they called Satan with his knife drawn, Susie screaming and screaming until Stafford clamped the still unloaded gun under his arm and scooped his wife up in a sheet and threw her across his shoulder, then backing out of the room while Merchant knelt before the crumpled man. And the detective rising and shouting "Now!" into his walkie-talkie and dropping to his knees and picking up green shells. The rest happened so fast that he recalled it only as a blur, the wild stumbling retreat down the dark stairway, with Susie clinging to him, and finally Merchant's heavy footfalls catching up with them, the pistol firing behind him. Then they were through the back door and the hole in the fence, where a young black man held the back door of a car open and closed it when Susie was in. The car disappeared down the driveway and Stafford and Merchant roared out into the street behind the fast receding taillights of the Camaro.

Finally he did manage a smile. "Me too. I'm glad we didn't need them." He looked over at Merchant. "What did you do with your knife?"

"It's in my pocket."

"No," Stafford said, "you pulled it out over him and did something."

"I left a mark on him."

"What kind of mark?"

"Just a mark on his chest, so that if they happen to find enough left of him they'll believe somebody else did this."

"What do you mean, if they find enough *left* of him?"

Merchant laughed deep and looked through the rearview mirror. "Well, the last thing I did on the way out of the room was squirt some lighter fluid on the wall and floor and light it. If we're lucky the New Orleans Fire Department will get a call along in a few minutes about a warehouse fire, and if we're even luckier, there won't be anything left of that place but a pile of smoking bricks by morning. Lotta that old building is pitch-pine on the inside, floors and all, so it should burn right nicely, if it caught. Air conditioner blowing right on the fire. By setting it on the second floor, there was plenty above it to burn. Shoulda swept right up the wall, across the ceiling, and into the hallway and—well, it should have gone up like a January Christmas tree."

"My God, Merchant, if the good cops work this way—"

"Easy, Jack," the big man said, shaking his head, "easy now. What went on tonight was what we got pulled into. We never asked for any of this."

"Do you think they'll suspect us?"

"I've covered things pretty well. The only thing that worries me is that there's a possibility the others will know that your wife was in the room with him when it happened. Now, Oswalt said he slipped her into the room and handcuffed her to the bed, still out cold. Said didn't nobody know about her at that point but him and Koontz. So it may be that Koontz decided to keep things on the sly until he made up his mind what to do with her. That's the best-case scenario. Or if he did say something about her, they may figure that he let her go sometime during the day. That ain't so good, since they might decide to try to find her and see whether she knows anything about what went down."

"What about those cars? Don't you figure some of those guys saw her?"

"I doubt it. Like I say, I imagine he tried to keep her a secret until he decided what to do with her. Those guys were just droppin' off money. Might not have even got out of the garage area."

"You knew all along what floor she was on, didn't you?" Stafford asked.

"Oswalt told me what floor, but I didn't want to take any chances. I wanted to be sure there wasn't a bunch of alligators on the top floors that could come piling down on us when the shooting started. Finding the room was just a matter of listening. And there wasn't but three air-conditioners hanging out windows, all on the second floor, so that narrowed it down. By the way, I don't know whether you noticed it or not, but there was some *kind* of heavy wiring on that second floor, and they got it started on the third. Looked like some ductwork being put in too, for central heat and air. I'll just bet you that several of them rooms were full of computers and stuff. That whole damned floor of the warehouse is nothing but offices and a couple of bedrooms like the one she was in. No telling what they were planning to do with it. Future headquarters of Satan Incorporated, I figure."

"Hell, huh?"

"Yeah, *Hell*. At least that's what your wife must have figured it was like. And if we're lucky, that's what it's beginning to look and feel like about now—one great big Pontchartrain of fire."

"And if they do suspect we were involved? I mean, if somebody did know she was there?"

"Well, as a precaution, I'd suggest the two of you take a vacation, go off to Europe or somewhere for awhile, take a leave of absence, let things cool down—quite literally—then come on back and resume your lives. Or get a job someplace else. Whatever. I don't see any reason to take chances."

Stafford laughed. "Jesus, Merchant, I don't have that kind of money. I don't make much as a librarian, you know, and I haven't saved *shit*."

Merchant reached beneath his legs and pulled his black bag onto the seat. "Open that."

Stafford set the bag on his lap and unzipped it. "And?"

"Take out them two pouches."

Stafford removed two long white zippered pouches, each over four inches thick. He held them out. "What are they?"

"Well, unzip one, man, and find out."

Slowly he unzipped one of the pouches, knowing what he was seeing even before the zipper was halfway across. Inside there were bundles of bills bound with rubber bands. "How much is in here?"

"No telling, Stafford, no fucking telling, but I'll just bet you that they're all hundreds in both pouches, and that makes a lot of money. Probably close to a hundred thousand apiece, if they *are* all hundreds."

Stafford pulled a bundle of bills out and flipped through them.

"Looks like all hundreds here." He unzipped the other pouch. "Hundreds here too. Holy shit, Merchant, this is a lot of money. He had all this with him?"

"Yeah, this plus the other stuff I saw bundled on the table. Looked like stacks of twenties and tens, smaller bills. The big stuff was in these pouches. Wish I'd had a bigger bag and more time. He'd been counting it and sorting right there in the room with her. Probably got a safe around there somewhere."

"I didn't see any money."

"Stafford, did you even see a table?"

"No, not really. I can't tell you *what* I saw in that room."

Stafford returned the bundles to the pouches and rezipped them and put them back in the black bag. "Jesus, why did you take it? That's drug money."

"May be, may be prostitution money," Merchant said, his eyes on the road. "May be Satan's petty cash fund. Whatever, I took it because if I didn't, it would have got burned up, and if they happened to get there before it burned up, they would know it wasn't a big-time hit. Those sonsabitches kill each other all the time, and they always take every dollar they can snatch before they leave, at least the big bills. You leave that kind of money laying around and they'd *know* somebody personally involved did it."

"What'll you do with it?" Stafford patted the bag.

"I'm going to take one pouch, give my nephew a few thousand, and I got a few hundred in expenses I got to pay. The rest of it I'm gon' spend on myself, fix up my house and boat, real slowly, over several years."

"Hell, Merchant, you can't do that. That's tainted money."

Merchant slammed the bag with his fist. "Don't you go getting sanctimonious on me, Jack. That money's from fat cats from as far away as New York and San Francisco—hell, from Japan and Saudi Arabia—who can afford drugs and five hundred or a thousand a night for a top-class New Orleans hooker. We just took it out of circulation is all. We can put it to nobler use than they can. Besides, like I say, it would have been burned up if I'd left it. And that's probably one week's income for him. Hell, maybe one *day's*."

Stafford shook his head. "Man, I can't believe . . ."

"The other pouch is yours," Merchant said.

Stafford looked at him. "*What*?"

"The other pouch is yours. You and your lady need to get the hell out of the country for a few months, go off to Europe, go on a spending spree, let things die down. I doubt very seriously that they would ever come looking for either one of you. If by chance they do know she was there, they'll probably think that whoever hit Koontz just took the woman and disposed of her to keep her mouth shut. Couldn't leave her body there for the cops to find. That'd just be inviting trouble. Thing is, if Oswalt was straight with me, Koontz had her brought in privately, just between the two of them, since he knew the senator wasn't too thrilled about that mess involving her anyway."

"But why take any chances by bringing her back down here?"

"To find out what she wanted, to play with her, to shut her mouth for good—hell, I don't know. He could have had Oswalt just kill her up there in Mississippi, but that could have got real messy too. Better to do it down here. But I'm just guessing. There's lots of shit I don't understand about all this. But what we do know, you and me, is that we got your wife back, Satan is deader'n one of them Goddamned rocks on Oswalt's desk, we got the money, and if we're lucky, that rat's nest is on its way to being ashes. Whether they know about her and will chase y'all or not, who can say? Probably *not*. But whether you take the money or not, if they decide to chase you, they'll do it. Might as well enjoy whatever time you've got."

Stafford sighed and slouched in his seat. "Merchant, I can't take that money."

"Oh, yeah you can, Jack. Consider it compensation for what they did to your wife. Hell, if you managed to get the sonsabitches to civil court and sued them for what they did to her, you'd get a hell of a lot more, and it would come from the same source. Just say that we won a judgment tonight—a small one, but it's better than none." He reached into the bag and took out one of the pouches. "Now, I haven't counted any of this, but I figger there's nothing but hundreds in both and they look to be about the same thickness. Gotta be a hell of a lot of money in'm. I'd figure somewhere around a hundred thousand in each. You can take either one. It's your draw."

"Jesus," Stafford muttered as he took the pouch. "This one's fine. Merchant—"

"Another way to look at it . . . ."

"Yeah?"

"If Susie really had been hooking at two thousand bucks a night, she'd have racked up more than that since they snatched her."

"Jesus, Merchant."

"And another way: that's about what the senator would have had to pay for a good, safe contract on Satan. So you see, anyway you look at it, we're entitled to the money. Merry Christmas, Jack."

Stafford balanced the pouch on his lap. "Merchant."

"Yeah?"

"Why did you do all this? I mean, if I were black—"

"In this jungle, man, color don't count. These animals go after anybody they want or anybody that gets in their way. Fact is—" He pulled off his cap and ran a hand through his thinning hair. His face looked very tired in the glow of the dash lights. "Fact is, my brother's got, or *had*, a daughter, sister to Oscar up there."

He pointed to the Camaro in front of them. "Finally caught up with'm. Told you everything was OK. This girl was married and with a kid. She got swept up in some shit out in Oakland, kinda like your wife did, innocent as a baby too—didn't have a Goddamned thing to do with the bunch of thugs that took her—and they found her floating in the bay, all cut up and bruised and so bloated my brother had trouble identifying her. They traced it all back to a big bad pimp that had got her confused with somebody else—thought she was working in his territory—but they couldn't pin a damned thing on him.

"Jack, this was just something I felt like doing. It *needed* doing. We got one bad cop out of the system, one bad-ass pimp off the streets, and, I hope, one enemy headquarters converted to ashes. Besides," he said, reaching over and slapping Stafford on the back, "I enjoyed the *hell* out of it. Man, what an adventure! It's the kind of shit a cop *dreams* about, like a soldier finally getting into a pitched battle with the sonsabitches his country's at war with. He finally gets to *do* something. First guy I ever killed, Jack, and damned if I didn't get the super bad angel. All of Heaven ought to be celebrating tonight. Ain't neither one of us going to forget this night, ever. Ol' Shotgun Jack blowin' the whole side off a warehouse—my ears are *still* ringing."

Stafford giggled nervously. "Mine too. And it's still an adventure, Merchant. God knows whether I'll ever feel normal again."

"Oh, yeah, man, you'll get over this. And the way I got it figured, she'll come out of it too, almost as quick as you. You gotta be a hero to her now. Comin' in there blowing that sonofabitch off of her. Her librarian with a shotgun! You done took that big bad burden off of her, more ways than one. That's the way she's gon' see it. Y'all will get off over there in Europe or somewhere and make yourselves little love nests all over the place, maybe down on the Riviera, let that Mediterranean sun bake the bad memories right out of your system. New Orleans will be just an old dead nightmare. You done come to what they call *closure*."

"New Orleans," Stafford sighed. "New Orleans." He noticed that the Mississippi line was only a few miles ahead.

"Let me ask you something, Jack."

"Sure."

"How the hell could you crack jokes while we were climbing those stairs in the dark back there? How in the hell could you be funny at a time like that? You know, the value shopping shit and all."

"To keep from screaming, Merchant, to keep from losing my Goddamned mind and screaming and charging up those stairs like a maniac to find Susie. I was role-playing, man, I was pretending to be cool."

"I just wondered. Man, you somethin'."

"Thanks, but I'd just as soon not to have to play that particular role again."

"You ain't to come back to the Easy for awhile, Jack. Promise me that."

"Don't worry," Stafford said, "don't worry at all about that."

"I mean, you can bring your kids someday, but only after they're in high school." Merchant laughed. "And, Jack, try to work out some safer fantasy routines."

Stafford nodded, but he couldn't bring himself to smile. "I intend to stay in the real world from now on. I'm throwing away every damned novel I've got, and if I play a fantasy game with my woman again outside our own bedroom, I hope to hell a lightning bolt zips out of the sky and splits me open like a melon."

The detective reached down and picked the shotgun off the floorboard. "You want to take this with you? I can spare it. Ship it back to me. UPS. Old Oscar might even deliver it. You'll feel better having it around for a few days."

"No, no, you take it on. I have a lady friend who keeps a pistol to kill her faggot husband with. If I think I need a gun, I'll borrow it."

Merchant held an empty shell out to Stafford. "This is a souvenir for you, Jack. Ol' Shotgun Jack. Put eighty Goddamn holes in the wall of Hell. And one other thing," he grunted, working something out of his pocket. "This." He handed Stafford a black-handled knife. "Says *Satan* on the side of it," he said. "Got a big nick in the handle where one of your bucks hit it."

Stafford pocketed the shell and knife. "Jesus," he said.

"Yeah, I rekkin Him and His daddy was involved. We were just instruments."

Stafford laughed at that.

"Don't forget to burn them gloves, Jack."

Just past the state line, the Camaro, followed by the pickup, turned back into the pines and stopped in a remote corner of the parking lot of the Mississippi Welcome Center. Merchant pulled up beside his nephew but left the engine running. He held a hand out to Stafford.

"Well, Shotgun Jack, it's time for us to part. It's been *real*, as they say. Take care of yourself and your lady, and y'all lay low for a few months. Everything will be alright. Oscar will run you on over to Biloxi. I'm gon' follow at a distance, just to be sure."

"Is he going to take us to the house?"

"Yeah. I don't see any reason not to. If the fire didn't take, there ain't nobody gon' find Koontz until sometime tomorrow, when he don't show up somewhere, and if it did they won't get things cooled off enough to find what's left of him until late tomorrow. If anybody did happen to hear the gunshots, they wouldn't have paid any attention—they hear that shit all the time down there. What I'd do, though, if I was you, is take off in the morning for parts unknown with your lady. Don't tell nobody—not *nobody*—where you're going. And if you write back from over there—and I hope you'll at least send me a postcard—be sure to use a fake name and mail stuff from the country you're leaving, not the one you're staying in. Y'all ought to be fine for quite awhile. It'll take you a long time over there to spend that judgment." He patted the pouch in Stafford's lap.

Stafford nodded, his vision blurred, and clasped the big man's hand tightly. "There's no way I can ever . . . ."

Merchant motioned with his head toward the Camaro. "Save your tenderness and sweet talk for the lady in the backseat of that car," he said. "She's gon' need it. Go on home, Shotgun Jack, be with your woman."

"Merchant." Stafford was looking away from him toward the car where his wife was.

"Yeah?"

"You said that day that I'd never get her back over the thresh-hold they pulled her across. You still believe that?"

"I don't know, Jack. I thought so then. Like I said, though, after what you did tonight—I mean, shit, man, you gotta be some *kind* of hero to her. That woman saw what went on. She was wide awake and givin' him a hell of a fight when we crashed in. And that wasn't a fuckin' book hero she saw blazing away with a shotgun, then swooping her up and hauling her out of there. Wasn't no fantasy. He was *real*."

"Even if I'm the one that threw her to the alligators to begin with . . . ."

"Jack, if women didn't forgive stupidity in their men, there wouldn't be one sound marriage in the country." He reached and laid a hand on Stafford's shoulder. "Give her a little time. Get off somewhere with her for awhile as far away from New Orleans as y'all can get. See if it don't come right. I'm bettin' it will."

Stafford shook his hand again and got out, shut the door, and stepped back from the truck. He popped Merchant a sharp salute. "So long, General," he said, "it was great serving under you. May the rest of the war go as well." He closed the door and did not look back.

When Stafford opened the Camaro door, the young Negro driving said, "Go ahead and get in the back with her. All she's been doing is asking about *you*."

"She *has*?" Then he had his sheet-wrapped woman in his arms, his face buried in her hair. They were both weeping like children.

XXV

When Oscar reached Stafford's house, he drove past, turned around a mile or so down the beach road, and drove back by.

"Taking no chances," he said.

"Yeah," said Stafford, "but you can't do this all night. I need to get her in the house."

"Just makin' sure everything's safe. What I was told to do." He glanced at Stafford in the mirror. "He give you a gun?"

"No. He offered me his shotgun. I know where I can get one."

"Me, I'd take a gun in with me. Anything can happen. Shit might happen before you can get ahold of one."

"I know where I can get one," Stafford said. "Go ahead and turn around and take us to the house. Please."

Oscar headed back east and as he approached the house he pulled over onto the shoulder across the road from it and sat for several minutes, lights off and engine idling, watching. Satisfied that everything was all right, he drove down a few blocks and turned back west, then pulled in behind the house. Merchant's pickup passed by in front.

Stafford leaned his arms on the seat in front of him. "Hope I'm not paying mileage."

Oscar laughed. "Naw, that's been took care of. That your car?" he asked Stafford. He pointed to Susie's Nissan.

"Yeah," Stafford said. "It's hers—*ours*. The other one's still at the college."

"Well, the best I can tell, everything's fine. You want to go on in and check it out while I'm still here?"

"I'll leave her in the car while I check the doors, but I'm sure it's fine." Susie had remained silent and still, but he could see her eyes shining.

Stafford went to the back door first, then to the front, and found them both secure, so he helped Susie from the car to a chair on the porch. He went back to the car and said good-bye to Oscar, but he kept his eyes on his wife, still huddled in the sheet he had scooped her up in.

They watched from the front porch as the Camaro disappeared into the night. A few minutes later the pickup drove by, the lights flashed twice, and it too was gone. There were no porchlights on, and the only light they had was from the streetlights along the highway.

"You afraid to go in?" he asked her.

She shook her head. "Not with you here, no."

He unlocked the door and they walked into the dark house. He flipped on a lamp before he locked the door behind them. Susie started upstairs, but he stopped her.

"Not till I've checked things out." He had his right hand in a rear pocket, in his left he carried the pouch.

She stood and watched as he eased up the stairs and turned on the lights, checked all the rooms and closets and upper porch.

"All clear," he said, descending.

She met him at the foot of the stairs. "Kiss me hello," she said.

"I kissed you in the car," he said, pulling her to him.

"I'm *home* now." Her face was pale and drawn, but the marvelous beauty was back, and Jack Stafford kissed his wife passionately for the first time in weeks.

He looked at her rumpled dress. "Where's your sheet?"

"I wiped my feet on it," she said, "and left it on the porch. "It's not coming in this house. I want you to burn it tomorrow. And this dress. It smells like vomit."

"Lotsa burning going on these days," Stafford said. "Go on up. That dress looks like it's been to hell and back."

"That's exactly where it's been."

"You might want to take a shower while I check things out down here. I'll be right up. Would you like a drink?"

"Oh my God, yes," she said, starting up the stairs. "Anything. One good stiff one. And fix us something to eat. I haven't eaten in I don't know when."

Stafford went to the kitchen and stuck the pouch back behind some packets of shrimp in the freezer. While she showered, he removed the gloves, shoved them down in a grocery bag with some crumpled newspapers, and burned the bag in the back yard. He watched the flames dance in a light breeze from the south while fine sparks streaked up and drifted up and over him, blending with the stars. He went back in and fixed drinks and sandwiches, then made some phone calls, all the while sipping on a stiff bourbon. When he had had his time in the bathroom, they ate dinner on the upper porch, with beer, and drank whisky for awhile, watching the boats out on the Gulf.

"I had forgotten all about food," she said after her second sandwich. "I'm still a little woozy from whatever they gave me, but I am *starving*."

"Yeah. Good ol' Southern meal: pimento-cheese sandwiches, tomato sandwiches, heavy with mayonnaise, and whisky. That combination lets you know you're home again." He felt a weary, vague euphoria, like a man snatched from a dark sea and dragged up on the sand to face another morning's sun, when a few hours earlier he had seen nothing but smothering blackness before him. The fear, all the misgivings and uncertainties, had simply evaporated, and whatever came into their lives now he felt would be mild in comparison, no more than minor nuisances.

"Should we have all these lights on and everything?"

"Yeah," he said. "Hell, we're home now and I'm not running another damned step—until tomorrow. Merchant said nobody would go in that place until tomorrow sometime."

"But we don't even have a gun here," she said.

He reached down beside his chair and raised a small black pistol. "Oh yeah. Bought Oscar's. Gave him a hundred dollar bill for it. He thought it was a good deal."

"Mercy, Jack Stafford, how very unlike a librarian." She looked at him above the rim of her glass of bourbon and water. Her eyes were twinkling.

"What are you thinking?" he asked.

"I'm thinking," she said, lowering the glass, "about my Pompeii Man standing at the door of that room with his gun blazing away. You had it down by your side and stuck up like that little guy with the—you know, the Pagan Penis from Pompeii—blazing away."

"Yeah," he laughed. "I killed a whole wall of roses and chains. Jesus Christ, I'm still having trouble hearing."

"Roses and chains," she said. "Glad you got to see my room, that little corner of Hell. God, what a chamber of horrors."

"Don't think about it anymore, Susie. It's gone from our lives. Gone for good, I hope."

"Did you kill him?"

"Merchant did, with his pistol. Just to set the record straight, though, I did shoot the knife out of his hand."

"I'm just glad he's dead. And who *was* that Merchant guy? I vaguely remember him from the hospital, and I believe he was the one who came by the house that day, when y'all talked on the porch."

"Yep. He's a New Orleans detective who took a personal interest in your case. Hell of a fine man."

"Did y'all hear what that—what Satan was saying to me?"

"Well, Merchant did. All I could hear was mumbling. He had his ear to that door for a long time listening to what was going on. I thought I would die waiting. He wanted to be sure we'd be able to nail him without hurting you. We didn't know but what he had a gun to your head and would pull the trigger when we busted in. So he waited and waited and waited, while I worked the Goddamned safety on that shotgun."

"Jack, he was going to kill me. He was going to cut me up with that knife and have those guys rape me again and throw me into a bayou."

"I know, Baby, I know. This whole damned thing is—well, it's been like a bad dream. But we're home now." He moved over beside her chair and took her hand. She had her hair wrapped in a towel and wore a white bathrobe, which had fallen open at the top. He rose to his knees and stared at the creamy curve of her breasts and then at the black cross.

"Tomorrow that comes off," she said.

"What?"

"The tattoo. I don't have to wear it anymore."

"Do you mean it?"

"Oh yes, I mean it."

He smiled. "I'm glad. Don't know about tomorrow, but we'll have it taken off."

"What do we do now, Jack? I'm scared."

"Don't be scared. I've already arranged for us to leave in the morning. We'll pack first thing and run over to the college and pick up my car, I'll get things squared away at the library, and we're off to Virginia. Already booked a flight out. I've got a friend we can stay with over there until we get a passport for you. Then we're going to Europe for awhile."

"To Europe?" Her eyes sparkled.

"Yeah, I thought you might like to see Pompeii for yourself, England, Paris, Rome. Rhodes—now there's a place I'd like to take you. Lindos Castle. We'll ride burros up a little winding rocky trail. Lord, the fun we'll have."

"Jack, how can we afford—"

"I'll take care of all that. I've got a little cold cash laid aside that I didn't tell you about. Let's call it mad money." He poured another drink for them.

"And what about your job and all our things?"

"Well, I'll work it out with the college, take a leave of absence or something, or I may never go back to that job. Frankly, I don't care. We can make it. After the shit we've been through, I'm convinced we can survive anywhere. I'll get somebody to store our things, the cars, and all the stuff in the house . . . ."

"God, I feel so free," she said. "Scared absolutely to death about the future, but so *free*. Like I'm alive again. It was like that cross he carved on me weighed a ton and I couldn't breathe for it. Now it's like it's just on my skin. Like a leech or something I can peel off. I can't wait to get it off."

"Just skin deep. Just on the surface. It won't take anything to remove it." He had turned to sit beside her chair again, and her hand came softly down to his head.

"Jack, I'm sorry about the call I made," she said. "I just had to try to get some sort of focus, and I guess I thought he could help me get it, could lift the curse, whatever. I had no idea he was—that he really was the devil incarnate."

"What you did wasn't nearly as bad as what I put *you* through. Me and my Goddamned fantasies."

"Jack, I don't think we need to talk about it anymore. As a matter of fact, I'd just as soon we never bring up any of it again. It's over. Let's bury it."

"Right," he said, "right."

Far out on the Gulf ships were moving across the starry horizon, blending their lights with the more distant ones. A plane moved silently from west to east. The night was soft, the wind gentle from the sea, slightly salty, and couples were on the beach walking hand in hand.

"I guess we have to leave for a while. But, Jack, I'd like to come back here. I really would. I'll miss the Gulf."

"Yeah," he said. "Me too. I wish we had time to go out to Horn again before we leave. But there are islands and oceans everywhere and the same stars above them. We'll find others."

She squeezed his hand. "Wherever my Pompeii Man wants to go will be fine with me."

"Except New Orleans," he said.

"Except New Orleans. I can wait awhile on that."

Then she excused herself and went to the bathroom. Soon Stafford could hear the hair dryer. He reached down beside his chair and picked up the pistol, hefted its reassuring weight. He walked into the bedroom and slid it under his pillow and returned to the drink on the porch. Susie came through the door, her hair combed out and fluffed, and kneeled before him and pulled his face to hers, moving it from side to side.

"You look like hell, Jack Stafford."

"I didn't sleep at all last night, worrying about you. Frankly, I haven't slept worth a damn in weeks and weeks, and I probably won't sleep much tonight, whatever's left of it." He looked at his watch and sighed. "I sure feel my age."

"And I feel a lot more than mine. Do you think you have the energy for one more fantasy, though?"

Stafford looked at her.

"Well?" She had turned from him toward the dark water across the road. Soft light from the bedroom fell on her hair, dry now and the color of sea oats.

"I've sworn off fantasies. What have you got in mind?"

"I'm asking whether Pompeii Man has the energy to play another fantasy game."

He slumped in his chair. "Susie, what do you mean?"

"Well, I was thinking that we might pretend that you had just rescued your lady from an evil man in the deep, dark swamp and brought her home again." Her back to the street, she released the tie on her robe and allowed it to fall open. She had nothing on beneath it. As his eyes traveled up her legs to her breasts, he saw a cross made of Band-aids where the black cross had been. "Or maybe Pompeii Man goes into hell and rescues his lover and brings her back home, something even Orpheus couldn't do."

He smiled and set down his drink and stood, pulling her through the doorway toward the bed. "No, no fantasy. What Jack

Stafford would like to do is take his wife Susie to their bed and hold her and wish away the horror. Maybe dream something nice for a change. And tomorrow we'll start over, just you and me, wherever and however."

Beyond their little house across from the beach the world went its busy way, far above and out over the dark water the universe spun on, the stars in their places and the sun in its circuit to another dawning, but neither was of consequence to a man and woman who, locked in each other's arms, had found the center again.

Paul Ruffin

Paul Ruffin's poetry and fiction have appeared widely in such prestigious journals as *Southern Review*, *Georgia Review*, and *Michigan Quarterly Review* and in such texts as Norton's *Introduction to Literature*, Harcourt Brace's *College Handbook of Creative Writing*, Little-Brown's *Introduction to Literature* and *Introduction to Poetry*, and *The Longwood Guide to Writing*. He is the author of four collections of poetry, the latest of which, *Circling*, won the 1997 Mississippi Institute of Arts and Letters Poetry Award. He has two collections of short fiction, *The Man Who Would Be God* and *Islands, Women, and God*. He has edited or co-edited eight other books.

Born in Alabama and raised in Mississippi, Ruffin lives with his wife Sharon and their two children in Huntsville, Texas, where he teaches creative writing at Sam Houston State University. He is the founding editor of *The Texas Review* and founder and director of Texas Review Press.